MYSTERY OF THE HORN

It was six inches long and sharp at one end. The other end was rough, as if it had broken off. Except for the fracture, it was unflawed: a smooth white surface with a fine grain that spiraled tightly up to a narrow, conical point. . . .

She looked up. "What is it?"

"You tell me." Sugar was enjoying himself.

BJ was too fascinated to feel pressured or quizzed. "It's either a horn or a tooth." Something floated up from a biology class she'd taken to get into vet school. A sea mammal, with a spiral tusk . . . "Does the animal have two of these?"

"Nope."

"A narwhal," she said suddenly with relief. "Is it a narwhal tusk?"

Sugar stared at her. "Not bad. Not half-bad. That's a hell of a guess. But it's still just a guess, and it's wrong."

Now she was lost. "Is it a land animal?"

"That much I'll give you." He was watching her face.

She barely noticed; the horn had taken her over. "A land animal. Antelope have two like this, generally darker. Goats have two, but they curve more in any of the goats I know—"

She had her first suspicion of what it was. She shivered, and the shiver turned into cold certainty. Of course. She should have guessed it long ago. It was obvious, except—

Except that there weren't any.

FIREBIRD
WHERE FANTASY TAKES FLIGHT™

THE MAGIC
AND THE
HEALING

Nick O'Donohoe

FIREBIRD

AN IMPRINT OF PENGUIN GROUP (USA) INC.

FIREBIRD
Published by the Penguin Group
Penguin Group (USA) Inc., 345 Hudson Street, New York, New York 10014, U.S.A.
Penguin Group (Canada), 90 Eglinton Avenue East, Suite 700, Toronto,
Ontario, Canada M4P 2Y3 (a division of Pearson Penguin Canada Inc.)
Penguin Books Ltd, 80 Strand, London WC2R 0RL, England
Penguin Ireland, 25 St Stephen's Green, Dublin 2, Ireland
(a division of Penguin Books Ltd)
Penguin Group (Australia), 250 Camberwell Road, Camberwell, Victoria 3124, Australia
(a division of Pearson Australia Group Pty Ltd)
Penguin Books India Pvt Ltd, 11 Community Centre, Panchsheel Park,
New Delhi - 110 017, India
Penguin Group (NZ), Cnr Airborne and Rosedale Roads, Albany,
Auckland 1310, New Zealand (a division of Pearson New Zealand Ltd)
Penguin Books (South Africa) (Pty) Ltd, 24 Sturdee Avenue,
Rosebank, Johannesburg 2196, South Africa

Registered Offices: Penguin Books Ltd, 80 Strand, London WC2R 0RL, England

First published in the United States of America by Ace Books,
The Berkley Publishing Group, 1994
Published by Firebird, an imprint of Penguin Group (USA) Inc., 2006

1 3 5 7 9 10 8 6 4 2

LIBRARY OF CONGRESS CATALOGING-IN-PUBLICATION DATA

O'Donohoe, Nick.
The magic and the healing / Nick O'Donohoe.
p. cm.
Summary: A veterinary student finds herself part of a special
rotation treating mythical and fantastical animals.
ISBN 0-14-240707-0 (pbk.)
[1. Veterinarians—Fiction. 2. Animals, Mythical—Fiction. 3. Fantasy.] I. Title.

PZ7.O252Ma 2006 [Fic]—dc22 2006040770

Printed in the United States of America

THE MAGIC
AND THE
HEALING

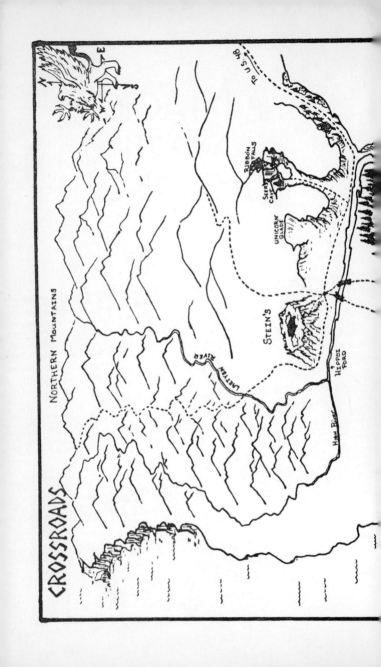

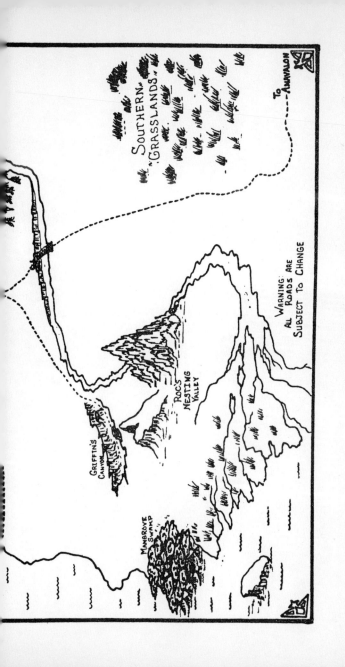

P·R·O·L·O·G·U·E

BRANDAL SAT NEAR the cave entrance, enjoying the late-afternoon sun coloring the cliff walls. To his right, Ribbon Falls split the cliff and dropped into a circular spill pool. Halfway up the cliff, ferns and moss grew where the spray cloud drifted from the falls. Nearer to him, the rapids below the pool watered a tangled field of flowers: asphodel and marsh marigolds, clematis and columbine, lady-slippers and lilacs, an impossible mix blooming all at once in the rich soil.

It felt lovely and peaceful, as though it had been like this for thousands of years and could go on undisturbed forever.

There was a rustle in the columbine, and a sudden outraged squeak. A white fluffy streak with blossoms tangled in it bounded toward Brandal. The flowerbinders, self-camouflaging cats who stayed kittens all their lives, had grown bored with lying in wait for hummingbirds and blue-backs; they were pouncing on each other.

The flowerbinder bumped into Brandal's kneecap and, confused, struck at it.

He bent down and patted it. "You should show more respect," he said severely. "I'm royalty."

The flowerbinder looked up at the man, assessed him quickly, and rubbed against his leg. Then it rolled suddenly on its back, paws in the air.

"Oh, all right." He rubbed its stomach, enjoying the loud purr as he moved his fingers around the vines and stems to tickle the white fur underneath.

"I have to go in, you know." But he didn't yet. He was happy here, and he hadn't rested this much in days.

A slow-moving shadow fell across them both. The flowerbinder cowered.

Brandal slipped the edge of his cloak over the cat and squinted toward the sun, half blocked by wings the size of a small cloud. "It's all right. That's one of the Great. I don't think he can land here." He scratched the flowerbinder's ears until it purred again. "He's not going to eat you this time. Anyway, he's not so bad; he's one of us."

He felt a bump as the flowerbinder pawed at his sword. "Careful. It's sharp. You've never seen one of these, have you?" he said quietly.

The shadow above Brandal lifted, and sunlight suddenly gleamed off his breastplate. He moved his cloak off the flowerbinder. It tilted its head for Brandal to scratch its jaw, then stopped and sniffed at his sleeve. The rough cloth had dried blood on it.

He pulled back. "Did I get any on you?" He looked the animal over carefully, finding a few flecks, and cleaned them off, even though the little carnivore wouldn't mind at all. It was very important to him to keep this blood out of this country.

Suddenly he scooped up the flowerbinder and, ignoring its struggles, hugged it close to him. "I'm sorry," he said, his cheek tight against its fur and the blossoms tucked there. "I never wanted any of this. For any of us."

The flowerbinder squeaked again. He let it go, and it bounded back into the flower patch and disappeared.

He sighed and entered the darkness.

O·N·E

BJ VAUGHAN KNELT before her locker, patiently and carefully emptying it into a row of paper bags.

Two things went into their own separate bags: her stethoscope, because it had cost so much and the diaphragm was delicate, and her coveralls, because after her large animal surgical rotation in the school barn she had felt that no amount of washing would ever make them clean enough to touch anything else.

She took out four three-ring binders (ABNORMAL REPRO, AB-NORMAL NEURO, AB GI, OPHTHO) and a paperback text of *Severin's Ophthalmology*, stuffing them in a bag. She laid her sunglasses from ambulatory rotation on top of them carefully; the sunglasses at least might be useful.

In a junk sack she put a hoof pick (it looked like a cross between a beer-bottle opener and a screwdriver) and a copy of *The Last Unicorn*. In with them she shoved her extra pens, two hemostats, her bandage and suture scissors, and her sun-faded Orioles base-ball cap.

Halfway to the bottom of the locker was her safety box of Ritz crackers, for nights when she couldn't leave the hospital for din-ner. She considered eating a handful, then tossed them out.

She sorted down methodically: past her three black books full of case notes, past a Zip-Loc bag with a spare penlight and bat-teries, past the Styrofoam Big Mac containers, to the bottom of the locker.

At the very bottom was a crumpled and stained packet, includ-ing a letter with the seal of the Western Virginia College of

3

Veterinary Medicine, welcoming BJ Vaughan to "her final year." She crumpled it and thrust it in the bag with the Big Mac containers.

For now, she kept the bag with her black books and course notes. On her way through the tunnel connecting the classroom building and the animal hospital, she smiled and said hello to a number of sleepy, strained friends in lab coats, all of whom asked, in overly sincere tones, how she was *feeling*.

She walked upstairs, past the hospital library and into the hallway off the exam rooms. A waiting client, a teenage boy holding a bedraggled cat too tightly, stared anxiously at BJ. She smiled encouragingly and glanced ahead toward the conference room where the small animal rotation was in session.

As she passed it, a woman's voice distracted her. "And I'd recommend withholding food and water for at least twenty-four hours, immediate I.V. fluid therapy at sixty milliliters per hour, antibiotics, and a bland diet afterward."

"Is that all?" The older voice, male, sounded amused and patient—almost kind.

The presenting student, Marla Schmidt, said uncertainly, "Those are my recommendations, Dr. Truelove."

"Pancreatitis is frequently misdiagnosed, young lady." He added with satisfaction, "One of the most misdiagnosed ailments in veterinary medicine. Are you quite, *quite* sure you're done?"

Marla muttered unhappily and inaudibly. Another student said sweetly, "Could I ask a question?"

Dr. Truelove said, "By all means, DeeDee."

The question was directed at Marla. "Why didn't you recommend repeating daily serum levels of amylase and lipase?"

Truelove said happily, "Good question, DeeDee. You hadn't said anything about follow-up blood work, had you, Marla?"

Marla fumbled. "I was getting to that."

BJ spun and walked away rapidly, immediately crashing into someone and spilling the paper bags.

It was Laurie, who bent over and deftly popped things back into bags, coming close to BJ's original order. "God, I can't believe how clumsy I am."

"It was probably me," BJ said, picking things up more slowly. To herself she thought, frightened, *It was probably me.* The hoof pick slipped through her fingers; she picked it up with great care, hiding her reaction.

"You look better. Did you sleep the whole weekend?"

It was the first sensible question BJ had been asked.

"I slept all day Saturday," BJ said.

She had stayed awake Wednesday and Thursday night, trembled all Friday morning, then gone to Dr. Truelove and said that she was too ill to take part in rounds.

While talking to him, she'd started crying and couldn't stop. He patted her hand, smiled sympathetically, and sent her home to sleep.

In the afternoon, a note in her mailbox informed her that she had just failed small-animal medicine, and would have to retake it. Sleepy and disoriented, she had called to confirm the message (Dr. Truelove did not answer his phone; a secretary confirmed it) and had gone back to bed.

BJ blinked and saw that Laurie was still listening. "I woke up feeling fine today, rested and everything. I'm okay now."

"Of course you are," Laurie said flatly. "You were okay before—just exhausted. Have you talked to anyone about what you're going through now? Friends? Family?"

BJ said flatly and without much friendship, "You know about my mother."

Laurie nodded. "I know what she did. It's commoner than you think, BJ, and"—she hesitated—"I've heard that she was terminally ill."

BJ nodded shortly. BJ hadn't known anything about that until her mother's note. That was the monstrous part.

Laurie said again, "So have you talked to someone?" Laurie Kleinman, an anesthesia technician, was too young to shepherd the other students, but couldn't help worrying about them.

At the moment, BJ was glad. "I called my brother." He had been sympathetic but disinterested; probably their mother's suicide had left him numb. BJ had been angry that he hadn't been more upset with her. "I'm not ready to talk about it to friends yet."

"You seem ready enough. I can't believe that you cleaned out your locker right away; I'd have done it when I came back three weeks from now."

Laurie spoke innocently, but her eyes were sharp. She had taught English before quitting to become a tech.

BJ said what she hadn't even told her brother: "I may not come back."

Laurie nodded. "I thought you might feel that way."

BJ almost smiled. "That's it? No shock, no distress, no pity?" There was more, but she wasn't ready to tell Laurie or anyone else.

Laurie smiled sadly. "You'll be throwing away your career."

What career? "Well, you did."

"You mean teaching? I didn't even like it. But you love animal medicine—"

"And I failed a course in it." But it was hard to make that matter; it was just one more, not very large thing.

"You didn't fail it; Dr. Truelove failed you." Laurie scowled. "He said if you had any trouble at all, you could talk to him. You talked to him—"

He had been paternal, attentive, and completely understanding.

"—and he flunked you by note. He's not only a pig, he's a gutless pig."

BJ said dubiously, "Everyone says he's an excellent teacher."

"That's because he says it; they're afraid to contradict him. Everyone also says that DeeDee Parris is a good student and a fine class officer."

BJ shifted uncomfortably. Laurie was generally perceptive, but Dr. Truelove and DeeDee had always been her blind spots. She called the one "vicious" and the other "scum."

Laurie sighed. "You don't have to believe me about Truelove, but you'd better believe that you're still one of the best students in the class. Most of us still do."

BJ's eyes filled up; she wiped them angrily. Not that it mattered now, but she would never cry in this building again.

Laurie looked around furtively. "Do you think anyone heard me talking about Truelove? I shouldn't have said anything. I hate when I do this." Whenever Laurie spoke her mind, she was terrified that someone was actually listening to her.

She lit a cigarette. All the anesthesiologists drank too much coffee and smoked; they liked stimulants. She turned to go, then added, "By the way, Dr. Dobbs is looking for you." Her smile was almost a smirk. "If I were you, I'd go see him. Maybe he's wearing a muscle shirt."

Laurie left. BJ sighed, rebalancing the bags, and trudged to Dobbs's office.

His door had three decorations: a cartoon of a red-faced cow slapping a man in coveralls and an arm-length palpation sleeve, a black-and-white nameplate that said DR. SUGAR DOBBS, and a hand-lettered sign that said, Knock Even If It's Open. BJ set down one armful of bags and knocked tentatively.

A man's voice said from inside, "A student who can read did that. Must be BJ. C'mon in."

She did, leaving the door ajar.

* * *

"Sugar" was short for Sugarfoot; Dobbs's family had loved horses. Far from embarrassed, he chose to use Sugar instead of his given name (Charles Franklin Dobbs) on veterinary conference programs.

Sugar, now in his thirties, never put any of his past behind him. In addition to his nickname, he still kept (and wore) a belt buckle from the Nevada Ropers and Riders, a holdover from his rodeo days. When he taught, his speech and manner came as much from his ranch past as it did from his surgical practice.

On the other hand, he wore pastel shirts and ties instead of embroidered western shirts. In the barns he wore Tingley black rubber boots, not tooled leather cowboy boots. On the rare occasions when he wore a hat, it was a beat-up baseball cap with no team insignia on it. He seldom talked about his rodeo and ranch days. "Sugar Dobbs," Laurie had observed once, "doesn't give himself away."

She had added, with a frankness that startled even her, "And isn't that a damn shame?"

Just now, BJ didn't find Sugar attractive at all. He leaned on his elbows, staring at her, and said, "You going away for a while?"

For one wild second she thought of saying, Oh, much more than a while. Longer than you can imagine. But she only said, "I might."

"You look rested now. All you needed was sleep. What do you want to do?"

BJ was silent. For the moment, with her life blown apart and confused, it didn't matter what she wanted to do. She wanted nothing.

He coughed. "Seeing as you're fresh out of plans, how about signing up for another ambulatory block of Doctors on Wheels?"

BJ nearly dropped her bags again. "Why?"

He grinned, fiddling with something that she couldn't see on his desk. "Because I need another student."

She was groping for a polite "no" when he added, "Set down your bags and close the door."

BJ closed it reluctantly. The office suddenly felt like an airless closet. Sugar, a married man who knew damn well he was good-looking, was scrupulous about keeping his door open during conferences with women. What was going on?

She faced him nervously. "I didn't know you were teaching another large animal ambulatory rotation."

"Sign-up is private." He nodded at the bags she was clutching to her chest. "Is that stuff heavy?"

"What? Oh." She set them down.

He pulled his hands off his desk, hiding what they held. "I've got something for you, and you'd better take it home in those bags and not leave it in your locker." He frowned. "Things grow legs and walk away around here lately."

BJ nodded cautiously. She'd been glad to find her books and stethoscope still intact, though she planned on selling them. "What are you giving me?"

"Oh, nothing much." He still didn't show it. "You might call it something to keep quiet about."

"Oh?" A gift, from Sugar? She felt threatened, though flattered. There were prettier students than she, and Sugar's wife was beautiful.

He added pointedly, "Until you do a first-day presentation about it at rounds."

"Oh." She didn't hide how she felt. "Presenting at rounds" had meant long nights and hard mornings, library time sandwiched between twelve-hour shifts of surgery and clinical care for animals. The presentations had to be broad ranging, but detailed; the faculty and even the other students grilled presenters over everything from dosages to nutrition, to whether a surgeon should use two-aught or three-aught suture on a particular wound.

Sugar stood up. "Don't knock me down climbing on board."

"Dr. Dobbs, I appreciate the offer—I know it's kindly meant, but I really think—"

"You really do," he agreed. "That's why I want you to look at this."

He handed her the object.

It was six inches long and sharp at one end. The other end was rough, as if it had broken off. Except for the fracture, it was unflawed: a smooth white surface with a fine grain that spiraled tightly up to a narrow, conical point.

BJ twisted it in her hands, making it catch the light at different angles. Sugar watched her. "Can't help doing that, can you? I couldn't, either."

She looked up. "What is it?"

"I won't always be here for you to ask. You tell me." Sugar was enjoying himself.

BJ was too fascinated to feel pressured or quizzed. "It's either a horn or a tooth." She added, "If it's a tooth, it's from something big."

"How do you know it's not a rock, or a toenail?"

"Most rocks wouldn't have this grain. Plus you wouldn't ask me to do a presentation at rounds about a rock."

"Let's hope not. I do fool people some. Why isn't it a toenail?"

She held it out. "Any animal with a toenail this big would scrape it unevenly by walking and digging."

"Nice work, Sherlock." Sugar meant it. There was never anything mean about his hard questions, and he always praised good answers. "But you haven't told me what it is, yet."

BJ looked at it, trying to think of where she'd seen anything like it. "Is the rotation a large animal block?"

"More or less. Some small animals kind of creep in."

She tested the point of the horn. It was sharper than any antler or horn she'd ever felt. "Is this an exotic animal block?" She all but held her breath. All of the potential zoo vets fought to get into the exotic rotation; regular students never had a shot at it. There was a chance of interning in San Diego for the koalas or Washington, D.C., for the pandas.

Sugar said, "Not the exotic rotation you mean, no. It has its moments." He was holding back, waiting for her to say something about the fragment in her hands.

Something floated up from a biology class she'd taken to get into vet school. A sea mammal, with a spiral tusk . . . "Does the animal have two of these?"

"Nope."

She could see the picture in her text: a whitish, spotted pelt. . . . It was an Arctic mammal—not a seal, but one of the permanently marine mammals—the *name*, dammit, what was the *name*—

"A narwhal," she said suddenly with relief. "Is it a narwhal tusk?"

Sugar stared at her. "Not bad. Not half-bad. That's a hell of a guess."

She smiled, feeling a ghost of the pleasure she had felt in her life and work a month ago.

He added, "But it's still just a guess, and it's wrong. Don't buy mukluks and a wet suit, 'cause we're not going to Greenland."

Now she was lost. "Is it a land animal?"

"That much I'll give you." He was watching her face.

She barely noticed; the horn had taken her over. "A land animal. Antelope have two like this, generally darker. Goats have two, but they curve more in any of the goats I know—"

She had her first suspicion of what it was. She shivered, and the shiver turned into cold certainty. Of course. She should have guessed it long ago. It was obvious, except—

Except that there weren't any.

She looked at Sugar. He looked back innocently. "Are you ready for another guess, BJ?"

She shook her head.

He said, "That's good. Vets guess a lot, but they're better off knowing."

She looked at the horn for reassurance. It lay in her palm, smooth and warm and completely impossible. She whispered, "I know. I think."

"Well, do you think, or do you know?" He tried to drawl, but his voice was tense, as though her answer mattered a great deal.

BJ swallowed. In the past four days she had wept in front of classmates and faculty, and been publicly humiliated for it; she had been watched and pitied; she had been ridiculous and completely ashamed of herself. She wanted all of it to be over.

She looked around at the Merck veterinary manual, at Sugar's diploma from Georgia, at anything that might help her make her answer.

In the end, the closed door helped more than anything. If she were a fool in front of one more professor, what did it matter now? "I know," she said shakily.

Then she straightened, looked Sugar Dobbs in the eye, and said in a controlled voice, "One thing I don't know: this came off an animal with an equine body and a"—What a time to go blank. What was the word for goats? Right—"caprine beard. Is the animal more goatlike, or more horselike?"

Sugar said nothing.

Instead, he took the horn from her and held the tip loosely in his fingers. He took his penlight from his shirt pocket and tapped the horn once, softly.

It chimed like a small silver bell.

Seconds went on, and BJ realized that the sound was growing, as though the horn received feedback from its own echoes. It was pure and full, as loud as a tubular bell, and as loud as a church bell, as a full carillon, louder and sweeter than any bell she had ever heard.

Sugar wrapped his hand around the horn. The sound was gone, with no echo.

He held the horn out. "Mostly, only show animals need horns grafted back on. This is what you'd call a special case. You take it home and study it, and make a presentation in one week, on Monday." He pulled an accordion folder from his shelves. "Here's some reading."

She looked at him helplessly. If she took the horn, she had to take the folder. If she took the folder, she was back in vet school, back to giving presentations at rounds and sitting up with dying animals and walking right back into an arena where she felt like a fool and a failure and a living mistake. And all for nothing, since she'd never practice medicine now.

If she didn't take the horn, she would never see where it had come from.

Without a word she took the horn, slipping it carefully into the bag with her stethoscope. Sugar handed her the folder; on the outside was one of Sugar's typical penciled notes to himself: "BJ Vaughan—first presentation." She glanced inside.

It was a battered book with a tooled-leather cover. The spine was split; a rubber band held the pages together. She slipped the rubber band off and opened the cover, which felt like suede but also like nothing she had ever handled.

She read the title page, printed in an absurdly ornate, antiquated Gothic block: *Lao's Guide to Unbiological Species*.

She read the first paragraph of the preface:

> An unbiological order, I call it, because it obeys none of the natural laws of hereditary and environmental change, pays no attention to the survival of the fittest, positively sneers at any attempt on the part of man to work out a rational life cycle, is possibly immortal, unquestionably immoral, evidences anabolism but not katabolism, ruts, spawns, and breeds but does not reproduce, lays no eggs, builds no nests, seeks but does not find, wanders but does not rest. Nor does it toil or spin. The members of this order are the animals the Lord of the Hebrews did not create to grace His Eden; they are not among the products of the six days' labour. These are the sports, the off-throws, of the universe instead of the species; these are the weird children of the lust of the spheres.

She put the rubber band back on and slid the folder into her bag of books. Sugar called out as she left, "See you next Monday."

His door had shut behind her before she managed to say, "I'll be there."

T·W·O

A PATH OF chiseled and cut steps descended between stalactites that varied from pencil thin to icicles, to colonnades the thickness of mature oaks. The rich colors, stained in by mineral salts, became quickly indistinguishable except near the torch.

At the first landing in the stone steps, Brandal laid down his sword and hung his armor on a waiting peg. His breastplate had a triskelion made of an arm, a hooved foreleg, and a feathered wing; there was only one scratch on it—acquired in practice. He tried, for the hundredth time, to polish the scratch out on his sleeve.

A reflecting pool paralleled the path here. On a ridge above it a lizardlisk, mimic of a basilisk, puffed its throat ruff at him. He smiled and stretched a finger out to the harmless reptile that looked so deadly. It hissed and fled.

At the second landing he put on his crown.

At the fourth he put on his robes: fur trim (tribute willingly sacrificed), feathers (willingly sacrificed), and hides and human skin (the same).

At the last he took a fresh torch from the waiting sconce and lit it from his own dimming brand. It sparked on his hand, and he swore, jittery from remembering his first visit here thirty years ago.

At that time he had tiptoed, awed, past the crown and robes he was too polite to touch. Below, the Seer had clicked its beak and said, "All hail, him who shall be king hereafter." Its yellow eyes fixed him, and he could see that it had once been an eagle.

"How do you know that?" He knew he was staring at its feathers as they ruffled endlessly in the breeze of the Pact of Air.

"I know what I know." It stared back at him, as fascinated with him as he with it, but also deeply unhappy. "And I know all."

"What makes you think I'll be king someday?"

"Well, I always said that someday my prince would come; why not you? Why did you come here?" It waved a branch, moist from the Pact of Water and dripping on its feathers.

"I needed to."

It nodded. "And no one else needed to."

He had been young and easily frightened. "Will I like being king?"

"Not much." It shuffled its smoldering talons, pained by the Pact of Fire. "Sometimes it will satisfy you. Sometimes it will set you on fire. Once in a great while it will make you heartsick. Why ask?"

He fled back up the stairs, saying, "I'll never come see you again."

"True enough," the eagle thing agreed, and laughed. "And I still say that you'll come here again, and we're both still batting a thousand." Its laughter, with no humor in it, followed Brandal the boy up almost to the surface.

Now the thing by the well said, "A second question, King Brandal?"

He stared. "I never saw you before. How do you know me?"

"True, but you above all kings should pay less attention to how things seem and more to what they are. Didn't I tell you that I know what I know—and I know all?"

"The eagle." The king stared at him. "He was you?"

It shrugged human shoulders. "He wasn't what I used to think of as me. Now I'm five-sixths of him, yes. But you were right then, sire: you never came to see him again. It makes no difference. You're still here again."

The Seer was mostly human, which made things worse. The king automatically looked for and found the signs of the Pacts of Six Kingdoms on the seer:

He had gnarled roots instead of feet (the Pact of Plants).
He kept much of his humanity (the Pact of Animals).
His left hand was stone (the Pact of Earth).

His singed and smoldering hair (the Pact of Fire) blew rest-lessly (the Pact of Air) into continually weeping eyes (the Pact of Water).

The Seer had traded a part of his body to each kingdom. In exchange, the kingdoms held no secrets from him, but they per-petually reminded him of his pact.

The king shuffled uncertainly from foot to foot. "All right, I'm here again. Just don't laugh; I hate your laughter."

The Seer nodded. "I hate it, too. Remember: I'm not laughing at you, I'm laughing about you."

"That makes it better?"

"Probably not. Explanations aren't always helpful. A great man, from a place you should know better, said that to understand all is to forgive all. I understand all—and let me tell you, the man who said that was an idiot."

"Do you really understand everything?" The king looked at him, thinking of the lost limbs and hair. "Why did you do it?"

"You came to ask that?"

"You know I didn't. But I've always wanted to ask."

He sighed. "Once, I thought being wise would be the best bar-gain I could make." His mouth quirked and he gestured around at the stalactites, at the tiny stream that ran from the well, and at the twin bats (Thought and Memory) hanging at either side of his head. "Who could pass up offices like these? And to think my mother wanted me to be a doctor or a pharmacist. Are you listening?"

"I'm listening, but it doesn't make sense to me." Somehow, in learning so much, the Seer had lost the ability to say things directly.

"Then listen for how I say things, which may help you more than what I say. A pharmacist is a drug dispenser on a different world. I think you know what a doctor is, even if we hardly ever see one." He cackled to the ceiling, "Sorry, I don't make house calls," and coughed, his eyes weeping more than ever as smoke drifted into them. He stared back to Brandal, and for a moment his eyes had the sharpness Brandal had remembered in the eagle-Seer's. "But some doctors still do. Remember that. What doctors still do?"

"Why are you talking about a world I don't know?"

"Why aren't you listening? Because my answers are of no use, but how I answer is everything you need. That's why how you ask is so important." The Seer grinned. "Think of your kingdom and do your best."

The king cleared his throat and stood up straight. He didn't have to remind himself; his kingdom never left his thoughts. "What's your name?"

"Why?" But the Seer was looking at him amusedly, and had seen through Brandal's attempt to stall.

"I'm your king. I ought to know."

The Seer bowed, awkwardly since his stone hand unbalanced him and his rooted feet limited him. "I was a man named Harral, sire. Much of me still is."

"I see that." The king looked at him, trying not to show the pity he felt. "It was brave of you to choose what you did."

"I was a fool," Harral said simply. It was true. He could now say nothing but the truth. "Why have you come?"

Brandal looked uncertainly at him, then sighed and said bluntly, "Crossroads is going to be invaded."

"Crossroads is always being invaded."

Brandal nodded, looking restlessly from side to side as though answers hung in the dripping limestone. "But most of them pass through, or settle quietly. Morgan won't do either."

"I know," Harral said. "Tell me what you must, and then ask what you must. The way you ask changes the answer."

The king stood still. "Could you explain how that works?"

"Certainly. Once a young woman told me, 'I marry tomorrow; will my husband love me more than life, all his life?'

"I told her that he would. At the wedding, a jealous friend tried to stab her, and he leaped on the knife." He chuckled. "You see? He was her husband, and he loved her more than he did life itself, all his life. That's how it works. So, as I said to you before, why ask?"

He was surprised at the bitterness in Harral's voice, but answered, "Most of us can't help asking. I'm surprised that you're not busy all the time."

"One hopes not," he said dryly. "No one who wasn't desperate would consult me."

The king responded immediately, "I'm desperate. Crossroads is facing war."

"You think so?" He sounded amused.

"I know so," Brandal said simply. "I've been in Morgan's camp outside Crossroads, as a volunteer."

"Really?" But Harral had clearly known. "Your subjects will make up a wonderful ballad, and several bad ones, about your heroism."

"I didn't tell them I went." He looked embarrassed. "I didn't want them to worry."

Harral's voice was suddenly gentle. "And instead you worried for them." He shook himself and added in his own voice, "They'll know anyway, if you choose another spy."

"Maybe I won't need one."

"Maybe not, but if you do, you can't keep the spying mission a close secret. It's not as though you can send the Inspector General." His lip twisted, even beyond its perpetual grimace of pain. "After all, he's a bit obvious."

"And I'd never risk him." Brandal was surprised by the heat in his own voice. How had he grown to love an officer legendary for cruelty, whose cruelty had once scarred Brandal deeply? "We need him in Crossroads."

"Well, you shouldn't risk spying for yourself again. If you go back now and you're caught, Morgan will torture you for desertion. Delightful."

Brandal shuddered. "While I was there, Morgan caught a man stealing military supplies—a barrel of salted meat. The troops tied the man to a stake, and forced chunks of meat down the man's throat until his body burst open; I didn't think that could be done. They punched a tube into his throat, to keep him breathing." He shuddered. "I have no idea where Morgan learned to do that."

"Get some idea where, and soon. So you won't be going back?"

Brandal said evasively, "I'd barely have time. Less than a month from now, Morgan's troops will march into Crossroads."

"And out, if you're clever. Remember when the Legion of the Ninth marched on us, up a road they called an *iter* and thought was taking them somewhere else?" He spoke casually, as another man might speak of last winter.

King Brandal shuddered. "You forget what year it is."

Harral considered. "Was that really two thousand years ago?"

"And Crossroads still remembers. The *milites* were a handful of well-trained soldiers, and they almost destroyed us."

"Right. And where were they from?" Harral shook himself like an animal. The bats shrank back as steaming water flew off. "But they marched on the Strangeways, and Darryl the Wise lured them onto a road out of Crossroads and to some other world."

"That won't work this time."

"Really? Why not?"

"Morgan is searching for a copy of *The Book of Strangeways*."

"Ah." Harral, perpetual tears and all, looked impressed. "You know that already? But the Strangeways aren't our only defense—just our best."

"We need a better one." The king said carefully, "I've been thinking of finding defenders elsewhere—along the Strangeways."

"Creative," Harral said. "But first you have to be able to tell heroes from villains. Then you'd better be sure you know what evils the heroes bring with them." He leaned toward the king as best he could. "Remember this and listen carefully: heroes are like drugs or drink; they bring problems you may not know."

"That's why I'm asking you before I risk anything: Is there anyone out there who can save us from the greatest threat this world has known?"

Harral, unexpectedly, gaped. "That's your question?"

"Yes."

Brandal regretted it as he spoke, but it was too late. Thought and Memory uncovered their faces and stared at him; they announced ritually, "Yes. Yes. Yes," and covered their faces again with webbed wings. Brandal thought that their fanged muzzles sneered.

Harral smiled. "After all these years, it's nice to be surprised. For a moment I thought you'd force a useful answer out of me. You want to know if such heroes exist?"

"Yes."

"And you want to know if they're coming?"

"Yes."

"And you want to know if they'll defeat the greatest threat this world has known?"

"Yes, damn you." Somehow, by misphrasing the question, Brandal had failed his entire world.

"All right. Yes, these heroes exist. They'll come without your having to do a thing, and yes, they'll save Crossroads from its greatest danger."

"Just 'yes'? That's it?"

"Of course."

"Is it the truth?"

Harral said without anger, "If you didn't know that I told the truth, you wouldn't have come."

"Then why can't I stop worrying?"

"Never stop worrying." The seer threw back his smoldering head and laughed: great, mirthless sounds echoing until the bats shifted and squeaked with discomfort. For a moment Harral seemed more than himself: the stone hand a mountain, the roots a forest, the hair a firestorm, the wind a hurricane, and the weeping eye more ocean-full than the well in front of him. The Six Kingdoms of the World were laughing at a poor human king.

Brandal fled. At the lowest landing he replaced the torch and heard laughter. At the next and the next he replaced his robe and crown, and heard more. At the last, putting on his armor, he discovered that he could still hear it.

He emerged into the valley at sunset. The shadows were already quite deep over the water, and trout leaped after the evening insects. Brandal walked stiffly to keep from putting his hands over his ears. Faint laughter followed him all the way to his bed.

T·H·R·E·E

MRS. SOBELL, HEAD reference librarian for Western Virginia University, finished patiently, "And that's how the Library of Congress cataloging system works. Do you have any questions?" She looked expectantly up at the student—not because she was seated and he standing, but because she was quite short.

The student, whose hair was moussed straight up and whose T-shirt said Unprepared for Anything, swallowed and looked blank. Finally he said, "Yeah, well, uh, you like, say you got these, you know, like, books, available in the library? They're not there, man."

Mrs. Sobell looked at him for a moment speculatively, then said with perfect poise, "Have you tried the card catalog and the Library System terminals?"

He burst out, "No, man, but I got friends." He wandered off, scratching his backside.

Mrs. Sobell thought to herself that, though the major drug years on campus were long over, there were still plenty of personal excursions going on.

She turned confidently to the next student. Mrs. Sobell had worked with thirty-five years of Western Vee students, and was always ready for a next one, no matter what the last one had done. No question, she often told the other librarians, was unanswerable.

The next student didn't look like a challenge at all. She had carefully combed dark hair, a laundered and sketchily pressed

19

green cotton blouse, and dark serious eyes. She smiled down at Mrs. Sobell, who smiled back. Here was a nice, stable student, no drugs and no crises. "May I help you?"

The girl's smile went away, and Mrs. Sobell recognized the "professional face." Graduate students wear it more than they ever will in their careers. "I have an odd question."

Mrs. Sobell said firmly, "No question is unanswerable." She waited confidently.

BJ said carefully, "How can I find practical medical material on unicorns?"

Mrs. Sobell looked at her for several seconds. Finally she said, "Did David in Science Reference put you up to this?"

BJ looked puzzled.

"Never mind. What sort of material are you looking for?"

She repeated, "Medical material."

"Yes." Mrs. Sobell repeated thoughtfully, *"Practical* medical material. Do you have a starting point—an author, a magazine article?"

From her blue backpack, BJ pulled the battered copy of *Lao's Guide.*

Mrs. Sobell opened it carefully, accustomed to rare and tattered books. "Flyleaf inscription—'For Sugar from P. Fields.' " The handwriting was terrible. "Title page. Privately printed, Arizona, nineteen twenty-one. It may not be in the National Union Catalogue." She opened it to the bookmark and skimmed the unicorn entry, carefully not looking surprised or interested. "Why unicorns in particular?"

Silence. Then: "I was curious about them. Why do you ask?"

Silence. Mrs. Sobell said, "Have you tried the veterinary library, or spoken with the faculty or staff?"

BJ said cautiously, "I have."

After another silence, Mrs. Sobell said with barely a quaver, "We'll do our best."

She began with the inevitable, "Have you tried the card catalog and the WVLS?" She gestured toward the computer terminals on the central table.

BJ said dubiously, "I tried under 'unicorns.' Most of it was folklore." Data searches, like library searches, made her nervous.

Mrs. Sobell, back on firm ground, said stiffly, " 'Unicorns' is too broad." She made some quick notes on scratch paper. "Enter each of these: author, subject, key words of title. Add to the list of search items every time you come up with an entry. Don't forget that you can do a global search based on the call numbers of any books you find."

BJ thanked her and went to the terminals. Mrs. Sobell felt like the center fielder on her beloved Orioles, stretching up and snagging a tough one just before it could sail over the fence. Just to prove a point to herself she dragged a stool over to the National Union Catalogue, which lists every work of which a printed copy is known to exist, and climbed up to check for *Lao's Guide*. It wasn't there, and neither was the author.

At a terminal, BJ keyed in "medicine, unicorns." Nothing.

"Veterinary medicine, unicorns." Nothing.

She requested a title search and keyed in "Lao's Guide."

The monitor went blank. It stayed that way long enough that she considered moving to another computer. Finally a new screen came up:

Author	Title	No. of Copies	Location
Lao,	Lao's Guide to the	0	Not
Shen-Tzu	Unbiological Species		Available

LISTING BY AUTHOR: None
LISTING BY SUBJECT: Crossroads
LIBRARY OF CONGRESS NUMBER: MBZ 1442.5 LAO
This is an unreal number.

She read it far more slowly and carefully than it deserved. It didn't tell her much. She tried the listing by author, even though the WVLS said there wasn't one. For her efforts she learned that the Western Virginia library had seventy-three titles relating to Lao-tzu and Taoism.

Without much hope she tried the subject heading, "crossroads." She had the sense to wait through the blank screen, even though it was longer this time. Ten titles flashed on the screen, with MORE in the lower right-hand corner. She read the first three:

1. Anatomy of species transferral between worlds: Natural re-selection and importation.
2. Bedrock, Reality Tectonics, and Crossroads.
3. Book of Strangeways, The.

She printed a screen-dump, called the next screen, printed that, called and printed the final screen, and, suddenly curious, recalled the first screen and pressed 3.

The screen stayed idle a very long time. If she hadn't already tried once, she would have given up or punched a key long before anything happened.

Finally the screen renewed itself slowly and deliberately, line by line from the top down:

Author	Title	No. of Copies	Location
Unknown	The Book of Strangeways.	1	Main Library

LISTING BY AUTHOR: None
LISTING BY SUBJECT: Crossroads
LIBRARY OF CONGRESS NUMBER: PYZ 1993.7 STR Ref.
                              This is a completely
                              unreal number.

DOES NOT CIRCULATE

BJ looked puzzledly at the number. Like most students, she was barely familiar with library cataloging; still, something didn't look right about it.

She at least knew that "Ref." followed by "DOES NOT CIRCU-LATE" was redundant.

She tried to print the screen, but something was wrong with the printer. She wrote the catalog number on her previous printout, tore the paper off the printer, and strode off to the elevators.

BJ's tastes ran to biology, chemistry, and old movies. She knew the geography of Roanoke, Virginia, of Kendrick, and of the places mentioned regularly on the news. She had never been to the map department of a university library. She walked through slowly, reading labels and looking for the right call numbers.

There were row on row of flat steel drawers with contour maps and aerial photographs. There were distribution maps of flora and fauna, census maps of endangered species, and largely conjectural maps of the widest ranges of extinct species.

There were geologic maps of mineral deposits and climatic maps of rainfall and snowfall, tundra and desert.

There were maps of this world and of the others: the moon, the planets, and a few maps of their moons. There were star charts and zodiac charts and even a rough chart of the known universe.

Closer to her call number, there were maps of legendary places—Atlantis, Eden, Hell—and old maps with sea serpents and chimeras filling in the unexplored areas. There was a folio of maps to the Lost Dutchman Mine, and maps to the Lost Colony, the Fountain of Youth, El Dorado, and the Seven Cities of Cibola.

She almost missed it. On a bottom shelf, between *A True and Factual Account of the Newlie Established Colonie of Virginia* and *Annotated Maps of American Exploration, with reference to Timothy Flint's Writings*, was a blank cloth spine. There was a piece of white tape on it with PYZ 1993.7 STR Ref on it. Nothing more.

She pulled the book out carefully, frowning at the dust on the top. She blew on it, and her eyes watered; some of the dust was pollen. The front and back were marbled paper, with no embossed title. She opened it, trying to examine it as Mrs. Sobell had *Lao's Guide*. The flyleaf was blank, and there was no title page. The paper felt as thick as parchment; BJ thought, unwillingly, of the books Peter and she had taken from her grandfather's library when they were children and he had been taken from his home.

She turned a page and was immediately disappointed. The book was nothing but maps. First was a town map of Kendrick, Virginia, including the Western Vee U. campus. Someone had gone to a lot of trouble to make the map look old. BJ automatically scanned the campus area.

It must be a fairly new map, she decided; the veterinary college, barely two years old, was shown in full on it. There was the classroom building, the hospital, the circular drive, and the two parking lots. . . .

She frowned. The back lot, its asphalt still oily from being freshly laid this week, was shown on the map. She looked again at the dust (pollen) on the book top, thankful that her eyes had quit watering and her allergies had not kicked in.

She ran a finger over the sketch of the parking lot, feeling foolish when it didn't smudge. Probably whoever drew the map had drawn it from the plans.

She looked at the rest of the map. She recognized most of the streets, but there were a few with no "street" or "avenue" designations. They all took odd turns, and they all seemed to go nowhere.

She leafed through and scanned the other maps, using the one of Rouen to test her high-school French. There were several in Russian, and a few in Arabic. One was in what she thought was Indian, and several were in languages she didn't recognize at all. They were all street maps. BJ turned to the back.

In the very back were two brief paragraphs, handwritten in a script that made BJ think of monks and quill pens:

Even familiar places have unfamiliar roads, and even people found at home can become lost after a wrong turn. But there are small wrong turns and large ones, and these last are the Strangeways.

Use this book, and good traveling, but remember that one good turn may not deserve another, and that two wrong turns may not make a right, and that there are many worlds of difference between "turn" and "return." For those lost at Crossroads, only a map will help them find themselves.

Clearly the book was miscataloged, since the other books in this section were all mythical or for exploration. Still she slid it back in place, wondering idly why "Crossroads" was capitalized.

It was past time for lunch, but BJ had one task left. On her way out she sat down at the Infotrac system—a computerized index, on laser disk, of current periodicals. The screen said uncompromisingly, in block letters, ENTER YOUR SUBJECT. She sat with her fingers poised over the keys, not wanting to type.

Finally she pecked out, steadily but slowly, HUNTINGTON'S CHOREA.

The list of entries was six screens long. She printed them all and quit for lunch.

On the corner opposite Mitch's, a leftover-hippie ice cream and natural food parlor on College Avenue, was a Greek lunch counter called Gyro's. By now (one o'clock) it was nearly empty.

BJ went there whenever she could; Stan (Constantine), the gray-haired man who had taken it over from his incredibly old immigrant father, knew her by name and chatted with her while she sat at the counter.

"Beej!" he said as she came in. "A gyro?" But he was already shaving lamb from the spit and throwing it on the grill.

"Hi, Stan. How's your father?"

He shrugged. "Over eighty. Other than that, he's fine." He said, a shade defensively, "Chris's mind is as sharp as it's ever been, though." She nodded. Even with her own troubles, she had noticed that lately the old man seemed disturbed and confused, especially when he was looking for utensils hanging from the rack he had used all his life. She understood, better than Stan knew, what Stan was feeling.

But she didn't talk about it, just clutched her backpack and moved to the booth by the side. "I need to do some reading, Stan."

"Okay, sure, Beej." He looked troubled. She felt guilty, but pulled the second printout from her backpack and began checking off the titles.

The popular articles she ignored for now. She put stars beside the articles in medical journals, knowing that some of them wouldn't be available in a university library where there was no medical school. Perhaps she could get printouts from Duke.

For now she could read the abstracts, which were lengthy. The first one was from the *New England Journal of Medicine*:

Huntington's Chorea is one of the most feared of degenerative nerve diseases. Its rarity (one to two cases per twenty thousand in the U.S. population) is small comfort to those who suffer its effects or to those born with the fear of developing it in their mid-twenties or, more usually, in their late forties (the age range over which symptoms are first apparent).

Huntington's Chorea is an autosomal dominant-gene disorder; offspring of victims have a 50 percent likelihood of developing it themselves. At present there is no cure, and little can be done to alleviate the often-horrifying effects of the illness. While tranquilizers and drugs such as haloperidol have had some effect against the involuntary spasms for which it is named, no known treatment retards the gradual mental decay from loss of motor control into depression, memory loss, and finally dementia. The course of the disease from its onset generally takes ten to fifteen years, with occasional variation in the order of symptoms.

Huntington's Chorea has been recognized since 1872, but research has been limited by the tools of observation and analysis for nervous and genetic tissue. A CT scan can determine the extent of atrophy and a PET scan the rate of deterioration in the cerebral cortex and basal ganglia; however, the PET scan is not generally available, and neither of these can detect the disease before physical deterioration has actually begun. (In some cases, the dementia appears first.)

A genetic test now available can determine whether or not offspring of Huntington's Chorea victims carry the short 4-chromosome deformity indicative of the gene having been passed on. Administration of the test is controversial. On the one hand, a knowledge of a degenerative and always fatal condition is devastating to the patient. On the other hand, allowing an unknowing victim to pass the same gene to offspring is immoral. At present medical ethicists are divided on the issue. Both sides recommend an interview with a genetic counselor before testing.

The test itself . . .

BJ read the rest carefully, wishing (not for the first time) that she had wanted to go into human medicine.

She took a notepad from her pack and flipped through it, nearly to the back.

There was a series of lists, carefully outlined. "Things to finish first" was written at the top of the first page. The lists were long and painstaking; BJ was quite thorough.

"Friends to write" covered a page and a half, and included people she had not written in years. It would, she reflected gloomily, be like doing thank-you notes after her college graduation.

In contrast, the next list, "Property," was embarrassingly short: a stereo, an aged and disreputable Chevette, too many textbooks. There was a person's name written after each piece. She passed this page. She didn't need it yet.

On the first blank page she wrote, "Find a genetic counselor." She chewed on the stem of her pen and looked back at the printout to see where she could find the article abstract.

But she had already refolded the printout, and the article title on top was "Terminal Illness and Suicide: The Uses of Donor Organs, the Ethics of Fatality."

She put the printout and the pad away. When Stan brought her gyro, she ate slowly and without enjoyment.

F·O·U·R

THE CONFERENCE ROOM wall was hung with a pink- and purple-stained cross section of joint cartilage, a line drawing of a horse's foreleg with arrows indicating the sites for nerve blocks, and a multi-panel diagram of abnormal presentations in bovine and equine fetuses.

There was a radiograph of a horse's fetlock, pastern, and coffin joints clipped to a view box, and on the antiseptic white counter were plastic models of exposed eye sockets and of a bovine G.I. system, with the brand names of pharmaceutical companies on them.

The counter had Styrofoam cups and a coffeepot half-full of cold coffee of indeterminate age. A wall clock said 7:20.

Everything looked normal and rational and ordinary, and had nothing to do with what BJ was carrying in her backpack.

The other students, familiar from a class of eighty-three people, looked ordinary and still sleepy. The woman in the corner, Lee Anne Harrison, was from a Clydesdale farm near Mount Airy, North Carolina. She never thought she could pass any courses, and she seldom got less than an A.

Lee Anne, who had been staring straight ahead, focused on BJ, nodded, and said curtly, "Good to see you. You feeling all right?"

BJ nodded. Lee Anne toyed with a ballpoint. "Did Sugar tell you where we're going?"

BJ shook her head. "I'm presenting today. I didn't think we'd go anywhere."

"Guess again," someone drawled from the doorway. BJ turned,

but knew the voice, and part of her died. Dave Wilson, a.k.a. Gunner Dave.

Dave firmly believed that being a maverick was just as important as being good, and that if you were good you could be as rude, as loud, and as irresponsible as you wanted to be. Someday a careless accident would make him ashamed—possibly ruin his career, probably kill an animal—but meanwhile, he was terrible to work with.

He said, "Sugar's getting the truck."

BJ said, "In front of clients, let's call him Dr. Dobbs."

Dave dropped into a chair, putting his boots on the conference table and tipping his Redskins cap over his eyes. "Sounds great. And we'll all be doctors too." He stuck out his hand and said in a booming false voice, "Hi, I'm Dr. Dave."

When no one else laughed he said, "Loosen up." He tilted his head up just far enough to watch BJ. "Sugar said you were presenting. What on?"

She moved a hand over her book bag automatically. "On our first case. Have either of you got anything to present?"

He stiffened, nearly bringing his feet off the table. "Nothing much."

It was fun, seeing Dave that unsettled. BJ felt better.

Lee Anne said, "You wouldn't believe me."

They sat in silence. Lee Anne read. Dave picked his teeth with a corner of notebook paper.

With her right hand, BJ felt quickly for the string she had run through the zipper of her book bag and started tying, untying, retying: one-handed square knots, surgeon's knots. Partly she was training for surgery, but mostly she was reassuring herself, proving that she was coordinated still.

DeeDee leaned in and said, "Good morning." She made it sound just bright enough that everyone felt obliged to smile back. "Which rotation is this?"

Lee Anne said, "Ambulatory. One of Sugar's."

DeeDee rolled her eyes. "Keeping the highways hot. Dr. Truelove asked me." She smiled sympathetically to BJ. "How are you *feeling*?" she said, almost intimately.

BJ blushed and said, "I'm okay now."

"Good, that's so good . . . where are you going today?"

BJ realized that Dave and Lee Anne were looking at her intently. "We don't know yet."

"Oh." DeeDee looked disappointed. "Dr. Truelove asked. Well, good luck." She left.

Laurie looked in on them, grinned inexplicably, and said nothing. Dave shifted uncomfortably in his chair; Laurie was the only woman in the vet school who could make him profoundly uneasy.

Sugar leaned in. "Move out." They jumped, and he grinned. He liked keeping people off base.

They trooped out to the ambulatory truck, behind the hospital, and stared at it. Dave, for effect, dropped his army pack.

The truck was an off white, with scrapes from tree limbs, and a Western Vee Vet Med logo on it. The students knew every creak in it, every squeak of the brakes and bone-jarring, bladder-starting jog of the worn shocks.

It was the usual double-cab truck with lockers and cabinets down the body. BJ had often wondered how anyone could possibly fill up all that storage space; it had more drawers and closets than her apartment.

This time she wondered how everything would fit.

Beside it, on the asphalt, were two gas cans, two bottles of thirty-weight motor oil, a gallon of coolant, five spark plugs, two spare tires, and a tool kit. There were a fire extinguisher, three canteens, a tarp, a coil of rope, and a Colman stove.

Beside these were a box of Ace bandages, two wound packs rolled and tied, a fetotomy Gigli wire for delivering dead foals and calves, another wire for bone sawing, obstetrical chains for deliveries, gauze, cotton balls, bottles of iodine, scrubs, a portable generator, surgical theater lights on C clamps, a collapsible stainless steel table, and an anesthetic machine the size of a small jukebox.

BJ moved her mouth but nothing came out.

Dave said, "Holy shit, we're doing field surgery."

Lee Anne said, "Why?"

Sugar spoke only to her. "We'll be pretty far back in the hills."

Dave poked at the auto equipment. "What the hell are we doing, fleeing Poland?"

Lee Anne answered, flatly and with complete assurance. "We're going a long ways from any mechanics, that's what we're doing."

Sugar chuckled. "The country girl scores again." BJ wished that Sugar could see how touchy Lee Anne was about being from the country.

Unless, of course, he knew, and was teasing her on purpose.

Sugar said, "If you don't know much about cars or trucks,

now's the time to learn. I never had much use for anyone who couldn't take care of his own truck."

"We'll do fine," Dave said, in a close imitation of Sugar's drawl.

But Dave was from tidewater Virginia; it sounded like a parody of Lee Anne's Carolina accent.

She snapped, "You may think so, Mr. Wilson, but you'd better hope to God we don't bust an axle or drop a trannie. Do you have any idea what can happen off road?"

He blushed and said back, "I can handle it." He tried to sound as though he could handle anything.

Sugar only grunted, "You'll have to. Load up." They began packing, each moving away from the other. BJ thought glumly that the next three weeks, with three people who weren't close friends and a teacher who wasn't easy, were going to be hell— and hell on wheels, at that.

When the packing was done, Sugar said, "Mount up." They climbed in, holding their book bags on their laps. Lee Anne and BJ fastened their seat belts tightly. Dave smirked at them and slumped, his seat belt unfastened.

Sugar, at the wheel and holding a photocopied road map, turned and said, "Ready?"

The right rear cab door swung open suddenly, and a woman's voice said, "Sorry I'm late." It was almost a girl's voice, soft and hesitant.

Lee Anne said, "Hi, Annie."

Dave rolled his eyes and mimed prayer.

Annie Taylor didn't see him, or pretended not to. "Thanks for waiting." She climbed in, a large knapsack in her right hand. BJ leaned back and helped pull her in.

Sugar called over his shoulder, "What took so long? Did matins run late this morning, or was the preacher long winded?"

She said without taking the slightest offense, "I wasn't sure where we'd be going, so I made some extra sandwiches in case anyone didn't have enough. We always needed them on the last ambulatory block." She smiled at BJ. "Thanks for the hand."

BJ suddenly felt that the block wouldn't be all bad.

They took a right from the hospital lot onto the campus access road; predictably, they turned onto the 480 bypass, headed for the Jefferson National Forest and Brushy Mountain. They passed the last few ranch houses on the edge of Kendrick, the first farmhouse with its battered, sawback rail fence, the sudden drop-off with a southern view of a twenty-mile valley.

Two miles down the road, Sugar turned left onto a battered gravel lane that dropped steeply, paralleling a stream that cascaded around rocks and roots. Dave bounced sideways and whacked his head. Lee Anne grinned.

Sugar, his eyes never leaving the road, said, "Start presenting, BJ."

"Here?" Her hands fumbled in her pack, and her stomach tightened. The ride was too bumpy for her to read her notes.

"Here," he said firmly. "This rotation y'all better learn to shoot from the hip."

BJ looked back at the others. Lee Anne and Dave looked back noncommittally. Annie smiled encouragingly, but expectantly.

What the hell. She pulled out the horn, stuffed the notes that fell out with it back into her backpack, and said, "This is a broken horn from a unicorn, species *unicornis*."

None of them laughed. BJ suddenly wondered what each of them was scheduled to present on, and realized that this could be one hell of an interesting block.

Sugar prompted, "What subspecies?"

"There are no subspecies," BJ said.. "At least none that I could find. I read *Lao's Guide*, and some classical sources in the university library, a few medieval legends, and"—she hesitated—"some essays in the library. They all give the same morphology, so I'm guessing there's just the one species, the Indian."

"Doctors don't guess," Sugar said automatically, but seemed pleased just the same. "Were the other sources much help?"

She shook her head, then realized that he couldn't turn to watch her. The road, now barely two ruts, forked often; he was concentrating on the map. "The essays were taxonomy, not medicine. The other sources sounded like folk wisdom. For instance, does it really take a virgin to catch a unicorn?"

"And what do we do if it does?" Dave commented. The students involuntarily looked at Annie.

Annie said placidly, "I could shock all of you just now."

"So could I," David said.

Lee Anne said, "Wouldn't surprise me, Dave."

After a moment's intrigued silence, BJ went on. "Assuming that we can catch the unicorn, we halter it—with an adjustable halter; I'm not sure how big they are. The hard part will be reattaching the horn." She tapped it with her penlight.

The ringing swelled, as it had in Sugar's office, until it seemed the metal truck frame was ringing in sympathy; she covered the horn and cut the sound.

In the silence that followed, the roar from the waterfalls beside the road was striking. The stream had grown, and they had gone downhill farther than BJ had thought Brushy Valley went.

"For a cow or goat, we would simply saw off the broken horn and let a new one grow in from the bud, but for some reason"— she hesitated, then plowed ahead—"the client does not wish that procedure."

"Mating time," Sugar said. "They don't breed every year, and the horn's part of the courtship ritual. It has to be in place and ring true, or no unikid."

BJ went on, as though she had anticipated the second condition. "For these reasons, it is important to reattach the horn as seamlessly as possible." She braced for questions.

Annie asked matter-of-factly, "What's the fracture like? Were there any fragments?"

BJ blessed her silently and held the horn sideways so the others could look at it. "No, it's non-comminuted and non-segmented, a fairly clean oblique break. Probably the horn snapped sideways while there was pressure against it.

"I'd recommend filing a slight bevel onto each side of the break, and filling the new space with methyl acrylate for bonding. That way there'll only be glue on the edges, and the horn-on-horn contact should still provide good sound transmission. Probably the bond should be reinforced with metal, either with two cerclage wire rings, or with similar bands, slipped over the horn"—she was winging it, and knew it—"with the bands to be made of some material with better acoustic properties than surgical steel has."

Dave raised his hand and said innocently, "Just what are the acoustic properties of surgical steel?" He poised his pen over his notebook.

BJ glanced at Sugar, who stared studiously at the map in his right hand. She said, "I suspended various plates from three-aught suture and struck them with a rubber hammer. They sound pretty poor." From her pack she took a flat plate with screw holes in it, hung it by the thread and struck it with her penlight. Klunk. "Ideally, we should make the bands from something other than steel, possibly from a bell metal."

"Bronze?" Sugar asked.

BJ shook her head again, automatically. "No. Bronze corrodes. Not silver, either. Silver tarnishes."

He said softly, "Any recommended metals, Doc?"

She was pleased. "Gold." She fumbled in her pack and pulled out a clear sandwich bag with two gold hoops. "I got these at Ryerson's jewelry on College Avenue. They had fourteen-karat hoop earrings of two different sizes; the large one should slip around the bottom." She suspended one of the hoops and tapped it; it chimed faintly. The hoops weren't very thick, but they were the most she could afford.

She slipped the small earring over the top of the horn fragment; it slid down to about an inch below the upper start of the break. "These should help hold the horn in place, especially if we run a line of glue around the tops of the rings."

Sugar reached into his shirt pocket and passed her two thicker, flatter bands. They were much heavier than the earrings. Close up she could see that they were woven from gold wire, then pounded flat. They felt fairly heavy.

"Pure gold," he said, "braided for strength. They'll fit over the horn, like you said. We'll use the acrylate, like you said, but capillary action should pull some of the glue under the band for a tighter bond.

"After mating season, the client"—he grinned at the word, but didn't elaborate—"will remove the horn, and a new one will grow in plenty of time for next season."

He added while the students carefully passed the gold pieces from hand to hand, "If you're gonna surgerize, you need to be a carpenter and a mechanic."

He held a palm out and pocketed the horn bands. "Any questions for BJ or for me?"

Annie said, "Where did the bands come from?"

Dave coughed. "Yeah. You must be talking a thousand bucks' worth of gold there."

Sugar said dryly, "If you ever need them for private practice, I'll tell you."

He added without humor, "And don't tell other students about them. We've had enough of a theft problem as it is."

He drove across the stream; the bridge was a single slab of stone with no guardrails, and looked ageless.

On one side of the road, which was now flat stone, was a rock wall with five-leafed ivy and occasional shrubs hanging from it. On the other side was a sheer drop to the stream, which descended in cascades broken by still pools.

The truck bounced down the stone road. Dave hung on to the seat in front of him as they approached a gap in the cliff ahead, where the valley walls almost closed together over the road and the stream, far below them. BJ stared ahead; beyond the cliffs, she could see a flat sheet of water.

Sugar spun his hands on the wheel. The truck swung right as the road angled through the gap and around the corner of the cliff face.

The river in front of them was half a mile across, placid and clear, with weeds trailing under the surface.

The cliff faces were overgrown with flowers: peach, blue, purple, dangling from vines against the sandstone. Blue-backed birds fluttered in front of them. The rock itself was studded with quartz, and the western bank flashed and glittered in the morning sun.

It was nothing like the New River in Virginia, nothing like the Jefferson National Forest just beyond the campus. It was nothing like any place they had ever seen.

They rode in silence, staring as every turn along the river brought a new vista: canyons cutting into the far bank, dunes below the roadway, almost alpine mountains far to the west. Finally Sugar slapped the wheel. "Aren't any of you going to say anything?"

Lee Anne said shakily, "If anyone has something smart to say, say it for me." She was pale.

Dave said uneasily, "How do we get back?"

BJ said, "How much further are we going?"

Annie, looking lost and a little dazed, still said nothing. Once she fingered the cross on her necklace.

Sugar stared out the windshield and smiled fondly, almost proudly at the wilderness ahead. "If you don't know the way, it's farther here and back than you can go in a lifetime."

He tucked the map carefully in his shirt pocket, but not before BJ noticed that the original had been drawn with the same penmanship as the maps in the book she had seen in the library.

When Sugar pulled the truck over, the cliffs had curved away from the river; they were in a bowl-shaped valley with a small stream running through it. The stream came through a narrow wind gap in the wooded cliff top. He shut the motor off and grinned at BJ. "Shouldn't we say hi to our client?"

The client was leaning against a low dry-stone wall. He was wearing what looked like loose khaki breeches and a broadcloth shirt. The trouser bottoms were hidden in a tangle of grass. He had a flat cap on over his dark curly hair.

Both shirtsleeves were rolled up; his arms were muscular and covered with dark hair.

He spoke carefully and rhythmically; to BJ it sounded like a

Greek accent. "You welcome back to Crossroads, Sugar."

"Always good to get back." They shook hands. "Folks, this is Mr. Fields."

Mr. Fields grinned. BJ had the strong feeling that wasn't his real name.

Fields looked them up and down and smiled. Annie put her clipboard in front of her protectively, and even Lee Anne looked daunted. BJ had the sudden urge to check whether her coveralls were zipped. She swallowed and said, "You own the patient?"

He looked shocked and said, "Not in any way, miss. Some things you work with but you shouldn't own." When he waved his hands while talking, he looked a little like Zorba the Greek.

Dave looked around. "So, where's the herd?"

"No," Fields corrected. "Always you should know what they are called." He recited carefully, "A murder of crows, an unkindness of ravens, a pride of lions, a pod of whales. A serenity of unicorns."

He stuck two fingers in his mouth and whistled up the valley. The sound was as echoing and piercing as that from the unicorn horn.

They walked down the wind gap quickly and carefully, with the minimal stepping height and easy precision of Tennessee walking horses. The splashing from their hooves broke into spray.

On level ground, they moved to the grass beside the stream. Without appearing to avoid it, they stepped across the trail that ran parallel to the stream and walked smoothly and evenly through the grass.

As they approached, BJ could see that they were smaller bodied than ponies: narrower, and more muscled. They looked like colts. Their hooves, however, were split like a deer's; their chins had goat beards; their tails were like no animal BJ had seen—a cow's tail, but lithe and graceful without being feline, ending in a light tuft like the tail of a deer.

They paused in front of the road, and stayed off it.

[*Lao's Guide* said:

Whether from a mythic animal's avoidance of the commonplace, or from a tradition dating back to some near-tragic event in species memory, or from objection to the acoustic properties of hooves on pavement, unicorns refuse to travel any but the road less traveled by.

Once, an entire circus parade was held up by an intransigent unicorn until a clown thought to slip his argyle socks over each of the unicorn's hooves. Whereupon the animal stepped forward as calmly as unicorns do everything, including kill. Apparently that specimen, at least, had no highly developed sense of fashion.]

BJ, with a sidelong glance at Sugar, stepped off the road. The truck didn't disappear, and she didn't turn to stone.

Mr. Fields scratched at the matted, dark ringlets under his cap. "I never see how you people travel that road so calmly, miss." He looked up it the way they had come and shivered. "One wrong turn, miss. Just one."

They all looked thoughtfully back the way they had come, and thought of all the turns Sugar had taken.

BJ looked at the unicorns. They stood in a group (a serenity), not bunched and not isolated, peaceably regarding her. Their irises were a cool indigo, the pupils black and endlessly deep. She shook her head to break contact. "Which one is the patient?"

Fields grinned at Sugar, who shrugged and said, "Most likely the one with the broken horn."

BJ winced, waiting for Dave's crack-jawed laugh. It didn't come; Dave was staring, openmouthed, at the unicorns. Lee Anne, beside him, looked less foolish but as absorbed. Annie at least looked alert, but she was gazing back and forth from the unicorns to the bearded herdsman, and frowning uncertainly.

BJ strode into the serenity. They parted just enough to allow her comfortable moving space between them.

Of course he was in the middle; he was being defended. BJ looked, appalled, at the graying, hollow breaking point of the otherwise white spiral. It was like a chip in Wedgwood china, or a crack in a Donatello marble; the flaw hurt the eye more on something nearly perfect.

The unicorn would not meet her eye, as though it were ashamed. BJ took the horn fragment from her backpack and held it in front of her; the maimed unicorn nuzzled it but made no sound. Sugar said, "What do you need?"

She was stunned. So were the others. He was leaving BJ in charge of the treatment, instead of making her assist.

BJ swallowed. "I need two people with a halter." She added hastily, "And a third with the files, the acrylate, and the gold."

Lee Anne, looking defensive, brought the halter. BJ couldn't tell if Lee Anne was proving her virginity or just trying to test herself.

Annie, without saying anything, quietly grasped the other side of the halter. Lee Anne frowned at her.

The herd fell away around them. Together they haltered the docile unicorn.

They held either side, and BJ turned to the herdsman. "Well?"

He shook his head and leered. He couldn't seem to help himself. "Not a fair test. It wished to be caught."

BJ said patiently, "I meant, should we restrain it more?"

He shook his head violently, a motion oddly like a bull shaking flies. "Don't try."

The other unicorns watched them, not moving. BJ was suddenly aware that all the horns were lowered and pointed at them. She swallowed. "David . . ."

"Yo." He swaggered through the serenity, trying to look casual. Once he raised his hand to swat the flank of a unicorn. It turned toward him and lowered its horn without apparent malice. He pulled his hand back. "Hey, if I'm the ring bearer, who's the flower girl?"

Lee Anne said, "I knew you weren't best man."

David muttered something and passed the gold pieces to BJ. "Here's a rat-tail file, and a flat bastard. Where do I start?"

"You?" BJ was floored.

He looked surprised. "Of course me. Were you gonna do it?"

"It's my presentation," she said flatly.

He put the thin rat-tail file in his jeans pocket and used the bastard file to level the break on the unicorn. "Whatever."

BJ looked at Lee and at Annie. Neither of them said anything. She held the piece of horn in her left hand and held her right out. "File."

"What?" But he didn't stop filing. The unicorn blinked with each motion, but stayed still. Unquestionably, Dave was good. Perhaps better than she was now . . .

She kept her hand out. "I need to do the broken end first."

The client raised his shaggy eyebrows. Sugar looked irked. "Are you just doing this to show who's boss?" Dave said.

Yes. "Of course not. If we do the fragment first, we can match it—and only work on the animal once."

Dave considered, sucking his cheek in. "Why didn't you do the fragment before driving out here?"

Lee Anne said quietly, "Before presenting? Even you aren't that crazy." She said it too softly for the client to hear.

He heard anyway, or at least he grinned. BJ hadn't seen human ears twitch like that; they made her uneasy.

Dave shrugged and passed the file over.

When the broken end of the horn was as smooth as she could get it, BJ passed the horn and file to Dave. "Match this."

He took it. "Sorry. I can only do better." But he turned it over and over, and finally admitted, "Nice job."

BJ was annoyed enough not to thank him.

She took the can of acrylate and, for something to do, reread the instructions. The others waited, none too patiently.

Finally BJ said to Dave, "I'll test-place the horn. You hold the head steady."

Dave said, "No, really? I thought I'd shake it around."

At first BJ thought that he was serious: the unicorn's head kept jerking sideways, the horn fragment twisting off its base. Dave made little exasperated grunts and finally said to Annie and Lee Anne, "If this is sex, get closer. If it's work, step back."

Fields snorted, but he looked worried. Sugar looked openly disgusted.

BJ just assumed that Dave was being difficult until she stepped, tentatively, closer to the unicorn to see if that made things easier. Suddenly it didn't seem possible that four people could have this many feet and elbows. The two holders were too far forward on the head, and even Dave was working at arm's length; they were too nervous to work well.

Of course we're nervous, she thought. We've never worked with one before.

BJ remembered, during her anesthesiology rotation last winter, when the team of Laurie and Sugar gassed and operated on a bear cub. It was one in the morning, during a party, when the state troopers had called: someone had hit a bear cub, breaking its leg. The trooper had hit it with a tranquilizer dart and brought it in to see if the vet school could pin the bone. Laurie took the call and immediately lit a cigarette.

BJ, DeeDee, and some of the others had gone to watch. Laurie had rolled the tanks over to the cub, confirmed the supply, and sat waiting for Sugar to say something. The library was locked for the night, nobody had the key, and Laurie, pride of the school though she was, had never anesthetized a bear before, let alone a cub.

Sugar had thought a moment, then said, "Pretend it's a really fat, really mean forty-five-pound dog."

Laurie had tied off one of the cub's legs and induced it through a vein with a shot of thiamylal; then she'd jury-rigged a large-dog mask by adding an extra strap, set up some extra restraints, and maintenance-gassed the cub with isoflurane. The cub had stayed under and recovered nicely.

And that was how to handle the new: relate it to something you already understood, and make your skills new, too.

BJ said confidently to the others, "Stop treating it like glass. Pretend it's a small horse or a large goat."

"It isn't," Dave said. But he shifted his arm on its neck, holding it tighter. Annie and Lee Anne, on halter duty, said soothing things in the unicorn's ears and scratched its poll, moving behind the head so that Dave and BJ had room to work.

It went smoothly after that. They had to refile BJ's piece a little, but even Dave couldn't pretend that was her fault. She pried the lid off the methyl acrylate can, poured a small amount out, and carefully, precisely bonded the horn fragment onto its base.

She tried to imagine what she would have said four days ago if someone had said that she'd be doing horn repair in a serenity of unicorns. She'd probably have wanted to laugh. Then she'd have wanted to call her mother to share the laugh.

BJ slid the gold bands down the horn and added a ring of glue, in tiny beads, to the top of each band. The beads subsided as the glue crept under the edges; the gold, a good conductor of heat, grew quickly warm.

She wished her mother could see the unicorns. There had been a stained-glass sun-catcher of a unicorn hanging in the kitchen while Paul and BJ were growing up; her mother had dropped it one day, trying to clean it with clumsy, uncontrolled fingers, and had wept more than BJ had thought it merited.

BJ imagined calling her mother, after all this was over and they were back home, and telling her, "Mom, I just treated a unicorn." Her mother would hang up—she always did—and they'd each make a cup of tea, and her mother would call back. Suddenly BJ's eyes stung, remembering her mother's last note: "BJ, this is the hardest letter a mother could write. This is even harder for me, knowing that someday you may face the same choice. . . ." The police had shown it to her, but had kept it.

She felt a grazing at her cheek, as soft as a leaf. One of the other unicorns had drifted close to her and was rubbing its horn against her, rhythmic and soothing.

Fields, watching her, said gently, "They care for innocence, you know. Grief is also innocence."

Lee Anne looked up from the halter. "Mr. Fields, if like you say these aren't your animals, why do you take care of them?"

He grinned at her—at all of her—and she edged behind a unicorn. "Maybe, miss, I like being with animals who can show me who is innocent." Then he shrugged. "Besides, that's how it is. In Crossroads, we help each other."

BJ asked, "Are they native here?" Fields looked confused; she tried again. "I mean, did they come from Crossroads?"

He shook his head. "None of us come from here, miss. We came to here." He smiled at her again, and lewd as his smile was, she could tell that he was also friendly. "If you're lonely, or the last of your kind, or you don't fit in anywhere, you can always come to Crossroads."

BJ, half listening, nodded and felt along the horn. The acrylate was no longer warm, and the rings felt firmly in place. "Brace yourselves," she said to Annie and Lee Anne . . .

. . . and lightly, with the rat-tail file, she struck the horn.

It rang softly, but rang clear and true. The herd turned at the sound. The damaged unicorn, without seeming to exert any force, snapped out of the bridle and held his head high.

When Fields spoke, it was with ungrudging respect. "That sound . . . near perfect. Thanks." He grinned again. "Maybe later this year, you'll come watch them mate."

After seeing his smile, she hated to admit that she wanted to. "Possibly." She looked to Sugar for advice.

This time he helped her out. "We might not be here then, but we'll try." He shook hands again with Fields, who looked suddenly worried.

"You be very careful this time here, Sugar. Some things are not normal just now."

BJ tried to imagine what "normal" meant here.

Sugar took it seriously. "Trouble?"

"I am not sure." Fields looked sorry he had said anything. He looked up and down the roads, hesitated, and said finally, "The Inspector General is back."

He looked at Sugar, waiting for a reaction. Sugar scratched his head. "I've heard of him. I don't know what he looks like."

Fields shook his head in the fly-shaking motion again. "Nobody does."

Dave said, "Then how do you know he's back?"

Fields looked amused and angry at the same time.

"I tell you how: because not far from here is a butcher who cheated people, who used his ring finger to tip, to add to the balance on his heavy, his—" His arms waved.

"Scale."

"Scale, weighing scale, that's it. And the man cheated poor people when he weighed at market, and he knew they'd be afraid to argue with him. And the Inspector General knew it, too, and this I know because the man was no more at market yesterday.

"And on the wall where the man used to put his table, the word *justice* was written in human blood with one finger, just like the finger used to tip the scale."

"Anybody could do that," Dave said.

Mr. Fields said, "True, young man. But only the Inspector General would leave the ring finger behind, wedged into the wall."

They all looked at each other. Mr. Fields, satisfied with their reaction, said, "Time for me to work." He passed a small sack to Sugar. "Payment, like you said." He grinned. "And another case, I think. My young friend Stefan has an itch. Maybe one of your young ladies can take care of it for him?" He laughed loudly.

Dave snickered. Fields added, "Or your young man." Dave stopped abruptly.

He bowed and tipped his cap. The tips of short, blunt horns flashed through his curly hair, then disappeared as he straightened.

The students, dazed, watched him skipping or trotting away through the grass. BJ was nearly sure that, if she could see under the loose britches, she would see a hock like a goat's on each leg.

The unicorns lined up quietly and each of them touched its horn to each of the students and to Sugar. For reasons some of them might have denied, they stood still for it, and watched the unicorns move swiftly and silently up the wind gap.

The vet students moved quietly back to the truck. Sugar did a remarkably careful three-point turn—he didn't want to get off the road—and headed back the way they had come. He double-checked each turn against the map.

It wasn't until they were back to the stream that he spoke. "Annie."

"Yes, Dr. Dobbs." But she sounded less sure of herself than she usually did, and she was staring out the window.

"How'd you like the horns?" Sugar asked. Annie turned. He finished blandly, "On the unicorns."

She nodded, trying to look composed. "They were beautiful." But she stared back to where they had met Mr. Fields, and she was troubled.

Sugar said gently, "Not everything fits into your little picture of the world, does it?"

Annie, staring out at a landscape unlike anything in her world, said nothing.

It was even more obvious on the way back how many side roads there were, forking off suddenly and twisting up or down on the cliffs above them.

Sugar hit the brakes as a deer crossed in front of the truck and leaped gracefully onto a muddy road, which dropped parallel to them. A bush blocked her line of sight briefly as the deer leaped; BJ watched out the side window to see the deer land.

It never reappeared. BJ craned her neck, staring; the deer was no longer there. The tracks in the mud stopped abruptly, near the bush.

BJ turned to look at the others. Dave had his hat over his eyes again; Annie was preoccupied and hadn't looked. Lee Anne, pale and wide-eyed, had noticed.

Sugar hadn't seen their reaction. He was concentrating on following the map, and BJ suddenly had no desire to distract him.

When he crossed the stone slab bridge and looked more relaxed, BJ said, "The library didn't have much on unicorns."

"I don't imagine," he said without looking around.

"Neither did the vet library."

"Well, it's a new library. The vet school hasn't been here but three years."

Lee Anne said suddenly, "I'm not finding over much on my case, either."

"Do your best."

BJ said, "Are we the first veterinarians in Crossroads?"

Sugar waited awhile before answering, possibly to avoid missing a turn. "You're the first vet students, anyway. I've been in before."

"But you didn't do casework." Once again, BJ was sure of herself. "The other articles about Crossroads were all research, not cases. Why are we needed there, all of a sudden?"

The wait this time had to be for Sugar to collect his thoughts; he didn't say anything until they passed their first Virginia county road number, on a signpost in the ditch.

As they all relaxed, Sugar looked sideways and said, "I didn't start these trips. Fields came and got me, just showed up at my office one day and scared the life out of me by tipping his cap. He said he needed animal doctors—that's how he put it. Then he said something that stuck with me. He scratched his head, right between the horns like you'd scratch a bull calf, and he said, 'Always before we knew what had happened when something was wrong. Now, maybe, we're lost, and in danger.' And I went back with him, and I agreed that something was wrong, and I formed this ambulatory block.

"That's why you're really here." He turned onto the bypass around Kendrick, and pointed to each of them in turn. "Dave, you're reckless enough to look places I wouldn't. Lee Anne, you've got more sense than the rest of us. Annie, you've got a feel for what other people and animals are feeling and thinking— I've seen it with animals, and I've heard about it with humans. BJ . . ." He paused, then grinned. "Let's just say I like how you think."

BJ didn't think he was giving them the whole answer, but before she could say anything, Dave broke in. "So, what did you think of our work?"

Sugar looked surprised. "So that was work? I'll be damned. It looked like a fight."

Dave, for once, said nothing. He went on, "It did to the client, too. Your skills were all fine, but that ain't worth much, is it?"

They rode back in silence: Dave pretending to be vindicated, BJ embarrassed, Lee Anne annoyed, Annie with her own troubled thoughts. As they exited the bypass onto the campus, Sugar warned, "I've shown you a big secret. I don't want to hear that you've told all your friends."

Dave snorted. "Like we'd be believed."

Sugar said conversationally, "Well, Dave, nobody believes what you say, anyway. The rest of you had better watch it."

Lee Anne smirked.

In the parking lot, as they unpacked, he added, "If you don't have a bedroll, get one. Keep it and a backpack ready; some days we won't come back here."

He looked at their excited faces and grinned. "Oh, yeah. This is gonna be all right."

Unexpectedly, Annie said, "Do you think we'll meet the Inspector General?"

Sugar looked out a long time, over the hills and fields they knew.

Finally he said, "This rotation is like nothing in a normal lifetime—for me as well as for you. It's the best thing I've ever been part of."

He turned and faced them. "But if I thought for one minute that we'd meet the Inspector General—whoever he or she is—I'd tear this map up and never go again."

He picked up his gear and went to his office. The others stood in the parking lot near Dave's motorcycle, each hoping someone would suggest going somewhere to eat or drink and talk about what they'd seen.

When no one did, they split up and headed home.

F·I·V·E

BJ WAS LOOKING out the truck window as the trees flickered past, changing from scrub growth to second growth to virgin timber. Lee Anne had her window rolled down and was sniffing the air like a farm dog.

The morning air was brisk; BJ wrapped her windbreaker around her tightly.

She needed sleep badly, but she still tried to read in *Lao's Guide* and make notes; Lee Anne needed it next.

Last night BJ had stayed up long enough to read some of the articles she had photocopied. "Terminal Illness and Suicide: The Uses of Donor Organs, the Ethics of Fatality" had concerned a disturbingly simple incident: a woman BJ's age who had discovered that both her parents had Huntington's chorea and that she was certain to have it herself had written a note indicating her wish to have her undamaged brain donated to Johns Hopkins. Then she had propped a 12-gauge shotgun against her chest and, leaning the butt against the wall, pushed both triggers in.

The ethical debate was complex, but the research value of the woman's brain was indisputable.

Because there are next to no tissue samples available from presymptomatic victims, tissue samples were taken and prepared even while the moral argument over the use of the donor source continued. It is unfortunate but inevitable that the availability of presymptomatic and undamaged brains for study is highly unlikely.

BJ had written shakily on her list of things to do, "Contribute to science?" When she slept, not well, she dreamed of the black-and-white Colin Clive/Victor Frankenstein raving to Igor, who was smiling at her.

This morning that article seemed far away, as though the drive to a new world left that part of her behind. They made the same steep turn into the valley and the same winding descent to the stone bridge. All of them except BJ had been staring out the window eagerly, trying to notice the break between Virginia and Crossroads.

Annie pointed out the first of the blue-backed birds; Annie, it turned out, had been a bird-watcher since she was five. Dave noticed the addition of a strange deciduous tree to the woods, but it was mixed in with the other species and simply became more prevalent. BJ noticed this time when the road gradually changed from gravel to cobblestone.

Once they made the last dramatic turn and were along the riverbank, Sugar sighed and looked away from the road ahead and from the photocopies—fresh ones, BJ noted—clutched in his right hand. "Presentation time, Annie."

Lee Anne turned around, her chin between her hands like Kilroy-was-here on the seat back. "So, what's the case?"

Annie said calmly, "It's nothing very dramatic. There's a flock of sheep—"

"Suffolks?" Dave said promptly. "Hampshires? Lincolns?" As an urban student, he was vain about knowing breeds.

She shook her head. "An older breed. Something like the specimens you'd find in Plymouth or Salem, Massachusetts, at the heritage farms. Anyway, they've suffered a sudden onset of anemia, unthriftiness, and exhaustion. The client supplements grazing with concentrates, primarily with the breeding ewes.

"As far as he knows, the herd has never been vaccinated or treated against any major diseases. The herd has not come in contact with any other sheep, and has shown no major outbreak of new parasites—"

"That's it?" Dave yawned. "Hell, you could see a case like that right outside of Galax, Virginia." Lee Anne, who had been born near Galax, looked resentful.

"Some cases are dull," Sugar said. "Get used to that." To Annie he said, "So, what's unusual about it?"

Annie looked disconcerted. "Possibly the client," she said. "I've seen a photograph of him." But she wouldn't say anything more about him.

"Have there been any abortions?" BJ asked.

Lee Anne perked up. "Fertility problems?"

"Any deaths?" Dave said.

Annie said, "This is all too recent to have much in that line. The ewes had already lambed before he noticed. That's really all I know right now," she said apologetically.

"Try to go in knowing more," Sugar said disapprovingly. "It's not like the sheep's gonna come up to you and say, 'My belly hurts: (a) nutritional deficiency; (b) toxicity; (c) infection.' "

"I agree," Annie said. "And I'm—I wish I knew more."

It sounded like the epitaph of every struggling vet student.

They rolled through the bowl-shaped meadow of the day before, then turned uphill when the road forked. The river dropped below them.

On the lower fork, a short caravan with a horse-drawn wagon was peering upward at the van. The people carried digging equipment: long-handled, double-billed sticks like hoes. Lee Anne craned her neck, staring.

"What are you looking for?" Dave asked.

Lee Anne looked excited but cautious. She only said, "The usual, Dave. Munchkins, leprechauns, seven dwarves."

"Don't look unless you want to see," he said, lurching as the van took a sharp right turn. The land had turned to rolling, rounded hills completely unlike the cliff terrain earlier. The road, stone paved, looked much the same, but branched often. Dave said to Sugar, "We're going farther in."

"That's right." Sugar scrutinized the photocopies. "Be still for a couple minutes."

Dave opened his mouth. Lee Anne nudged him hard, and he grunted and shut up.

They took three turns during the ride through the hills, and they passed several more. They rounded a final bend and Sugar sighed and said, "There." He pointed into the valley below.

Once they'd seen it, it was so predictable that they nearly laughed: a crossroads, really a hub where five roads intersected. Overlooking it on a small, nearly circular hill with rock outcroppings near the top was an inn.

It seemed to be made of hand-hewn wood, and the windows were narrow, with heavy shutters. It had been added onto several times; rooms at each corner jutted blockily out from the original building, spoiling the lines.

The building was built like a ranch house, but L-shaped with an overhang nestled between the long and short wings. A large square tower topped the corner of the L. The rear abutted a stone cliff, and on the far side a wide stream with a rapids tumbled and roared. Nearly matching ponds lay above and below it on the stream.

BJ thought that it was an inconvenient place for an inn; the approach lane wound up between two rock outcroppings, and the building itself was far enough removed from the main road that it needed a second sign, a picture of a drinking stein, on the road below. A few carts were pulled off the road beside it.

One man (or at least, BJ reminded herself, he looked like a man) was stumping determinedly uphill with a walking stick, headed for the low log wall that topped the inner circle of rock around the inn. As he arrived, he dipped almost out of sight, his head showing as he passed through the gap in the wall.

A sheaf of wheat, dried and kept from the winter crop, stuck out from the sign-picture over the inn door. "What's that for?" Annie said, pointing.

"It's a message," BJ said. "For people who don't read. I'm not sure what it means."

Dave said suddenly, "It means there's fresh-made ale." The others looked at him and he said, a little guiltily, "It's in Robin Hood. It was my favorite story as a kid."

"I hope they have something non-alcoholic," Annie said wistfully.

"Cider." Sugar licked his lips. "Some of it's gone hard over the winter, and the rest has a bite, but it's mighty fine."

"The golden apples of the sun," BJ said softly, and wished she hadn't. "Are we staying there?"

"Eating there," Sugar said. "We're staying outdoors. Tomorrow we'll drive back, and you can take the rest of the day off."

The truck rolled to a stop. As they reached for the door, he said, "Hold it."

They stayed in place. Sugar looked at them, troubled. "It's not something I think about much. If something happens to me in Virginia, you can drive back. Hell, if you had to, you could walk back."

He folded the photocopies in half with one hand, around his index finger, then opened the glove compartment and slid the maps in. "If anything happens to me, follow these back home. If you can't get to these, find Fields and ask him to walk you back. It's risky, but it's better than nothing." He grinned. "If you can't find me and you can't find Fields, make nice lives for yourselves."

They got out quietly. BJ resolved to take a closer look at *The Book of Strangeways* and get safety copies of all route maps.

Fields was standing and waiting, but instead of watching the vet students, he was looking at a flock of twenty or thirty sheep as it spilled around the side of the hill. The flock was ambling and confused, always on the edge of dissipating, but something was driving it forward without panicking it.

A slender figure appeared among the rocks, peered down at Fields, and shouted: "Io!"

He shouted another word they didn't know and bounded over in short hops that BJ could feel in her arches. He hugged Fields, laying his head full across Fields's chest, though he was nearly as tall.

He was much thinner than Fields: wiry and muscled, with fine dark hair on his arms and a thick down of curly chest hair showing under his brown vest. On his back was a canvas knapsack, much patched, with the webbing straps of old GI packs.

He wore simple shorts, like jogging shorts but homemade, and the dark hair continued down past his ankles, which bent strangely.

Fields laughed and ruffled the boy's hair, and the small horns showed clearly. BJ stared at the cloven hooves on the young man's legs.

Fields released the faun and said, "Now in English, Stefan. These are the doctors."

Annie smiled weakly. "We aren't doctors quite yet." She was clearly shaken.

Dave nodded curtly.

Lee Anne said, "Sir, are you the patient?"

Stefan laughed, showing strong white teeth, and shook his head. He was very excited, on the edge of dancing. "I can show you." His accent was even stronger than Fields's. "The sheep are behaving strangely, and one of them is hurt. One—" he thought, and finished carefully, "shoop."

Dave snickered. BJ said, "We understand, but the word is 'sheep.'" She held up fingers. "One sheep, two sheep, ten sheep, all the same."

Stefan frowned, concentrating. "Are you sure? One goose, two geese; one moose—mouse, two mice."

"I know, but English doesn't follow rules, even its own rules." She added, because he looked embarrassed, "You speak English very well."

He brightened. "I practice, by myself and to the sheep." He pointed. "Even to one . . . sheep."

A deep indigo finch was landing on the back of one of the sheep; it flapped its wings frantically and drew back as a white paw swept up between the woolly bodies and snatched unsuccessfully at it.

Stefan bounded into the flock, doubled over, and returned with difficulty, his arms wrapped around a pudgy white kitten the size of a German shepherd.

He set it down but held on to it to keep it from returning to the flock. "Daphni, you shouldn't do that," he told it reproachfully.

"You shouldn't name her," Fields commented. "Worthless animal."

Stefan scratched between the kitten's ears until it purred and rolled in the dust, waving its paws in the air. "Don't listen to him," he said to it, and to Fields, "She only wants to eat."

"Ummm. You've been feeding her again."

Stefan said defensively, "She wouldn't chase birds if she weren't hungry."

Annie and BJ were entranced. They bent down and tickled the kitten's stomach. Dave watched with distaste. "How big is it when it's full grown?"

"She is full grown," Stefan said in surprise. "Haven't you seen one before?"

"None of us have," Annie said. She was looking at the kitten instead of at Stefan. "What kind of cat is she?"

"Flowerbinder." Stefan gently rolled the cat on its side, exposing a few fresh blooms. "They put them in their fur to hide. This one has taken most of hers out; she's trying to hide among the sheep." He tapped her nose reprovingly. "Naughty Daphni." But the flowerbinder pawed at his hand enquiringly. "Just a minute; let me see. . . ."

Stefan rummaged in his knapsack and pulled out a small paper-wrapped strip of meat. "Is this yours, then?" He waved it over her. The flowerbinder snatched at it, one-inch claws out, until she snagged the meat, tucked it into her mouth, and bounded off to eat it in peace.

"Why do you mind her eating the birds?" Lee Anne said. "She's just being a cat."

"But it's bad for the sheep," Stefan said earnestly. "First, the hunting makes them nervous when the bird struggles. Besides, I want the blue-backs to come roost; they eat ticks and lice."

"Then you should chase the flowerbinder away," Fields broke in, amused.

Stefan gave in. "I know." He looked sadly off at the flower-binder, who was done eating and was studiously tucking pink-flowered vines into her fur. "It is hard. Well." He shook his head. "Work calls." He looked at them expectantly. BJ realized that he was more excited by seeing them than they were by seeing him and Fields.

"It's my case," Annie said. Her forehead was puckered, and she was looking dubiously from Stefan to Fields. She stepped carefully by them and into the herd.

The lambs, still unweaned, bounded in and out of the flock, bleating anxiously at the intrusion.

Stefan pointed out the one that was limping, its left hind leg stiff. Annie quickly felt the leg and said with relief, "I'm sure it's just a sprain. Let it rest, if you can."

"That's hard to do." Stefan knelt concernedly, feeling the sheep's leg himself. "The Hippoi would say, ford a stream with it. If it can't swim across, butcher it." He patted the sheep. "Well, I can sell it to Stein." He glanced at the inn up the hill. "I was going to sell one anyway."

The vet students were used to the mix of concern and cold-bloodedness that people who work with meat animals often have. They were surprised, however, when Stefan said calmly, "Well, good-bye, Karyata," and kissed it on the nose. Fields dropped a halter on the sheep and dragged it, bleating, up to the inn.

"Now," Stefan said, standing up, "what about the others?"

Dave walked quickly into the flock. "You check those; I'll check these." Annie looked frazzledly at him, but was too off base to say anything.

Lee Anne glared. Before she could say anything, BJ, to her own surprise, stepped in front of Dave and said to Annie, "I'll help too, Annie—if you want us."

Annie smiled. "Thanks. Thank you both." She pointed. "Dave, why don't you check the rams. BJ, help me with the ewes. Lee Anne, would you mind checking lambs?"

"Glad to." She smiled at Stefan and walked straight into the flock. Of all the students, Lee Anne, who had grown up on a farm for Clydesdales, was the most at ease with large animals. Possibly that was because she didn't consider anything but a Clydesdale to be large.

Dave singled out a ram, listened to it, prodded it, looked at its eyes and mouth, and announced, "A clear case of ADR."

Stefan looked puzzled. "ADR?"

"Ain't doin' right." Dave gestured at the herd. "Off its feed, tired, skittish. Nothing else wrong."

"But there is," Stefan said. "I live with them, all day. I can feel it."

"Mmm." Annie considered. "Have they had any exposure to swine?"

"A little, four or five days ago. We met a herd at a farm fence." Stefan looked puzzled. "Could that make them sick?"

Sugar said nothing, but raised an eyebrow.

"Pseudorabies?" Lee Anne murmured. "Coach, that's a little farfetched."

"Yes," Annie said without looking up. "And they would have died within forty-eight hours, so that's not it."

Her curly-haired head suddenly popped up beside a ewe, her expression worried. "Unless those things work differently here."

"In which case," Lee Anne pointed out, "we're wasting our time anyway."

"This one's in bad shape," BJ announced.

"So's mine." Annie stared at BJ and they said in unison, "The ewes."

BJ checked another ewe; it was weak but in much better shape than the others. "I don't get it," she said, troubled. "This one seems fine."

Annie said, "This one's not doing so well—hi, little fella." An anxious lamb, runty and underdeveloped, nudged her aside and moved stiffly for the ewe's teat.

Something clicked in BJ's mind and she looked longingly back at the truck, where she had left her black book. She moved quietly next to Annie. "The nursing lambs are the worst, aren't they? Stiff, below size . . ."

"Yes," Annie said flatly. "Stiff, recumbent—low selenium. Stiff-lamb disease." Annie was full of the relief a doctor gets in a clear, sensible diagnosis with an easy treatment. "They're exhausted, the lambs are still nursing but not enough, and the ewes are range grazing."

"Is that bad?" Stefan said puzzledly. "They have always nursed and grassed."

"Grazed. No, it's fine, but they're using up more energy, and they've got a mineral shortage while they're lactating."

Stefan scratched his head, a gesture oddly like a calf rubbing against a fence. Fields said a few quick words in Greek and Stefan's face lit up. "Then you can give them something for that?"

"For the lambs and the ewes both, yes. Mineral supplements.

Probably 0.5 milligrams of selenium, repeated twice a month apart. We can bring it in next time." She glanced cautiously at Sugar, who nodded. "For now, we'll take blood samples and double-check the diagnosis." Her relief over, Annie was staring at the rest of the flock. "But you still need to know what's tiring them all out. Could something have chased them?"

They all glanced involuntarily at Daphni, who was now nearly hidden in a cross weave of vines.

Stefan shook his head. "She couldn't. When they first ran, she would run away, always."

"Well, you don't think any are missing—"

"I know none are missing."

"And even the hurt one isn't bitten or clawed. If anything chased them, it did it for fun."

There was a brief silence while Stefan took this in. BJ tried to remember what animals would hunt for fun. Wolverines would kill without eating, and weasels . . .

A cloud-shadow passed over them, and BJ shivered. There were strange animals here, and some might have odd ideas of play.

Annie shrugged. "For now, can you watch them by night, or get a sheep dog?"

"A dog," he said happily.

Fields groaned. "Another pet."

"Well, maybe," Stefan said, deflated. "But I can pen them by night, and sleep by them. It's no trouble. That could help." He was standing next to Dave, beside whom he looked remarkably skinny. A closer look showed that Stefan's slender arms and chest were solid muscle with hardly any fat.

Dave glanced over at him. "So, how's farming?"

"This isn't farming," Stefan corrected. "If you said that to a farmer, he might shout at you." He pointed eagerly and asked, "Please, may I listen through your stetheoscope?"

"Stethoscope. Sure." Dave passed it up to him. "Let me place it." He put the tympanum against the ram's chest. "Hear that?"

Stefan's ears, though they looked human, cocked forward like an animal's. Dave nearly dropped the head of the stethoscope. Stefan whispered, "It's so loud." He suddenly looked concerned. "It's faster than mine. Is that normal?"

"I don't know what your normal heart rate is," Dave said. "And the sheep's probably stressed. Sheep heartbeats even at rest are slightly faster than a human's, around seventy to ninety a minute—you know what a minute is, right?"

Stefan shook his head. "But I can tell fast and slow by listening. And did you hear that *swoosh* sound?"

Dave took the earpieces back, surprised. He listened carefully. "The murmur, right?" he said grudgingly. "Bad mitral valve. I forgot to mention it." He grinned back at Stefan, but the grin was forced. "Nice ears, Doc."

Stefan didn't notice. "A real heart with a bad valve."

He shook his head, laughing at himself. "It's so wonderful that I'm meeting real veterinarians. I can't believe it. Are there many of them in your world?"

"Loads," Dave said. "Most of them have the jobs I want."

Stefan's eyes were shining. "And you have schools for them, where anyone can be a veterinarian?"

"We mostly just say 'vet,'" Lee Anne muttered.

"But where anyone who wants could study and become a veter—a vet?"

"It's hard to get into a school," Lee Anne said—she had applied twice before being accepted—"but sure, they take anyone who's qualified. Do you really want to be a vet?"

BJ recognized the disillusion in Lee Anne's voice; did all of them feel it by now? She felt a sudden ache, remembering when she had felt as Stefan did now, absolutely sure that if she could become a vet it would all be magic and wonderful.

Stefan said shyly and with an odd formality, "If I could become a vet, it would make me very happy. I work to learn how." He reached into his knapsack. "I asked for books from—"

"I got him books," Fields rumbled.

Stefan looked at him and said quickly, "Oh, yes. From . . . from Fields." Fields nodded to him and smiled.

Stefan pulled out and displayed a battered paperback with a Greek title. BJ recognized the cover picture: *All Creatures Great and Small*, by James Herriot. He put it back and withdrew an even more battered paperback, handing it to Lee Anne. She opened it.

In the first chapter, every third word was underlined, or followed by a question mark, or tied by a line to a clumsily lettered definition or page reference in the margin.

Lee Anne leafed through it, mouth slightly open. Annie, BJ, and Dave looked over her shoulder. None of them had annotated a textbook that carefully in their lives.

Sugar, who had moved behind them, whistled. "Keep watching this boy. You might learn something."

Lee Anne stood frozen over the book. "Stefan, are you sure you need us at all?"

"Yes, yes." He waved his hands; he was blushing, but pleased. "I work very hard at it, but still it isn't so easy to know for me."

BJ said, "Not for us, either."

He laughed. "No, but look at you. You walk up to a shoop— to a sheep—and you know what to look at, the gnostics."

"Diagnostics?" Annie asked.

"Yes, diagnostics, you see the mistakes I make, and that is only the word." He reached out to touch her hand.

She drew it back sharply. He pulled his hand back, hurt and embarrassed. He stared at her, puzzled. "I mean—what I mean, I can't really gnose, can't diagnose, at all, when I make mistakes of small things."

BJ opened her mouth, but Lee Anne plunged ahead. "You do just fine speaking." She shot Annie a withering look. "I figure learning the terminology took me most of my first year, and I was doing it full time."

He smiled at her uncertainly. BJ ached for what he was feeling: looking at a strange new world, and wanting desperately to be approved and liked.

She said, "We'd be glad to help you. Do you have any questions for us?"

Belatedly she realized that Sugar was behind her. She couldn't have set herself up better for an oral exam.

Fields laughed and rubbed her shoulder affectionately. His hand felt warmer than a human's, and his fingers seemed to caress everywhere they touched. "Young woman, that one will keep you answering until you are older than Sugar."

Stefan shook his head violently, curls springing back around his small horns. "No, but if I don't ask, how will I learn? Even if I read alone." He turned back to BJ. "For instance, what are cancers?"

"They're lots of things." BJ felt as though someone had just asked her what animals were. "Basically, a cancer is a set of cells—you know what a cell is?"

He nodded quickly. "A walled body usually," he stumbled a little, "char-ac-ter-ized by having a nucleus, protoplasm—"

"Okay." She saw his expression and added, "That's very good. A cancer can be caused by environmental conditions, and in some cases by an inherited predisposition—meaning, certain offspring are likelier to get certain kinds of cancer that their parents had— but what it all comes down to, really, is abnormal cell growth in one area of the body or another."

He smiled blankly at her.

She tried again. "For instance, an organ will grow abnormally, or there will be skin growths or—"

He was nodding in that patient, hopeful way people use when they're listening in the dark, without a clue. She tried again. "Maybe you've seen it in the flowerbinders. They'll have a squamous cell carcinoma—well, a red, ulcerated raised growth—at the tip of the ears. It's common in white cats, especially those who get a lot of sun exposure."

He was still trying to smile, but his dark eyebrows had pulled together until they looked like Fields's single brow. "I don't think I have seen that."

She glanced back at Sugar's impossible-to-read grin, then sideways at Fields's genial but slightly concerned smile. Both men were watching Stefan.

She gave up. "I'm not much of a teacher. Maybe I can look up more on it, and try again. Is there anything else?"

"Yes," he said immediately, daunted but still game. "Please, what is myelopathy?"

"Myelopathy." BJ felt, for one wrenching moment, as though she were back in Dr. Truelove's class. "Degenerative myelopathy is a condition of nervous tissue degeneration in which myelin dies back—do you know what myelin is?"

He nodded happily and recited verbatim: "The sheath around the nerve cell—"

"The sheath, right. You're very smart."

"In the book was a picture. I want to see like that, under a microscope. Do you have one?" He looked at her pockets.

Fields laughed loudly and looked at her jeans as well, but with obvious and entirely different thoughts.

"Not on me." She said it without mockery. "The good microscopes are too large; they're back at the school. So you know what a myelin sheath is, and you know that myelopathy means that it dies away."

He just looked at her.

"Wears away. Deteriorates. The back legs of the dog go lame, because the brain doesn't get any nerve impulses from the paws or from along the legs. Mostly German shepherds—right. Mostly a special breed in my, um, home gets it. They turn their paws under when they try to walk." She said slowly and carefully, "Degeneration. Wearing away of the cell material. You understand?"

He looked at her unhappily. "I'm trying very hard."

Dave was putting things back in the truck, and Annie, mostly to avoid Stefan, was helping him. Lee Anne was leafing through Stefan's textbook.

BJ suddenly took the book from Lee Anne's hands and flipped through it, looking for question marks. "Do you know what a meningioma is?" He shook his head. "An astrocytoma?" Again. "Tell me about the degeneration of the heart muscle."

He spread his hands helplessly. "Please . . ."

But BJ flipped through the pages relentlessly. "Define inherited epilepsy." Nothing. "Lissencephaly? What about the following motor disabilities: Locomotor ataxia, myasthenia gravis, muscular dystrophy."

She stopped. Everyone was staring at her, and Stefan had tears running down his face. "I'm sorry," he almost whispered. "I don't know. I try hard, but some things I don't understand."

Fields said softly, "The boy laughs and cries easily, like all his kind." But he was staring at BJ.

BJ lunged forward, handing Stefan the book, and took his free hand. "I shouldn't have pushed you like that. You were wonderful, and you're a terrific student. You should be proud."

Stefan looked wonderingly at her. "You're not making fun of me?"

"I would never," BJ said sincerely, and suddenly knew it was true.

Stefan squeezed her hand and suddenly let it go, looking at Fields. "Did I do anything wrong? I did not mean to."

Fields's reply was gentle, but laced with regret. "Stefanopoulos, you did nothing wrong at all. You only answered a few questions." He looked at BJ, smiling sadly. "And I let you."

"Perhaps you're getting senile," BJ said.

The other students gasped. The cardinal rule, almost above Don't Screw Up, was Don't Be Rude to Clients.

When Fields didn't react, she said, "Don't you want to know what that means?"

He smiled at her again, with barely a leer at all this time. "If you told me, I think maybe I still wouldn't know—and then you would know that. Young lady, Sugar chose a little too well for this study trip."

He shook hands with Sugar, said good-bye to the others, and he and Stefan were gone, driving the flock back up the hill. Stefan looked back over his shoulder once at BJ; she smiled but did not wave.

When Fields and Stefan were out of earshot, Dave said to

BJ, "Nice shooting, Tex. What made you decide to gun the kid down?"

Lee Anne said, "Nobody talks to a client that way."

Annie said, "No matter who or what he is, you shouldn't have hurt his feelings."

BJ turned to Sugar. "Aren't you going to yell at me?"

But he was watching and waiting, and she knew again that she was right.

Annie said, "Why did you ask those questions?"

"Because I needed to know something—and doctors shouldn't guess, if they can know." She turned back to Sugar. "There's no cancer here, is there? And no nerve degeneration, no myasthenia"—she took a leap to human ailments—"no senility."

"No Alzheimer's," Sugar continued, as though he had begun her thought. "No muscular dystrophy or MS."

He looked around at all their open mouths and finished, "And we haven't done any AIDS tests, but we're pretty sure there's none of that, either."

For a while there was no sound but bird calls and the sheep herd in the distance. Finally Annie whispered, "Why? Why here?"

"Why not." But he didn't grin. "Honest, we don't know. We've taken back skin samples and organ biopsies, and run blood tests and cultures and a couple of full necropsies on things that you wouldn't believe, not even after the last two days. We've pulled strings at Duke to get tests run without people knowing why, and we've pulled even more strings to get somebody on leave from Duke. We've done it all, over and over, and all we ever come up with is that most of the sicknesses that still cause heartaches to doctors and heartbreaks to patients at home never happen here at all."

Lee Anne said, "Sir, I don't mean to sound disrespectful, but why don't you just turn the whole mess over to Duke? They've got the equipment and the facul——the facilities."

"Meaning, they've got people doctors." Sugar nodded. "If this were official research, with official university resources, I'd do just that."

Dave waved an arm at the equipment around him. "What do you call this, outlaw research?"

"That's as good a name as any." He grinned at Dave. "I forgot to mention that."

There was a brief silence.

"If you look at your transcripts," Sugar said easily, "you'll see that this is an independent study, graded but untitled. If you go to the Maintenance Department and look up the records on this truck, you'll find that it's in storage. My salary time is listed as research, and the medications we use . . ." He paused. "Let's just say that they're tougher, but we can get them, so it ought to be tougher still."

He looked at all of them. "Can you imagine what would happen to this place the moment it got out that the species born here were immune to viral diseases like feline leukemia, equine viral encephalitis? That they never got degenerative nerve disorders, even the inherited ones? We'd all destroy it, trying to find out about it . . ."

And BJ missed the rest of his sentence as she thought suddenly, No Huntington's chorea.

"No nerve degeneration at all?" she said to Sugar when he paused.

He shook his head. "Not any. If we could find out why . . ."

He didn't finish the sentence, and didn't need to. BJ, her eyes stinging, thought bitterly, if we had found out why twenty years earlier, my mother might not have killed herself. If she'd only been born here, she'd never have gotten sick.

She felt ashamed and selfish for her next thought, but while it was still fresh and desperate she said, "How soon do you think you'll find out why? How soon do you think . . ." She trailed off. Sugar was staring at her. She blushed at having spoken so intently.

Finally he said slowly, "BJ, you know how research goes. I'd like to say, maybe a year, but I doubt it. Most likely more than ten years. Or twenty. Or longer."

She nodded without speaking, the sudden flash of hope fading almost as quickly as it had come. In twenty years, she would probably be beyond help.

Sugar added, "If you're gonna be vets, you'd all better learn to be patient." He slapped his hands together, as though smacking the dust off them. "Let's go get some food in that inn."

BJ joined the others back in the truck, barely even seeing the impossibly green and beautiful landscape around them. If I'm ever really a vet, she thought bleakly, I'll be more patient than anyone I've ever met. I promise. Just let me live and be well.

S·I·X

THE FRONT DOOR of the inn was propped open—a good thing, since it was hardwood paneled in two cross-grain directions; it would have been nearly as heavy as the truck the vets had driven up in.

The inside hallway was narrow, paneled with strips of hardwood. Small vertical slits pierced the walls, but opened on what looked like closets to either side; BJ decided the slits were decorative, like the iron studs set into the thick doors on each end of the hallway.

In the middle was a wooden stand with a tropical parrot perched on it. The bird was bright blue, red, and white, with a deep black beak. On the wall across from the bird was a tray of biscuits.

The parrot cocked its head at them and said a high, fluting phrase they didn't understand. It paused, then made several clicking sounds, which it followed with *"Ert' Magyar?¿Habla español? Capisch'?* Speak English?"

"English," Dave said quickly.

The bird settled back on its perch, flapped its wings, and coughed like someone clearing her throat and said mechanically:

"Welcome to Stein's. The following rules are in effect:

- Hippoi are welcome under the overhanging roof outdoors, but not inside.
- It is not polite to ridicule another's race, world, speech, or unique body parts.
- People here speak many languages. Please do not curse, even in your own tongue; for your own safety, please assume that all insults may be overheard.
- Only talking species will be served.
- Gambling is permitted and encouraged. Cheating is fatal.
- Only recreational fights are allowed; all others must go outside.

"Because of its policies, Stein's has never had a fatality on premises. Please help us to continue this proud tradition."

The bird stopped and looked expectantly at the tray of biscuits beside the door. Lee Anne picked up a biscuit and held it gingerly between her fingers and the parrot's wicked curved beak.

The parrot promptly snatched the biscuit with one of its claws, pecked Lee Anne, and laughed raucously. "STOO-pid."

Sugar opened the inner door to Stein's. "Watch yourselves," he said flatly.

The meat smelled strong. Some of it was clearly organ meat, and the chalk picture of a pie made BJ wonder queasily if it was steak-and-kidney pie.

Even above that was a strong breadlike smell from the bottling of the ale; it must have been done in the inn itself. BJ, already swallowing uneasily from the smell of the pies, was grateful that the grain of the ale wasn't bothering her hay fever.

The people talking at the tables didn't look at them. The vet students stared at the people.

"You'll need money." Sugar reached into his jeans pocket. "Don't spend more than you can afford."

He opened the bag Fields had given him on their first trip into Crossroads and passed them each a few coins.

The coins were hexagonal and lined to break into pieces. On each piece was a different symbol: earth, air, fire, water, plant, animal. On the back of each was a stylized crossroad. The coins shone brightly, but were very scratched.

Dave dented one with a fingernail and said incredulously, "Gold?"

"Pure enough to work easily." Sugar broke one of the coins. "Here's how to make change. One of these ought to cover your food and drink."

Lee Anne stared, fascinated, at the coins in her palm. "Is this how we're getting paid?"

Sugar smiled cynically. "How the school's getting paid. I'm on salary, and you're enrolled."

He glanced over his shoulder. "I have some business. 'Scuse me." He strode quickly through the public room and up a flight of nearly vertical wooden stairs near the far wall.

BJ looked up as Sugar knocked and a trapdoor opened. She had a brief, tantalizing vision of a wall full of books before the trap shut beneath him.

She turned to comment to the others, but stopped as she saw their open mouths. She looked around the room, and her own jaw dropped.

There were more people inside than the students had yet seen in Crossroads. The people were wearing breeches, dresses, kilts, and cloaks. The small windows let in enough fading sunlight to show a rainbow of colors and patterns: stripes, spots, plaids, and the most common design, a white jersey broken with rows of inverted pyramids above upright pyramids. The effect was disturbingly like abstract fangs, and the flickering light from the hanging wheels slung with oil lamps made the fangs move.

At one table was a woman nearly eight feet tall, her face either painted or tattooed with a stylized bird head. Beside her table lay a pack and frame as long as Annie.

Nearby was a table of small brown men dressed in green caps and leather jerkins. The eldest had a carefully trimmed golden beard and no hair; the others were smooth faced but had flowing red hair to their shoulders. From time to time they glanced at the woman admiringly.

One person in a cloak had either a backpack or wings underneath. She saw BJ staring and raised an eyebrow; BJ, embarrassed, turned away.

Another woman, completely nude, had greenish tinge bark wherever humans have body hair. She had nothing in front of her but a glass of water; she was with a fat, pink companion who was happily gnawing at the meat pie in front of him. His mouth, full of pointed teeth, went back nearly to his ears.

Beyond them, there was a large black being that looked faintly like a human tadpole; its human companion raised a glass to it and affectionately called it something like "pook." The pook-thing twitched, turned toward the watching students, and grinned nastily.

BJ said into Dave's ear, "What else did you learn about inns from Robin Hood?"

He answered slowly, looking from table to table, "That people aren't always what they seem. That you can end up paying more than you expected if you're not careful. That you shouldn't gamble with people you don't know or with games you don't know."

"Good advice," Annie said.

They moved cautiously to an empty table. A young woman with goat feet, tapping quickly past them, dropped a bowl, a jar, and a steaming, cloth-wrapped bundle in the center of the table.

The cloth fell away; it was fresh dark bread. The bowl held soft butter.

Dave reached for it, but froze when Annie said, "Wait."

She looked at them earnestly. "I feel silly but . . . remember in fairy tales, how people always got in trouble by accepting food from strangers?"

"If you're gonna worry about it," Lee Anne said pointedly, "I'll take your share." Still, she didn't take any at all.

They stared at the loaf. Steam was rising from it, and it smelled maddeningly delicious.

Dave tapped his fingers on the table. "Look, we could starve in front of all this if someone doesn't have the guts to start."

Annie argued, "Why risk your life for a meal?"

BJ, shrugging, tore off a small chunk of the bread, dipped it in the soft butter, and put it in her mouth. The others watched as she went wide-eyed.

Annie said quickly, "Are you all right?"

BJ's only reply was to reach for a second chunk.

The jar turned out to be honeycomb honey. They dismantled the loaf quickly, Annie eating only after a muttered (and fervent) saying of grace. They received and dismantled a second loaf, and quit worrying.

An old man with straight white hair, combed back, walked up to their table. He was in his sixties; he looked thin in that way the old get whether they eat or not, but he was carrying a tray of steins, which, if full, must have weighed forty or fifty pounds. He didn't look strained. He set the tray down and looked at them quizzically, saying nothing. His face was deeply wrinkled already, but his eyes were very sharp.

Dave said slowly and loudly, "I would like to have some ale."

"All right, all right," he said. "So you'd like a beer. I'm not deaf."

He had a Polish accent. Dave gaped at him.

Lee Anne said, "Sir, I'd like a hard cider and we'd all like to see a menu."

He smiled toward her, his tired, sharp-looking face lighting up. "No menus. I just tell you what we have. A good-looking young lady like you, I'd bring her a glass of wine on the house if I were only younger."

He bent at the waist, kissing her hand, and froze over it. "Nice watch," he said coldly. "So, are you tourists?"

"We're veterinarians," Amy said, and corrected herself. "We're fourth-year vet students."

He looked at them each curiously. "So? Is this your usual course of study?"

They shook their heads numbly. BJ said timidly, "Mister—"

"Call me Stein." He was smiling, but he was watching them carefully, as though each of their responses were important to him.

"You own this place, then," Dave said.

He shrugged. "I built it." He was unable to keep the pride out of his voice.

"And named it after yourself?" Annie asked.

"Actually, I'm named after it. The tavern is named after those." He pointed to a wall rack of steins, each hanging by the handle from a peg. "When I first built the place, a woman made them for me. Baked in a little brick kiln, hand glazed and fired. I thought they'd be my trademark, so I called the place Steins—no apostrophe.

"Then people started calling me Stein." He waved a hand. "Why not? So now I'm Stein. There are worse places to be named after."

A voice nearby said, "'Scuse me."

A young man with stag antlers growing out of his smooth brown hair had stopped at their table. "Is that a real faun serving the bread? Wow. I thought they were legendary."

Lee Anne said shakily, "We're pretty sure she's real. Does everybody here speak English?"

He laughed. He had even, white teeth—he had no incisors at all. "Not like I do. I learned in San Francisco. At college." He pointed to his T-shirt, which they now saw had a faded USF on it. "I majored in anthropology." He touched his antlers. "Everybody just figured I was into some religion."

They watched him leave. Annie said with surprising bitterness, "California!"

Lee Anne asked, "Do normal folks live here?"

The man with stag antlers sat at a table with friends. He put his arm around a singularly doe-eyed woman.

"What," Stein said, deadpan. "You don't find us normal?"

He waved an arm. "How normal can you get? There are Cambodians who fled from the Khmer Rouge and the Killing Fields. There's a family founded by a couple who walked into the woods of America during a witch trial in Salem; they had to be plenty afraid to do that."

Annie nodded earnestly. Stein noted her but went on. "There's a boy from Lebanon and a college-age girl from China. He ran down a lane during an Israeli raid on the camps, and she ran up the wrong alley—or the right one—during the massacre in Tiananmen Square. Maybe they'll both stay."

He looked at them earnestly. "And those are just the human stories. Look around."

"We have," Dave said.

"Look closer."

BJ did, and noted for the first time the small scars, the broken antlers, and all those who were walking with canes.

Stein saw her eyes. "That's why, in Crossroads, there is mostly peace. That's why, in my home, there is nothing but peace. People come here to find it."

He saw the students looking at him, their mouths slightly ajar, and chuckled with embarrassment. "I'll leave that story for Owen. He tells it better."

Dave wiped ale foam from his lips. "What story? Who's Owen?"

"It's the story of the Stepfather God. Owen's . . ." He shrugged. "A good man. A trader. Probably the best one there's ever been. He takes a cart up and down the Strangeways—" He cut off and looked at them. "Well, let's just say if you've ever dreamed of it, he can find it. And if you don't mind the price, he'll sell it to you."

He sounded amused and affectionate, but BJ wondered again about fairy tales and the price you pay. Crossroads seemed to remind her of that a lot.

Dave said, "If he'd sell me something to eat, I'd buy it." He added quickly, "No offense. If you've got something I know I can eat—"

"Dinner? Tonight's Anglo night, so it should look familiar, you know." He grinned. "Come back some other night for adventure. Anyway, I have steak-and-kidney pie, very nice—"

"I'll take that," Lee Anne and Dave said at the same time.

"All right. And side roots and greens with everything: earth-heart, turnips, rutabaga, collard, rampion—"

"Let down your hair," BJ murmured.

Stein shot a quick look at her and finished, "But the treat of the house is from the roast fireplace." He gestured proudly at it.

They could hardly have missed it. One fireplace had a stew caldron hanging from a pot hook. The other was a walk-in hearth, its fire kept down to embers.

At either end of the hearth, two upright wagon wheels supported either end of spits latched to the spokes. A belt coming up through a slot in the stone floor went around one wheel hub, turning both wheels slowly and evenly. On the spits hung a number of small poultry, game, and cuts of larger meat.

Stein beamed at them. Before he had seemed withdrawn, even hostile; now he was like an excited boy showing off a tree house.

"I run a trough inside from the upper pond. It runs over a bucket wheel to turn the spit. Watch." Fat dripped from one of the red meat cuts onto the chicken, which smoked in the high heat below. "See? This way they baste each other. A cooperative effort, like most of Crossroads."

"Burning fat on coals," Annie murmured. "Carcinogenic."

"Not here," Lee Anne said quietly back.

"What are the meats?" Dave said. BJ grimaced. She hadn't wanted to know.

Stein pointed to the items as they turned.

"Chicken, of course. The small birds are squab and year-ling blue-back. The meat cuts are venison, mutton, Cockaigne pig—"

"What?"

He spelled it. "Wait 'til you see one. Wonderful animals. And the other body is—" he hesitated, "rabbit, more or less. Also, nice fresh mutton, nothing like it."

BJ and Annie looked at each other. Dave said hollowly, "Well, good-bye, Karyata.'"

BJ ordered venison, Annie the lamb stew. Lee Anne frowned as Stein left. "You two should hang around a farm; you need toughening up."

"I'm tough enough," Dave cut in, "and I'm from Richmond."

"Maybe. But you're only tough to prove it to yourself. These two don't need to do that."

The pies came, and BJ had to admit that they smelled delicious, if strong. There was an overscent of pepper and onion and some herb BJ couldn't readily identify.

Lee Anne saw her face and passed the pewter fork over. "Try some."

She did. Suddenly she was sorry she hadn't ordered it. "I wonder where they get the spices."

"Don't talk with your mouth full," Dave said. "Probably they get them anywhere they want."

BJ passed her fork back. "I'm not talking, I'm mumbling."

The female faun hurried back with steaming bowls of vegetables. Lee Anne took collards after looking dubiously at the earth-heart. BJ took an earth-heart, bit a chunk off it, put butter on it and mashed it up, and scraped her plate for more when it was gone. She also ate rampion, and caught Annie smiling at her as if sharing a joke. BJ reached back and let down her hair, which was short and had a single elastic in it, and Annie laughed.

"Where were you last week?" BJ asked her.

"Public practice." Annie put on her polite public face. "I inspected dairies with regulatory agents. I did California mastitis tests, and that was the most exciting thing that happened."

"Pathology." Dave moved his knife like a saw over his kidney pie, mocking Dr. Vendreau's whiny voice. "How do you think it died, David, hmmm? Was it reeeenal amyloidooosis, or urolithiiiiiasis?" He cut apart a kidney, pretending to look for stones.

"It's a kidney pie, isn't it?" Lee Anne said. "Pylonephritis."

"Life changes us," Annie said wonderingly. "I used to play with my food; now I post-mortem it."

"Gotta post it," Dave said firmly. "It's dead, ain't it? We can't *pre*-mortem it."

BJ sipped her hard cider. "Life changes us," she said. Her hand slipped once on the stein; she gripped it tighter and told herself that the pottery had, after all, been wet and slick.

The carrots and onions were smaller than back home and, BJ

thought, tastier. The turnips were strong and there was another dish of yellow mashed vegetable, which Lee Anne said was rutabaga; BJ didn't much care for it. The rest was delicious.

Stein stopped by again with another round of drinks. "No longer on me, but I can see you need them. Is the food all right?"

"Oh yes." BJ found to her surprise that she loved venison, peppered and eaten with chunks of the dark bread.

Stein nodded quickly and left with the tray.

Annie gave her a bite of the lamb stew, which, spiced with mint and browned with fresh butter, was delicious. BJ caught the tree woman frowning with distaste as she watched them eat. She caught BJ's eye and looked away quickly.

Stein, his business elsewhere concluded, dragged a bench sideways and straddled it at their table. "So, do you like it?"

They nodded vigorously, their mouths full. Stein raised an eyebrow. "Don't all of you talk at once." But he looked pleased.

The parrot flew through, pecked a bit off Lee Anne's plate, chanted, "STOO-pid, STOO-pid," and dropped to the floor, walking a rolling gait back to his perch.

He sighed loudly. "You've met my parrot."

Lee Anne said, "Where did he come from?"

"He flew here one day. No one else wanted him, and he said he needed the work." He leaned toward Lee Anne. "Do you know anything particularly fatal to parrots?"

"No sir," she said.

He shrugged. "Well, I can hope."

Lee Anne said abruptly, "You're a Jew, aren't you, sir?"

Stein turned to stare at her, and she looked uncomfortable. "If I phrased that wrong, I apologize. It's only a way of speaking."

Stein looked squarely at her: not hostile, not friendly. "I've heard many ways of speaking. Some like yours, some worse. You're Americans, aren't you? From the south."

Lee Anne bristled. "Is that a problem?"

Stein said easily, "It shouldn't be, should it? People there are people here, and everything is just a way of speaking."

Annie said unexpectedly, "When did you leave our world, Mr. Stein?"

Stein smiled at her. "If you're trying to distract me, young lady, you didn't do so bad." He raised his mug in a salute. "I was Polsc——" He paused. "I was Polish."

He added quietly, "My name wasn't Stein then; it was Stankewicz." He nodded to Lee Anne. "And as you say, I am a Jew. I grew up, quickly, in Warsaw."

Dave looked up. "During the war? World War II?"

"Yes."

"Were you in the Warsaw Ghetto uprising?"

"You've heard of it," he said, startled.

David said eagerly, "We read about it in history. The ghetto fighters had only seventeen rifles, and they pushed back the first wave of Nazi troops anyhow. I read a book about it in high school, too. It must've been exciting . . ." he trailed off, watching Stein.

Stein was smiling tightly. "It's history now. That's wonderful. And yes, it was exciting. I was ten, and my brothers and sisters all in their teens. They trained me, and I fought as best I could. I killed my first man that year."

He watched their faces, still smiling. Now the smile was warmer, as though the students were long-lost friends from his childhood, and they were reminiscing together. "It's true. I had a pistol, an old thing of my grandfather's from the Franco-Prussian War. It shot balls instead of cartridge bullets. I cleaned it myself and found a flint and loaded a ball into it. I should have turned it in so someone else could use it, but I was proud of it.

"I was a messenger—what that means, you see, is that I was small enough to crawl through the sewer under the ghetto wall, which ran right down the street. On that morning I came out in an alley two blocks away from the ghetto. Careless of me to come out so close.

"I heard a noise at the end of the alley, and I hid behind a box. And when a man in a Nazi uniform came down the alley, I stood up and shot him in the chest. I'm lucky the gun didn't blow up in my hand. He dropped his gun and clutched at his chest, and down he went." He stopped.

"And then?" BJ said.

"Then I threw away the empty pistol and ate a chunk of bread."

"Right then?" BJ said, stunned.

He looked surprised. "Of course. I was starving. He had a chunk of bread, sticking right out of his shirt pocket under the hole I'd made. And I brushed his blood off of it and ate as much as I could swallow in one gulp. And then I cried," Stein said simply, "because he was dead and had eaten bread once.

"That was how they found me, empty-handed and crying beside his body. That was why they didn't kill me then; they didn't think I'd been the one who shot him. They beat me with rifle butts and sent me home. Charitable, for Nazis."

He sighed. "There isn't much to say about the time that came next—days, weeks—people died every day, shot or starving. Finally the Nazis took us to the rail station and loaded us in box cars while other Nazis made chalk numbers on the outside. Our car had splinters and cracks, it looked like bomb damage, or maybe shrapnel from somewhere. Then they shut the door and locked it. We were too crowded to sit, and the heat and stench were terrible.

"In the car I was in, two men managed to break a hole in the roof. I don't know, maybe the car had taken more damage than the Nazis knew. So they pulled on the hole, with everyone yelling at them, but they couldn't make it big enough for a grown-up. A skinny girl squeezed through the top, and they started passing children up to her one by one. I was last; my older brother Avram lifted me up and passed me over people's heads. He didn't say anything, not even good-bye.

"When I got up, it was cold from the wind, and I could smell the engine way up front. It was so bright, after the car, that I could hardly see, but I could tell I was right on the edge of the car, with the ground rushing by way below. The girl, I remember she had red curly hair and freckles, was holding me near the edge.

"And then she kissed me, right on the mouth like a lover, and she threw me off the side of the train. I screamed. I thought she was trying to kill me."

He took a sip of cider. BJ noticed that his hands were shaking.

"I hit on my left side, on a rock. I heard my arm snap, but I didn't feel it, not even when I rolled down the embankment into the mud at the bottom. I stood up, and tried to move my fingers." He grinned wryly. "That I felt.

"By then I could barely see the train. I looked behind me, but I didn't see any other children; they were too far back. I walked to the crossroads and started up the road, not even thinking about Germans. I guess I was in shock. I thought, I need help, I'll find a town somewhere.

"But I didn't. I took a few turns, and the trees got taller and older, and it got dark, and soon my whole side was damp with blood and I was shivering and half-crazy from the hurt and too tired to be afraid. There were no towns. I knew I was going to die, but it didn't matter to me anymore.

"And then the hairiest man I'd ever seen knelt down beside me and said something I couldn't understand. He touched my arm and I screamed. He set me on his shoulders and carried me over a mile to his hut."

"I thought, This is finally the end; I'm going to be killed. But he bound up my arm and he bandaged the cuts on my other hand and he spoon-fed me soup. I didn't ask him whether it was kosher or not. I didn't ask him where in Poland I was. I didn't even ask about my family; all that was gone from me already."

He smiled at BJ. "Your hands are shaking, darling. I don't mean to scare you."

She pulled her hands off the table quickly. "It's all right."

But it wasn't at all. Her hands were shaking, and she hadn't been afraid. In a moment they subsided, but now BJ was shaking inside, trying to control her own hands. *Oh, God, she thought, not now, not like Mom and Grandpa. Please not yet. I've just found something wonderful.*

Stein looked at her thoughtfully but went on. "Four years later, I walked back into Poland. Not the wisest idea, or the safest, but . . ." He shrugged. "I had to know. I thought I'd ask someone about my family, someone I knew."

"And you couldn't find any of your family?" Annie asked quietly.

He smiled at her, a smile more melancholy than any BJ had ever seen. "I couldn't find anyone I knew."

They sat in silence. He went on, "I walked four, five days through Warsaw, asking names. Sometimes I'd hear how someone died. Mostly they had just disappeared, but sometimes someone knew. I told them about my family and the train to Treblinka, and everyone said they had gone up the chimney. That's what they called it: the bodies go in the ovens and the people go up the chimney."

Lee Anne shivered. Stein said quietly, "I'm very sorry, young lady, but it's true. I grew up in a city neighborhood and I knew maybe five hundred people by name, a thousand by sight; I was a friendly boy. Out of that neighborhood, the Germans killed fifty thousand and more in one year. The buildings were shelled, the people were dead, my world gone.

"The last thing, my last question, I asked a man my father's age about my brothers and sisters. He asked where I had last seen them and I told him. He hit me on the ear hard enough to knock me down.

" 'And you live?' he said. His face was jumping on one side. 'You live?'

"He bent over me and shouted in my face, 'I was at Dachau, boy. The Germans made me sort shoes, children's shoes, thousands of pairs. From Treblinka, from Auschwitz, from Majdanek and the others! And you live!' He stood ready to hit me again. I got up and walked away."

Stein sighed. "Now I understand; I didn't then. He was really saying, Why did I live when they died, and why do you share that with me? But I hadn't known about it all, not long.

"I walked out of Warsaw down the rail line, and walked back into Crossroads. When I was old enough, I built the inn." He spread his hands: end of story. A forty-five-year gap, an abandonment of an entire world, explained only with spread hands.

Lee Anne said slowly, "And you haven't been back?"

He shook his head. "Others bring me books, bring me news. I don't need to go back."

Annie looked lost. "I can see grieving, or even being angry, but giving up a whole world?" She looked at him squarely. "Giving up your religion?"

"Listen, pretty-head," he said angrily, "I was ten when I saw my last rabbi, heard my last prayer. So don't talk to me about what I gave up. And don't judge me, don't ever judge me. Do you know what it's like to lose your family, even to know that no one alive can understand what you suffer?"

He looked around the table at Dave and Lee Anne—and locked suddenly on BJ. "Ahhh." He seemed astonished. "Now? Still?"

The others were looking at her. BJ shifted uneasily. "You're so serious. You don't laugh, do you?" she said to Stein.

Stein nodded, smiling. "Of course I laugh. Every Monday, someone brings me a week-old Sunday *New York Times*. I read about Ethiopia, about the Middle East, about the craziness in Ireland and Eastern Europe and all over your world." He was still nodding terribly, still smiling. "And I laugh."

He seemed to see, for the first time, how uncomfortable he was making them. "But you're done eating; there are better things to do than listen to me. Have you tried the games?" He gestured into the corner.

The small brown men, two at a time, were whipping what looked like stylized forks into a pockmarked wooden target. The others were keeping score with charcoal on a section of white-washed wall.

A second pair walked up to the throwing line and took off their belts, then lashed them overhand at the target. The belts flew across the room; the fork ends (buckles, BJ realized) stuck quivering in the target, both near the center. The two little men ran up to the target.

"Nice, huh?" Stein said proudly. "I designed those belts myself.

Now they're in fashion; I can't make enough of them. Over twenty different sizes, four colors. Available on order." He waited expectantly, then sighed. "Well, maybe you'll want one later."

The two little men, measuring the target with their hands, were shouting at each other. One of the scorekeepers walked over, folded his arms, and said something that made one of the other men bounce up and down and chatter like a squirrel.

"The games are for wagers, aren't they?" Annie said politely.

"You're quite right," Stein said smoothly. "Plus there's a small fee to rent the equipment, and a modest house fee for breaking the rules if you play wrong."

They watched as the rest of the scorekeepers bounded to the target, chattering themselves. The hair on one of the little men fluffed like a cat's fur. The people around them edged forward to watch.

"Still," Stein said, speaking quickly, "game playing is good for people. Coordination and training. Builds character. Excuse me a moment. Melina," he called to the female faun, "cover for me."

He moved swiftly to the target, where the brown men were jumping on each other's shoulders and shrieking.

Sugar dropped back by the table. "Having fun?"

"You bet!" David said loudly.

Sugar grimaced. "Don't have too much. You need to be in shape for tomorrow." He patted his pocket. "Stein told me where to meet your client."

Dave belched. "Cool." Sugar shook his head and went back upstairs.

The doe-eyed woman passed the table. Dave leered at her. "Hey, Bambi, wanna frolic?"

She looked back at him, shy and frightened. BJ winced, wanting to calm her. Dave only laughed.

A shadow fell across him. The stag-man in the USF T-shirt had pulled her aside and was standing in front of Dave, one leg braced forward as if in a starting block for a track event. He was glaring, his head hanging low, at Dave.

"Hey," he said bitingly, "that was incredibly uncool, man." The insulting emphasis on *man* hung in the air.

Dave rubbed his jaw confusedly, looking at the stag-man's hands. The man's palms were open; he wasn't making a fist.

But the stag's head was lowered, and BJ realized that he was preparing to charge. The antlers that had looked foolish a moment before gleamed in the oil-light; he was an eight-point buck, and every point was razor sharp.

Lee Anne pulled quietly behind Dave. Her hand, BJ noticed, was inside her knapsack.

Two more stag-men were behind the one they knew.

Stein appeared out of nowhere. "So, how's everybody?" He surveyed the group quickly. "I think maybe it's time for a little game. Target or stick?"

"Stick," the stag-man said immediately. "Up close and personal." But he was already calming down.

"Sticks it is." Stein turned back to Dave. "Young man, I think you should know that we always put money on these games. House rules. Is that all right with you?"

The others looked hopefully at Dave, waiting for him to refuse.

"Suuure." Dave was on his third stein of ale. "We'll give it a shot."

Annie said quickly, "I'm sorry; I don't gamble." Lee Anne looked relieved.

"No problem." Dave broke off a sixpiece and slapped it on the table. "Will this cover her?"

Stein raised an eyebrow. "Generous of you." He made a small hand signal, and the other team quickly moved the table away.

Dave and the stag-man, side by side, looked awkwardly at each other.

Dave said, "Sorry. I didn't mean to be rude."

"Hey," he said, "we all do it once in a while. I should be easy when it happens. What's your name?"

"Dave. Yours?"

He made a soft fluting sound, and said, "In San Francisco I used 'Rudy.' "

Dave stuck his right hand out. Rudy took it, but also tipped his head back in a sort of reverse-nod. BJ remembered that a handshake was to show that your weapon hand was empty; Rudy was showing that he wouldn't charge.

The others lined up. The doe-woman gave way to another stag; BJ couldn't tell whether that was her idea or theirs. Stein came forward with a small bowl for the wager stakes and a bundle of what looked like kindling. "Catchlets. Each take one."

BJ turned hers over. It was some hard wood, nothing but a smoothly polished stick about a foot long, worn smooth by constant striking. Each stick had a cross-piece with upraised ends.

Stein held an extra catchlet. "The object is to hook the other person's stick on the bar and then tap him on the side with your stick before he breaks free." He twisted his against Rudy's, effortlessly flipping Rudy's catchlet up in the air, tapping Rudy's rib cage, and grabbing the other catchlet with his free hand. He passed it back to Rudy. "So you try."

"Wouldn't that be easier with two sticks?" Dave objected.

"Naturally," Stein said tiredly. "It would also be easier if he had a stick and you had a gun, but that's not how the game works, right?" He raised his catchlet in a mock salute, like a fencer. "Begin."

Dave looked blank. Rudy lunged at him, and Dave barely caught Rudy's extended catchlet. They each twisted a wrist at the same time and found themselves hooked together. BJ, staring, barely brought her own catchlet up in time as one of the other stags engaged her.

She twisted the catchlet correctly, but it shivered sideways and fell from her hand. She stared numbly at her empty, disobedient fingers as her opponent's catchlet tapped her side.

The humans quickly lost. The stags, barely breathing hard, locked antlers with each other in mock combat, laughing. Rudy turned to Dave and said eagerly, "C'mon, let's do another."

"Go for it," Dave said woodenly, and tossed another broken sixpiece out. BJ saw Annie grit her teeth.

They spent the rest of the night playing and replaying. When, after two hours, they began winning, even Annie looked happy. Only BJ, sweat beading on her forehead and her tongue between her teeth, was still straining to perform the wrist twist. Twice more she dropped her stick.

Once Lee Anne, with a quick spin, hooked BJ's opponent's stick until BJ could pick up her own.

The other time, Annie, who had taken some fencing, did a double disengage around her opponent and performed a quick parry to save her.

Dave called over his shoulder, "What's with you, kid? Can't walk and chew gum at the same time?"

"Shut up," BJ snapped, surprising him.

By the end of the night they were down only two sixpiece. By this time, the stags were buying drinks for them, and the little men and the tree-woman were watching and cheering. The fun ended only when Stein beat a ladle against the nearly empty stew pot and called, "Time to sleep."

Paying travelers moved back to their tables and took bedrolls down, laying them under the tables. Locals headed for the door, waving to each other. Rudy's girlfriend, having had a few drinks, put an arm around Dave and then stunned him by affectionately licking his nose with an absolutely huge, thick, rasping ruminant's tongue. Dave stumbled into the night; his companions followed.

They pulled their sleeping bags from the truck; Annie helped Dave with his. A few feet above the upper retaining pond was a bed of moss in the middle of low floral shrubs. It looked, BJ thought, like a tiny protected fort. They laid all four bags in a row, fairly close together.

Dave crawled into his bag fully clothed, closed his eyes immediately, and snored.

Lee Anne crawled into her sleeping bag and discreetly struggled out of her jeans, tossing them out. Annie, with an aplomb BJ hadn't expected, simply dropped her jeans—within inches of Dave's legs—and crawled into her sleeping bag. BJ did the same. The night was mild; she barely needed the bag.

She lay under the clouds, thinking about Stein's story and about her own. Why do some people live and others die? Why should Huntington's chorea happen to her mother, maybe to her brother, maybe even to her?

Lee Anne rolled over to go to sleep but stiffened and said, "The stars."

The clouds had blown away, and above them, a belt of stars spun across the sky in a wide spiral. As they watched, one fell—not quick drop and fade, like the Perseids or the Leonids back on earth, but a slow, lazy glide that seemed to go on forever. "Make a wish," Annie said to herself.

BJ, testing her hand that had failed so badly earlier, wished quietly and fervently to herself and fell asleep.

S·E·V·E·N

TO AN ONLOOKER, it would seem that Brandal had simply turned a corner and come into sight on the main road of Anavalon. The road, however, appeared straight.

Brandal trudged patiently and steadily onward without the slightest stealth. To either side, the land seemed gray in the predawn light.

The sun rose, but the hills of Anavalon remained gray. The trees bore shriveled fruit; the weeds and shrubs had dusty green foliage. Below the road lay a brackish lake. The sedge was withered from the lake, and no birds sang.

Once, Anavalon had been ruled by a wounded king who, according to legend, sent his bravest, truest, and purest knights on a quest to find a cure.

The knights had never returned. The king had died, and his land remained barren.

Brandal walked the road, looking from side to side as guiltily as though he had been the failed king and thinking (as always) of Crossroads.

Just before the camp, he turned off into the underbrush and walked between two dark-leaved shrubs, called (in Anavalerse) *thearnficht*. Brandal wrapped himself in his cloak to avoid the finger-size thorns. There didn't appear to be a path.

Once inside the low grove of *thearnficht*, he walked quickly downhill, always angling to the right when he had a choice. The walking was difficult, particularly because he had to keep his balance while keeping one hand on his sword. He coughed from the dust; Anavalon, even after a rain, was always dry.

Finally he broke free of the shrubs. He was standing on a steep rise overlooking a valley. In the valley lay a camp of crudely made huts.

Brandal stared, disheartened at the change while he had been away. The hide-and-wicker shelters still looked the same, but there were far more of them. The size of the camp had nearly doubled. Anavalon was a good place to recruit an army; any way out seemed worth trying.

The huts had been moved so that they were laid out in a grid. Brandal wasn't sure why that disturbed him.

A hand grabbed his sword arm, tight enough to pin it to his side, and spun him around. "Here now," the voice said gruffly.

Tall as he was, Brandal was staring into the man's shoulder. He winced at the jacket buckles, but was pressed too tight to speak. He could feel a beard tickling the top of his head.

With his free hand, the man tilted Brandal's head back and up, then broke into a gap-toothed smile.

"Curly!" he shouted happily. "Thought you were gone for good. Dead like the best of us, or jailed like the rest of us." He gave Brandal a squeeze that nearly dislocated the smaller man's shoulders.

"Good to see you, Reize." Brandal was bemused by, but not surprised at, the strong smell of wine on the big man's breath. At dawn in a camp with limited resources, Oghannon Reize had done well by himself. "Half-drunk, are you?"

"I'm too great a man, Curly. Only half of me can be drunk at a time. And fully drunk costs too much." But he added hopefully, "How'd that run you made go?"

Brandal shrugged. "Not good." But he passed over two sixpiece. "Here's your share, as promised."

He smiled, showing several blackened gaps in his teeth. There was hardly a complete set of teeth in the camp. "My fair share? What would I find if I turned you upside down and shook you?"

Brandal said levelly, "Your own huge guts, spilled in the dust. But if you could do it, you'd find six more like that." His hand drifted toward his boot, where he had a dagger hidden.

Reize laughed and slapped his shoulder. "I believe you." He sighed loudly, and a small lizard nearby sniffed the air and looked up at him reproachfully. "I should have asked for half."

"Half? What did you do, besides answer for me when anyone asked?"

"Ah, but that's gotten harder to do." He laid a finger beside his nose. "We look nothing alike, you know. No offense to you."

"None taken. But everyone else thinks I never left?"

"So true. I mussed your bunk, ate your food, drank all your wine—"

"All of it?"

"I had to make sure no one was suspicious, right? And they weren't. By the way, this is yours." Reize handed him a scrap of parchment.

Brandal turned it over curiously, and said finally, "Payment?"

Reize guffawed. "You're smarter than most of us. Taburnal wiped his ass with his, and now it's worthless. She calls it 'scrip.'" He said the odd word carefully, short as it was, and Brandal pricked up his ears at how foreign the vowel sounded in Anavalerse.

"And this is my full wages?" he said, looking straight into Reize's face.

Reize looked down uncomfortably and changed the subject. "Now that people know what it is, it's as good as gold or brass. Better, really. You can fold it in your pocket. You can gamble with it, buy wine with it, buy a whore . . ." He reached casually at the female mercenary who passed, a small full-figured woman with strong arms and a slight beer gut. She knocked his arm aside without slowing down.

He chuckled. "Well, once you find one, you can buy a whore. There's a few in the camp now."

"No."

Reize nodded, wide-eyed. "Oh, yes. Whores, gambling, stoat fights, scar-etching artists—comforts of home, really. If you come from that sort of home."

"Not quite." Brandal looked uneasily at the camp as they approached. Reize saw his expression.

"We could still go it alone." He laid a hairy arm across Brandal's shoulders. "Think of it: nights under the stars, except when it rains or snows. No deadlines, no hurries except for running from the authorities. Burglary, robbery, assault, hardly any murder unless you want it. Set your own work schedule, be your own boss." He dropped his arm and said wistfully, "I could never make it work alone, but with a partner . . ."

Brandal patted the big man's shoulder. "Let's stay with the army. It's more secure."

"Security." Reize sighed loudly. "Men like you and me, Curly, we never get ahead. Dreamers on bedsteads, never on horseback, that's us. Take me." He waved his arm expansively, as though genuinely offering himself to be taken. "Clever, but never educated. Courageous, but never armed or trained. Filled with the potential goodness of a saint for all stars, but badly brought up."

"Very badly."

"Damn badly." Reize's eyes filled with tears. "All that potential, wasted. Given the right luck, I'd have been great beyond bearing, like a fat ass on a milk stool." He patted his own buttocks. "Kings would have wept at my death. Instead"—he sighed hugely, enjoying himself—"unknown through the whole world, but known too well by all who know me." He burped. "Oghannon Reize, the Turd of Fortune."

Brandal thought of pitying Reize, but knew he couldn't compete. The big man pitied himself more completely, and with more satisfaction, than anyone else ever would.

"What's the patch?" He pointed to a triangle on Reize's shoulder.

"Right." Reize swore softly and picturesquely, something involving egrets and small boys. "Good you noticed. Here's yours."

Reize placed a triangle on Brandal's shoulder and aimed at it unsteadily with a brass pin. Brandal snatched the pin hastily and fixed the patch on himself. "Does everybody wear one?"

"The triangles, only unlucky scum like you and me. Higher up? Squares, pentagons, hexagons; even a few circles . . . watch who you smart off to, Curly. The patches tell you which ones to fight, which to flatter, which to bribe—"

"Badges of rank."

"That's it. Not of merit, though." Reize shook his head mournfully. "Here I stand . . ."

Brandal barely listened.

As they approached the edge of the camp, Brandal stared right and left at the new shelters and the newly imposed grids of order. A pockmarked man with a sword scar running across his face glanced sideways at Brandal. "Been away?"

"Not even a day," he answered flatly.

The man shrugged. "Suit yourself." He walked on.

Reize belched, a terrible sound like falling rock. "I wouldn't trust that one, Curly. Jaeken is here only for himself, doesn't care who he sells."

"And you do."

"I have strong values," Reize said stiffly. "They should never come cheap."

"They'll fetch a good price," Brandal agreed, but he took more care to be subtle in looking around.

They stopped at the water station, a small pool under a spigot in a barrel. A ladle hung beside the spigot.

Reize passed the ladle to Brandal first. "Here's to the dead." He added courteously, "And to your health."

Brandal sipped cautiously. The water tasted better than it had, but was still tepid. He looked at the shallow ditch leading from the brook; now it was lined with stone, and flowed into a barrel full of a mix of lime rock and charcoal.

He passed the ladle back. "Speaking of health, how is it here?"

He scratched. "Better. Nobody gets the runs anymore. Well, nobody dies of 'em, now." He added, struck by it for the first time, "Less flies around, too. Well, that's natural; we're cleaner." He dismissed it as unimportant.

Brandal said, "Who does garbage now?"

"Everybody. No, I'm not joking; you'll get your turn." Reize threw a dirt clod at a long ditch beside the camp. "Gather it, fill it in; gather it, fill it in. You'd think we were in a city."

Brandal looked around. "We are."

Reize snorted. He had been here all along, and hadn't registered the rapid growth of the camp. "Someday, Curly, I want to show you a real city. The fires! The women! The strange animals!" His eyes glowed. "The fiery women with strange animals!"

A slender figure trudged by: a young man with angry eyes, still full of the hurt that comes with learning for the first time that crime is your only way to get ahead. Brandal turned to watch him automatically.

"Oh, him." Reize waved an arm dismissively. "Sold his body last night, I'd guess. Does it a lot. Wants money to send home, only gets scrip. He's something awful committed to victory now."

Brandal, considering, realized that the scrip ensured men's commitment to the army. It was an imaginative way to buy loyalty. Aloud he said, "At least it's better than rape."

Reize lifted an eyebrow. "Don't say that word too loud. There's a new camp punishment for that." He made a cutting gesture at crotch height.

Brandal blinked. "That ought to discourage rapists."

"At the very least," Reize said, squinting judiciously, "it's cut down something dramatic on second offenses. It's nearly drill time, Curly; best we get weapons."

Brandal's short sword was hidden under his cloak. "Don't folk carry their own?"

"Nah, nah." Reize squinted at him thoughtfully. "And don't you. Twenty lashes if they find you with a sword—first offense. Don't ask about second offense; I'm not strong this morning." He tried to look sickly, but spoiled it by hiccuping.

The weapons racks were half-empty; the camp was full of life now. Reize sorted through five swords before choosing a dented veteran with a blunt edge; Brandal pantomimed pulling his own sword from the rack. They both took battered but serviceable shields from a pile nearby.

"How's the nightlife?" Brandal asked casually. "Still full of fights?"

Reize frowned, his shaggy red brows coming together. "Not as many, now you mention it. No point to it, unless you can choke a man. You can be flogged for using a dagger without orders. Fights happen, but they're nothing, now. A few kicks in the crotch, some broken noses—it's just not the same." He sighed loudly. "Waste of time, really."

Felaris shouted, "Gather."

She was a tall, bony woman with burn scars running down one side of her face. Her chief fame, prior to her captaincy in Morgan's army, was a large jar she carried with her, which she claimed was half-full of ears she had bitten off opponents in fights. She was hoping to fill the jar.

The soldiers moved forward quickly, half running. Brandal was astonished; this crowd of starvelings and cutthroats had always moved sullenly and indifferently. He ran with them, and stood beside Reize on a line in the dirt.

A single man, dozing in the sun, still lay apart. Felaris walked over, smiled grimly at those already in place, and coughed loudly, nudging him with her buskin. Brandal could clearly see the circle patch on her shoulder, and the cross-draw dagger sheath just beneath her left arm.

The big man looked up at her, suddenly pale, and scrambled to his feet.

She shook her head, pretending to be sad.

"Too slow, Barlien."

The others, already lined up in formation, snickered.

She handed him two rocks, put a sword to his throat, and shouted in his face, "Twenty."

Barlien raised and lowered the rocks while she counted. By the fifteenth repetition, his face was red and his jaw shook as he struggled to lift.

She looked sympathetic. "Need help?" A dagger flicked into

her other hand and spun in it, pausing with the blade in his groin.

Not surprisingly, he redoubled his efforts.

At twenty, she grunted, "Over there. Now," and took the sword and dagger away.

Barlien sagged—but he ran into formation.

Felaris called, "Up."

The unkempt soldiers, a knot of forty or fifty, stood uncomfortably close together for humans. They didn't seem to care.

Not one of them had weapons.

"Left." They turned. "Right." They spun right. "March." They moved forward at an easy, oddly inhuman lope that looked as though it could last all day. "Circle the camp."

They trotted out of the camp, their weaponless hands hanging uselessly at their sides.

Brandal stared uneasily at the loping soldiers.

After ten circuits of the camp, most of them had their mouths wide open, panting, but they still didn't look tired.

He muttered to Reize, "They never stop, do they?"

Reize panted, "Look at them. Nothing to do but trot. No sword work, no obstacle work—that's not soldiering."

Brandal said politely, "Could you do it?"

"If I trained," he said dubiously. He glanced involuntarily at his belly. "Soon enough, I could. You never know."

"Could you beat one of them in a fight?" Brandal said.

Reize eyed him disbelievingly and dropped the subject.

She turned and faced them. Brandal noted that she had one foot behind her, poised to move away. "Right. Forward drills. Sword."

Each fighter clapped a hand to his sword but didn't draw it. Brandal imitated them, but didn't see the point: why tell a man when to touch but not draw his sword?

"Draw."

They drew, pulling their arms back until the sword hilts touched their ribs.

"Thrust."

They each thrust forward, nearly identically.

"Shield."

They raised their shields and put both hands behind them, pushing forward with a loud grunt.

"Ten. Charge."

With loud yells and raised swords they came forward exactly ten steps, finishing in nearly as good formation as they had begun.

"Ten. Charge. Ten. Charge. Ten. Charge."

It was as beautiful as a dance, in its own strange way: hundreds of warriors, moving at the same time in the same direction. Brandal felt as though he were part of a festival.

"Close."

They pulled together again, and were as neatly in formation as when they had begun. Brandal sneaked a look behind him and realized how far from the camp they had come. Behind him, not far from the tents, the squadron of unarmed men trotted by, panting but not slowing down.

Reize lurched to a stop beside Brandal. "I'm old for this," he panted. "I should leave. Work up some cash, have a nice, quiet wayside inn. Serve rich food and strong drink to needy strangers—overprice the food, underfill the glasses, and choke the stray rich orphan—nothing wicked, really. A nice place, if you're not very nice to start with . . ."

Brandal listened patiently. Reize was off on a dream again, and there was no stopping him. Once he rode the same dream all the way to a throne made of wine bottles and gold goblets; coming back to himself on a dirt floor had not been easy.

Brandal was exhausted by the time they stopped for lunch. He slumped in a dry gully not far from the camp and watched the dust they had kicked up as it blew away.

Brandal passed him some bread. "A little extra." He swigged from the goatskin flask and satisfiedly exhaled wine. "What would I do without it?"

Brandal smiled. "We'll probably never know. Has it been like this every day?"

Reize lay back with his eyes shut. "Every day. This feels longer than the other days, but they all do." He rubbed his face and scratched futilely at his burning red nose. "I shouldn't be here, a man my age. This is for you youngsters."

"But you have so much more experience at it," Brandal said earnestly. "Shouldn't you be doing this every day without even breathing hard?"

Reize waved a feeble hand at him. "Ah, you're talking like a man with an eagle up his ass."

Brandal shifted his stiff muscles on the sparse grass, looking for comfort. "What's the point of all this work?"

"Drill, man." Reize opened one eye, raising a bushy eyebrow and making it look like more work than Brandal had done all morning. "Drill. Makes you strong and makes you fast; makes your breath and muscles last. Gives you courage. Gives you gas."

He demonstrated loudly and chuckled.

Brandal stared, brooding, at the collapsed soldiers lying across the field in either direction. Even at rest, they looked different now, less like robbers and more like an army. A few were gambling, some were singing, but they all seemed to have one ear cocked, waiting for the next command.

It disturbed him how constantly *ready* they all looked.

"The most terrifying thing an army can bring against you," Stein had told him once over ale, "is obedience. An army that has it won't run away, and it won't think, and it won't do anything stupid until you tell it to." He raised his own stein and swallowed. "Like kicking a beehive. Fight one, and you fight them all."

Like most inhabitants of Crossroads, Brandal had never seen more then four people fighting at once. He had never seen any organized effort to fight. Until today he could barely imagine it.

He still couldn't imagine any cooperation between them.

Felaris shouted, "Gather!" and they all stood tiredly.

The afternoon was worse, a seemingly endless repetition of combat skills. For a while they broke into pairs and sparred with swords, then worked with shields only, then swords and shields.

Brandal found Reize a surprisingly strong opponent. The big man was quite strong; for a while at least he was fast. Reize finally said, panting, "Curly, you're better than I dreamed." He added quickly, "You need polish, but I could teach you that in time. Where did you learn to fight?"

"Inns and taverns." Brandal, seeing an officer looking their way, swung his sword at Reize.

Reize grunted and raised his shield. "We should work together for ourselves. Greater risk, greater glory. How long would it take us to make something of ourselves?"

He drifted off into daydreams again. Brandal noted that even in dreams, Brandal ended up doing most of the work and Reize took the profit. The daydream, finishing in a palace with kings and queens offering women and tribute (to Reize), took the rest of the afternoon.

The other combatants around Brandal looked uninspired but steady, a frighteningly obedient force. The entire time, the pack of gaunt men and women circled the camp, never slowing down and never resting.

A man shouted, "Meals."

The men and women with Brandal grunted with relief and stored their swords and axes against the wood rack. A subordinate with a square shoulder patch supervised; Brandal waited until the woman yawned, then rattled the rack loudly as he mimed putting back his sword.

Brandal noted, though, that none of the daggers were returned. He furtively checked his own; the sword was only for dire emergency.

The unarmed men and women trotted into camp, panting loudly and their sides heaving. Otherwise they seemed indifferent to the rigor of their all-day drill. "If I'd run that hard," Brandal said to Reize, "I'd be half-dead."

"Nah, nah. Get you in shape." Reize scratched his belly where sweat had stained his shirt. "Best thing for you, really."

The group of them went to the water trough, ignoring the ladle and scooping water in their hands, splashing it over their faces and hair. They grinned and shook their heads, letting the spray fly. Then they ambled over and stood by the meal tent in an unnaturally close group.

Brandal, lining up with the others, took his ration of mutton and a half jug of wine, and stood waiting to see where everyone else ate. He sniffed at the mutton approvingly; cooking standards had definitely gone up in his absence, or he was hungrier.

Many of the others, tipping the jugs up as they walked, walked toward where the unarmed men were standing, and halted behind them, waiting. Brandal joined them, slipping in besides Reize. "What now?"

Reize said, "Right. You were gone when they signed on." He chuckled. "Watch this."

The waiting group of unarmed trainees bunched together around a few individuals. The ones in the center collapsed, out of sight; cries of pain and whimpering went up. Brandal peered between the surrounding people, who were facing out in defense of the ones in the center. He couldn't see anything.

The cook came out from under the canopy with two massive uncooked haunches, both scored and gashed. To carry them at all he dragged them in the dirt. Brandal's nose wrinkled and, as the cries in the center of the group changed, he had a sudden terrible suspicion.

The cook laid one haunch in the dust, then swung the other by the leg and heaved it into the air, shouting, "Now!" The haunch sailed up; he had the second one behind it before the first dropped nearly to the ground . . .

. . . And was caught by two frantically growling muzzles.

They tugged together and growled fiercely at the two other wolves.

Those surrounding them, metamorphosing now that they had defenders themselves, whimpered and pushed, trying to get closer to the meat. They snapped at each other but, by some pack consent, never broke into fighting.

Brandal turned away, sickened. These soldiers had never needed arms.

Jaeken, nearby, said disinterestedly to the woman beside him, "Yesterday was better." The two of them turned away.

Brandal looked questioningly at Reize, who looked uncomfortable. "Yesterday," Reize said awkwardly, "the poor bugger was still alive. Mentioned everybody's mother and four armies on the way down, and cried out for his own mother when the fangs hit him. I felt bad myself. Would have choked him, if it weren't for the group pressure just to watch."

"Deserter?" Brandal tried to sound casual.

Reize shook his shaggy head. "Thief. The deserters are hanged half out of reach, and they have to leap for them. Takes longer. Curly, we shouldn't be here. We ought to be someplace wholesome, throttling rich orphans and whoring women who still have their own teeth."

Brandal wanted to object, but anyplace at all seemed more wholesome during feeding time.

The wolves were nearly done. One of them came forward and pawed at Felaris, looking up desperately. She threw a stone at it. It came back again, head lowered, horribly servile, and pawed at her leg.

"All right," she said finally. "I'll get her." She went into Morgan's hut.

The hut was made entirely of dark stone, and twice the size of any of the others. The entrance flap, of leather stained dark red, was full height. Brandal was unsurprised; Morgan would never stoop.

The crimson flap drew aside, and Morgan herself strode out.

Even now, knowing everything that he did about her, Brandal's breath caught in his throat. Her auburn hair flowed behind her, and she swung her long, superbly muscled arms as she walked almost as though she were pulling herself along. Morgan walking moved nearly as quickly as a horse trotting; she moved with the march of someone who would always be unhappy with where she was at the moment.

Brandal ached, watching her; she was beautiful in motion.

But her face was set unsmiling, and her hair when it moved exposed streaks of gray. An angry red scar creased her neck.

She looked indifferently out at the eating troops and turned away, walking alone.

He kept his distance; Morgan knew him too well to be easily fooled.

The soldier Barlien was sprawled in her path. A friend, or at least a well-wisher, called out a warning to him and he sat up abruptly, scrambling almost out of her way.

Her right hand flashed down. It had looked empty, but Brandal knew better; Morgan's hands were never empty. The man gasped, clutching at his neck, and fell.

Morgan pulled her bloodstained hand back, never breaking stride. The only sign that she noticed what had occurred was the slow, caressing way in which she rubbed her right hand over her left, washing them both in blood.

She gestured, and the wolves followed her as obediently as any lap dogs might. They fell into a line—Brandal wasn't sure of the hierarchy in the pack—and waited outside a stone outbuilding near the camp.

The other watchers drifted away. Reize wiped his lips, glanced down automatically at his goatskin, and said, "Join me later, then." He walked off toward his hut, his left hand reaching down to the goatskin as he went. He had not invited Brandal.

That was fine with Brandal; he had to see the inside of Morgan's hut. He edged nonchalantly over, checking for both posted and surreptitious guards. There were none; evidently, Morgan felt secure from violence. Given the brutality of camp discipline, she was probably right.

There was a snarl and a pained yip from the line of wolves at the stone hut. All heads turned, and Brandal slid quickly into the hut.

The inside was spare; the bed was little more than a camp cot, and the writing desk folded for travel. No rug covered the dirt floor, and the only light was a tallow lamp, still burning. Morgan could live like a soldier.

It hardly surprised him that there were weapons everywhere.

There were a short sword, a scimitar, and a broadsword. There were a hunting bow, a longbow, and some sort of small bow on a stick with a crank attached. There were nine daggers in the rack, some straight, some curved, one a triangular stiletto, and one with a wicked S-shaped blade with a groove to let out blood.

There was an empty space for a tenth dagger in the rack. Brandal decided to hurry.

He glanced at the shelving beside the writing desk and his heart froze. There was a stack of books with very old bindings.

Brandal spelled the titles out with great difficulty: *Gallic Commentaries*, by Caesar (with an annotated English translation), a book called *On War* by Von Clausewitz, and the translated writing, on infantry tactics, of a General Rommel. There was also a book called a Department of the Army Field Manual. Several other books related to training and disciplining soldiers.

He looked at each of them blankly, then opened the Caesar. The left-hand pages were in a language he didn't know. The right-hand pages used English, but for some reason were too complicated to follow. He turned pages and discovered an illustration showing movement of something called a phalanx. He read the text again, and suddenly it was clear: a squadron of soldiers, shifting to the left and right as needed for attacks. There was a black-and-white print of a Roman foot soldier, labeled in English and then in Latin: *milites*.

"Stepfather God," he whispered, and he was not swearing.

The last time a small force trained as the *milites* had come to Crossroads, they had been isolated, confused, frightened, and cut off from supplies. They had nearly conquered a country anyway. Morgan's forces would be less confused, less frightened, and, if Morgan could get *The Book of Strangeways*, less cut off from supplies.

Beside the books was a brooch: a stylized representation of a griffin fighting an armed man. Rubies showed blood from the griffin; the man's spear was deep in the griffin's side.

Brandal, looking at it, smiled strangely. The first time he had seen the design, he had assumed that it was simply a fantastic decoration. He had loved it.

He shook his head and stepped back outside. The line to the hut was greatly diminished; the wolves were still entering one at a time. The waiting animals were too intent on moving forward to look at him.

The wolves leaving the hut were disoriented. Brandal thought he saw one of them drool, but didn't go close enough to find out.

"Wyr," he said to himself unhappily. Morgan could not have found a better alliance to attack Crossroads. But why were they willing to serve her? The Wyr, as they themselves were proud to point out, were neither loyal nor tame.

Brandal carefully tucked his cloak over his sword and strode toward Reize's hut; he would need help leaving again. Brandal would definitely need to question Stein about arriving strangers. Brandal grimaced unhappily. He should also speak to the seer again.

"The Road Crews," he whispered to himself, "will be very busy from now on."

E·I·G·H·T

THEY WERE RIDING back on the road to Virginia. Dave was wearing sunglasses, and clearly his head was killing him.

Nonetheless, he was trying to hold his own in an argument that had broken out before his presentation and which Sugar, amused, was letting happen instead of directing discussion back to Dave's case. Dave had made the mistake of beginning, perhaps for effect, "All we've seen so far are ordinary cases with a few twists."

"You can't just say they're ordinary," Lee Anne insisted. "New breeds bring new problems; why wouldn't new animals?"

BJ, staring out the window ahead, noticed a small herd of deer grazing in a clearing. There were two bucks, two does, and two fawns. A week ago she would have been more excited to see them, and they were still wonderful. The grass around them rippled slightly as a faint cloud shadow moved over the clearing and stayed over them.

"So?" Dave lifted his sunglasses and rubbed his temples. "You can still treat a dog as a dog if it comes in."

"You can start there," Lee Anne insisted, "but you'd better not stop there, even with dogs. Dachshunds get spinal troubles. Labs get hip displasia. Those rotten little Shih Tzus get skin fold pyoderma."

BJ noted idly that the cloud-shadow had stayed over the deer, and was getting darker. The bucks froze, antlers high and ears pricked. The does nudged the fawns under the brush.

"Remember how BJ handled her case? 'Think of it as a horse

91

or a goat.' That worked, right?" Dave folded his arms.

"Okay." Lee Anne frowned. "But it still wasn't a goat; we just *thought* of it that way."

The shadow was getting larger and darker. The does crouched over the fawns. BJ sat up as the truck came closer to the deer.

"We're winging it," Lee Anne said flatly.

The truck was nearly opposite the deer. The shadow over them was developing solid edges.

"We need to face," Annie said softly, "that this is not a world we should be in."

BJ heard a sound of something whistling down.

"Sugar?" she said uncertainly. Sugar slammed on the brakes as the others stared at her. BJ didn't call teachers by their first names.

The whistling grew. BJ rolled her window down to stick her head out.

Dave grabbed her and pulled her back. She tried to twist free, turning to glare at him. Annie, Lee Anne, and Sugar were watching the two of them.

There was a sudden, loud rush of air and a screaming noise. They all shut their eyes in the wind. When they opened their eyes, the shadow in the field was getting smaller again.

Lee Anne stuck her head quickly out the window and stared upward. She pulled back in, blinking and wiping her eyes. "There's a dot against the sun."

BJ was looking out into the field, waiting desperately for the deer to get up. Let both fawns get up, she prayed to herself. Please.

She saw one fawn rise awkwardly and bound off, then another bounded past it. The does nuzzled them in passing, and BJ sighed in relief.

The two fawns moved to a place where the grass and plants were smashed flat, as though a great wind had struck a very small area. They sniffed at the grass curiously.

The other buck was missing.

Dave said, "Sorry I was rough, BJ." He looked sorry; his glasses had slipped, and his sweat-beaded forehead had a vertical headache-crease running between the eyebrows.

BJ looked out at the crushed grass. "Thanks for doing it. You probably did me a favor."

Annie said to Sugar, "Do you know what did that?"

Sugar, staring out the window, shook his head. Finally he reached for the keys and started driving again.

They recovered quickly, and stared interestedly out the window at the woods. It looked wilder than Virginia forest, more gnarled and twisted; the trees were often four or five feet thick, and in several cases had small streams, their courses changed, flowing through the roots. The forest seemed incredibly old.

Of course, it helped their recovery to know that nothing very large could dive at them between the tree branches.

Annie said to Dave, who was peering eagerly through the windshield, "Are you looking for something in particular?"

"My client," he said, "and my patient. Or at least the patient; nobody's really come forward as the client." He looked questioningly at Sugar, who shook his head.

"Maybe it's one of those deals like Fields and the unicorns," BJ said. "Stein, looking after an animal. What kind of animal is it?"

The truck maneuvered around a bend, and Sugar hit the brakes. They sat and stared.

Annie whispered, shaken, "That's not real."

BJ whispered, "Dave, is that your patient?"

Lee Anne said in a normal voice, "What are you gonna think of that as?"

"As an eagle," Dave said, and added unnecessarily, "and a lion."

Sugar, staring out at it, muttered, "One hell of a big lion."

"Is there a client?" Dave looked out at it, then at the halter he'd already pulled from the back of the truck this morning. The halter looked hopelessly flimsy. "Is there anybody to help?"

Sugar said flatly, "If you don't feel up to it, I'll take over."

Dave stared out the windshield and licked his lips once to wet them. Finally he shook his head. "It's my case." He looked at his notes and slowly opened the truck door.

"It's just vet work," he said firmly. "I'll think of it as an eagle. And a lion." He smiled weakly, stepping out of the truck. "And a whole lot smaller."

The Griffin stared at him; its eyes were golden and piercing. Its head was the size of a panther's, and its wicked curved beak was nearly a foot long. Its wings were folded, but had a strange double fold to them; BJ tried to imagine the full wingspan and thought, with a wrench, of the missing buck.

Dave approached the Griffin slowly and easily, no sudden movements. The Griffin cocked its head like a sparrow looking at a crumb—not hopping, but not friendly. A breeze rippled the brown feathers and tawny fur, and BJ shivered.

Once he was by the Griffin's side, Dave tucked the halter in his belt and reached out his hand. It was, BJ noticed, his right hand; Dave was left-handed and wasn't taking any chances on losing his career. "Easy," Dave said, patting the Griffin's body. He stooped, checking for the griffin's genitals, and added reassuringly, "Easy, boy."

The Griffin turned. His eyes, golden and perfectly circular, looked under tawny, angled ridges, which, BJ reflected, would make his face look perpetually angry.

Lee Anne said, very quietly to BJ, "You make sure my folks know how much I love them." She stepped from the truck confidently and slung her arm over the Griffin, just behind the massive wings. "If it's okay with you, I'll restrain the patient."

The Griffin gave no sign that it had felt anything. Lee Anne put a hand back for the halter; Dave wordlessly passed it to her, and she said quietly, "Here goes." In a single easy motion she slid it over the Griffin's head.

The Griffin whipped its neck backward as the halter slid down, bit through the rope with no apparent effort, hooked the bridle strap with its beak and bit three times, and looked at her solemnly as the severed pieces of rope smacked the roadway.

After a moment, Lee Anne said, "Okay, no halter. Stay quiet, boy." To Dave she said, "Do me a favor and warn me before you do anything rash."

"You got it." He was feeling better now, moving his hands up and down the Griffin and rubbing the fur backward. "No flea dirt, no scabs. No skin parasites at all. He's pretty clean. . . . Quite the scar here. You been fighting, boy?"

He patted the Griffin's chest, pulling his hand back when the leonine muscles twitched and the tail lashed once. "Okay. Don't tell me." He slid his hand down the furry belly. "More scars . . . don't try to tell me about the Peaceable Kingdom."

BJ watched nervously. Sugar, not relaxed and not tense, stood by the truck, one hand in his pocket.

"Belly feels good . . . solid muscle . . ." Dave arched his hand, feeling. "Okay, there's his bladder. Damn, it's the size of a cantaloupe. Is he blocked? Does anybody here know how big a lion's bladder is?"

"We figured you'd know," Sugar said casually. "Isn't it your case?"

"Just asking," Dave said quickly. "I didn't get a chance to feel up a lion before we came here." He probed again with his fingers. "It feels normal to me. Maybe a tad large . . . hang on a minute."

"I wasn't going anywhere," Lee Anne said. She sounded calm, but her coveralls were damp at the armpits. "What do you have in mind?"

Dave moved to the truck, grabbed a palpation sleeve, and slipped it on. "Cover me. I'm going in." He moved directly behind the Griffin, grabbed the Griffin's tail right-handed, and raised it high. "This is gonna hurt you more than it hurts me, fella."

"Not necessarily," a dry, cultured voice said.

They looked around.

"I am," the Griffin said acidly, "something of an amateur surgeon myself."

His talons, easily three inches long, raked through a granite road stone as though it were sod.

Dave swallowed. "I'd like to check that bladder again," he said carefully.

The Griffin turned his head, and BJ could have sworn his beak was smiling. "Yours or mine?"

Dave smiled weakly. "Got me there."

Lee Anne, still holding on, said, "Let me apologize for myself and my colleague. We had no idea you were a talking—well, that you could speak."

"Stones have been known to move," he said softly, "and trees to speak. Do you recognize the quote?"

After a moment's silence, the Griffin shook his head. "Shakespeare, *Macbeth*. You mustn't neglect your education in favor of your studies." He added lovingly, " 'It will have blood, they say. Blood will have blood.' Lovely idea."

BJ said timidly, "Where did you read Shakespeare?"

"Stein's," he said. "He has a marvelous library. I recommend it to you for your copious spare time."

BJ decided that he was being sarcastic.

Lee Anne said, "Do you have a name we can call you?"

"Of course I have a name," the Griffin said loftily. "Surname and family name. Quite a prestigious family, too. Which is why I don't give it out for common use."

Dave scratched. "What should I call you?"

"Simply call me Griffin."

Lee Anne said, "But what if we meet another griffin—" and shut up.

The Griffin, looking her in the eye, said slowly, "Most people do not meet more than one griffin in a lifetime. Most humans, in fact, meet with a griffin exactly once, and briefly. Until you prove yourself an exception to that rule, you may as well address me as I see fit."

It made sense, BJ reflected. When you meet someone who can disembowel you in seconds, you address him as he sees fit.

His entire body twitched, and he dug quick parallel furrows through the stones, striking a shower of sparks. He turned his head slowly to the left and glared over his shoulder at Dave. "Was that last prodding strictly necessary?" he said coldly.

Bloodless as Dave already looked, he went still paler. "I was just expressing your anal sacs," he stammered. "They were pretty blocked up, and I—"

"All right, all right," the Griffin said testily, looking around. BJ thought that he might be embarrassed. "Carry on, then."

"I just thought of something." Lee Anne looked disturbed. "Griffin, what if you need a prescription? How will we get it back to you?"

"Stein, I imagine," Annie said. "Or . . . he mentioned a trader named Owen."

"Owen is an interesting man," he said approvingly. "If you have ever wanted anything and are willing to pay, tell him. If it exists and can be moved, he'll find it." He raised one feathery eyebrow slightly. "You must be willing to pay the price, however."

BJ thought to herself about Rapunzel and Rumpelstiltskin. "Is he"—she almost said "wicked," which seemed the right word in Crossroads—"is he a cruel man?"

"Dear, no." The Griffin's head circled like a cat's as he watched a blue-back fluttering from branch to branch in the cedars beside them. He added indifferently, "If anything, he's far too kind."

Annie said, "So far, everyone we've met has been kind." She sounded dubious.

The Griffin said, turning and regarding her solemnly, "And you're quite right to mistrust that. Some people in this world are cruel and quite frightening. The Inspector General, for instance."

Lee Anne said, "We've heard he's around again."

" 'Around'? Nonsense, young lady. He is always 'around.' " He considered, tipping a claw to his beak. "I would say rather that he is making rounds, much as you do."

The blue-back flew too close. The Griffin's head snapped up and sideways, and he reached up with a claw and delicately tucked the remaining limp, blue wing into his beak. "And I myself would not want to face him."

He looked into their appalled faces with satisfaction, then turned to Dave. "Well? What next?"

Dave shook himself and thought. "Lessee. I've palpated you, I've done a skin check—wait." He straightened up, grinning. "This is a chance we don't ever get. You're the patient: is there anything you want looked at?"

The Griffin stared directly at Sugar and said flatly, "My foot hurts: (a) broken bone; (b) infection; (c) idiopathic; (d) nutritional cause."

Sugar said without batting an eye, "Your call, Dave: a, b, c, or d?"

Dave looked back and forth between the feet. "Which foot?"

The Griffin held up his right taloned forefoot. Dave knelt and ran his hand over the index claw cautiously, then hissed and put his finger in his mouth. "Damn." He squeezed his finger, staring at the ball of blood on the end of it, and asked the Griffin, "You got any venom on that?"

The Griffin said demurely, "Do you think I need any?"

Dave nodded. "Okay." He turned back to the foot.

Lee Anne said, "Sir—" and bit her tongue. It had been automatic.

The Griffin said gravely, "Madam."

She plunged ahead. "Sir, you're mostly feline—"

"Leonine."

"Leonine. How do you groom yourself, when you have a beak?"

For answer, the Griffin twisted his head, owl-like, almost completely backward, using his razor-sharp beak to preen his own neck feathers. He also deftly smoothed his fur right next to Lee Anne's arm. "Don't be so ready to denigrate beaks. They can be quite useful." He arched his neck, looking down on her like a teacher to a young student. "On your world, for instance, an eagle uses his beak to tear out the liver of Prometheus the God."

Annie said, "That's a myth." She said it as firmly as she possibly could.

"Absolutely," the Griffin said dryly. "And we all know the firmness of the dividing line between myth and reality." He stretched his massive wings once and turned, admiring them. They shaded both Dave and Lee Anne. He turned back to Annie. "I myself can't see where they begin and end; can you?"

"Actually," Annie said, "you're not mythical. You're a chimera."

The Griffin said mildly, "There's no need to get personal."

"It's a biological term for two species mixed together." Annie added, "Usually it's applied to plants."

He nodded gravely. "No offense taken. For the record, however, I'm not a graft."

"Maybe not," Dave said as he turned the foot over, "but I'm treating this part like an eagle."

" 'He grasps the crag with horny hands, and like a thunderbolt he falls.' Tennyson. Paraphrased."

"Why is it," Lee Anne said, annoyed, "that everybody who sounds educated quotes literature? Doesn't science count?"

"Of course it does, my dear. However, quoting it would be monumentally boring. Probably because most of it is written badly." He added, "However, it is fashionable now to speak affectedly of chaos theory, catastrophe curves, and the occasional fractal. Much as your grandparents would have invoked Einstein's name over cocktails." To Dave he said, "Aren't you examining the wrong foot now?"

Dave looked up unhappily. "Your foot isn't cut, scarred, or fractured. I wanted to see if it's exactly like the other foot, maybe related to walking too much on eagles' feet—"

"Talons."

"Sure, talons. But there's nothing external. . . . Has it bothered you a lot?"

"Not yet, but it soon may. It's been worse of late." The Griffin sucked in his breath sharply as Dave twisted the foot, then did it again as Dave poked it. "Those do hurt equally, if that's what you were trying to discover."

"It's not a break. It's not a sprain. Something birds get . . ." He snapped his fingers. "Gout. I'll bet anything."

"You needn't sound so happy about it."

"I'm just glad I could figure it out."

"Gout. Oh, dear. Are you quite sure?" He sounded genuinely disconcerted.

Dave shook his head. "Nossir. A blood test would help."

"Possibly not . . . I'm told that griffin blood is fairly unique." The Griffin blinked, a membrane passing over his golden eyes while he thought. "I believe gout is related to nutrition."

"It's controlled by diet." Dave scratched his head. "Just, uh, what is your diet?"

The beak seemed to be smiling. "I don't think we have time for all of it. Perhaps I could show you some other time."

"Yeah, that would be great." Dave shuffled backward gradually. "Listen, if you want, I can bring some diet guidelines back here and leave them with Stein. Probably he can help sort out what . . ."—he struggled, trying to match the Griffin's educated sound—"what, uh, local delicacies are bad for you."

The Griffin nodded approvingly. "An excellent idea. I see Stein often; we enjoy each other's company."

BJ tried to imagine the sharp-eyed but kindly-looking innkeeper as a friend of the bloodthirsty Griffin and realized, to her discomfort, that it wasn't hard to imagine at all.

Dave was much more relaxed now that he had reached a diagnosis. "I'll draw some blood and we'll do some lab work. . . . Is that okay, Dr. Dobbs?" He added tactlessly, "Do you have somebody you trust to do the lab work?"

The Griffin raised a feathery eyebrow. Sugar said to him, annoyed, "Just so you know, the lab work at Western Vee is top-notch. My *student* here"—he leaned on the word—"wants to know if we can use the lab for the blood work and not compromise your existence."

The Griffin nodded. "You seem resourceful, Doctor. I imagine you can." He peered narrowly over his beak at Dave. "It's not my duty to tutor you, young man, but not all conversations are appropriate in front of a client."

"Right. Sorry." Dave stood and moved away. "We'll get the results to Stein—never mind. Dr. Dobbs will see that you get them somehow."

"Much better. I suppose this is good-bye, then. Thank you for coming."

Clearly, it was a dismissal, and from a patient. The others went back to the truck, fascinated but glad to be leaving in one piece. Only BJ stayed behind. Finally the Griffin said, "You have a question."

She nodded. "I'm wondering why you didn't speak at first."

"And you think . . . ?"

"That you liked having the advantage."

"I'm a predator," he said. "We prefer the advantage. You know, you really should be more afraid of me."

She shook her head. "I don't think you'd eat anyone you talked to. Sort of like Alice being introduced to the pudding."

He raised a feathered eyebrow. "I beg your pardon?"

She smiled. "Lewis Carroll. It's a relief to find something you haven't read."

The Griffin laughed, a throaty sound that reminded her of a muted roar. "I have quite a lot to learn myself, Doctor."

She was pleased, and didn't correct him. "Anyway, I don't think you'd eat anything that could think unless it gave you just cause. On the other hand, did you happen to eat a deer this morning?"

"I beg your pardon? I do eat venison on occasion. . . ."

She gestured back up the road. "No, I mean swoop down and snatch away an entire buck."

"Ah." He looked solemn. "You have been in the presence of the Great. How fortunate that you weren't hurt; it is often like an encounter with fate."

"I've had an encounter with fate," BJ said. "Recently." The Griffin's diction was infectious. "One is enough."

The Griffin cocked its head at her, an oddly catlike pose from an eagle's head. "You remind me of why I occasionally like women."

"For breakfast?"

"For conversation." He offered his talon, an oddly courtly gesture. "Please give my warmest regards to anyone who seems to know about me."

She shook her head. "I don't think I should mention you to anyone, just in case."

He looked into her eyes. "I trust your discretion," he said, and suddenly she felt quite charmed by him, not at all afraid.

Back in the truck, Dave let out a long breath and sagged. BJ felt like putting an arm around him, and so, clearly, did Lee Anne.

But it was Annie who leaned forward, hugged him, and said, "You did a good job."

He leaned back into her and patted her arm. "Man, I was so scared."

"You didn't show it," BJ said.

"Much," Lee Anne said. "You're pretty tough."

He grinned at her. "Gotta be. It's a tough world."

But BJ saw him suddenly as she would have twenty years from now, looking at their yearbook: smooth faced, innocent, traces of baby fat still under his cheeks. This is how he'll always look to me, she thought unhappily. If I kill myself now, I'll never see what he turned into. Or any of us.

Sugar drove awhile in silence. Finally Dave, unable to bear it, said, "How do you think I did?"

Sugar stared at him. "You, or the team?"

Dave looked blank, then turned around. "Right. Thanks, L.A." Lee Anne grinned.

Sugar grunted. "It went better than I expected. You thought on your feet, all right. Make sure you learn how to plan ahead."

Dave said desperately, "I mean my grade."

"Sure. I didn't mean to forget the important stuff." Sugar drawled, "Physical, a B minus. You did fine, but you quit when you found one thing wrong. What if it's not the only thing?"

"Okay," Dave said tiredly. "So I could have missed something. How did I do other than that?"

"Well, there is one more little problem."

Dave stiffened.

Sugar went on, "You kinda forgot your own presentation."

Dave paled. "We got distracted."

"Yep. *We* didn't talk about it again. Which is kind of a shame, since *you* were being graded on it. Half your grade."

Which meant that Dave would be failing the rotation. BJ bit her lip, and Lee Anne and Annie stared sympathetically but helplessly at Dave. There was nothing they could do.

"However," Sugar went on, "this is kind of a strange rotation, and it probably shook you up some, so I'll cut you slack. Do a post-presentation tomorrow morning. The rest of you show up for it. Sorry, no full day off, after all."

They nodded. Dave looked so desperate that BJ couldn't resent him.

Sugar frowned. "You remember: hot-dogging doesn't count for anything unless you can play by the rules, too. Being a maverick is fun, but mostly it's a waste. Got it?"

"Yes, sir," Dave said, but he sounded more relieved than sincere.

Sugar looked up in the mirror. "How about the rest of you: any comments for the case jockey?"

Lee Anne and Annie shook their heads. BJ said thoughtfully, "Just one."

Dave frowned. "What else did I forget?"

"Nothing." BJ stared out at the trees, watching the gnarled virgin timber blend into second-growth Virginia pine. But she said suddenly to Sugar, "You knew all about him, didn't you?"

After a moment, Lee Anne and Annie started to laugh, and Annie said, "Right. He quoted you."

Dave stared, openmouthed, at Sugar, who looked back innocently. "What's wrong, Dave? You thought I'd let you work on an animal that big if I didn't know him?"

"But you hadn't worked on him yourself," BJ said firmly.

Now it was Sugar's turn to gape. "What tipped you off?"

"He knew what gout was, but not that he had it. If you'd looked at him, you would have noticed his gout."

Sugar shook his head back and forth, grinning. "I'm glad

you've got that much faith in me. You're a pistol. You got any more snappy answers?"

"Just another question. I wonder," BJ said thoughtfully, "if the Griffin wasn't checking us out more than he wanted checking out by us."

Nobody had anything to say to that.

Beautiful as the scenery was, the students dozed off. They woke when Sugar slowed down suddenly and the road became nothing but bumps.

"Are we off-roading?" Lee Anne said.

BJ bit her lip, thinking of what "off-roading" could mean in Strangeways.

Ahead of them, the road itself was gone. To the left was a large, hastily thrown-up pile of rock, underlying gravel, and clay: the remains of a road that had looked, to BJ, thousands of years old. Plus it was their only way home.

(The only way home they knew, she reminded herself.)

To the right, men and women with pickaxes, shovels, and a strange double-billed half-hoe half-ax were tearing up sod and chopping through roots, laying a path between the trees for a new road. To people accustomed to freeways and bypasses, the changes made no sense. The new road doubled back on itself and forked twice, its end and the forks disappearing into the trees.

A woman bearing one of the double-bill tools over her shoulder tapped on the window of the truck. Sugar rolled it down the rest of the way. "Yes'm?"

"Where you going?" she said simply. Sugar looked at her. Finally he said, "Just down the road a piece—"

"Really going?" she said bluntly. She seemed amused by his unwillingness to say.

Sugar said uncertainly, "A place called Kendrick, Virginia. We're gonna join up with 480 outside the Jefferson National Forest—does that make any sense to you?"

She nodded. "Giles County line, still in Floyd County."

Lee Anne chuckled. Sugar nodded shortly.

The woman said flatly, "Road's different. We'll show you."

After a short silence, she gestured at the others. "Changed it."

Annie said suddenly, "What's the tool you're holding?" She took it off her shoulder and held it out proudly. "Twybil."

She turned it quickly, the sharp hoe blade and the razor-honed ax blade. "Best tool in the world." She whipped the handle sideways, letting it slip through her hands, then caught it at the last minute and swung it sideways, chopping a small branch off a nearby bush without looking at it. "Does everything."

Lee Anne said, "Can't we just walk the old roadbed and find our way?"

She laughed then, and her dust-smeared face crinkled around her hazel eyes. "Best not."

Lee Anne pointed. "We can see the other road from here. Couldn't we just cut across between the trees?"

The woman with the twybil grinned.

To make her point, she threw a rock down the new road, straight at the tree where the road turned.

The rock never hit. BJ never saw it disappear, but never saw it land, either.

She grinned at them. "New twists."

"I guess," Lee Anne said, shaken.

The woman stood on tiptoe, reached in, and tweaked Sugar's photocopies. "Need a new map," she said disapprovingly.

Sugar said, "I wouldn't try to come back without one."

She frowned and pursed her lips. "Best not." She sounded remarkably like a relative of Lee Anne's, and BJ realized that the woman's English was probably leakage across the Crossroads-Virginia border.

She walked in front of the van herself, stopping occasionally to throw rocks. About half the rocks vanished without seeming to. She stopped periodically to check the slack on a piece of twine tied to her foot and pegged back in Crossroads. Along the way she waved nonchalantly with the twybil to other workers.

She waved to the last one, a fat man wearing Levi's and carrying an eight-pound maul for breaking rock. He was wearing a faded Copenhagen Snuff T-shirt, and he had a long, curly beard. He nodded back to her.

They drove by him, and he looked at them. "Which way to Kendrick?" Sugar called out.

He pointed with the maul, as though it were light as a ball-peen hammer, and grunted.

"Thanks," Annie said.

He grunted again, but he was smiling under the beard. He shouldered the maul and strode up a side road, into the woods. BJ watched him, wondering if he was headed back to Virginia or up another strange road of his own.

Sugar drove in the brand-new, final driveway of the new parking lot and stopped. They stepped out stiff-legged, aware for the first time of how much riding they had done. Only Sugar seemed limber, if slightly bowlegged.

He stopped when Lee Anne said urgently, "Dr. Dobbs."

"Go on."

She swallowed. "I don't mean to be rude, and I have faith in you—I've spent more time in the hills than the rest of you—"

"Like we couldn't tell," Dave said.

Lee Anne shot a look at him that, in his present weakened state, might have killed him. "Point being, sir, I'd like you to be sure and get the right map. Getting lost is funny on the freeway, but . . ." She waved an arm at the Appalachian Mountains, which faded into blue on the horizon.

Dave rode off, gunning his bike throttle loudly. He hadn't had a good day.

Annie walked with BJ to the cars. "She did have a point," she said, and shivered. "I'm sorry. I keep thinking of that disappearing stone."

BJ, fumbling in her purse, had other things to think about. She dropped her car keys trying to get them out, and had trouble getting the key in the ignition. She drove away very carefully indeed.

N·I·N·E

BJ WAS MORE cautious this time than she had been before. She searched for twenty minutes to find a library terminal with no line in front of it, and looked both ways before entering CROSS-ROADS in the subject category. She wrote down only the Library of Congress numbers, none of the titles, and she put the list inside a manila folder.

Assembling the books themselves took more than an hour, and quite a bit of walking. Twice she passed Mrs. Sobell, who smiled up at her in recognition. BJ tried to look friendly but bored.

By ten-thirty, she had a stack of ten manuscripts, nearly all typewritten on red-margined thesis paper, none of them published. She had been to the stacks in geology, physics, biology, mathematics, and comparative religion. She sat with the stack and a Nestle's Crunch bar, the candy carefully hidden as a leftover high school reflex, reading quickly.

"Reality Tectonics and Continental Drift" presented a devastatingly simple theory: that worlds drifted like tectonic plates, touching at various eras (Atlantean, Arthurean) and having a permanent vortex relationship in "the area known as Crossroads." It was by a man in the physics department who had taught the only course BJ had taken as an undergraduate for the simple love of learning. Estevan Protera was easily the best professor BJ or most of the others had ever had.

BJ knew from a friend in computer publishing that Estevan, the sponsor of Lambda House, the Western Vee gay fraternity,

105

was also known (for reasons not published in the Lambda House newsletter) as "Señora Esther." Converging realities might be a fairly comfortable concept to Professor Protera.

"Toward a Science of Magic: The Laws of the Physically Impossible" took the position that "by proceeding from quantifiable results to hypothesis and prediction, we can develop a gradual understanding of phenomena contrary to known natural law. In this manner, we can probably uncover the nature of forces which were hitherto discussed, but never scientifically. An entire new field of physics may come of this process."

The writer, a graduate student named Fiona Bannon, was clearly quite excited about the possibility of obtaining a research grant for sorcery. BJ resolved to look her up someday and see how her work was going.

"The Extinct and the Mythical: Symbiosis and Natural Reselection" argued that the long-term effect of what it called "second-chance species" in Crossroads would be an explosion of unstable diversity. "While symbiotic partners are, in tandem, likelier to survive a hostile environment than are non-symbiotic species, the partners are more vulnerable to environmental change. Comparatively small changes in moisture, temperature, or food supply can throw the symbiosis out of balance."

She thought of Fields's simple declaration: "Besides, that's how it is. In Crossroads, we help each other." The truth of symbiosis seemed a massive injustice.

Or perhaps she was inclined to see injustice in the world just now. . . . She pushed that thought aside and read on.

She had saved the mathematics article for last, sure that she wouldn't understand it. With a sigh and a fervent wish for lunch, she opened the binder and scanned it, not sure what to expect but quite sure that it would be completely incomprehensible.

Instead she found a simple title: "Catastrophe in an Open System: Chaos Theory and the Ultimate Instability of Crossroads." It was written by a current member of the Western Vee math department, a dour and perpetually confused woman named Harriet Winterthur whom BJ's undergraduate friends had frequently laughed at. BJ had seen her up close once: gray hair falling on all sides, papers stacked every which way, struggling to keep her lunch perched on the loose stack while she opened the door of a badly corroded Volvo. Chaos, BJ thought in retrospect, suited her well.

But Professor Winterthur's writing was simple and graceful, and her prologue was disturbingly clear:

The Buddha's last words were that all things decay. Pope wrote that the world is subject to decay. In the nineteenth century, entropy was the topic of etchings as well as of essays. Humanity is as fascinated with whimpers as with bangs, but only recently have we been able to quantify as well as glorify randomness in systems. . . .

Unfortunately, the consequences for a system in which randomness is artificially increased from the outside, and seldom counteracted, is spectacularly rapid decay into catastrophe. In a nuclear reaction, bombardment promotes collision creates fission; the process is as dramatic on the superatomic scale.

The unpredictable entrance of species and of individuals will inevitably destroy Crossroads. Conscious attempts to delay destruction are simply another random element in a system which has, we shall see, no real chance for survival.

There was a quick reference to fractal theory, an exfoliation, which left BJ completely lost, and a series of mathematically laid-out hypothetical cases involving types of introduced species. Beginning from models involving rabbits in Australia, kudzu in Virginia, and African bees in South and Central America, Professor Winterthur dealt with variables of population, food chains, and predator relationships to extrapolate starvation, disease, extinction, and desolation.

Her conclusion was tragically brief:

This essay has little rigor, and is not a proof. I suspect that it is possible to prove that Crossroads is unstable; I have not the heart. Suffice it to say that whatever value Crossroads has for us, we must extract it quickly and prepare to mourn what little magic we have been allowed to see.

BJ put the essay aside, thinking about their own invasion of Crossroads and the injuries they had witnessed. Was it possible that the instability Professor Winterthur had predicted was taking its toll already?

She resolved, feeling guilty and selfish but sensible, to be even more cautious to avoid observation when working with materials about Crossroads. She went back to the terminal she had used and double-checked that she had cleared it after leaving.

The Book of Strangeways was on its shelf in the same place as last time. BJ touched it, then quickly slid it back and picked up the book next to it, then picked up *The Book of Strangeways* again. It had a slight static prickle, like walking across a dry rug on a cold day.

She opened it and, sorting through the foreign (and, she now suspected, entirely alien) maps, found one map labeled Jefferson National Forest. It showed the interstate, and the varying forest roads, and even the fire trails. It included a turnoff marked only CR.

BJ was barely average with maps, but she traced the road down until the main branch of it crossed the stone bridge, near the edge of the page.

She wondered why Sugar had taken a fresh copy for both places they had gone. Wouldn't it make more sense to photocopy the entire book at once?

She took it to one of the other copy machines on the second floor, cautiously carrying the book protectively with the front cover against her chest.

The third copy machine she went to was working, and there was no line. She placed the book facedown on the glass, lowering the rubber cover mat carefully so as not to damage the spine.

She looked at the photocopy with the map's finely crosshatched lines well reproduced, and exhaled. She hadn't realized how afraid she'd been that the copy would be blank.

She flipped back to the map of Kendrick. It wouldn't hurt to have a copy of that. She found it and looked for the vet school, as people always look for the most familiar place—

And froze, staring.

The third driveway to the new parking lot now showed on the map. When the driveway hadn't been completed, it hadn't been on the map.

A voice behind her said plaintively, "Are you still using the copier?"

"What? Oh. No." She moved aside, clutching the book tightly.

The undergraduate behind her, a copy of *Road and Track* in his hands, stared at her.

She took the stairs down to the map area and passed the stacks, back and forth, unwilling to let go of the book.

She sat a moment with it, looking carefully at the first turn into Crossroads from the national forest. This time she double-checked the turn marked CR. She wasn't good with maps, but it looked as though the new change, made by the Road Crew, was already on the map.

One of the new side roads was labeled MOCKPA. Another was labeled in odd squiggles and, under that, AGRA. Another had nothing but a stylized symbol on it, reminiscent of a lizard with wings. She shuddered and slid the book back on the shelf.

She ate lunch at Gyro's, slowly and thoughtfully. Today she sat at the counter.

BJ wanted to sit in the corner, but was still feeling guilty from having ducked Stan the other day. Having secrets promoted guilt. She hopped up on a counter stool and said, "How's it going?"

"Pretty good." He glanced sideways at his father Chris, who was looking at them alertly but with little understanding. "A few problems."

"Me too." She glanced at her book bag involuntarily.

He laughed. "Beej, you been having problems since you were a freshman. Work again?"

"Well, medicine."

"Dr. Beej." He shook his head, running a spatula across the grill. "It's finally gonna happen."

She shook her head. "Stan, I'm not there yet."

He grinned at her. "That medical problem gonna hold you back?"

She munched her gyro and stared across at the campus. "It might."

On her way out, she waved to Chris, who waved back jerkily. He watched her go, but never even tried to speak.

The health service was in the same building as the foreign language department; space on campus was tight.

The woman at the desk, in her mid-thirties, smiled politely but not maternally and said, "Your name, please?"

"BJ Vaughan." BJ showed her ID. "I have an appointment with Dr. Hitori."

"This way." But she sounded sympathetic now; normal students made appointments with GPs and GYNs, not with neurologists.

Dr. Hitori was dark haired, Asian, and in her late forties. She scanned BJ's previous records (which contained fairly mundane information about strep throat and a mononucleois test), smiled rather distantly to BJ, and said in a surprising Tennessee accent, "We surely have something to talk about, don't we?"

BJ nodded timidly. Dr. Hitori had the worst doctor-patient rapport she had ever seen, and she talked too fast.

"I was able to verify that your mother had Huntington's chorea." BJ was surprised but said nothing. "I couldn't find anything on your grandfather, but it stands to reason that one of her parents had to have it. Under the circumstances, I do recommend genetic testing."

BJ suspected that Dr. Hitori found this conference a formality. "Should we do anything else?"

Dr. Hitori was scribbling quickly on the form in BJ's student folder. "I have some paperwork for you to sign, and Duke will set up to test you."

"How quickly will I have the results?"

"A week, tops." She looked sharply at her. "I know you're thinking that positive test results would be the end of everything. It's just not that simple." She paused, choosing her words carefully. "Have you ever seen a Huntington's chorea victim"—it sounded more sensible than "patient"—"in the final stages?"

On separate holidays and increasingly sporadic visits, BJ had seen her grandfather sink from madness into depression and paralysis, and had seen him completely immobile, and still conscious, at the very end. That last had been during a short visit to Raintree Hospital in the company of her grandmother. BJ's mother, after she found out about it, didn't speak to BJ's grandmother for a month.

BJ remembered the suffering, conscious eyes, too alert for the indifferent muscles around them.

Aloud she said only, "I've seen one."

"I've seen several. In fact, I've seen people fight it all the way." She was speaking even faster.

BJ said, "They don't win, of course."

Dr. Hitori said bluntly, "Depends on what you call winning. They had longer lives than Keats did, some of them longer than Mozart; that's plenty of time to do something worthwhile, feel things." The speed, BJ realized, was anger, directed at the appointment more than at her.

"Time." BJ's voice was trembling. Talking about it with someone made it more real. "Does it ever start early? Like my age?"

The doctor hesitated, then nodded. "It's more common to see the onset when the patient is in late thirties to early forties, but the early twenties is possible. Late teens is possible, but not common." She reopened BJ's folder and sat poised with a pen. "Does something make you think you have symptoms already?"

"Just like that? A list?"

Dr. Hitori looked surprised. "You seem pretty bright. You've done enough reading to make the appointment. So, got any interesting symptoms?"

"Depression."

"Bullshit."

BJ smiled, picturing exactly what Sugar would do to her if she said "bullshit" to a patient. "Why bullshit?"

"You mentioned your mother's suicide in the request for testing. Plus you're in a fourth-year medical program; I can't remember a time, my last year, when I wasn't sleep deprived and depressed. Right? So, what else?"

"Shaky hands." BJ held one out and, damn it, it wasn't shaking.

She tapped the pen, considering. "Not a sufficient symptom by itself. You could have drunk too much caffeine, or you could be exhausted—"

"All the time?"

"For more information, see my comment about medical school. Tell me what happened."

She stumbled, careful to leave Crossroads out of it. "I was playing—it was kind of a stick game, with friends, half like tag and half like fencing—and I kept dropping the stick. And losing. And I couldn't get my hands to do what I wanted them to."

"Had you played this game a lot before?" BJ shook her head. "Ever, then? That could just be a symptom of being human, then. Everybody's clumsy at new things." Dr. Hitori sighed. "Listen, I'm not trying to pretend it's nothing to worry about. Plenty of disorders cause reflex problems. If you come back negative for Huntington's chorea, we'll still check out your coordination, run reflex tests, the whole nine yards, just in case."

"You're saying I might have early Parkinson's disease or Lou Gehrig's disease or something?"

"I'm saying you might have nothing wrong at all. I'm saying we'd run tests one by one. But given your family history, we'd start with a genetic test; it's the first, certain, test to tell us what we might be looking for." She glanced at BJ's folder again. "It says here you're in vet school. You should know that you rank your rule-outs and do the least invasive tests—and the least expensive tests—first. In your case, the genetic test is indicated. That's all."

BJ nodded unhappily.

"Stick out your tongue and keep it out."

BJ looked at Dr. Hitori strangely; the doctor smiled. "This isn't sophisticated, but it's a ball-park test. You see if you can hold it out, or if it pops in by itself. I don't believe in it myself, but patients like it. Kind of the home reassurance test."

BJ popped her tongue out.

Dr. Hitori added casually, "Of course, sometimes the dementia appears first, but you seem pretty down-to-earth for that."

BJ had a wild desire to tell her about treating a unicorn and talking to a satyr and a faun.

Dr. Hitori frowned. "No, keep it out."

"I *am*," BJ protested, and realized that she was talking clearly.

Dr. Hitori shrugged. "Try it a few more times on your own. Like I say, I don't buy it. And now," she said easily, "let's talk test results. Once you know, then you have to think about tough choices: do you risk having children?"

"I've thought about that one," BJ said flatly. "No."

She spread her hands. "Okay. Tougher, then: beyond student coverage, do you have health insurance? It won't be easy to get now."

BJ bit her lip.

Dr. Hitori, watching her, said only, "Having Huntington's chorea doesn't eliminate planning for the future. In some ways it intensifies it. The gene test is conclusive, but it doesn't say when you'll get ill. It could be years."

She leaned toward BJ. "I'll bet you've thought about suicide, right?"

BJ held her neck completely rigid, and would not nod or speak.

"Most people in your shoes do. I hate to shoot your plans, but many people live a long time before the first symptoms develop."

"How would that shoot . . . any plans?"

"Like I said, better people have been given shorter lives. Don't waste it."

Dr. Hitori's callousness was getting to BJ. "All right, I'll be blunt. Assuming I want to kill myself while I still can, how much warning will I get?"

Dr. Hitori, unoffended, considered the question. "Some tests can tell you about the onset of brain deterioration. It's fairly identifiable. For instance, a CT scan will show you the choreic brain pattern after the onset of atrophy; it's unmistakable. We call it a butterfly pattern."

She waved her fingers, thumbs together, to show what she meant. BJ felt sick.

"Beyond that, there are reflex tests—"

"Like the one with my tongue."

"Yes, but more sophisticated," she said sharply. "Look here, miss, I'm a professional. I know all about Huntington's chorea. I know that nobody wants to rave or be paralyzed or fall down or be depressed all the time. And to know that there's no chance of getting better, ever again."

BJ's stomach lurched. She had known that the appointment would be difficult, but Dr. Hitori would be difficult in an appointment about earaches.

"So"—the doctor tapped BJ's folder—"we've talked about the test a little, about suicide and depression, about deterioration . . . anything else you'd like to cover?"

BJ shook her head numbly.

Dr. Hitori slapped the folder shut. "That's it, then. By the way, it's standard in cases like yours to have a genetic counselor before you receive test results. You can also get depression and suicide counseling." She looked over her glasses. "I recommend them. You have no idea how upsetting people find this stuff when you talk to them about it."

"Really?" BJ said. And left.

She went straight to Mitch's for an ice cream cone, coffee mocha in a sugar cone. Normally she watched her weight, but it seemed foolish just now, and she definitely needed a treat. She sat on the bench in front of the ice cream parlor, between Stan's place and the movie theater, and stared broodingly at the campus.

Mrs. Sobell came suddenly around a corner, walking very fast. She spun on her heel in front of BJ. "You." She stood, full height, glaring straight into the seated BJ's eyes.

BJ paused, ice cream cone in the middle of her face, tongue out. She was startled, as students often are when they see faculty and staff out of their natural habitat. Worse, Mrs. Sobell's gray hair had drifted down over her left ear, and her white-knit sweater was shockingly rumpled. One of her knee-high stockings had sagged to her ankle.

She tugged at BJ's sleeve and said distractedly, "What have you done with it?"

"With what?"

"With *The Book of Strangeways*."

BJ dropped the cone. "It's gone?"

Mrs. Sobell nodded. BJ turned and ran to the library, followed closely by the older woman.

Mrs. Sobell fell behind, but found BJ at the shelves, double-checking where Mrs. Sobell had just checked. She watched as BJ sorted down the shelf frantically.

She raised a respectful eyebrow when BJ ran to the back of the book shelf, took out four books, and felt around in the gap. Finally, when BJ checked the orange reshelving area, Mrs. Sobell said, "Don't you think that I would have done that before I tried to find you?"

"Could someone have walked out with it?"

"Possible." Mrs. Sobell agonized, "I should have found a way to protect it. I didn't mind people making notes from it, or—"

BJ said suddenly, "The copiers."

BJ ran up a flight of stairs, then two more, and stopped, panting, in front of the last row of copiers on the sixth floor.

Mrs. Sobell stepped off the elevator and walked quickly to the copy area. BJ was still panting, looking with relief at the reshelving table.

The Book of Strangeways was underneath two magazines and an almanac.

Mrs. Sobell quickly picked it up, hugging it much as BJ had before. BJ gasped, "How did you know to come here?"

"I didn't, but it's the best place to start." She opened the book automatically, then shut it. "I find walking down to the other copiers much easier than walking up."

"Aren't you going to check it for damage?"

In her relief, she laughed. "Dear, you'd need to be awfully resourceful to damage this book." She pulled a pen from behind her ear—BJ, in the excitement, hadn't noticed it—and dragged it across one of the maps.

BJ gave a small cry, but watched as the ink-mark faded and gradually disappeared.

Mrs. Sobell said with delight, "It won't burn, either. Isn't that wonderful, a book that won't burn?"

"And can't be harmed." BJ looked around, but no one was watching. "Do a lot of people know it exists?"

"Researchers. Not many of them." Mrs. Sobell hesitated and added, "I think you're the only one who has found it by accident, so far. That's why security wasn't tighter; there's really no use for the book, except for traveling."

BJ dived through the wastebasket and fumbled through the copies. She found several relating to human medicine, a few from economics, and one from the *Sports Illustrated* swimsuit issue, but none from *The Book of Strangeways*.

She said disappointedly, "I was hoping for a clue to where they were going."

"I think I know." Mrs. Sobell pulled the book tighter to her chest, looking a little like the way BJ had appeared earlier. "And now we'll put it back, downstairs."

"Why do you leave it on the shelves?"

"This is a library. Where else would it go?"

"The rare book room." BJ had not been in it since the library tour her freshman year, but she had seen it from the outside: glass walls, separate climate and air control, remarkably neat and spacious shelving.

"Impossible. That area is too well documented. It's also too hard to get at the materials. Users would always have to keep explaining themselves." Mrs. Sobell showed distaste. "That's fine for books whose principal value is that they're old and rare, but—well, some users might find it hard to explain themselves."

She did not elaborate. BJ didn't ask her to. "What about special reference?"

"Those books are too well used. Librarians, graduate courses, even the occasional faculty member," she finished without sarcasm. "No, the best place to hide it is out in the stacks, where it's available to everyone and hardly anyone will bother, since it doesn't look special."

"The purloined letter," BJ murmured.

"Yes." Despite her worry, she brightened. "Do you read Poe?"

"Some." Lately BJ had found herself thinking about "The Masque of the Red Death" and "The Premature Burial."

"He lived in Baltimore for a time, you know. I grew up not far from where he lived with his aunt. He wrote some of the poetry there, and fell in love."

BJ dutifully tried to look interested. Mrs. Sobell was very easy to like.

"Well." The librarian sighed. "Back to the shelf." She patted the book fondly, looked back up, her eyes suddenly sharp behind the upper half of her bifocals. "You know, dear, I wouldn't be angry with you if you told me that you were really the one who left it on the copy machine."

"I wasn't," BJ insisted. She added thoughtfully, "And you know what else? Dr. Dobbs wasn't, either. He always puts books away."

Mrs. Sobell smiled. "And he would have spoken to me. He always leans over the desk on his way by and says, 'Hey, good looking.' " She said it with Sugar's easy drawl.

"He would. All right, it wasn't him. He."

Mrs. Sobell's smile faded slowly, and she said quietly, "No, it wasn't Sugar Dobbs, and it wasn't you, was it?" She looked at the book in her hands. "Either of those would have been too easy."

BJ looked at Mrs. Sobell, hesitated, and made up her mind. "You know that *The Book of Strangeways* is special."

"It's extremely unusual."

"And I think you know more than you're saying about Cross-roads."

Mrs. Sobell said placidly, "I've been a reference librarian for thirty-three years. I know more than I say about nearly every-thing."

BJ tilted her head down, fixed Mrs. Sobell with a no-nonsense stare, and said, "Are you a dwarf?"

Mrs. Sobell smiled politely. "Most of us these days prefer the term 'small person,' dear."

BJ turned bright red and fell apart. "I'm so sorry. I honestly didn't mean to be rude—"

"Please don't worry about it. It happens all the time."

But BJ, blushing and stammering, apologized twice more flee-ing quickly down the stairs.

That night BJ slept badly. She dreamed of Poe's black cat, crouched on her chest and staring intently into her skull: the CT scan. She felt feather-light, ragged-edged wings, beating inces-santly behind her eyes, as the brain butterfly struggled vainly in her skull.

T·E·N

SUGAR WAS DRIVING, a student presenting. It had already begun to seem routine.

"I have a normal case." Lee Anne said it simply, as though it weren't a major disappointment. "A foaling mare." She looked sideways at them. "The client's a tad strange, though." She described him briefly. They nodded without sarcastic comment.

She described potential problems in foaling mares, and gave several notes on the difficulties of working this far from electricity and a sterile environment, particularly with a nomadic client. Sugar interrupted her three times: once to ask a pointed question about the fescue grass diet in mares and amniotic sac suffocation in newborn foals, and twice so that he could concentrate as they were conducted on new routes by members of Road Crews, twybils in hand.

BJ noted that the humans on the Road Crews came in several different sizes, and that at least one worker had staghorns; the crews were recruiting from farther afield. There was no time to comment before Lee Anne resumed presenting.

At the end of a simple, straightforward presentation, she said, "Is that about it, Dr. Dobbs?"

"If you say so." He was watching the map as they approached Stein's, looking for a turnoff in the valley. "Hang on one second."

He swerved into a short lane and they bounced over well-grazed hills until they stopped on a plateau across from the hill Stein's sat on. "End of the line."

Lee Anne looked around. "Is the client meeting us here?"

"Actually," Sugar said, "the man who contacted me for the client is meeting us here."

"Not Fields?" BJ asked.

"Not Fields. This man made the appointment, through Stein, for the client. Sometimes the telephone would make things a lot easier."

Annie asked delicately, "What sort of person is he?"

Sugar grinned at her. "Oh, nice enough, in his way, I guess Never met him myself."

They heard a call from the lane below and watched a man with a cart trundle slowly up the hill. Dave started down to help him but, at a gesture from Sugar, stayed put; Crossroads was not a good place to meet strangers alone.

The man looked harmless enough. He was pulling the cart himself, walking between two parallel shafts and whistling happily. BJ didn't recognize the tune, but that didn't surprise her.

He stopped beside the truck, locked the stand-legs of the cart in place, and smiled at Sugar and the students. "Where are you from?"

"Earth," Dave said.

"Virginia," Lee Anne said.

The man considered, then stuck out his hand. "I'm Owen. Your world would say I'm in retail."

"Mobile retail," Sugar said.

"Traveling sales." He gestured proudly at his cart.

His cart was graying hardwood, sun-dried and scarred. It looked well made, but also well used. By contrast, Owen seemed fresh and innocent: a man in his thirties, with boyish blue eyes, an unweathered complexion, and an untroubled serenity. He had the air of a man who was completely happy with what he was doing just now.

Lee Anne looked over the closed cart interestedly. "It can't be too heavy, if you can roll it without a horse. What kind of goods do you sell?"

With a flourish he lifted the lid of the cart, sliding a slat to pin the lid upright. With more effort he turned out a second panel, dropping a leg from it to expose a table with small doors in its surface. Lastly he pulled a small rack up from the front of the cart and pegged it to the table. "If a world makes it, and if it's worth selling somewhere else, I have it."

The upright was covered with pegs and hooks. On the hooks were knives: Swiss army knives, a curved cleaver with a pearl handle depicting a dragon, a fileting knife made of some red alloy they had never seen, a bottle opener that seemed to be a semihuman doll with a windup key.

On the pegs were what had to be toys: flying birds, butterfly-winged people, which had to be whimsical even in Crossroads, a game involving pouncing mechanical cats, and a wheeled wooden mouse.

There were hats, mittens, and gloves. BJ counted the fingers on the smaller gloves; most had four fingers and a thumb. She looked at the hunting scenes embroidered on the larger gloves, shuddered, and chose not to ask about them.

She was, however, intrigued by the cart. "There's another cabinet below the bottom. What's in it?"

"My bedroll, clothes, food, and personal items," he said lightly. "I keep the real marvels up here, where they'll find buyers."

Sugar peered at the odds and ends. "Any bargains?"

Owen looked hurt. "Sir. Anything on the cart is a bargain, unknown to your world."

Sugar poked at the can opener, exposing the sticker, which said, KROGERS: $1.29.

"Except those things which are from your world, and rare to others," he finished smoothly. "I wouldn't expect you to buy them here, since you'd be paying unnecessary freight."

Annie looked blank. "Is there really much market for can openers in Crossroads?"

"Not so far," he admitted in a stage whisper, "but once I find it, I can sell them cans, too, and have the entire market to myself."

"What's special about the red knife?" Sugar asked.

"Ah. You have a good eye. Pick it up—*carefully*—and test it on a stick."

Sugar lifted it off the hook lightly, with his thumb and forefinger, as though he were going to throw it. Owen watched him uneasily.

When Sugar made as if to test the blade with his finger, Owen said quickly, "No!" Sugar raised an eyebrow and swung the blade lightly into a fallen branch . . .

. . . And through it, with no effort at all. He examined the cut, which was as smooth and even as could be done with a table saw.

"What's the blade made of?"

"Blood." They stared at him, and he added, "It's a very special process."

Annie stared into the blade. "Can you imagine bone surgery with one of those?"

Sugar clearly could. He stared into it for some time before putting it back with regret. "It'd ruin my technique," he said apologetically, "and then someday I'd lose the knife."

"Got any magic tricks to impress my friends?" Dave said brightly. Lee Anne shot him a nasty look.

Owen, not seeming to notice the sarcasm, considered. "I have a few things. . . ." He rummaged along the side of the cart, then rolled up his sleeves and sifted through the pile in the bottom.

"A scroll of curses." It was sealed with something that looked like a cross between fur and feathers. He opened it up and recited thoughtfully, " 'May your spawn brothers spread fungus among your sister's . . . ' No, that wouldn't be much help to you." He rolled it back up hastily and tossed it back in.

More rummaging produced a pitted, bent flat steel bar nearly four feet long. He pulled it free by the blunted point, tugging to free the crosspiece at the far end; it was a crude sword.

"What is it?"

He held it by the hilt. "This," he said solemnly, "is the legendary Glarundel, the Sword That Was Useless. Guaranteed to render its bearer vulnerable. It's priced to sell," he added hopefully.

"I'll pass," Dave said.

Owen tossed the sword back in the cart and dug in the bottom of the cart for quite some time. Finally he engaged one end of a time-blackened leather thong, looped over other odds and ends. He pulled on it gently and steadily, and a worn piece of stone with the thong through a hole in it emerged from the cart. He held it forward.

Dave and the others examined it. The carving was very worn. It looked like a frog, and a little like a lizard, and very little like anything any of them would want to wear.

"Where did that come from?" Annie asked dubiously.

He lifted it and examined it thoughtfully. "I really couldn't say."

"Can't you remember?" Dave asked.

"I didn't say that," Owen answered mildly. "I said that I really couldn't say where it came from."

BJ watched it swing back and forth, suspended from Owen's finger. "Is it magic?"

"So I was told."

"What does it do?"

"The same thing each of you does," he said, amused with himself.

"Treats animals?"

"Actually, heals them. And people, too, if it really works."

"How does it work?" Lee Anne asked. Annie looked at her warningly and shook her head.

"Ah. How does it work." Owen put a hand under his chin in mock contemplation. "Well, if we knew that, would we still call it magic?"

"No, I mean, how do you use it? Sir," she finished, remembering her manners even in her annoyance.

"I think you just wear it." He demonstrated, dropping the leather thong over his own neck. "Doesn't that make sense?"

Dave snorted. "Not really, no."

"Pity." Owen took it off and looked at it sadly. "It's said that it can cure everything but loneliness and bad tempers. If it really works, of course."

BJ said suddenly, "How much is it?"

Owen was taken aback. "To be honest, no one's ever offered me anything before. Still . . ." He turned it over and over in his hand, rubbing the worn face with his thumb. "If it doesn't work, it's just a rock, and I've overcharged you. On the other hand, if it does, then it's priceless and I've sold it for next to nothing. Somewhere between the two, then," he said, as if it were settled. "Two sixpiece."

BJ paid out from the gold Sugar had given them each for expenses. She leaned forward, and Owen carefully hung the amulet on her neck. Annie looked appalled, Dave disgusted. Sugar, oddly, was unreadable.

"Enough business." Owen clapped his hands and whisked the cart shut again. "Time for medicine. My friend should be here shortly. I'll introduce you, then be on my way." Owen looked at them, scratched his head, and finally added quietly, "In Crossroads it's rude to make too much of another race's oddities. Have you met the Hippoi?"

"We've heard of them," BJ said, remembering the parrot's speech inside Stein's.

"Ah. They're fairly unusual, and their sense of humor is . . . different. They laugh less than we do. They live hard lives, and are proud of it."

Lee Anne said, "*Lao's Guide* says that they breed once a year, and that one mare—one woman—may have fifteen or twenty colts in a lifetime."

"And why," Owen said sadly, "do you think that Crossroads isn't overrun with a stampede of Hippoi?"

The answer was painfully obvious to anyone who had read Darwin or Malthus, however hard it might be to associate the hardships of natural selection with a thinking species.

"Infant mortality," Lee Anne said promptly. "Predators. Disease—that might not be as true for Crossroads. War and starvation—why did they leave the place they came from, if it's so bad here?"

"Once, they lived in your world, I think in what you call the Middle East. Is Syria in the Middle East?"

Annie said tactfully, "I don't think our history says much about them anymore."

"It says that they were wise," Dave said, "and dangerous. Some people say that the myth of centaurs came from foot soldiers panicking when they first saw cavalry—" He stopped in confusion.

Owen chuckled. "If your world is like the others, it's the other way around: horseback riding was an imitation of the Hippoi."

They heard hoofbeats, coming from below them on the hill. Owen said quickly, "Be ready for anything; they may surprise you."

Dave grinned. "Don't bet on it. We're hard to surprise now."

The hoofbeats grew louder. Carron came over the edge of the hill, and Owen was right: they weren't ready for him.

It makes sense, BJ thought as she stared up at him. If centaurs can be part horse and part man, why wouldn't there be a Clydesdale centaur?

His hooves were half-hidden by a fringe of white hair; at the top, his muscular legs were almost as thick as BJ's body. His back—his horse back—was over four feet wide, and more than five and a half feet off the ground.

That meant that his human torso was also four feet wide, and rose to a height of more than ten feet. He looked down at them sternly. His companion—probably his mate—followed.

The Hippoi looked Arabic: dark skin, sharp dark eyes, dark curly hair. They made Stefan and Fields look light complected. Polyta was Arab in another sense: a beautifully proportioned horse body, with the musculature of a racing thoroughbred. She was also, BJ realized belatedly, pregnant herself.

The flat human belly had fooled BJ; the horse belly was full on both sides, and her rear legs were ever so slightly splayed to accommodate the weight and the bulge.

From Carron's attitude, BJ was willing to bet that it was his child, colt, whatever.

BJ turned to Dave to make a comment and saw his slack-jawed expression. She was puzzled for a moment, then followed his upturned gaze.

A human body, to blend with a horse's body, must be fairly sizable. This means that all the features of the human body must be fairly sizable.

Polyta's human torso was the size of a heroic statue. Even if she had been only of normal human stature, her breasts would have been impressive.

"No one," Lao had written, "would have the temerity to call the human mammaries of a centaur vestigial."

And she was topless. Dave was, frankly, mesmerized.

In addition, she was undeniably gorgeous: flawless dark skin flowing over tight cheekbones, huge dark eyes with thick lashes, lips fuller than most humans can attain without surgery. And as the Clydesdale's face was marked by its sternness, hers was shaped by an innate kindness.

Carron coughed once to get Dave's attention. He didn't get it.

Lee Anne stepped forward unhesitatingly and, apparently by accident, nudged Dave. "I'm the student on the case, sir. Are you Carron?"

"I am Carron," he said quietly, but with authority, "but my name is Nesyos." He gestured. "My love is Polyta."

Dave shook his head, trying to refocus. "Nesyos—Nessus," Dave said thoughtfully. "A ferryman. The most helpful centaur to humans, except that he tried to run off with Heracles' wife."

"You do a lot of odd reading, don't you?" Annie said.

"I used to," Dave admitted, "but who has time in school?"

"What about Carron?" BJ said. "Is that also your name?"

"It's a title." Carron eyed them sternly.

"Carron, Carron . . . got it." Dave snapped his fingers. "Charon, with an *H*. The ferryman to Hades, boatman of the dead . . ." He trailed off, looking speculatively up at Carron, who nodded curtly.

He folded his arms and smiled down on Dave. "Don't be afraid. I choose the dead only from the sick, the old, and the evil. And only from my own people." He touched Polyta's shoulder tenderly and caressed her human back, down to the start of her horse back. "Believe me, I would only choose death for those I love most."

Sugar and the students stared at him.

Owen said cheerily, "Now that you know each other, I'll be on my way. Glad to help. Maybe we'll meet at Stein's." He left, whistling.

Carron watched him wheel his cart away, then turned and said bluntly, "When I asked for you, my mare was fine. She began foaling, and is in trouble. Please come see."

Polyta was already galloping down the crest of the hill, into a sheltering grove.

Lee Anne packed a medical kit for carrying; Sugar supervised. Dave picked up a halter; the others split the gear, and they trooped downhill after Carron.

The mare was in trouble; she looked exhausted, and her eyes were wild. Polyta had an arm on her back, and was speaking softly to her in a language that sounded like a cross between Arabic and whinnying. Some of it, BJ decided, was simply comforting sounds for the horse.

Lee Anne took one look and said to the others, "Hold her." The other three moved quickly into position: Dave slung the halter on, and BJ and Annie put one hand on the halter and one on the horse's neck. Dave held on to the lead rope. Sugar lounged against a nearby tree, watching.

Lee Anne was already at the mare's hindquarters. The mare's vulva was swollen, but her vagina was dangerously dry. Something was wrong; the foal wasn't emerging.

Lee Anne put a sleeve on and, with her free hand, took a squirt bottle full of Nolvasan from the medical kit. She applied liquid to the mare and to the sleeve, and stretched her arm into the mare.

Carron, trying to see, edged closer than he should, and his hindquarters brushed Lee Anne's shoulder.

"Out of the way. Get along." She slapped Carron with her free hand on his flank, hard. Carron, startled, backed off, and Lee Anne put her free hand to her mouth. "Sir, I am about as sorry as I can be. I'd forgotten you were the client—"

"It's all right," he said stiffly.

But Polyta, her own hand to her mouth to hide it, was giggling. BJ had the feeling that Carron's dignity did not sit well with all of the centaurs.

Lee Anne stopped feeling and went very still. Sugar, who hadn't appeared to be looking, said instantly, "Trouble?"

"Hoof," she called over her shoulder. And, quietly a moment later: "Rear hoof."

Colts were normally born in what BJ thought of as the Superman position, diving headfirst from the womb. Any other position prevented the body from emerging easily, and increased the danger to the mother.

Sugar moved in quickly, pulling a sleeve on, and felt briefly inside the mare. "The presentation is wrong," Sugar said to Carron and, BJ noted, to Polyta. "In our world, we'd call it a breech birth, rear first."

Carron waved an arm. "I've seen it before. It happens not so often, but happens. I knew to call you, before I even knew this. Sometimes you know."

"I wondered why you called us for a foaling," Lee Anne said. "Most foals drop right out. Real horse people know when something's gone wrong." She didn't notice the accidental joke; she was too concerned for the mare.

So was Carron. He walked up to the front of her body, his hand flowing down her back, calming her. He patted the trembling mare, and moved to hold her muzzle in both hands. He bent, at the waist like someone doing toe touches, and kissed the bony bridge of her nose, speaking softly and indecipherably.

Then he let go and said casually to Lee Anne, "You have chemicals? Kill her."

After a moment's stunned silence, Lee Anne said, "I'd prefer to do a Caesarean." She added unwillingly, "Sir."

"A Caesarean," BJ said quickly, "is a lateral cut on the mother, through which the foal can be removed. Afterward the mare is sewn up and, after she rests for a while, she's as good as new." BJ added hopefully, "It's named after one of our world's great leaders, who was born that way."

Concerned though he was at the moment, Carron smiled at her. "Do I seem easily flattered? No, Doctor," and he clearly knew that calling her "doctor" was also flattery. "If you cut the mare open, we'd still need to kill her. How could we stay with her, when the Hippoi move constantly? Better to kill her now, with mercy."

Sugar said, "We can cut the colt apart."

Polyta looked horrified, Carron interested. "While it's still inside?"

Sugar pulled a thin wire from the surgical pack. "With this. It's called Gigli wire or fetotomy wire. We can reach in, saw the legs off the colt, deliver the pieces. The mare will need watching, but should be fine."

Carron nodded. "Can you kill the colt first?"

"Not really. Saline would take too long." He scowled. "Normally we'd saw the head off the colt—kills it right away." He added, "Vets in our world prefer not to do this."

"We'd rather not, as well." But he gestured to Lee Anne. "Kill the colt, if you can save the mother."

Lee Anne said, "I'll check for life signs first."

Carron, obviously not sure what she meant, frowned.

Sugar moved up beside her and, coincidentally, between her and Carron.

"That would be dead right in our world, and I want you to go ahead. Just as long as you know that either way, you have to kill it."

She looked over her shoulder at him, her eyes wide, her expression unaccepting. She turned away and strained, moving her arm inside the mare.

Finally she said with relief, "No life signs." Annie's shoulders slumped, but she didn't let go of the horse.

"Go on to the next step." He held out the fetotomy wire.

Without another word she pulled her arm free, took the wire, and moved back inside, this time with both hands.

BJ and Annie held the mare steady; Annie spoke soothingly to it. Polyta stroked the mare's nose from time to time; Polyta's beautiful eyes, nearly as large as the mare's, were full of grief.

They knew exactly when she began cutting: the shift from an uncertain fumbling, to a cautious repositioning of her arms and feet and a bracing of her body, to a sudden set of her jaw and sideways motion of her arms. The mare tried to turn its head. Polyta, hand on its mane, did more than the halter did to keep the mare calm.

Lee Anne worked for several minutes, her face showing the strain that her hidden arms did not. Dave was the first to offer. "I'll spell you."

"If I need it," she panted. "Thanks." Her arms were tight together against the sides of the horse's vagina; the sweat on her face and the strain in her shoulder muscles seemed incongruous when she seemed to be moving so very little.

After five minutes, she said, "Dr. Dobbs? If you don't mind, I'd like for Dave to spell me. It'll be over faster that way. Otherwise, I can keep on."

"You four work it out," he said. "You're the team."

Lee Anne pulled her left arm free, gasping with the effort. Her arm was red almost all the way up. Her other arm was the same; she pulled it out with the fetotomy wire in her hand.

There was a thin, bony leg in her other hand. She laid it gently on the ground.

Dave had already taken the wire from her and peeled back the sleeve, putting it on his own arm. She took off the other sleeve thankfully, passed it to him, and looked at Dr. Dobbs. "Sir, I know it's my case and my decision, but I'd like to consult with you before Dave finishes the other leg."

He said, "That's all right."

"Do I need to retropulse to pull the . . . the foal torso out?"

"Not if Dave gets the other leg clear; not much of a push, anyway. The mare's gonna fight you all the way if you try it; she wants that foal out, not pushed back in."

"Thank you." She turned back to Dave. "Cut the leg off as high as you can. Don't let the pushing motion bother you; that's the mother. When you're done, I want the sleeves back."

"I'd be glad to—"

"I know, and thanks, but it's my case."

This time Sugar didn't look disgusted, and the client looked impressed with Lee Anne.

The others comforted the mare and watched. There was nothing to be done.

Very shortly, Dave said, "Got it." He pushed back, then pulled, twisting his arm slightly, and removed the other leg hoof first. He passed the gloves to Lee Anne, who put them on in silence.

Sugar said only, "Need help?"

"No, thank you, sir." She put both hands in, reaching down; she closed her eyes, groping, and suddenly leaned forward, giving a hard push. The mare snorted and shifted. Polyta, BJ, and Annie struggled to hold it in place. Lee Anne relaxed her body and lifted her hands up, guiding the fetus.

With an ease that seemed a bitter joke after what had come before, the foal torso slid free and dropped. Dave grabbed it with Lee Anne, and the two of them, grunting, settled the weight on the ground.

Lee Anne knelt by it a moment, then looked up. "It was a filly."

Carron gestured to the others, holding the mare's head. "She needs to know. Show her."

Silently they led the mother around by the halter. She fought only enough to turn her head and see behind herself.

When she saw the remains of the colt fetus, she froze in place, planting her feet and nostrils flared and sniffing. BJ and Annie held tightly to the halter ropes, half expecting her to buck.

Instead, milk streamed from her teats, splashing on the ground in a sudden single flow.

BJ had seen the reflex in mares when seeing their colts for the first time. She shut her eyes.

Carron watched expressionlessly.

Polyta watched, her face taut with grief. Polyta's hooves, BJ noted, were planted in a twin of the mare's pose.

Carron stared down at the small body in the field. "Do you know, if she were my own, I would lift her in my arms? It's a tradition." He held his empty arms out. "I would raise her up and say to God, 'Bend down and bless this body. This one is yours, but also mine.' "

"And mine," Polyta said.

Carron looked at her, and she stared back without flinching. Finally he said, "And yours, of course."

Lee Anne wouldn't look at him. He ambled over and put an arm on her shoulder. He said to Lee Anne, "You think us hard."

"It's the only way you know," she said woodenly.

"We know others," Carron said. "This is best for us. Think."

He pointed to the horizon. "If griffins or the Great flew over us now to attack, and my people had to run or defend themselves, how could we, if some of the Hippoi or their animals couldn't even walk? What if some of us couldn't run, or couldn't see, or couldn't breathe well enough to fight or run?"

Lee Anne burst out, "I see that, sir, but it's a whole lot easier for you to see it that way now, while you're healthy."

He dropped his hand. "I am healthy now, that's true. And someday, when I'm old, the Hippoi will move south for the summer. We'll pack our small rolls, and the toys for the Poloi, and we'll walk together to the High River fording, not far from here. Have you seen it?"

The others shook their heads.

"It's a rapids, leading into Laetyen—the big river. High River divides the western half of Crossroads, north and south, as Laetyen divides the whole land in half. Farther north, it's nothing but a stream over man-size rocks, except when there's a flood. Below, in Laetyen, it's easy to swim the river, if the autumn is as dry as usual. But there's a ford there, near the mouth of High River, where the valley is narrow and the current is swift. Below it is a waterfall.

"And all of the others will cross, and they'll stand together and watch me try to follow. Maybe I'll fail and be swept over the falls. Or maybe I'll try two or three times before I give up.

"If that happens, Polyta, if she feels strong enough to cross three times, will swim back across and say good-bye. Perhaps she'll take a few of my belongings. Then she'll cross again, and leave me to die alone the way my father did."

Lee Anne turned her head and looked at him almost defiantly, and he said, "Oh, yes. My mother died fleeing the Great, and we built a fire at her death. But my father lived a long time, and when I was young, I saw him stay behind, willingly, to die at Laetyen. He waved good-bye to me."

Carron's left hand moved in a phantom wave good-bye. "I wouldn't wave back, because he had died of his own free will. Then I was angry; now I understand. I can't even be sorry that it's so."

Polyta murmured, "Carron, look at her face." But she was looking at BJ, not at Lee Anne.

BJ mumbled, " 'Scuse me," and turned to go. Her foot landed squarely on a rock extending barely an inch above the soil, enough for most people to notice but not to be bothered by.

BJ fell. Carron bent forward, practically a low bow, and caught her under the armpits like a lifeguard doing a cross-chest carry. He lifted her effortlessly and set her on her feet, but did not let go of her shoulders. "You stumbled."

"I'm all right." But he looked searchingly and frankly into her eyes, and she was ashamed of the lie.

"Are you sure?"

"Of course." Actually, she was unsure of a great deal. "If there really were something wrong with me, wouldn't you say that I was better off dead?"

"Oh, you wouldn't be better off," he said seriously. "You'd be dead. Dead is dead."

Concerned though she was, Polyta smiled behind her hand at BJ's expression.

"But I would try to help you," he went on earnestly. "You might need me, you might be afraid and needy. I couldn't know, you see, and I'd have no way to know."

Polyta was looking up at him now, and her expression said a great deal about why she put up with him.

"As long as you need me," he finished, "I should help you. I will help you. You're sure that you're all right?"

"Very sure," she said to him. "And thank you. But if I were one of the Hippoi, and I'd stumbled for a reason?"

He waved a hand dismissively. "Oh, I'd have you killed."

Carron paid, and though he did it with dignity and grace, they somehow felt mean and cheap accepting payment. Sugar said, "Would you like to meet us at Stein's?"

Carron and Polyta looked at each other. Polyta explained quickly, "They don't know our customs." To Sugar she said, "The Hippoi never go indoors."

"Never?"

Carron said, "Rarely. We move south with the change in seasons, so winter is not a problem." He hesitated, then said bluntly, "When one of the Hippoi dies, his body is burned on the spot to keep it from predators. It's one of the First Laws."

Dave murmured to BJ, "I'll bet it came from health. If you left the bodies around, predators might get a taste for you."

Polyta said brightly to them, "I'm sure you'll all wish to clean up. Stein lets us swim in the pool below his inn—never in the pool above—and we'd be glad of company." She looked first at Lee Anne.

"Thank you, ma'am, but I think I'll just wash up and eat."

A swim sounded good to BJ, but a quick look at Lee Anne changed her mind. "That sounds good to me, too. Thanks, though." Annie declined.

Dave said, "Cool," and amended, when Polyta looked confused, "I'll go swimming. You go ahead; I'll catch up."

He was staring admiringly at Polyta again.

She looked inquiringly at Carron, who smiled at the students a final time and thundered off, Polyta following more slowly.

Sugar regarded Lee Anne coolly. "Do you always pick fights with people four times your size?"

She looked him square in the eye. "I grew up around Clydesdales. They don't scare me."

"This wasn't a Clydesdale; he was a client. He rides you, not you him. Make sure you don't forget that."

Lee Anne, clearly not caring, said, "Yes, sir."

"You did a fine job. Nobody could have done better." He looked at the others as well. "Remember when I said in class that eighty-five percent of your patients get well, no matter what you do? That leaves fifteen percent. A few of those die, no matter what you do. I'm sorry, but it's so."

He turned away and said, "Pack up. I'll see you at the truck."

They watched him stride energetically away. When he was out of earshot, Lee Anne said bitterly, "Old High-pockets there is in a fine mood, isn't he?"

"He feels as bad as you do," Annie said. "It makes him angry. He's like Carron, I think—trying not to show it."

Lee Anne considered. "I like Polyta's way better."

"Polyta," Dave said thoughtfully. "I'll bet her full name is Hippolyta."

"You," Lee Anne said in the same tone, "are a smartass."

Dave subsided. After a minute, Lee Anne turned around in the seat and said, "Don't feel too bad. At least you're smart."

Dave, pleased but embarrassed, said, "Gotta go." He jogged after the centaurs.

Lee Anne watched him go, then sighed loudly and said to BJ, "So, should we have you killed?"

"Not just yet," BJ said.

E·L·E·V·E·N

SUGAR AND THE students washed up at the water wheel connected to Stein's upstream pond. Dave had excused himself and headed, with enthusiasm, for the pond just below Stein's, where Polyta and Carron were already splashing peaceably.

The rest trudged back toward Stein's, bemused. Lee Anne said, "What's the point? He's already seen Polyta naked. He's not thinking straight."

BJ said delicately, "I know Polyta's pretty, but I think that he's forgotten an important detail about her anatomy."

Sugar snorted. "Her 'natomy? It ain't her 'natomy I'm thinking about. If he had half a brain left, he wouldn't get naked in front of those two. Believe me, she's seen better."

They considered. "Wow," Lee Anne said finally. "And Carron's a Clydesdale." She snickered.

Annie said, "I think this discussion has gone far enough."

In the narrow entry hall, the parrot leered at them and began, "*Ert' Magyar? Capisc'? Sprechen sie—*"

"We know the rules," Lee Ann said. The parrot cocked its head at the biscuits suggestively. "And I'm not feeding you this time, so tough."

It snapped its beak at her several times, then said a word in a strange language and laughed raucously.

"If I ever find out what that means," Lee Anne said, "you're a fryer."

The parrot shut up.

Dinner hour was in full noisy swing. Melina, tray in hand, waved happily to them. Annie waved back cheerily and said under her breath to BJ, "How proud my mother would be. I'm known on sight in a tavern and gambling den."

They found an empty table near an isolated pillar in back. BJ glanced at it curiously; unlike the care shown in the rest of the carpentry here, this pillar had a diagonal saw cut partway through it at the midpoint. Probably no one wanted to sit near it. She looked up nervously—this part of Stein's was nearly under the upper pond—but the roof seemed firm enough.

They had just sat down when Dave, his hair barely damp, slunk in quietly. Sugar, walking by the table, said, "Did she laugh much?"

Dave flinched and said in a broken voice, "I would really, really like a beer." Sugar grinned and went off to chat with Stein.

Rudy came over and slapped palms with Dave. "Hey, man. High five!" They slapped. "On the side!" They slapped. "Head butts." He lowered his antlers, then raised them. "Just kidding."

Rudy's doe-eyed girlfriend came over, too. She was wearing a print halter-top and cutoffs, and looked very Californian. "Hi, Dave."

"Hi, uh . . . hi."

"You can call me Bambi," she said, smiling.

Rudy said, "I took her to it in Oakland. She cried buckets." He frowned. "I never thought Bambi was a male name."

"It sounds better on women," Dave assured him, and said to her, "It suits you."

"Thanks. It's good to see you."

"Sure. Um, you aren't going to lick my nose again, are you?" She laughed. "We'll see." They went back to their table.

Melina brought a tray of steins over, but smiled and waved their gold aside. "It is paid for."

Owen slid to a seat beside them. "I promised Carron that I'd check on you tonight." He smiled at BJ, a careless interested smile that made him look younger than she, though he was easily twice her age. "Is the amulet working yet?"

"Give it time," she said.

Lee Anne said, "Mr. Owen—"

"Just Owen."

"Sir," she said stubbornly, "how can all these people get here?"

"On foot mostly." He sipped at his own ale, then held up a worn shoe to illustrate. "A few ride, but that only means that the creatures they ride have to walk, doesn't it?"

"No, I mean, how do they find their way here?"

He considered, and shrugged. "Some use maps. Some come by accident." He shivered. "I prefer maps."

As he talked, he was waving at each of the other tables. Everyone seemed to know Owen and like him.

BJ held the stone amulet in her hand; it still felt strange and new at her neck. "We haven't asked why they all come here."

"Ah." Owen signaled, and Melina brought over an enormous clay pitcher of refills, and, with a smile to Annie, a small pitcher of cider. "There's a story behind that. Have you heard of the Stepfather God?"

Their faces were blank.

Owen set his stein down. "This is the story of a world's beginning," he said musically, "told the same way, in the same rhythm, for all time. For the story came before tongues came here, or it came with the first of them.

"Your world has a mother." All but Annie nodded. "Many worlds have mothers—they are called Gaea, Mother Nature, or Demeter, and their nature is in the way that they cherish. So it is with the Father worlds.

"But there was a world with no parents, and no children. It was green and fertile but there was no child there. And this world went on, dreaming fertile dreams alone, until one day the Childless God entered it.

"Among the world gods of that time, he alone wandered from world to world, for he had no child and no home. And when he came to the empty world, he surveyed it and said, 'This will be my home, for it and I are empty.' And he sat on the banks of its river, and grieved."

BJ started. Up until the meeting with the Hippoi, she had given little thought to having children, and none at all to being denied them.

Owen went on, "One day, walking in the empty world, he found a child. Some say it had horns, some antlers; some say it was a thinking child, some an animal. The Father only noticed that it was hungry and forsaken.

"And the Childless God picked it up and carried it to another world. And there he held the child up to Gaea and said, 'Will you feed this child?'

"But Gaea poked at the child and frowned. 'This is no child of mine.' And she cast them out.

"Then the father walked to another world, and asked Demeter, 'Will you feed this child?' And she, too, said, 'This is no child

of mine,' and cast them out. And the child clung to the Childless
God and wept.

"And so it went in all the worlds, mother and father alike. And
in the last world, the Father held the child up to the father of that
world and said, 'Will you feed my child?'

"And the Father said only, 'If he is your child, feed him yourself.' "

"And the Childless God looked down at the child and said, 'So
I will.' And he returned to the empty world, and became the
Stepfather God, and fed the child. And later he named the empty
world Crossroads, and built the Strangeways, so that every child
who was cast out might come to him."

Owen looked at them all earnestly and finished, "And so it is
today. Whoever is lonely, or broken, or has no hope left, sooner
or later will come to Crossroads."

He drank his ale and said in his normal speech, "Have you
tried any of the games here?"

"We've played." Lee Anne looked at the bickering brown men
with distaste. "We're not real good at them yet."

"Did you say so to Stein?" Owen, lazily stretching out a foot,
hooked the apron strings of the quick-moving innkeeper.

Stein whirled and ducked, disengaging the foot and grabbing
it in his right hand. Owen found himself tipped half off his chair,
helpless. "He's really quite fast," he said deadpan, as he slid to
the floor.

"Faster than you." Stein tossed the catchlets on the table. "Not
so much to ask, when you think about it."

Owen thumped the table, sending the sticks flying into the air,
and caught one in his hand. "Ready?"

But Stein saluted him with the catchlet he had snatched from
the air. "Of course. Teams?"

Without waiting for an answer he gestured to the right and
left.

"Mine. Mine. Mine."

Owen did the same. As the bar gathered around, they all joined
in the teams: brown men, the green woman, Sugar, even Melina
put down her tray and joined.

Following Owen's and Stein's leads, the players split to either
side of the bar. The students edged uneasily with them: BJ and
Lee Anne with Stein, Annie and Dave with Owen.

Stein held his arm forward, bent for lunging, stick held easily
and loosely in his hand. "Remember, guard low and strike high
with the small ones, guard high and swing under with the tall.

Not so difficult, right?" He called out in the soft, fluting tones Rudy and Bambi used to each other, then dropped to one knee and chattered, making an upward jab that looked faintly obscene. The brown men snickered.

"Ready?" Owen called, and charged forward before Stein could answer. Dave whooped and followed him.

The brown men on Stein's side, who seemed to like Dave, screamed a challenge and bounded forward.

BJ moved forward cautiously, swinging her stick left and right. This was chaos.

A brown man screamed, "Yaaa!" and leaped from a tabletop at her, lashing the belt end of his target-belt down at her stick.

BJ ducked automatically, then stuck her fist, stick clenched in it, into the brown man's hard little belly and pushed. He cried, "*Oooofff!*" and landed in a corner, dropping his weapon. He moved glumly to the sidelines.

BJ turned forward and barely had time to parry her next opponent, Rudy. The stag-man was easier than she thought he'd be; facing an attacker, he tended to duck his head automatically for a charge. She rapped him sharply between the horns and knocked his catchlet down when he brought his hands up.

To one side she could see Sugar, grinning and fighting with Annie and Dave. Owen was laughing as he leaped, ducking and turning in front of Stein; Stein had his usual thin smile as he beat back each of Owen's thrusts. Anyone else in the place would have fallen to either of them.

At this point she took a nasty knock on her left elbow. With great effort she avoided dropping her stick.

Melina made a second attack. BJ parried, stumbled, put her arm up to keep from being struck again, and dropped the stick. Melina smiled apologetically and leaped after another opponent.

At the end, Stein and Owen were facing off alone, the entire inn cheering and shouting. Owen was still leaping, dodging, putting as much pressure on Stein as he could; he was panting. Stein, moving as little as possible, was barely breathing hard.

Finally Owen stepped back, gasping. "Okay, I give up."

Stein saluted him. "I keep telling you, don't wear yourself out so early." He held his palm out.

Owen reached into his breeches pocket and took out three gold pieces. "Usual stakes?"

"We didn't say." Owen started to pocket the gold, and Stein finished quickly, "Let's assume so." He took the coins, then grabbed a tray himself and said loudly, "Refills, anyone?"

When the refills went around, someone raised a stein and said, "Hail Brandal." The others said "Brandal" with various other words. Stein clinked his own ale with Owen's and said, "To the King." Owen smiled and drank, but BJ noticed that he did not toast back.

The game had realigned and melded the small groups of customers into large groups. Dave sat with Rudy and Bambi a while, then bought a pitcher of hard cider for the little brown men, who bowed and chattered at him. Melina introduced Annie to the Cambodian refugee, and translated for them each patiently. Lee Anne got into a lengthy conversation about door-to-door sales with Owen, trying to explain why it barely existed in America anymore.

BJ stopped at the table to ask, "Owen? Who is King Brandal?"

"Ah." He refilled her stein from a pitcher. "An extraordinarily wise king. He rules best by leaving everyone alone."

"But he lets the Inspector General do what he wants."

Owen frowned. "Who told you that?"

BJ fumbled, and he interrupted, "The Inspector General does what he must. Only once was Brandal foolish enough to interfere with him, and—"

He stopped for a moment, staring into the distance while he thought. Finally he said, "Listen, I don't like to talk to strangers about this. But not too long ago, in my lifetime, there was a woman named Morgan in Crossroads. No one knew where she came from. Everyone knew that she was beautiful, and everyone but Brandal—"

"King Brandal," Melina corrected, passing the table.

"King Brandal," Owen went on, grabbing a pitcher from her, "is the only one who didn't realize how cruel she was. And one day"—he looked around before speaking, and lowered his voice—"the Inspector General came to him and said, 'My liege, you must see this.' And he took the king to a hillside where there was a mass grave: Hippoi, fauns, humans, horses, even a unicorn. All killed by Morgan."

"If everyone knows this now," Lee Anne said, "why are you whispering?"

Owen looked around again quickly. "Stein does not like to hear about mass graves," he said quietly. "I've never discussed his reasons—"

"He has good ones," BJ said. "So did the Inspector General kill Morgan?"

"The king wouldn't let him. He ordered the Inspector General to wait until he, Brandal, could interrogate Morgan. And because he waited," Owen said bitterly, "Morgan took her opportunity and tortured one more animal nearly to death. She was caught, and Brandal still wouldn't let the Inspector General kill her. Instead, he exiled her." He sipped his ale in silence.

"And that's the end of the story?" BJ persisted.

"I doubt it very much," he answered. "Morgan is still waiting outside Crossroads, lost and furious and looking for a way in. And if she ever finds one, she'll kill the rest of us." He finished his ale and wiped his mouth. "I know everyone else here toasts Brandal, but I'm sorry, I can't bring myself to."

He turned back to Lee Anne abruptly. "Now, what was it you were saying about telephone sales pitches?"

BJ wandered through the inn, listening to snatches of conversation and carefully holding her stein in two hands. She was unsure whether she had dropped her stick because of Melina's attack or because her hand wouldn't do what she wanted.

Eventually she wandered outdoors, taking her drink with her. The night was beautiful, with a waxing moon casting enough light that she could see the valley. An owl called from somewhere, and a wolf, or something like it, howled from a nearby hill. BJ walked around the outside of the inn, enjoying the quiet.

Stein was sitting on a rock by the upper pond; Fields was with him. The older man sighed loudly. "A time of change."

"We've lived through other changes. This one, this could be trouble, but I think we'll do fine."

Stein shook his head. "I don't know sometimes. The things I'd hear, you'd swear it was the end."

"I've heard that before," Fields rumbled.

Stein put his arm around Fields's waist and said as if quoting, "Tammuz, when you come to Pylades, tell them that the great God Pan is dead."

Fields chuckled. "Not a time so rough as that, I think."

He put his arm on Stein's shoulder and there they sat, looking like father and son in silhouette; the older man was slight enough to seem like a child next to Fields.

"You know what?" Stein said finally. "I like it here."

"That is because you have a good nature."

"I think it's because I was well brought up."

They both chuckled, though BJ couldn't understand why. She smiled, in the shadows, and turned to move back to the inn, then froze in place as Fields said, "So. What do you think of the new ones?"

Stein said thoughtfully, "I don't know yet. The doctor, he's a thoroughly knowledgeable man, and skilled. The students are still learning—"

"You know what I ask." Fields leaned in. "Will they be able to help us?"

"You're asking me? What do I know? They have skills, but I don't know what they'll learn." His voice got sharper. "I'm not sure how much we want them to learn."

"You are always suspicious."

"And so far, at least, I'm still alive."

Fields said, troubled, "If they are a problem, perhaps the Inspector General—"

"Not yet." Stein waved his hand, cutting Fields off. "I hope it won't come to that. There's been enough blood in Crossroads these past few months."

"Too much blood." Fields added, with a sadness that chilled BJ, "Well, the Inspector General will keep watching them, and if they are trouble . . ."

He trailed off. BJ waited for them to say more, then drifted quietly back into the inn.

T·W·E·L·V·E

"THANKS FOR GOING with me." Annie, glancing down from time to time at scribbled directions as she drove, looked oddly like Sugar headed for Crossroads. "I just didn't feel like going alone."

BJ looked out the window. "I was glad to." Actually, she felt awkward. BJ hadn't been a churchgoer since she had first moved away from home, and she felt especially awkward because she had the feeling that Annie might be worried about BJ, and hoping that church would help her.

But she had worked on the Big List for as long as she could bear the night before. She had itemized her books and put a name beside each title on the list. She had done the same with her records and cassettes (foolishly, she was doubly grateful that she had never invested in a compact disc player). She had written several more letters to friends, addressed them, and put them in the box marked OPEN IN THE EVENT OF MY DEATH.

It's sad to think of dying when you have so much to live for, even worse when you feel your life amounts to little. BJ was now painfully aware of exactly what made up her life; she was grateful to get away from that awareness for a while.

She watched as Annie slowly and laboriously took a right-hand turn, very wide of the drop-off on the passenger side. BJ had to lean out to look down, checking the rock-strewn slope. "You don't much like back roads, do you?"

Annie laughed, not very convincingly. Her tongue was sticking out between her teeth while she concentrated. "I hate them."

"How are you able to stand Crossroads?" BJ regretted saying it almost instantly.

"Quite a bit about Crossroads bothers me." That was the last thing Annie said for quite a while. BJ settled back and watched the oaks and cedars flicker by, and enjoyed the lazy Sunday-morning feel of warm sunshine filtered through the green.

She could smell, above them on the hill, the pines and the years of decaying needles. An occasional birdcall and the crunching of gravel under the tires were the only sounds. BJ wasn't sure how you could tell this countryside from Crossroads, except for the graded road, but there was a definite difference.

BJ had nearly drifted off to sleep when Annie slowed and said satisfiedly, "There it is."

The church looked exactly as BJ had expected: unmarked white wood siding, a small steeple with what looked like an old schoolhouse bell in it, and a well-kept graveyard in the pines beside it.

The people filing in were dressed well but not stylishly. The sport coats all were heavy, the ties a range of patterns from different years.

The older women wore . . .

BJ felt suddenly wistful, looking at the gathered families. Only when she was very young had there been any three-generation gatherings in her family; later there were none, and family reunions were unheard of. Now that she knew more of her mother's family, she understood why.

BJ's thoughts drifted to her own brother, in Chicago.

He had answered last night on the tenth ring, and had been hostile as soon as she'd said hello. "Jesus, it's midnight here. How late is it there?"

"Two," she said. "Listen, Peter, I want to talk about Mom's death—"

"Well, I don't." His anger was defensive, half-guilty. "She wanted to kill herself, didn't she? That's her business. Leave it alone, BeeGee."

She winced at the nickname, which, for no reason, had aggravated her horribly when they had both been living at home and she had been twelve and thirteen. "She left behind some unfinished business."

"No shit. Me, for instance. And you," he added grudgingly. "Look, I know it's hard. Believe me."

Listening to his tone, BJ did.

His next words stunned her. "But it's later than hell, and I have to get up in the morning. You take care. Call me if there's any real news."

And he hung up. BJ, who had fought with her brother on and off, but had always known or thought she knew that he loved her, stared, unbelieving, at the phone.

BJ stepped awkwardly out of the car. She was wearing nylons for the first time in months, and her navy skirt and jacket were too dressy for any service but Christmas or Easter. Plus she felt that she had on too much makeup. Four years of vet school had left her unable to dress well without feeling self-conscious.

Annie looked nervously across the car hood and brushed quickly at her hair, which was tangling in the brisk spring wind. She said lightly, "Time to go in," and BJ realized that Annie felt much the same.

They scurried to a pew as the service was about to start. BJ barely had time to glance around. The inside (it had no apse, and was too small to be called a nave) was as plain as the outside; the white-painted, uninsulated rafters dropped down to plaster walls with no paintings, and windows with no stained glass. The only ornament, near the pulpit, was a bulletin board labeled in cutout letters, TELL ME ABOUT JESUS and seven enthusiastically crayoned pictures from, BJ assumed, a Sunday-school class.

The last of the stragglers were coming in. A young woman with dark eyes and long, dark, curly hair to her shoulders stepped awkwardly down the aisle to the pew opposite. She was dressed in a hand-sewn white blouse and a dark, homemade long skirt, and unlike the other churchgoers, she was wearing sneakers and bulky sweat socks, as though she had jogged here. No one seemed to mind.

An older man caught her elbow as she stumbled trying to edge sideways; she smiled nervously and thanked him. BJ looked with pity at the girl's feet; her sneakers were splayed at angles to her body.

The pianist bobbed her head determinedly and began the intro for the first hymn. It was an old folk tune, what BJ's mother, back in her guitar-playing days, would have called a shape-note hymn. BJ was sure that she'd heard a record of it: "Talk about suffering."

The congregation sang:

> Oh, can't you feel it brother,
> And don't you want to go?

And leave this world of trial
And trouble here below.

The dark-haired girl stood, with help, but did not sing. She looked blankly at the hymnal and smiled politely while those around her sang. BJ daydreamed about her brother again.

BJ, without guilt, tuned out most of the service. She had done that at church since she was a little girl, going with her mother; it didn't bother her now except for the mild worry that Annie might later ask specific questions about the service.

She did, however, look around again at the other singers when they began the collection hymn. It reminded her, somehow, of Crossroads: "I come to the Garden alone . . ."

The dark-haired girl brightened. She opened her mouth, singing sweetly:

And He walks with me,
And He talks with me,
And He tells me I am His own . . .

BJ's head snapped sideways toward her. The girl had a Greek accent.

The rest of the service seemed interminable, but probably only took fifteen minutes.

As they filed out, Annie stopped to shake hands with the minister and give greetings from her own minister in Maryland. The minister, an older man, looked delighted and pumped her hand vigorously. BJ edged on outside.

The other churchgoers were talking in knots. The dark-haired girl was speaking shyly to an older couple in rumpled dress clothes. Once, the woman made her laugh; her voice sounded like music.

BJ kept the girl in sight long enough to be sure that she wasn't leaving soon, then tiptoed around the churchyard, looking for anything unusual.

The gravestones were normal; there were fifteen family names: Rickers, Johnson, Hudnall, Greene, and other good British Isles names. BJ peered at the older carvings, but saw nothing unusual in the worn gray stone.

A set of cracked and mended concrete steps led down a covered entry into the ground outside the church. BJ checked to see that no one was looking, then walked quickly down the steps into the basement.

It was a distinct disappointment, even for a church basement. The usual folding chairs stood in rolling racks against the walls, and a group of tiny wooden chairs huddled close against a portable blackboard, which was erased but needed washing badly. A pass-through window at the far end, with a steel counter under it, showed where the church kitchen was.

On the far wall was a painting, clearly done from a photograph by a loving if amateur artist. It was of an elderly woman with a walking stick and knapsack, carrying a Bible in her left hand. She was above a name: Elizabeth (Hetty) Hudnall, 1924–1989.

The painting was, BJ reflected, unusual in a church that did not seem to approve of decoration.

The woman's face was crisscrossed with thickly drawn wrinkles. Her smile looked tight and determined, and her hair was blowing free of its tight bun.

The landscape looked fairly Virginian on the right, but on the left the hills were too high, the birds too large. A figure dancing in the woods had legs that bent the wrong way.

"A bad artist?" BJ said aloud, and shook her head. "No," she said to her own echo, "a bad artist working from a photograph."

When she returned to the front of the church, the dark-haired girl had nearly disappeared, dancing uphill quickly even on the gravel. She didn't seem to be limping at all, and her body swayed in the long skirt.

Annie finally emerged. "Thank you for waiting," she said. No comment about BJ's ducking out on introductions and polite conversation.

BJ flushed. "I didn't mean to run out. I wanted to check something. Let's go."

In the car, BJ said, "Drive uphill, not down."

"Is there anything up this way?" It was unlikely, and it was fairly easy to get lost on country roads in the hills. BJ, in her undergraduate days, had loved getting lost. Clearly Annie, brought up solely in the suburbs, would never love it.

"There should be someone walking. Did you notice that dark-haired girl who had trouble getting up the aisle?"

Annie said, "I wondered if she weren't praying to be healed." She added, just a trace defensively, "I prayed for her to be, too."

Then she looked stricken. "People are letting her walk from church? The poor thing could barely keep her feet straight."

"It wasn't her feet," BJ said flatly. "It was her shoes that were crooked. And I'll bet any money, that is if you were a gambling woman, that she'll be carrying those shoes. We've seen her before, Annie."

Annie said in simple shock, "The barmaid."

"Melina, right. At Stein's."

They caught up with her at the first turn. Annie pulled over; BJ opened the rear passenger door. "Hop in."

The girl stood stock still, trying frightenedly to hitch her blouse down. Her navel and midriff showed, but now her feet were covered. BJ had been right; the tennis shoes, stuffed with the socks and the laces tied together, dangled at her chest.

BJ said, "You'd better go back in by road, with us. The Road Crews have been changing things again."

Melina bit her lip. "Always there is a chance of that." Her accent was thicker than Stefan's.

"More than a chance," BJ assured her. "Come on. It's faster anyway."

Melina lifted her right foot, revealing an elegantly curved, shiny black bifurcated hoof, and stepped into the car. "You are very sure you know this way?"

"Completely sure."

She sighed and settled in. Annie did an agonizingly careful U-turn and they began the slow, twisting descent toward the highway.

BJ said, "I remembered you from Stein's. Melina, right?"

She nodded, looking more comfortable. It's good, in a foreign setting, to meet people who know your home.

Annie said as naturally as BJ would ask about road signs, "How did you find Jesus?"

Melina smiled mischievously. "I didn't. He found us."

Annie waited.

Melina went on, "There was a woman. A wonderful woman. From this church. She grew up in the hills, and she walked everywhere, and her name was—"

"Hetty Hudnall," BJ said.

Melina turned to her eagerly. "She touched you, too? She came to you?"

"Oh no," BJ said with too much haste. "That is—I saw her picture in the basement."

Melina said shyly, "How did you like it?"

BJ had the wit to say, "It was wonderful. Expressive. I'm surprised they let you paint it, though; they're not much on saints or images here."

Annie was looking back and forth at them, nearly lost.

"I begged," Melina said simply. "I had help with the letters, but the rest was from my heart." She looked back at Annie. "They say in Crossroads that she is our only missionary to have come to us since the monk Brendan, a thousand years ago maybe."

"Why did she do it?" Annie raised her hands, then dropped them quickly to the steering wheel. "Why would she come to bring Christ to people who were—" She stopped suddenly.

"Of different shapes?" Melina asked.

"Well, yes."

Melina answered slowly and thoughtfully. "I met her only once, when I was little. She told me stories of Jesus, and she sat with me while I played. She showed me a picture. . . ."

She put her hands up in the air, trying to sketch a twisted outline. "Her son. His body was very strange, like it had melted to one side or the back had bubbled. She said he had been born that way."

Annie said, thinking aloud, "Sounds like spina bifida."

Melina wasn't listening. "She told me that she had prayed and prayed, but God had never changed her son's back. She told me that for years she tried, but God never did anything."

BJ had a quick vision of the hard-faced woman in the wall mural dragging her son to camp meetings in patched canvas tents, to radio and television evangelists, dragging a frightened young boy across stage after stage for men and women to shout and wave their hands over him. She wondered how many times, in how many generations, it had been done in her own family for failing older relatives. She said, "Sometimes God doesn't heal you, that's all."

"I know. It is what Hetty said." She stared out the window. "At first she thought it was something she had done, drinking bad water from the mines or eating tainted food. Then she thought it was a punishment. She said that for a while she doubted God's plan—I hope you aren't mad with me, my saying that."

And Annie surprised BJ more than most of Crossroads had by saying placidly, "Of course she doubted it. Probably more than once. I have, too. Everybody does."

Melina, relieved, went on. "So. Finally, she told me, she asked, 'What good would God expect an old hill woman to find, that would be worth His breaking her son's life in half?' And one night, dreaming, it came to her: that He wanted her to see other shapes to His love."

"So she went searching for Crossroads. She had heard stories; people living here have all heard the stories. She cut a walking stick, and she practiced on all the roads in the hills, and she spoke to everyone she met about her mission and asked for guidance." Melina's eyes shone. "And she said she always prayed for guidance when she walked. And the guidance came, because finally one day she walked into Crossroads."

BJ said, "And did she have some kind of map?"

Melina thought. "She showed me one she had sketched, one day, but she never had the true book of good maps." Melina smiled nervously. "I don't, either. Hetty told me always to pray and let God set your feet on the right road, but always to mark on paper the shape of the road you took, in case you wish to come back."

Hetty sounded immensely practical to BJ. "Do you come out every Sunday? Aren't you afraid of taking a wrong turn?"

"I fear wrong turns always. But so far I have come home safe." She smiled at BJ, who was looking awed. "Every Sunday. Several of us have been born anew—"

"Again. Born again," Annie said dazedly.

"Yes, born again is right, but I am the only one who walks to church this often. Maybe I am the only one who needs it so much."

Annie said, "So you don't believe in the Stepfather God?"

She laughed out loud, musically and without hurt. "Of course I believe in him, and love him. I just don't worship him." She said with affectionate rebuke in her voice, "It would be hard to."

They had returned to the highway. BJ pointed quickly to the right, nearly missing the turn, and Annie, gritting her teeth slightly, began the now-familiar descent toward Crossroads.

BJ asked, "Do you know a faun named Stefan?"

She nodded quickly. "I know him. He wants so badly to be an animal doctor."

She smiled suddenly at BJ. "You must be BJ."

Annie smiled back, but she raised an eyebrow at BJ, who was surprised to find herself blushing. "That's right. Could you double-check us on these turns?"

BJ didn't ask again about Crossroads. Melina, tongue protruding slightly as she concentrated, pointed the way for Annie.

At the stone bridge, Melina said, "Stop, please."

Annie did so. "We could go on—"

"No. Please." She put a hand on Annie's shoulder. "This part is very bad if you have got it wrong. You should not risk your lives, just because I so wanted church."

She kissed them each on the lips, which made them both

uncomfortable. "The peace of Christ be with you both."

She slung her knotted tennis shoes back over her neck, skipped lightly down the road, and disappeared without seeming to, directly in front of them.

They didn't say much on the way back to the highway. Finally Annie said in a small voice, "Do you ever feel as though you only thought you knew the things that you thought you knew best?"

BJ took a second to sort that out. "All the time, this rotation."

"Not just in vet school."

BJ repeated, "All the time."

Annie sighed loudly. "And when my mother calls and asks how church was, I'll say, 'It was just fine.' That's all." She drummed on the wheel, thinking. "Sometimes I feel like God is laughing at me."

"Einstein said God was subtle, but not malicious. Maybe it's a good joke."

Annie considered and smiled. "Know what? My mother will also ask if I had Sunday dinner with anyone." She looked down. "And we're both dressed up . . ."

BJ laughed. "And they serve a great Sunday brunch at the Ramada across from the campus."

Annie thumped her flat stomach. "This dress will never fit again, and can we afford this?"

"Oh, yeah." BJ had a sudden, quick vision of being able to spend her savings, but pushed the thought away determinedly. This was the pleasantest Sunday she'd had in a long time. "Bring on the buffet."

Annie, turning toward the Ramada, sped up. BJ saw the look in her eye and wondered idly, relaxing, how a woman who clearly loved food so well could keep in such great shape.

T·H·I·R·T·E·E·N

THE MORNING CASE had taken all of an hour: a quick prenatal check for Polyta, who had been willing to meet them halfway. By mutual consent, Lee Anne had been allowed to continue with the case. Dave had been embarrassed and shy until Polyta kindly mussed his hair and said that she was glad to see him again. Thereafter he had been insufferable.

Now they were stuck, halfway on the road between Stein's and the unicorn field, with a second case late in the afternoon. "How are we going to kill five hours?" BJ said.

Annie said, with a sensuality that caused Dave to raise an eyebrow, "Lunch."

After that it was simply a matter of finding a place to picnic in a land almost entirely made up of good spots. They argued amiably over choices while Sugar drove until Dave said, pointing to twin wheel ruts by a rapidly running stream, "Where does that road go?"

Sugar checked his map and replied, "Nowhere; it just stays there."

On any other world, that would have been a bad joke. Here it was welcome news. They turned up it, and Sugar stopped when the wheel ruts turned grassy and faded out.

The stream had come from a second, hidden valley between two cliffs hung with vines and ferns. At the far end was a ribbon waterfall that ended in spray in a pool large enough to be calm at its far end. Rainbows flickered above it as light breezes whipped the spray.

To either side of the pool, grass, shrubs, and flowers sloped gently up to the cliff base. It was midmorning, and the place was alive with sunshine.

Sugar turned to Dave. "I don't know if you can navigate roads, but you can sure pick 'em."

Dave beamed.

Free time inside Crossroads was rare, and welcome. Almost immediately, Annie, Sugar, and Dave were swimming (with bathing suits) in the pool by the falls.

Lee Anne and BJ lay in the grass, talking. BJ would have joined the swimmers, but it was traumatic wearing a bathing suit in front of Dave and, frankly, she was feeling too lazy.

Lee Anne lay back against a mossy, practically padded, tree stump. "Doesn't Crossroads have any ugly places?"

BJ lay on her back. "I'll bet it has plenty of them. And since the good parts are prettier than anything we've ever seen, I can just imagine the bad parts."

"I'd rather not." Lee Anne added meditatively, "Parts of farm life felt like this, when I was growing up. Later there was more work and less rest, but some of it"—she patted the grass appreciatively—"was just like this."

In the distance, a flock of blue-backs flashed in the sunlight, diving into the flowers. A number of them backed out immediately, squawking. A few didn't come out at all.

Lee Anne squinted up at the flowerbinders hopping in the grassy slopes to one side of the pool. "A couple of them are limping."

Clearly, they were. One was three-legged lame; another was favoring one paw.

Lee Anne looked at BJ. "I'm gonna go look them over. You want to come?"

"Hang on." BJ put on her sweatshirt, then popped Betadine, some gauze, a towel, several ointments and dropper bottles, her penlight, a thermometer, a jar of Vaseline, and, as an afterthought, *Lao's Guide* into her backpack. "Okay."

Lee Anne grinned at her. "Ready for anything, are we?"

They were ready for anything but catching a flowerbinder who didn't feel like being caught. The giant kittens were as perverse as real cats; the healthy ones pounced at the student's knees, rolled on the ground to be patted, and generally got in the way. The lame flowerbinders hid in the brush, bounded awkwardly off, and ducked behind their healthy companions.

Lee Anne panted, "What's wrong with these guys?"

BJ rose to her knees after an unsuccessful dive onto a flowerbinder who had wriggled free, squeaking, and was now looking at her dubiously from six feet away. "Whatever hurt them must have scared them. Or else they're just being annoying."

Lee Anne grabbed futilely at a flowerbinder that bounded by on three legs. "I vote for choice two. Let's try going after the same one."

That worked. Lee Anne, waving her arms and being intentionally scary, drove a flowerbinder directly toward BJ, who managed to grab it by the scruff, push it down on its belly, and hook an arm around its waist. The animal kicked frantically, its floral camouflage rustling; BJ was grateful for her sweatshirt.

Its leg was scratched, not deeply; a two-inch thorn hung in the top end of the wound. Lee Anne pulled the thorn, checked the scratch for swelling and for fur loss (they take a few days to develop), disinfected the scratch, and, from the new good habits they were all developing, did a quick once-over of the animal.

BJ scratched its ears, comforted it, and tried to calm it. "Why did he go through a space he couldn't navigate?"

"She," Lee Anne announced, lifting the tail. She did a double take, crossing her eyes as she peered at the end of the tail. "Whoa." She bent the tail toward BJ. "Somebody's been after this guy."

The tip of the tail was gone completely, a badly healed stub marking where it had been taken off.

"It could be an accident," BJ said. "Sure, it looks like she was running for her life and dived into a thornbush, but—"

"Describe the natural accident that lops off an inch and a half of tail," Lee Anne said. "I'm real curious to hear it."

"Predators," BJ said finally.

"Any sane predator would eat more than a nibble of tail. Plus we'd see more damage in the rest of them." She sighed. "Can't do much about it. Okay, sweetie, you can go."

She bounded away aggrievedly and cleaned herself between the vines woven in her fur.

Catching the second one was marginally easier. Lee Anne drove it toward its lame side and eventually it overbalanced within reach of BJ. It seemed listless.

Moreover, it had let the plants around its hindquarters wilt and dry, making the camouflage ineffective. "It's too stiff to clean back there," BJ said thoughtfully, "or something."

She tugged the dried stems around the flowerbinder's hind leg. He squeaked angrily, then followed up with a yowl of real pain. "Hold it. Let's take a look."

BJ trimmed dead foliage away from the favored leg until all that was left was a narrow strip across the healing gash. Lee Anne looked closely at it. "Wow."

The dried stem had been driven into the wound. The clot had formed over it; bits of plant stem and specks of dirt were mixed in with the granuloma.

"Look at the dirt in here. We've gotta open it up again, else it'll scar even if it doesn't fester."

"Terrific." Neither of them had been expecting to run into a job this size.

"Kitty," Lee Anne crooned, "this is gonna sting a bit, but we'll make you better." She stood upright and bawled down the hill in a voice that might have shaken loose rocks, "*Dr. Dobbs?! What's a good local anesthetic for flowerbinders?*"

Dave, preparing to dive off a rock shelf, lost his balance and toppled in. Sugar waved, cupped his hands around his mouth, and shouted back in the same voice, "*Flexedine. We haven't got any.*"

"*Thanks.*" Lee Anne grinned back at the openmouthed BJ. "Anybody who's ever had to call folks in from the field can do that."

"I'm impressed," BJ said, and meant it. "Now, who can do this?" She traced the ragged leg wound, which started in the rump and streaked across the back of the leg, growing shallower as it went.

"Not me." Lee Anne considered and finally announced, "Know what I think? Somebody grabbed Kitty by the butt, Kitty jumped, and somebody's teeth weren't in deep enough and pulled out through the leg." She grimaced. "It's like something a junkyard dog would do, maybe a rottweiler that's been hammered on and turned mean."

"Kitty," BJ mimicked Lee Anne, "this is gonna sting more than just a bit. We're sorry." She clamped the flowerbinder firmly under her arm and tried to present the leg for Lee Anne to treat.

Between them, they got the leg wound reopened and the scab removed. After some debate they settled for Lee Anne's picking out the ingrained dirt and plant material, rather than removing healthy flesh. After the initial struggle, the flowerbinder was surprisingly docile, and the work went quickly.

They were nearly ready to rewash the wound and wrap it when a soft wind picked up in the valley, and a shadow, faster moving than any cloud BJ had seen outside of a hurricane, passed over the stream and the underbrush.

Instantly the other flowerbinders crouched, tucked still more leaves and blooms around themselves, and curled into tight balls. Where big white kitten-cats had been visible seconds before, now there were scattered blossoming hummocks. Only the occasional twitching tail betrayed them.

BJ suddenly had a struggling, scratching bundle of panic under her arm. Startled, she let go. It bounded immediately into a tangle of vine and fern on the rock wall behind them.

Lee Anne scowled. "Roundup time again."

BJ, rubbing her scratched arm, walked quickly to the cliff face, knelt, and moved the leaves aside. "Look at this," she said quietly.

Lee Anne peered over her shoulder and pulled the vines aside, peering into the dark hole in the cliff.

BJ said, "We can't leave it like that. It needs a bandage."

"You're gonna follow it in there?"

She pulled her penlight from her backpack. "For a little ways."

Lee Anne said, "Don't go too far." She looked at the cave and shivered. "I don't feel like going in after you."

"If it's dangerous, I'll come right out." She ducked in, even though the cave roof was well over her head. "Give me ten minutes before you panic."

The cave was cool and moist, fairly pleasant after being out in the sun. Dust-laden rays streamed between the vines covering the entrance. BJ looked back, then squinted forward.

She was in a chamber the size of a small bedroom; it was roughly oval. The floor was dry, and the worn stalactites didn't look as though they had dripped in years. A rippling water mark on the floor descended away from the entrance and toward the rear of the chamber.

The flowerbinder was nowhere to be seen. BJ moved to the rear of the chamber and shone her pen in the dark tunnel there.

The small beam showed a flight of carved steps, well worn in the middle, descending into blackness. A stone banister, little more than a notch midway up the left wall, followed the stairs in parallel. Far below her, she heard a loud mew.

She considered, then went back to the entrance. "Make it twenty minutes."

"Don't want to," came back. BJ smiled, but her smile faded quickly as she picked her way down the narrow stairs.

The penlight picked out a ribbed column; BJ ran her light up and down it briefly, trying to imagine the mineral colors in a stronger light. She continued down.

The path leveled, and her torch shone on water. BJ had never seen a pool so completely still, unruffled by wind. She waved the torch back and forth to be sure where the path went and paused: there was an iron peg, hammered into the wall.

Somehow that was more disturbing than the existence of steps in the first place. BJ tiptoed down, checking between stalagmites and pillars for the wayward flowerbinder.

The path became steps again, and this time a tiny stream from the pool above followed them. BJ descended with exaggerated care. If I fall here, she thought, no one will find me.

The path leveled again, but this time there was no pool, just a narrow channel of slow-moving water. BJ moved the torch to one side and saw the crown.

It was a simple gold band, broken in three places by etchings: A hooved leg came down on a grassy emerald. A feathered wing flew under a sunny topaz, and a thumb and forefinger grasped a ruby.

She heard another mew below her; she continued down.

She regarded the robes at the fourth landing disapprovingly; they had fur, feathers, and several kinds of leather. She looked with more interest at the waiting (unlit) torch in the sconce at the last landing.

At the end of the stair was a chamber too large for her light; she flashed it around futilely, then lowered it. She took a deep breath and turned out the light.

She was quite correct; though she could detect no light source, there was enough light to see a vast hall, with the stream running into the center of it and converging with another. She looked this way and that, finally seeing him.

The flowerbinder was facing away from her, crouched behind the broken stump of a stalagmite and lashing its tail back and forth as it watched two immense bats, hanging to either side of a man.

He was at least partly a man. BJ stepped forward, staring in disbelief.

Her clinical eye took in the tree roots, the stone hand, the burning hair and weeping eye, as well as the breeze that came from nowhere to ruffle the man only. At the same time, she thought to herself, God, the *pain* . . .

The flowerbinder struggled to rise up on its rear legs and paw at the bats. They flapped their wings suddenly and chittered at the cat. The man-thing turned to each of them. "Thought! Memory! Don't tease." He added, without bothering to look at her, "Ahh. The doctor is in. Tell me, Miss Vaughan, how do you like the accommodations?"

BJ stared at him without answering.

The flowerbinder was struggling to stay on its rear legs, pawing upward at the two bats, who seemed undisturbed.

The thing between the bats said, "I assumed you would arrive. You may ask me one question, and one only. Be assured the answer will be true. What do you want to know?"

BJ looked in horror at the stone hands, the rooted legs, the burning hair, and perpetually weeping eye. "Can I do anything to help you?"

He opened his mouth, closed it, considered momentarily, and said, "I had known you would ask that, but I refused to believe it. You may choose another question."

"I don't want another question; I want to know what I can do to help you."

He said unsteadily, "Anything you can do to ease the pain would help. Thank you for asking."

BJ dumped the knapsack out on the floor, checking what she had. "Are you under a curse or something?" It felt silly even to say it.

He smiled wryly. "Far worse. A blessing."

"Talk to God about that sometime." She climbed his gnarled tree-legs and stood on a bole growing from one of his hips to examine his face. The two bats shifted away and chattered at her resentfully; she tried not to notice. "Let me see."

She had a bottle of eye drops with a steroid; she checked his reddened eye to be sure there were no ulcers, and applied the drops to the insides of the lids, on the sclera. "This is for animals, but it's safe for humans, and it's all I have with me. I can leave the bottle with you, if you can apply it."

"I'll find a way."

"Who are you?" she said, simply to occupy him while she treated him.

"My name is Harral. I'm a prophet. That is the gift whose price you are presently ameliorating."

She stepped back down. "How's that?"

"Better." His eye was still tearing continually, but that seemed to be a permanent attribute rather than a sign of discomfort.

"All right. Does your hair always burn that way?"

"Always."

"Well, then." She stepped back up and used part of the gauze roll to tie a headband for him. "Only the tip of the hair burns. This should keep the burning off your flesh." Even saying it felt surreal, as though this would turn out to be a nightmare and any minute Dr. Truelove would enter and criticize her work. "Is anything else bothering you?" she said lamely.

"I'd like to see the sun again."

She glanced around the dripping cavern, the ribbed colonnades and the still-forming stalactites and stalagmites. "I can't change that. I'm sorry."

"I'm frequently sorry for what I can't change. Thank you for what you've done."

"Can you tell me what happened to you? Will you ever get better?"

"Will you, Miss Vaughan?" Harral said.

She froze, nearly as still as Harral himself. "I don't know yet. That was unkind."

"I'm sorry. Unkindness is what I have left."

"In that case, I'm sorry, too." She bent to pick up the flowerbinder.

"Wait." He genuinely sounded anxious. "I may still be able to do something kind, in return for what you did for me." He turned to each of the bats. "How much shall I tell her?"

The two bats shifted sulkily, watching her.

Harral turned back to her as well. "Miss Vaughan, not because it is tit for tat but because your kind nature merits it, I am going to tell you three things about your future. I will be oblique, because that is the nature of prophecy."

BJ said, "Why can't prophets be direct?"

Harral responded immediately, "Because if we said 'Turn left at the light and sell RJR the next time it splits,' we would change the future, instead of predicting it. We would also be consultants, instead of prophets."

"Oh. Thank you. What are the three things?"

"The first: Why is gold in your world more precious than lead?"

"Because it's in shorter supply."

"Then how precious is the rest of your life, and are you willing to risk making it more precious yet?"

She looked at him in startled silence. Finally she said, "I think so."

"But you don't know. Doctors should know. And avoid the

obvious meaning; remember, I'm prophesying."

He shook his head, careful not to dislodge the headband. "The second: Why don't you feel betrayed when a flowerbinder looks like a bush?"

"That's easy. Because I know that it's a cat."

"True." He leaned closer. "But blue-backs feel betrayed, when they're killed and eaten. They see the flowers and not the cat."

BJ said, "Is this related to Crossroads, or to my life back home?"

Harral said amusedly, "You're being confused by the flowers again, Doctor. Everybody has only one life. Don't be fooled by flowers, no matter where they are or how pleasantly familiar they seem."

BJ decided that prophecy was unpleasantly oblique. "Is any of this related to Morgan?" She added, "Here or back home, either one?"

There was a pause, and Harral said, "Very good. I wish that King Brandal were so astute." Thought and Memory chirped at him, and he said testily, "All right, all right, I'll leave it at that."

"The third: A song." He sang in a terrible, grating voice, "*Fas et nefas ambulant/Pene passu pari.*" He stopped suddenly. "Tell me your thoughts."

She thought that it was like talking to the Griffin, without the charm. "Is that Latin? What does it mean?"

"Oh, I can't tell you what it means. But it says, roughly, 'The good and the evil walk side by side.' Learning to tell them apart is the trick." He folded his arms. "Do you have any questions?"

BJ said in a small, tight voice, "Can you tell me whether I'm ill or not?"

The bats moved back and forth agitatedly. Harral, after a long pause, said, "No. I can't."

"Then you have nothing important to tell me." She added politely, "Thank you for trying."

"It makes no difference." He looked sadly down at her. "In the end, prophecy is accurate without being helpful. This time, at least, I tried very hard to be helpful. Good-bye, BJ, and remember that while dealing with the crisis of death, you must still survive the problems of life."

She pulled extra gauze out and left it on the stalagmite nearest him, then nestled the eye ointment bottle in the cloth.

The flowerbinder, tired of yearning for the out-of-reach bats, was leaning over the lip of the well. It swiped at the cave fish as they swam near, then shook its paw disgustedly to get the water off.

BJ scooped it up, holding it against her sweatshirt. "C'mon, let's go." She looked at Harral uncertainly. "Will you be all right?"

"I can be nothing but right. Go on; Lee Anne is about to go get help."

"Good-bye then." BJ walked briskly away, nestling the flowerbinder as close to her body as she could to make carrying it easier. There were a lot of stairs ahead.

Her arms ached before she broke into the sunlight to find Lee Anne and a dripping Sugar, Annie, and Dave waiting for her. Sugar was holding the flashlight from the truck, and he had a coil of rope around his shoulder. "Where the hell have you been?"

BJ was reminded of the tone her mother used to take when she'd been worried about BJ. "This little guy ran farther than I thought he would."

"Hurry up and finish him," he grunted. "We still have to pick up Stefan; he has a breeding ram that needs stitching. This one's special—not to us, to him; Stein got him a Merino—and he'll do anything to have it whole again."

BJ looked at the four of them and thought with a rush of warmth, "I'd care as much about any of them." She hadn't thought, at the start of the rotation, that she could ever be so close to any of them. They were riding back to meet Stefan when BJ, still basking in the glow of friendship, remembered Harral's warning about betrayal.

On the drive out of the valley, Dave suddenly shouted and pointed up. Sugar slammed on the brakes and they piled out of the truck, staring at the rock wall.

The body was slender, male, and unclothed. Its ankles were pinned together, and it hung from a protruding branch. Incongruously, a pair of blue-backs perched above it, singing.

One of the man's legs was scratched badly, with a thorn protruding from the top of the scratch. His other leg had a deep gash, torn into his buttock and growing shallower down the length of the leg.

BJ said with flat certainty, "That's the man who hurt the flowerbinders."

Lee Anne shook her head violently. "No way on earth could a human being bite into flesh that way. Plus which, what kind of justice is this? Why should he be dead?"

Annie said, "Are we sure he is?"

Sugar stood on tiptoe and, straining to reach the man's head, flipped the body around so that the chest faced out.

Dave, staring, made a sick sound in his throat at the sight of the exposed organs.

Annie, because she looked away, noticed the huddled body of a flowerbinder nearby. Its stomach had been ripped open, in exactly the manner of the hanging body.

And BJ, because she had been expecting another language, was the first to understand the import of the fact that the word JUSTICE had been written on the body in English: they had been meant to find it.

It had been done while they were here. The slain flowerbinder had probably been killed while they were here, the good and the evil, walking side by side.

F·O·U·R·T·E·E·N

THE OPERATION ON the sheep was, compared to what they'd been doing, quick and easy. It astonished BJ how calm and experienced they all seemed to feel.

The ram had been savaged in several places. Because it was a breeding animal, Stefan couldn't afford to let it die, and because it was unique, they chose to operate at the vet school.

The ugliest wound and easiest repair was the torn rear thigh, which BJ worked on. The most delicate-looking job was the rip in the scrotal sac; the right testicle was hanging against it. Fortunately, the tunic wrapping the testicle was still pearly and unruptured. Dave, folding the rip back carefully and delicately to double-check the tunic, made a crack about "Rocky mountain oysters," but BJ thought he looked pretty green.

Lee Anne grinned at Dave. "Lucky boy, isn't he? Came within an ace of losing his ram-a-lam-a-ding-dong."

Dave smiled, not very convincingly. Together he and Lee Anne clipped the wool, cleaned the wound, and debrided it, clipping its damaged edges.

Lee Anne, with one smirk at Dave's face, took over the gluing of the rip, from the top down (proximal to distal), with a surgical adhesive.

"Leave the distal third of that unsealed," Sugar said from behind her. "You'll want it to drain in case an abscess develops."

"Don't trust us?" Dave said.

Sugar replied, "I want the pus to have an out, and, if at all possible, I don't want the testicle to adhere to the scrotum. How would you feel if it happened to you?"

Dave shut up.

Stefan, watching the ram from a low riser at the end of the table, said anxiously, "Will it hurt him?"

"Not a bit," Sugar said, moving to the opposite side of the table so that Stefan could get a better view. "The anesthetic needle probably hurt, but nothing did after that."

"It amazes me," Stefan said seriously, "what you can do with syringes. So many different chemicals, with so many applications . . . How do you know them all?"

BJ, holding a hemostat, said, "We look them up. Over and over again. Eventually, we'll remember the dosages for the ones we use every day."

She saw his expression and finished, "The ones we use on the animals every day."

He laughed uncertainly and peered anxiously but with great interest at his ram. Stefan was wearing a surgical cap; he had worn a baseball cap in the vet school halls.

His legs were covered by loose-fitting overalls, and his hooves were encased in sneakers with inserts. BJ wondered, with a stab of jealousy, if he had learned that trick from Melina.

Annie finished exploring the abdominal area and said with relief, "Nothing but superficial damage. No apparent organ trauma, no heavy bleeding."

Lee Anne, reassembling the scrotum under Sugar's direction, said finally, "He'll be okay." She turned to Stefan. "We'll need to keep him here at least a week to observe that wound. It needs to heal by itself, open."

"Healing by second intention?" Stefan said shyly.

They looked at him, startled. Sugar chuckled. "Keep an eye on this one. He might outshine you."

Stefan looked at him anxiously to make sure he wasn't being made fun of, then blushed proudly. "Lee Anne, what should I do when he comes back to the flock?"

"You're gonna need to keep an eye on him. Isolate him from the others for a while once we bring him back, all right?"

His confusion changed to understanding when BJ amended, "Keep him apart from the others. You don't want him fighting or breeding until he's healed."

Stefan nodded and said with mock severity, "Did you hear that, Dmitrios? You be a good boy for once."

BJ announced, "I'm done. He may be lame for a while." Her forehead was dotted with sweat. She had used a Ford interlocking pattern on the thigh, and she had mistrusted her fingers the entire time.

Dave snorted. "It's about damn time. How long can it take, when it's just needlework?"

Sugar said, "BJ's bought a lot of pizza." It was a standing rule in third-year labs that the last student team done suturing had to pay for pizza for the staff. "But I've never seen one of her incisions dehisce, either. Can you folks say that?"

Stefan stared at her, impressed, and BJ felt a sudden surge of warmth toward Sugar.

"That's that." He checked the ram's breathing. "You people get cleaned up, and come back in here in five."

The exodus was fast. BJ, as she often did, took the side door with the observation window.

She nearly knocked over DeeDee, who had been looking through the window of OR. "Whoa." DeeDee reached out and steadied her.

BJ was startled by the touch. DeeDee had always seemed a dry, distant person, despite her constant smile and bubbly chatter. "Thanks."

"No problem." DeeDee stared at her with disturbingly clear blue eyes. "I can't believe Sugar's been letting you do this much surgery. What are you guys, real gunners? How did you get on that rotation? Do the clients mind?"

BJ said, "For me it's a make-up rotation." She suspected that it was true. "The others are in because of their skills, I think." She suspected, though she couldn't be sure, that that was only partly true. "And it helps a lot to actually cut, instead of watching."

DeeDee wagged a finger. "You're avoiding the question, but that's okay." She leaned forward. "Who's the client? He's awfully cute."

"His name's Stefan. He's Greek." She added unnecessarily, "A shepherd."

"How interesting," DeeDee said vaguely. She looked BJ in the eye. "Can I give you some advice?"

"Sure." BJ was startled.

"As a friend, I mean."

That seemed even more unlikely. "Of course."

DeeDee looked up and down the hall, suddenly hesitant. "Watch out for Dr. Truelove."

"Why?" BJ involuntarily looked both ways herself.

"He's been asking questions about your work. And about this rotation you're on, this independent study." DeeDee hesitated and said finally, "And I know that you two didn't see eye to eye."

"I always got along with him," BJ said. "I was always polite, and I worked hard." She added, her ears bright red, "He just failed me, that's all."

"Well, I don't think he feels that's the end of it. I don't know why." She tapped her feet nervously. "I just thought I should tell you. None of my business, really. Sorry."

"Thanks for warning me." BJ was confused, particularly because DeeDee's kindness had always been an empty polite expression, never an expenditure of effort. "I thought that you and Dr. Truelove thought well of each other."

Her eyes went artificially wide. "Oh, we do. That is," she added with obviously false modesty, "I think highly of him." Her stare went vacant again, and she frowned. "But lately he's even been questioning me. I think he's trying to find something out, and I think it's about you."

"Thanks," BJ said abruptly, and, "I'd better get back."

The others, having cleaned off and removed their scrubs, were back in the sheep barn. The ram was already moving from anesthesia into natural sleep.

Sugar, sighing, said, "That's all, folks. Move him to a holding pen, and then it's time to go home." He looked hard at Stefan. "Do you need to get back tonight?"

Stefan smiled. "My flock is cared for." He looked at the clock, which meant little to him. "Is it before midday?"

"It's three o'clock. You've been watching for half a day."

He shook his head and smiled embarrassedly. "I didn't notice . . . so fascinating." BJ was reminded of the other students' expressions, on seeing a unicorn for the first time.

Sugar said to Stefan, "We won't be able to get you back before sundown. Dave, can you board a client for the night?"

Dave swallowed. "Hey, I'd love to. I mean, you know I'd love to, but my apartment is kind of small, and I've got this . . . friend coming. . . ." He trailed off weakly.

Even Stefan understood. He put a hand on Dave's shoulder. "If you have a woman coming to you, David, I can turn my face to the wall. I promise, it won't bother me."

Annie's expression was even better than Dave's.

"He can stay with me," BJ said finally.

Under Sugar's amused stare, she added, "I have a fold-out couch."

"I didn't ask," Sugar said.

BJ took Stefan on a quick tour of the hospital facilities, sidling around corners to be sure they'd be alone before they went into rooms. She realized that this looked more furtive than a client visit should, but she wasn't sure that Stefan could carry on a lengthy conversation without revealing himself.

He was fascinated by the pharmacy, and asked why things were kept locked. BJ explained the sign-out system and the range of drugs they kept on hand.

The micro-photography in the conference room astonished him. Anxious as she was to get him out, BJ took him to an empty lab and let him look at his own blood through a microscope. He laughed with delight when he could make out the blood cells; probably no person since Leeuwenhoek had been so swept up by the view through a lens.

Encouraged, she showed Stefan the blood donor dogs. "This is Sam, and this is Maizie." She let them out of their kennel; they bounded eagerly about the room, casting wistful eyes at the two leashes on the wall. BJ ruffled Sam's fur and beeped his little rubber-nose, then patted Maizie.

"Hello." Stefan kissed each of them, and they licked him back. He ran his hands over each of them, checking them with a quick sensitivity that BJ, with four years of graduate experience, envied. "You're both good, good dogs. . . . What kind are they?"

"Greyhounds. Retired from a racing kennel in West Virginia. We keep them to donate blood."

"How good of you." He was talking to the greyhounds, who loved him unreservedly on sight. BJ was feeling jealous when he looked up. "You like Sam better than Maizie."

"Yes," she said, startled, and guiltily: "Does Maizie know?"

"Of course." He ruffled her ears. "She doesn't mind. Do you feel bad for them, that they are penned up and bleed for you?"

"We take good care of them. We're each assigned to walk two, and we give them love. I may be wrong, but I think they have a better life than they had when they were racing dogs. Stefan," BJ said slowly, "if you're going to go to vet school, there's something else you ought to see."

She took him down to a room of stainless steel kennels. The dogs here, of all sizes and breeds, all saw her enter. Some barked loudly, but others thumped their tails listlessly or did nothing. Some of the dogs had splints on, or gauze bandages on their stomachs. Some were groggy from anesthetic.

Stefan walked from cage to cage while she spoke. "In the lab courses, we worked on dogs like these—there's a company that supplies them for research and medical labs. We do only three surgeries on each animal, then put them to sleep."

Stefan stuck his slender fingers inside a cage and stroked an Airedale whose belly was partly shaved. He said nothing.

"Look, we hurt them as little as possible. They're all anesthetized. Plus we've all pushed to eliminate unnecessary labs, wherever we can, and use videotape instead."

He said without interest, "What is videotape?"

"I'll explain later. In this case, it lets us watch earlier labs as they happened, without having to kill another animal to duplicate them." The class before BJ's had fought, unsuccessfully, to eliminate the poisons lab in which dogs were dosed, allowed to develop acute symptoms, diagnosed, treated, and then put out of suffering. BJ's class had fought and won; their lab had been videotaped, for three abysmal hours, to produce a tape for the next class. The Old Boy teachers thought the students unnecessarily squeamish.

Stefan continued stroking the Airedale until it turned stiffly and gave his hand a cursory lick. "I see the need," he said finally. "You must practice on living animals, yes. But do you care for them, and do you say good-bye before they die?"

BJ felt guiltier than she had at any time except lying to her mother about dates in high school. "I used to. We all did, at first."

Stefan frowned. "You should still."

BJ was going to explain about professional detachment when she remembered Stefan kissing his lame ewe good-bye. She shut up. "That's the end of the tour."

Before they got to her locker, a rich bass voice called, "BJ!"

There was no way to avoid him. "Hello, Dr. Truelove."

He bent down farther than needful, as though he were talking to a five-year-old. "How are you *feeling*?"

"Fine now, thanks." She had all but forgotten her public crying jag until DeeDee had brought it up again.

"Good, good." He patted her shoulder, sliding his hand off it a shade slowly. "You get lots of rest, and I'm sure you'll do fine." He turned to Stefan. "And who is this?"

"Stefan Andros," BJ said, grateful that Sugar had insisted on giving Stefan a last name. "He brought in a breeding sheep that had been attacked by dogs."

Stefan looked shy and embarrassed. BJ was glad that she had lied for him, instead of letting him try on his own.

Truelove nodded. "Pleased to meet you." But instead of offering to shake hands, he said with mock severity, "You know, where I was brought up, we were taught to tip our hats when we were introduced."

BJ held her breath. Stefan sorted out the meaning of the sentence, considered, and delicately lifted his cap three inches off his dark curls, then back down.

"Very good," Truelove said jovially, and BJ couldn't tell whether he was disappointed or not. "And how do you like our little school?"

If Truelove wanted praise, he wasn't disappointed. "It's wonderful," Stefan said simply. "Now, more than ever, I want to be a veterinarian."

"That's fine," he boomed back at Stefan, patting the faun's shoulder. "Just fine. Well, nice meeting you. Good-bye, BJ." He strode purposefully down the empty hall.

Stefan stared interestedly after him. "Who was that?"

BJ said, "Let's just go."

She walked him through the tunnel to her locker, showed him how the combination would have worked (she had left it unlocked, as most students did when they were in a hurry), opened the metal door, and froze in place.

Stefan looked over her shoulder and chuckled. "So messy."

Someone had gone through her locker.

BJ sifted through the papers and books quickly, trying to see what was missing. Her backpack had been emptied out. She was grateful that she had taken her books home, then had a moment of panic trying to remember if she had *Lao's Guide*, or had passed it to one of the others—Annie. Annie had needed it for the flowerbinders, and had taken it yesterday.

Annie was the only one who knew that, wasn't she?

BJ didn't take time to check what else was missing. "Stefan, let's leave now."

He cast several longing backward glances at the school building as they crossed the freshly laid parking lot. He sang happily to himself in Greek, a tune strange enough to have been a thousand years old; he skipped clumsily in the padded sneakers.

At BJ's car, his hat fell off; as he stooped to pick it up, his horns showed clearly. No one was around to see; BJ sighed, thanking God, and opened the door for him. There was so much she wanted to show him, but she was beginning to realize that tonight was not going to be easy.

F·I·F·T·E·E·N

THE WALK DOWN the stone steps was faster. Brandal had not been wearing his battle gear, and did not bother pausing until he was in front of the Seer.

Harral, who was wearing an odd new headband, regarded him with one reddened eye. "Hail the well-trained hero."

"Too well trained." Brandal sat on a comparatively dry rock near the lip of the well. Several small fish, startled by his movements and the unexpected torchlights, dashed madly away to the safety of deeper water. "We can defend ourselves, but we can't fight an army. If she finds a way to attack with her full force, she'll win."

"Ah." Harral scratched absently with his stone hand at the place where his flesh merged into roots. "Morgan, strategy, and boot camp. A terrifying combination, isn't it? Tell me," he said with apparent indifference to the answer, "do you ever wish you had agreed to her execution?"

Brandal raised his eyes, staring tiredly at the Seer. "I wish she were dead. I still don't feel I could have ordered her death, and I don't wish to kill her."

"You also still don't wish to see me. And here you are."

Brandal considered. "If she should get a copy of *The Book of Strangeways*—"

"She hasn't," Harral said flatly. "She has found it, and is trying to steal it. If she succeeds, she will have it within ten days."

"And if that happens?"

Harral recited it as though it were past history—which, Brandal reflected gloomily, the future is to prophets. "The Inspector General will die two days after she acquires the book. She hopes to kill him earlier."

"He can defend himself," Brandal said firmly.

"True. Unfortunately for himself, he can also defend others. In addition, the innkeeper Stein will die the day she acquires the book; the children of the Great will die within a year. Coincidentally, the last of the Great die fifty years to the day after the last of their young. You, O King, will live long enough to be punished as a deserter by the Wyr in Morgan's service."

Brandal waved that off. He had lived with that threat for some time now.

"The Stepfather God will be killed in a celebration the following spring."

Brandal was on his feet.

"Are you so surprised? She intends to kill all of Crossroads; could she succeed while he was alive?"

Brandal was numb. Murder for him was abhorrent, regicide (for obvious reasons) taboo; deicide was beyond comprehension.

"And what if we keep *The Book of Strangeways* from her?"

Harral spread his grotesque hands. "Then she fails, but only at the last possible moment. You haven't asked how she moves from world to world presently."

"The Wyr lead her, of course. I wouldn't trust them to lead troops, and apparently neither does Morgan. But they obey her; why?" He spoke with the hurt that, for Brandal, would always accompany betrayal. "I never expected them to be loyal to Crossroads; still . . . what's her hold on them?"

The Seer said only, "You haven't asked about the visiting heroes you were so anxious about last time."

"I know more about them," Brandal said glumly. "They seem nice, knowledgeable, and mostly moral. They don't look as though they could save a world."

"They don't, do they?" Harral smiled without mirth. "Nor do they look as though they could betray it."

The king stared. Harral went on, "Strictly speaking, it wouldn't be betrayal, since this isn't their world."

Brandal said slowly, "You didn't say that they were heroes, and you didn't say that they were villains. But Morgan's training manuals are in their language—"

"And they come and go so quickly here, to quote one of their own loved works."

The king was still thinking. "You won't tell me directly—"

"Directness spoils prophecy. It's like the observation changing the event."

"Whether they are the heroes we need or the villains we need to kill."

Harral said in mock surprise, "Could you have them killed?"

Brandal didn't speak for a long time. He held so still that the half-blind fish in the well drifted back onto the lip near his feet.

When he spoke, his voice was soft and regretful. "I will wait until the evidence against them is incontrovertible. I will let the Inspector General, whom they don't know, examine them closely.

"But I will tell him that when he decides they are guilty, he should kill them without remorse."

Harral nodded. "Hail, mighty king. Morgan has taught you something, after all."

"A great deal," he said bitterly. "Should I thank her?"

For once, Harral was silent. Brandal turned away, frightening the fish a last time before disappearing up the long staircase.

S·I·X·T·E·E·N

BJ HAD WORRIED about how to occupy Stefan in Kendrick, Virginia. How could you do anything to entertain someone who worked around satyrs, unicorns, and giant kitten-cats?

She had been foolish to worry. The answers were obvious in Stefan's excited cries as she pointed out a drive-through bank, a six-story dormitory, an airplane.

The university library was a special treat. He had never seen so many books in one place; he stood in the stacks with his mouth open, not knowing where to go. She showed him a few of the holdings on Crossroads, avoiding the pessimistic article on Crossroads' fragility. He looked at the books and articles for a few minutes, then handed them back with regret and embarrassment. "I'm sorry. I cannot understand them."

"Me neither," BJ said. He laughed politely; he didn't believe her.

She stopped at the reference desk when she saw who was there. "Mrs. Sobell?"

She stood up and came around the desk, smiling. She did not appear to recognize Stefan; BJ had wondered if she would. Perhaps the librarian had never been to Crossroads.

"Mrs. Sobell, this is Stefan Andros." BJ added politely, "I'm BJ Vaughan."

"I remember you, dear," Mrs. Sobell said almost affectionately. "You come here often." She turned to Stefan. "And where are you from, young man?"

"I am from Greece," he said, and BJ's heart nearly stopped as, remembering Dr. Truelove's admonition on manners, he removed his hat. His horns showed clearly.

After a frozen moment, Mrs. Sobell nodded. "Of course you are, Stefan. Why don't you keep your hat on? It's so easy to forget them here; Lost and Found takes in hundreds of them."

He put it back on hastily, tucking his hair under it in order to pull it down tightly. "It was good to meet you," he said seriously.

"And you," she said, and meant it. She turned to BJ. "And what are you planning to show him?"

"After this? I'm not sure." They had two hours to kill until dinner. "I thought we'd watch a video upstairs—"

Mrs. Sobell cut in, "Do you mind my making a suggestion?"

She stretched on tiptoe and whispered in BJ's ear. BJ nodded vigorously. "That's a wonderful idea."

"If you don't think he's seen it before," Mrs. Sobell said. "In Greece."

"No, I don't think so. Thank you."

"Nice meeting you," Stefan said, remembering. BJ tugged on his arm and dragged him off before he took his hat off again.

They signed up for a booth in the video library. Stefan stared into the blank screen. "Does something swim in here?"

"No." She enjoyed watching him jump as the first picture came on. "Keep watching. You'll like this."

It was "Singin' in the Rain." BJ was surprised at how many questions he had; she hadn't thought about his not having heard of videotapes. He initially accepted the idea that tiny people were performing just for BJ and him, but was excited rather than disappointed when she explained. "You mean we could see it all again, just the same as before?"

"The same every time."

"Who is that wonderful man?"

"That's Gene Kelly," she said almost reverently. "Watch this next bit."

He liked the songs, but the dancing captivated him completely. Twice she had to push him down in his chair to prevent his imitating the action on the monitor.

When they left, Stefan was practically uncontrollable. He danced on the sidewalks. He danced into the street until she warned him not to. He danced under the marquee of the Lyric Theater, and stopped to stare at the poster and stills under NOW SHOWING.

"Is this a movie in a big building, like the one in the little tiny movie we saw?" He turned around. "Can we go see it?"

BJ remembered that movies were mentioned in James Herriott's books. Probably Stein had explained them to Stefan; he might not have been able to explain television.

She put an arm through his, only partly to hold him down. "Let's eat first." She led him to Gyro's.

Before going in, Stefan touched one of the old-fashioned lamp-posts, reproductions that the Chamber of Commerce had pressed for to make downtown Kendrick look attractive (and to keep business from the University Mall). "Like the movie."

"Very like." She pulled him in. He pretended to fall on her, and they swung through the door, laughing.

"Hey, Beej." Stan, as always, was glad to see her. "Been a while. I thought you graduated."

"Nope. Flunked out," she said, and was gratified at Stan's and Stefan's laughter. "Stan, this is a friend of mine. Stan, Stefan; Stefan, Stan." In quick desperation, she patted Stefan's head. "Leave the hat on; Stan's informal."

"Sure." He shook hands with Stefan. "And this is my father, Chris."

The old man had been standing in the background, nodding vaguely. He came forward now and said something in Greek.

Stan winced. "English, Pa."

But he was astonished when Stefan spoke back in rapid-fire Greek. Chris looked confused, then delighted. He leaned across the counter with more animation than BJ had seen him show in weeks; he gestured, he laughed, he cupped a hand to his ear to make sure he didn't miss a word.

Stan threw the meat for two gyros on the grill and swung back, wanting to see it all. "Where did you find this guy? He talks like a native—his accent's a little funny, but he's really Greek."

"Oh, yes. He's a client."

"And that's all." Stan grinned at her. "Don't try to kid me."

Chris pointed to a spot on the map of Greece and fired a question at Stefan. BJ watched anxiously.

Stefan pointed at the map, made circles around several mountainous areas, and shrugged. Chris laughed and patted his cheek.

Two minutes later they were still talking. "Now we're getting all the old stories," Stan commented dryly. "About being a shepherd and butchering your own meat."

Chris was nearly as lively as Stefan now, gesturing a cross cut with a knife, then down through the skin. He extracted a pretend pile of something, threw it over his shoulder, and pantomimed a snarling dog shaking it. He and Stefan laughed uproariously.

Stan said delicately, "Now he's talking about throwing out—"

"The entrails," BJ said. "Yes, I got it." It amused her that Stan, who cooked meat every day, was more squeamish than BJ, who barely could afford to eat it.

Stefan asked a question and Chris smiled, but looked more serious. He talked for a long time; Stefan listened raptly.

"He's telling how he met me, in Greece," Stan said quietly. "I was born in the old country, during World War II. Pa was starting the restaurant here in Virginia. He went back once, got married, came back, and the war broke out. He didn't know he had a son till I was three, and he was wild to get to me. I could already talk the first time I met him."

Chris waved his arms wide and spoke in a squeaky child's voice. Stefan looked at Chris and laughed.

"And I saw him hug my mother, so I ran up and hit his legs and said, 'You let her go! I'm guarding her for my father!' Stan turned to his father, whose eyes were moist. "Don't get so excited, Pa. Here, sit down while I feed these two." He helped his father back to one of the stools near the grill, then dished up two plates for BJ and Stefan.

They took their food to a booth. Stefan said, "They're very nice, BJ. You have good friends."

"And you make friends fast." BJ hesitated, then said softly, "Tell me: how was Chris's speech? Did he have any trouble? Did anything strike you as odd?"

Stefan considered, frowning. "He spoke well. Sometimes when he pointed to things, he started pointing to the wrong thing. BJ, I think he talks well, in Greek at least; I think maybe he's getting lost somehow." Stefan looked confused and worried. "I've known many old men, but none of them had problems like him, and the bent back and weak knees. You see how he walks? BJ, what's the matter with him?"

BJ remembered that Stefan would not have seen nerve and tissue degeneration, except in people who passed through Crossroads. "I'll tell you about it later. It's kind of complicated."

He frowned. "I would understand."

"Oh, I know. It's just—" She broke off as Stan approached with a tray covered by a napkin which bulged upward in two places.

Once out of sight of the windows, he whisked the napkin off with a flourish to expose two elegant stemmed glasses of white wine.

"No charge," Stan said to Stefan. "I don't got a license, anyway. It's Pa's. He loved talking to you." And he winked at BJ. "Plus, Beej is a favorite customer."

He left quickly. Stefan said with quiet amusement, "Beej?"

"Drink your wine." They clinked glasses softly.

It was raining when they left Gyro's, a nice, quick downpour like the one in the movie. The streetlights, on now, glistened. Stefan took one look at them, spread his arms, and sang in his clear boy-tenor: "I'm singin' in the rain . . ." He spun and danced, and BJ recognized with delight how close he was to Gene Kelly's choreography. He could not only sing by ear, he could dance on sight.

"Your friend is amazing," a voice said in her ear. She turned sideways and saw DeeDee staring in fascination at Stefan.

"He's happy. His case at the hospital went well." BJ tried not to speak quickly, which she tended toward when she was hiding something. "Sugar said to show him around."

"Lucky you." But DeeDee didn't look romantically or sexually interested, either one; she had an odd fixed look, like a cat at a window watching an insect fly against the pane. "Is he a dancer?"

"He looks it, doesn't he?" she admitted. Stefan, ignoring them both, scuffed down the brick sidewalk and suddenly, smoothly, leaped up on one of the old-fashioned lampposts.

BJ watched in horror as he extended a shoeless right rear hoof. Somewhere, one of his shoes had fallen off.

Quickly she turned to DeeDee and locked eyes with her. "DeeDee," she said solemnly, "we need to talk."

"About what?" DeeDee stepped back involuntarily.

"About the thefts at the vet school." BJ wondered what she could say about them off the top of her head.

Stefan's singing cut off abruptly and he began retracing his steps quickly.

She was saved by the rain. "Are you confessing to them?" DeeDee joked uneasily. "Listen, I'm drowning out here. I'll talk to you later." She skipped past Stefan, who, BJ noted with relief, had found his missing shoe and was determinedly tying it, frowning like a small child with the effort.

DeeDee barely glanced down at him—his cap was on, thank God—and then back at BJ. "Have fun," she said wistfully, and BJ wondered whether or not DeeDee, who never seemed interested in anyone but herself, might be lonely.

Stefan looked after her with interest. "She's a doctor, too?"

"Not yet," BJ said. "Come on. I have one more surprise for you." She escorted him into Mitch's.

It would have been worth almost any amount of effort to see Stefan's face when he ate his first spoonful, ever, of hot fudge sundae.

BJ let them in, sorted her mail quickly ("Junk—junk—junk"), and showed Stefan the apartment. He loved the refrigerator, clucked over the sad shape her plants were in, and tested all the furniture with his hands.

Then he bounded up to her and said, "Thank you for the best day of my life, BJ."

"I'm so glad." And she was. "What did you like best?"

"The dancing," he said without hesitation. He added shyly, "Can we try, together?"

BJ tensed. "I'm clumsy. I don't think it's such a good idea—"

"Please."

She sighed and looked through her cassettes, finally picking an oldies tape with Motown on it.

"I got sunshine," the speakers sang softly, "on a cloudy day . . ." Stefan unhesitatingly stretched out an arm to her, led her across the floor, and she was dancing.

She stayed in step. She bit her lip, watching her legs move and waiting for the inevitable stumble. She relaxed and leaned against him as he pulled her close, spun her out, pulled her in again. He wasn't just a dancer: he was a perfect teacher and leader, and she felt like she was flying.

Finally he spun her out the length of both their arms, hard enough that her short hair pulled away from her head. He snapped her to a stop and she leaned away like a ballerina; then, praying the entire time that she wouldn't fall, she spun back into him. His slim, strong arms caught her, stopped her, folded around her tightly.

The music came to an end; the cassette player stopped.

And suddenly they were face-to-face, their eyes wide open, arms tight around each other and bodies taut against each other. They stayed frozen that way; then slowly, almost as if holding back, he began kissing up and down her neck, by her ears, at the line of her jaw. . . .

Part of her was relieved when his tongue turned out to be a normal human tongue, and not a ruminant's. Most of her seemed not to be thinking clearly. She ran her fingers down his damp shirt, across the V-neck and touching his chest, down his sides to the sweatpants over his waist and legs . . .

. . . And she saw, in her mind, her mother's note again—but this time it was in BJ's own handwriting, and was addressed to Stefan.

She pulled back, gasping. "Hang on."

He looked stricken. He held his arms out, but dropped them when he saw her face.

She took his hands. "I'm sorry," she said. "I like you very much. I like you more than I've liked anyone in a long time. But there's an important reason that I can't be involved with anyone just now."

"You have a lover?"

"No," BJ said firmly. "If I wanted someone—" Honesty forced her to amend, "If I could choose someone at all, it would be you. I can't. I really can't. I'm sorry."

"But do you like me?"

"More than anyone," she assured him. "You're wonderful."

He looked at her dubiously. "It is not just because I'm not human?"

"Not at all," she said flatly, though she suddenly wondered what sex with Stefan would be like. "And it isn't because I'm older."

"You are not so much older than I am." He looked at her wistfully. His eyes widened, and both his ears twitched. "It is because I'm not educated."

"Stefan," she said, exasperated, but he had convinced himself.

She tried to hold him. He said politely, "Thank you, but you don't have to do that for me."

"I want to."

"I think maybe that is not good just now." In his hurt and his distance from her, Stefan's accent was becoming stronger. "I think maybe we should wait for when you feel better, like you said."

"All right," she said finally. "Listen, I'll get you some blankets for the couch. I just need to check my answering machine for phone messages."

"Phone?"

"Telephone. You remember telephones from James Herriott's books?"

"Oh," he said dully. "That's right. Telephone." He smiled at her, not doing a very good job. "You go check your machine."

"I'll be right back. I promise."

She went to her bedroom, wondering if he would follow (perhaps he wouldn't think that way of bedrooms), and trying to make up her astonishingly confused mind about what to do next. She looked at herself in the mirror, brushed futilely at her hair with one hand, and played back her answering machine.

There was only one message. "Hey there." The voice was unmistakable. "This is Dr. Hitori. Here's my number." She gave it. "Please call so we can set up another appointment, as soon as possible." A long pause. "Please call soon." That was all.

But Dr. Hitori had called for herself, instead of letting a receptionist do it, and she had sounded angry. There was no question what that meant. BJ felt sick.

When she came back to the living room, Stefan was already on the couch, his back to her, pretending to be asleep. His pose all but radiated hurt.

BJ turned out the light, went to her bedroom, and lay rigid until morning.

At eight-thirty the next morning, she called Dr. Hitori. She saw the doctor, received the news she expected, and was back by ten.

Stefan, who had been awake since dawn, was leafing through her textbooks relentlessly, his brow furrowed and his lips moving as he read. "So," he said, when she came back. "Are you going to take me home?"

She nodded. He saw her face and said anxiously, "BJ, have you been crying?"

"A little," she said. "People do sometimes. It's nothing to worry about."

S·E·V·E·N·T·E·E·N

ONE DAY LATER, they were headed back into Crossroads.

With Sugar's blessing, they had all slept on the first part of the ride. They had all needed the sleep, and, amazingly, they were accustomed enough to the ride into Crossroads not to be excited anymore. BJ had kept to herself, but the others were too tired to question it.

BJ had awakened, briefly, at the border. A Road Crew conferred with Sugar and walked them through the new turns. Sugar carefully sketched them on his copy. It seemed to BJ that there had been Road Crews on almost every road they traveled nowadays: digging and chopping with twybils, talking, following a road plan that only the crew leaders and *The Book of Strangeways* knew.

BJ fell back asleep, but she woke up again after passing Stein's. It was midday. They turned southeast at the main crossroads.

The road arched over a stone bridge, which took them back across the main river, over a gorge which seemed as deep as the Grand Canyon. Shortly they were driving through grassy highlands, something like the American Great Plains and something like *National Geographic* footage of the steppes. One could see for miles from the truck cab; the wind rippled across the tall grass like a succession of waves, and cloud shadows dotted the gently sloping mounds clear to foothills in the distance.

Sugar said, "Rise and shine. Annie? You need a few minutes to pull together?"

"I'm ready," she said quietly, and BJ realized that Annie had been awake for some time.

Annie gave a thorough, clear, straightforward presentation. She discussed the nature of the patient, the procedure for the exam, and the reason for the call.

"Of course, I haven't seen the patient, but I suspect he has a lipoma. Given what we know about Crossroads"—she glanced at Sugar questioningly as she finished—"it must surely be benign.

"Still, just as a matter of sound practice, I recommend a biopsy. Dr. Dobbs, can we send a sample to the lab?"

"Sure, if you don't mind taking one."

The sun shone brightly on the grasslands they drove through. It all looked cheery and peaceful and ordinary.

Dave said, "Any chance we can use a rabies pole?"

The rabies pole was metal and over eight feet long, with a steel cable running-noose at the end. To use it, one slipped the noose over the animal's neck and tightened, holding with the pole.

Then, presumably, one person muzzled the animal while another held the pole. There was quite a lot of trust involved on the part of the muzzler.

Sugar frowned. "There's a little question of pride. Roping might annoy the client."

"Great," Dave said. "Let's make him mad."

Annie, staring out the window at the empty grasslands, said mildly, "I think that would be a bad idea."

They watched the three-foot grass to either side of the road. It waved and bent with the wind; their own passage caused barely a ripple.

A man rose straight up out of the grass, arms folded.

He had very dark straight hair and high cheekbones. His nose was long without being at all comic, and his eyes were deep blue, their lids slightly Eurasian. His chin was completely hairless, as though he had shaved moments ago or undergone electrolysis.

His build was slender but his forearms were muscular; his legs were hidden by cloth trousers, but he had no shoes on. His feet looked normal enough. He looked at them calmly, not at all disconcerted by the truck, and made no effort to approach them.

Lee Anne surreptitiously unzipped her backpack, checked it, and rezipped it. She swung it off the truck with her when they got out. Sugar stepped down and went forward with Annie to greet the client. Dave sauntered after them, mostly to feel involved but partly, obviously, because he felt protective of Annie.

BJ waited until Sugar and the others were out of earshot, then turned to Lee Anne. "Smith and Wesson?"

Lee Anne stared at her and said shortly, "Colt."

"Thirty-eight?"

"Twenty-two." Lee Anne smiled sourly. "Eensy-teensy, cute little bullets."

"I wouldn't bother taking it, then."

"You think I need silver bullets?"

BJ said thoughtfully, "I wonder whether that's a matter of bullet weight or a toxic reaction to silver. Either way, we don't have any on us."

Lee Anne sighed. "You probably don't pass the rotation if you shoot a client anyway." She slung her backpack through the truck window to the backseat. "How'd you know?"

"You reached for it in Stein's, too." BJ said diffidently, "Do you really know how to shoot it?"

Now her smile was friendly. "Sometime, do you want me to teach you?"

BJ said, "I can't believe some of the stuff you're able to do."

"Most of it is useless in vet school." But she seemed pleased. "Some of it's helping here."

They walked up to Annie and the others. Sugar had offered his hand to the client, who merely stared at it without unfolding his arms. Annie had been asking questions, but not getting much from the man's answers. He seemed unable to put together more than three or four words, all blunt. His accent was thick and had traces of Eastern Europe in it.

Annie smiled at him. "What is your name?"

He didn't smile back. "I have two. You need one. My name Vlatmir. Of Tribe Szdolny. From the bitch Magda." He stood even straighter. "We are the Wyr."

["The Wyr," Lao wrote, "derive their name from the Latin *virus*, and seem to have confused it with *virtus*. Unlike the commoner 'wer' in 'werewolf,' it is not so much a question of etymology as of attitude. Where some might question the right of a race of lycanthropes to call themselves people, the Wyr regard themselves as the only true people.

"Perhaps, however, this is an ethical survival mechanism, enabling the Wyr to regard all other humans as food animals. . . ."]

Annie, used to Crossroads by now, said, "I assume that you are our client. Are you also the patient?"

For answer he took off his shirt. His chest was completely hairless and smooth, like a small boy's.

He reached over his own shoulder. "This is the bump. It moves, but it doesn't go away." He held it between slender fingers with remarkably smooth skin: unmarked and uncreased, like a baby's.

Annie looked at it carefully. "I'll have to see it—" she swallowed and finished calmly, "in your other form."

He turned and stared straight into her eyes. He wasn't angry, but it seemed challenging anyway.

Annie stared back peaceably. "I'll need your consent now to remove it, just in case. If it needs removal, I'll be giving anesthetic."

"An-es . . ." He gave up. "What is that?"

"Painkiller."

He gave an explosive, barking laugh. "Painkiller!" Then he smiled, a wide cynical grin that seemed to go back almost to his ears. "There are no painkillers."

But he reconsidered, struck by another thought. "This anostetic. Is shot?"

Annie said, "Yes. It won't hurt much." She bit her lip. "It's a quick needle jab."

"Yes, then," he said. "The needle." He removed his shirt and trousers, standing naked.

Quickly he dropped to all fours. His eyes rolled back in his head, and the whites blossomed pink as all the blood vessels on them ruptured at once.

When his eyes came forward, the irises were silver gray.

Annie had quoted from *Lao's Guide* that werewolf metamorphosis was acutely painful. Despite any number of dramatic scenes in movies and television, involving prosthetics, makeup, and animation, BJ was unready for the real thing.

In order to grow forward freely, Vlatmir's jaw dislocated with a loud pop. His nose and upper jaw developed with open, quivering, extended sinus cavities, which grew closed afterward.

His fingers and thumbs fell off and lay in the dirt. There was no blood in them; it seemed like leprosy. Vlatmir swung from side to side wildly, looking at them. Paw pads developed on his palms, and claws on the phalanges, which re-formed from the stubs of his fingers. The base of his thumb slid under his skin and receded, under a bump like a cartoon mole, up his forearm until it stopped and a dew claw ripped through the flesh.

His tail grew rapidly from the base of his spine, naked at first and growing fur as it extended.

He screamed and fell on his side. Annie started forward, but Sugar said, "Just watch."

His body shook constantly with muscle spasms. At first he looked like a human in convulsions; then he looked more like a dog having a seizure. Gradually the convulsions became smaller and further apart. The screams became whimpers.

The whimpering stopped. He lay on the ground, panting.

Annie dropped to her knees and edged to the wolf's heaving side. She listened through her stethoscope, frowning.

"We'll have to wait," she said finally. "I can't give him anesthetic yet."

But while she was waiting, he lunged forward, grabbed his cast-off fingers from the dust in front of him and swallowed them whole.

Then he turned to look at Annie, and his wolf's jaw seemed to be grinning at her. In a dog it might look playful; on Vlatmir it looked like contempt.

Dave murmured, "Have you ever seen a grown canine with teeth that clean?"

Lee Anne said, "Not even after cleaning them." They were blinding, and the fangs were unnaturally sharp, unworn, like a puppy's new needle-sharp set.

Annie said to him, "I'm going to look you over head to tail. It's just to make sure nothing else is wrong. Okay?"

He made a soft woofing noise, not at all friendly but not angry. He held perfectly still as Annie, nervously at first and more firmly thereafter, went over his head, limbs, and torso.

"Teeth perfect . . . eyes bloodshot but apparently that's normal . . . No evidence of ear mites; probably very few parasites can survive your changing form." She felt his legs. "Wups. Maybe I spoke too soon; that feels like scabbing from bites on your front legs, around the joints. How about it, fella; have you got fleas?"

She had fallen into the light pet-talking voice small-animal doctors use to keep animals calm. She reached up to ruffle his ears.

This time the noise he made was anything but soft. She pulled her hand back. "Excuse me."

For the rest of the exam she was terse and matter-of-fact, sounding herself a bit like Vlatmir.

At the end she returned to the shoulder. "There's the tumor." She probed it. "About the size of the ball of my thumb. Just under the skin. Feels movable, superficial, symmetrical. It feels like a fatty tumor; nothing to worry about."

He turned his head and chewed at it.

"No," she said, and when he growled, "No, I mean it. It has to be dry there, so that I can clip you and sterilize it and so you won't get an infection."

Clearly, he understood. He stood patiently while she used manual clippers and clumsily trimmed a minimal amount of fur from the area, though, as Dave pointed out, "Since he can revert to human form if he doesn't like it, you could probably do his whole body."

"Now for the Surital," Annie said grimly. She expected the wolf to be trouble.

But he held his foreleg up for the injection, and for a moment looked almost tame. She tied off the vein quickly, and BJ was frankly envious, now more than ever, of how steady Annie's hands were and how smoothly the injection went. Vlatmir didn't so much as twitch when Annie inserted the needle and pressed the plunger. He lay in the dirt, apparently resisting unconsciousness.

"That's it," she said. She stroked his back, though clearly she didn't like patting him. "Relax."

It took longer than she expected, but he went out. Annie said with obvious relief, "Unroll that surgical kit, and let's do this quickly."

"Do you want these?" Dave asked.

She looked up. Dave was holding one-by-one-inch splints and tape from the truck. "We could rig up a restraint."

"Or hog-tie him," Lee Anne said.

Annie smiled and shook her head, looking professional still but very young. "We'll be done before he wakes up."

Dave kept the splints out anyway.

The surgery was simple: a quick lateral incision, a swipe with gauze to clear away the blood momentarily, and a deft twist of a small, blunt dissection scalpel and scissors underneath the tumor. She lifted it out with a forceps and placed it in a jar. "There you are, Dr. Dobbs. Will that be of any use to you?"

"Or to somebody," he said. "Good thought. Seal it up and we'll take it back."

She looked longingly at the healthy flesh exposed in the incision walls. "I suppose it would be unethical to take an unneeded sample without consent."

"Yep." He added, "But we need one anyway, to biopsy the tumor. How can we tell that this is benign if we don't know what his normal flesh is like? Make it a small one." He frowned. "And make it quick; he doesn't seem very far under."

She took it very quickly; Vlatmir's breathing was getting more rapid. Annie pinched his foreleg to check for a reflex, and was disturbed to see a twitch.

"You want me to give him more?" BJ said.

"No," Annie said decisively. "I gave him Surital; the amount shouldn't matter. Let me just finish quickly."

She reached into the pack and took out a small curved needle and some zero-aught gut. She took the needle in a needle holder, threaded the needle, and twisted it under the wolf's skin.

Waking, he gave a full-throated growl and snapped his jaws up and sideways.

Annie pulled her arm back nearly fast enough. Teeth raked down the side of her arm.

He licked the few drops of blood on his muzzle and sprang at her.

Sugar slid in front of her, jacket wrapped around his forearm, and stuck his arm between the wolf's jaws. With his left hand he tried to grab the wolf by the neck, but it was too large and too furious to control one-handed.

The wolf snarled, wrenching Sugar's arm this way and that. Unable to bite, he rammed suddenly into Sugar's solar plexus. Sugar doubled over, and the wolf leaped at Annie, who was still dazedly holding her arm.

From either side of her, Dave and Lee Anne stepped forward, bringing up the splints in their hands like billy clubs. Dave struck Vlatmir on the lower jaw; Lee Anne, much harder, in the throat.

The wolf fell back, choking.

BJ, behind them, brought up her own stick. It bounced in her suddenly uncontrolled hand and fell into the dirt.

Vlatmir snapped at each of their splints. Neither of them was foolish enough to let him get a purchase on the sticks. Lee Anne rapped him on the muzzle, hard, and snapped, "Lie down."

The look he gave said a great deal about his intelligence, and nothing good about his nature.

"We have us a pole on the truck," she said, "with a steel choke-noose on it. You want us to get that out, or you want to behave?"

Vlatmir, red-eyed and fur hackles raised, ready to spring, crouched in front of Lee Anne.

Sugar tried to say something to her, but he was still gasping for air.

BJ put a hand on Lee Anne's shoulder. "Lower the stick. Slowly."

"Don't want to."

"Do it anyway. Please."

Reluctantly, Lee Anne lowered her stick. The wolf did not spring, but nothing else changed. He looked up at Lee Anne, snarling furiously.

BJ added, "And stop looking directly into his eyes. He thinks it's a challenge."

"It is a challenge," Lee Anne said stubbornly.

"Well, unless you can rip his throat out with your teeth, cut it out."

Reluctantly, glowering, Lee Anne lowered her eyes. Vlatmir relaxed from his crouch and grinned at her, teeth showing and tongue hanging out. He appeared to be laughing.

Then he howled as his teeth cracked audibly and fell out.

He crouched, shivering, as his fur fell out and his tail fell off, twitching in the dust. The open hole at the base of his spine grew over without scarring.

He turned around, picked up the tail in his rapidly swelling paws, folded it, and swallowed it whole, this time with a semi-human face. BJ watched, sickened, but now she understood the mechanism: preserving as much mass as possible.

Moments later, Vlatmir the man pulled himself upright in front of them. He was covered in a sheen of sweat, and his muscles were taut with the pain.

He glanced at his shoulder, which was clean and unscarred. "The cut. Still there. On the other me." He ran his fingers over the smooth skin. "I feel it."

Annie swallowed and said fairly calmly, "I was unable to close."

He was staring into space, troubled. Finally he said, "I bit you."

She nodded, eyes wide.

He looked at her, head cocked to one side. "But you live," he said, puzzled and unrepentant.

"We stopped you," Dave said.

"Did you?" He stared at Dave in surprise.

Lee Anne said, "Yep."

Vlatmir stepped toward her. "How?"

"Don't be concerned, sir," she said. "It wasn't hard at all."

He looked at her with his eyes narrowed, and for a moment the glinting blue eyes looked silver. "I remember. And I will remember."

Annie, all 105 pounds of her, stepped between them. "Perhaps we should finish the consultation." She held up the still-intact jar with the tumor in it. "We'll take this for a biopsy, if you wish—"

He casually swept the jar from her hand and smashed it against a rock.

After a frozen moment, Annie said, "Well. No biopsy, then. That's probably all right; it seemed like a fatty tumor, and you really didn't need to have it removed." She swallowed. "I have some post-surgical advice for you, but you may feel that it isn't needed."

"I heal." He grinned at her, showing his beautiful, clean, and unworn human teeth. "See?"

"I see." Annie said with barely a tremor, "Now that you've bitten me, will I become a . . . one of the Wyr?"

Vlatmir laughed shortly and loudly, not bothering to hide his contempt. "You?"

She colored. Annie was exceptionally patient, but everyone has limits. "I'm relieved. Do you wish to transform back so that I can suture the wound?"

"No. Not twice." He smiled again, and she stepped back. "I hunger enough." He looked perceptibly thinner than he had been when they met.

"In that case, be sure to keep the wound free of dirt if it comes back when you . . . when you metamorphose again. Avoid licking it, and don't roll in the dirt until the wound is closed."

BJ listened, impressed. Annie was doing quite well on her feet, considering that she was giving instructions to a naked man who had just tried to tear her throat out.

"And send us another message through Stein's if you need us again," she finished. "That's all."

"Yes." He bent over and felt in his trousers. "Money." He held it out to her as another man might hold a disagreeable snack for a hungry pet.

Annie said, "Dr. Dobbs?"

Sugar came forward and took the gold. "Thanks. One other thing." He paused.

"Yes."

"Tell your people that if they can't guarantee their good behavior, they don't get medical care. And from now on, they'll submit to muzzling."

Vlatmir said in a dangerously soft voice, "The Wyr never submit. You insult us."

"That doesn't matter," Sugar said, unwavering. "These students are in my care. I don't intend to put them at risk again."

"Not at risk?" He looked at them, and laughed low in his throat, like a growl. "Not at risk?" But he turned back to Sugar and curled his lip back. "No muzzle. Not for the Wyr."

"It's not open to discussion. Tell them."

Vlatmir turned away.

He dressed with his back to them, not so much out of shyness as contempt, daring them to attack. When he was done, he loped away through the grass without a backward glance.

They stood watching while he turned onto the roadway, paused at a signpost (sniffing it, BJ thought), and turned down a lane. He seemed to vanish into the distance while they were watching him.

Annie said irrelevantly, "But I love dogs."

"I even love wolves," Lee Anne said. "Got pictures of them from all over, and articles about the red wolf being reintroduced to the Carolinas—I even got a T-shirt of a wolf howling at the moon." She grinned at BJ. "Want it? It'd look nice on you, and I don't like it as much anymore."

BJ only said, "If he despises money, where did he get it?"

Dave said, "You tell me where he went just now, and I'll tell you where he got the money."

"Okay. Now: Why did he take the money, and why did someone give it to him?"

Sugar said, "Do you have any guesses of your own, BJ?"

BJ said flatly, "He didn't need that tumor off, and he knew it. He got the money specially for his appointment. Why did he get the appointment?"

"To check us out, you're saying?"

"And why did he want to check us out?"

"Maybe he's a cop," Dave said. And froze.

And in a second they were all remembering a bloodstained body with the word *justice* written beside it. And no one could tell them what the Inspector General looked like. . . .

Sugar was the first to recover. "I don't think he's the . . . that he's a cop. He looks more like a candidate for the other side of the law." He changed the subject. "Not a bad job fighting with those splints, people."

"Thank you, sir." Lee Anne added, "The practice at Stein's probably helped."

"Most likely. BJ, you might need some more practice. Is that hand giving you trouble, BJ?" Sugar asked indifferently.

"I'm just clumsy."

"Nice job cutting, Annie."

"Not so good with the anesthetic."

"What was the dosage?" Sugar asked.

Annie said helplessly, "A four percent solution of Surital, one milliliter per five pounds. That's twice what I'd give a rottweiler, about one and a half times what I'd give a normal wolf."

"Maybe he reacts differently to it."

"I think—" BJ said, and shut up quickly.

Sugar turned around. "You think what?"

"Nothing," she said. "I think his metabolism might need more pain resistance than a normal wolf his weight, that's all."

But she had thought something else: When Vlatmir had stretched his human arm out to hand Sugar the money, she had seen small bluish purple points on Vlatmir's arm: needle tracks.

That was, of course, impossible. There was absolutely no way to bring drugs into Crossroads.

Except that the vet school had a pharmacy, and Sugar could release drugs from the school.

BJ had an extremely uncomfortable ride home.

E·I·G·H·T·E·E·N

THEY WERE CAMPING again, although they were only a little ways inside Crossroads; Sugar wanted an early start in the morning. They had set up camp in the field where BJ had treated the unicorn. It was a little after sunset. The tarp, slung between two small trees, was purely a precaution; the night promised to be warm, clear, and possibly even free of bugs.

Dinner, a stew made from lamb donated by Fields, was excellent. Annie had found some sage and some parsley growing near the camp, and Lee Anne had packed salt and pepper shakers. Dave, with a flourish, brought out some fresh-baked bread he had purchased at Stein's that day.

Sugar, after seeing them settled, had driven to Stein's; he was, as he said, "down on sleeping with students, even bedroll to bedroll." Plus he had a free bed waiting, and had some magazines to drop off to Stein. He warned them to be sensible and said he'd be back in the morning.

Dave had made ominous comments about predators, and had gone through the motions of volunteering to stand watch, but they couldn't take the threat seriously enough. They had taken out their bedrolls and were now lazing against them, too relaxed to bother unrolling them just yet. BJ listened to the stream nearby, drifting off easily and peacefully.

The shrubs near the camp rustled, and a voice said, "Io!"

"Hello, Stefan," Annie said cheerily, and as he bounded into full view, "Wups."

Stefan was naked except for his backpack. He was definitely a faun, and quite definitely male, though his genitals were half-hidden in the thick wool at his loins.

He glanced down. "Excuse me," he said easily. "I will put on shorts if you wish."

"That's okay," Lee Anne said, and Dave said amusedly, "No sweat." Even Annie protested politely, but Stefan shook his head and fumbled in his battered pack until he could pull out a pair of gym shorts from their world. In full view of the female students, he put them on. "There," he said, satisfied. "That is modest."

He turned to BJ and said in carefully rehearsed words, "It is good to see you again, BJ. How are you?"

"Fine."

"I would like very much if you would go with me," he said eagerly and awkwardly. "I have something I would like to show you."

Dave snickered.

BJ stood. "Okay. Should I bring a flashlight?"

Stefan looked confused. She picked it up, clicking it on and off.

"A torch," he said. James Herriot had left his mark on Stefan's language. "No, better we go in the dark."

He gestured to her and receded into the underbrush. Annie said, "I'll set up your bedroll for you. He's in a hurry."

She scrambled after him.

It was almost completely dark. The moon, though full, was still behind the plateau to the east. Stefan was headed up the winding trail by the stream.

It seemed to BJ that every third rock was in her way. She nearly ended up in the stream several times. Once she gave a quick cry and fumbled for Stefan's hand; he grabbed her barely in time to keep her from going headlong into a pool.

He slowed down after that, though he was clearly too excited to want to. "We don't have much time before it starts."

"Before what?" By now she was using her hands beside the stream; Stefan, alongside her, was having to hold himself back from bounding from rock to rock in the increasing upgrade.

"Before the unicorns."

Wobbly balance and all, she was alongside him instantly. "What about them?"

"Before they mate."

BJ had a wild, heart-rending flash of imagination: "Hello, Mom? Make a cup of tea and call me back. You'll love this."

Aloud she panted, "Do they have a long mating season?"

"It is only tonight, for a few minutes. It must be during the spring eclipse."

BJ's astronomy was vague. "How often is that?"

"Every few years. Other years, nothing."

It was well past moonrise, and finally the moon was above the cliffs. BJ had accepted as natural the same sun rising in the same part of the sky, but was startled to see the moon showing its usual face. She thought of it as exclusively the earth's moon; this was as though it were being unfaithful. Besides, the stars had been different, hadn't they? She made a mental note to tell Dr. Protera, author of the reality tectonics article, about the moon when she got back to Virginia.

She skidded twice trying to get over the rock lip by the waterfall. Stefan had laughed at her slips down below, dismissing them; now he seemed politely concerned, offering her his hand to pull over the ledge.

Stefan tiptoed down into the small bowl of the glade. BJ stood staring, amazed.

The rock rim of the cliff widened out and sloped upward, making a natural bowl. Years of erosion and plant growth had left thick, black soil on the rock. BJ and Stefan were at the edge of a small hollow with trees at either edge, a meadow and a pool between them, and at the far end of the pool, a forty-foot cliff and a wall of waterfalls, broken every few feet by the rock face so that it dropped almost noiselessly into the pool it had worn for itself. Ferns grew on every rock projecting near or out of the spray; the falls were framed in and dotted with them. BJ could imagine it in sunlight. A path wound up between the ferns, close to the falls.

The meadow was awash in flowers, which looked blue even in the moonlight: pansies, irises by the water's edge, and lush, velvety blossoms BJ didn't recognize.

The small woods at the edge of the bowl had willows by the water, pine and oak by the cliffs, cedar in between. The air was rich with pine, cedar, and the sweet smell of the blossoms.

Stefan led her to the nearest trees, gnarled cedars with a soft bed of ferns beneath them. He leaned against one tree and gestured at the neighboring one. "Now we wait."

BJ leaned back. The tree, its broad trunk slanting sideways from the wind at the cliff top, provided a perfect chair back. She half closed her eyes, listening to owls, spring peepers, some sounds she half remembered from camping, and the inevitable crickets throbbing softly in the warm night air. Soon she was nodding as rhythmically as the blossoms in the bed of flowers.

She opened her eyes slowly and sleepily, and rubbed them. Her hand brushed wool; Stefan had taken a sweater from his pack and wrapped it around her as she slept. She smiled to herself, and tried to discover what had awakened her.

Looking up, she saw that the full moon now had a crescent bitten out of it. The glade was darker, and the eclipse was beginning. Could that have registered in her sleep, when it seemed so much like a dream already?

Then she noticed how quiet it had become. The owls and frogs were silent, and the crickets dying away. Shortly the last of the crickets fell silent.

"You are awakened," Stefan said quietly in her ear. His breath tickled. "Good. It begins." BJ leaned forward, peering through the fading moonlight as the light in the glade softened and grew fainter.

"They come," Stefan said, barely making a sound at all. She saw his arm, half in shadow, pointing ahead.

Two serenities of unicorns moved silently into the glade. One group wound down a path by the waterfall and strode through the pool to the glade. The water lilies seemed to part for them and glide together behind them.

The other serenity stepped between the willows on the far edge of the pool and followed a path along the shore. A flash of metal flickered in the moonlight from the horn of the third unicorn in the new serenity. BJ leaned forward, trying to see her former patient better.

The unicorns regarded each other across the field of blue flowers. They lowered their horns and tested their neck muscles, shaking their horns slowly back and forth. BJ watched, concerned; it looked as though it would be a fight, similar to mating ritual combat in other herd animals.

Then the two serenities moved toward each other, breaking apart as they came. Each male sought a female, each female a male, and they strode forward unhurriedly, horns lowered.

The first pair met. The male presented his horn forward, and as BJ caught her breath, the female swung her head sideways and struck her horn against his.

Their horns rang with the single bell tones BJ had expected, but roughly a third apart. The two of them held their positions for a moment, then lowered their horns and let the flowers

deaden the sound. They nodded to each other, forelegs bending in an almost-bow, and parted to try a pairing with another
unicorn.

Soon the glade was filled with the soft reverberation of horns
striking on horns, sometimes making a harmonious interval, sometimes (rarely) a terrible dissonance. The unicorns whose pitches
would be unharmonious nearly always instinctively avoided each
other.

Two quite close to Stefan and BJ struck, and BJ gasped as a
single powerful note throbbed and rose from the two unicorns.
The other animals turned their heads to listen, delicate white ears
pricking up.

Then the female laid its horn across the male's neck, the male
across the female's, and the sound died away. He moved beside
her and, sides touching, they walked quietly into the woods
beyond the pool.

Quite close to BJ, the unicorn with the mended horn came to
a female.

She put her hand to her mouth like a heroine from a melodrama,
afraid to breathe or move. What if his horn broke when he struck
his against hers? What if the note from it had come untuned since
the mending?

She grabbed blindly at Stefan's hand; it clenched her own.

The unicorn with the mended horn swung its head sideways and
struck against the horn of the female. The single note, perfect and
echoing, rose and swelled until they each lay their horns against
the other's neck.

Stefan happily laid an arm on her shoulders. "You did it,"
he said. "I would give anything to be able to do that for a
unicorn."

BJ was all but flying herself. "What are the chances now that
they'll produce a . . . a foal?"

"A kidling," he corrected, and his eyes were shining as he
looked at her. "Always. Once they mate, always. Congratulations, Dr. BJ."

"Thank you."

They watched the unicorns chime and leave together, through
the eclipse. Finally, a single unicorn was left alone. She lowered
her horn, struck it on a stone beside the pool and raised her head,
letting the sound ring and peal throughout the glade.

When no male came, she dipped her horn in the water and let
the sound die away. She strode alone back into the pool and made
her solitary way up the path by the waterfall.

"It's over," Stefan said. "Now they go to mate. Later they will return to their serenities, and in the fall the females will all bear kidlings."

"What about the one who didn't find a mate?"

"She will try to mate again when there is another eclipse in the spring."

"Will that happen again next year?"

"I don't know," he said honestly. "Did you like seeing it?"

"It was . . ." she faltered, looking for a word.

He looked stricken. "You can't say anything good? You didn't like it?"

"I loved it. It was wonderful." She watched as the lone female unicorn disappeared over the top of the waterfall.

"I'm glad. I wanted you to see it."

"Thank you so much," she said back. On impulse she kissed his cheek.

He kissed her cheek shyly, then moved immediately to kiss her lips.

She was kissing back when her mind made a sudden, horrid leap back to the reflex testing in Dr. Hitori's office: trying to keep her tongue out, being unable to.

She pulled away. "This is not a good idea."

He was hurt immediately. "Why not?"

"Because I'm—because I don't think it's a good idea." How could she tell him that she didn't dare start a relationship? He'd ask why, and she wasn't ready to tell anyone. Plus Stefan, whose feelings ran close to the surface, would be devastated.

But he didn't look for another answer. "All right," he said petulantly. "Perhaps you think I'm strange. You don't need to explain." He turned away. "Time we should start back."

BJ nearly fell in the dark several times. Once, trying to step over a fallen log, she fell sideways into the brush. Stefan helped her up carefully, avoiding touching her body.

"I may be strange," Stefan said with just a trace of hurt malice, "but you are clumsy." She had no answer.

BJ tiptoed back, but inevitably she knocked into one of the packs in the dark. It fell over with quite a bit of noise, for being stuffed with clothes and books.

"And people make rude remarks about me," Dave said sleepily as she slid into her sleeping bag.

"As well they should," Lee Anne said as sleepily.

"Are you all right?" Annie said quietly after the others had subsided.

BJ lay in her sleeping bag, facing away from everyone so they wouldn't see how close she was to tears. Oh, I'm just dandy, she thought. I'm dying, I'm losing my motor skills, and I don't dare fall in love anymore.

"I'm okay," she said aloud.

N·I·N·E·T·E·E·N

SUGAR WOKE THEM by honking the horn and bawling out the truck window, "Daylight in the swamp!"

"What swamp?" Dave said, but could not help glancing down the road, as though the landscape might have changed in the night. They rose stiffly and packed quickly.

In the car, Sugar handed them pieces of brown bread with fresh cream butter melted into cuts in it. The bread was still steaming. "Can't have you fainting on me. We've got a case today."

They were suddenly alert. Annie could not help glancing at the copy of *Lao's Guide* on the dashboard.

He tucked it in his black satchel. "Not today." He swung onto the road, checking his map—this time, BJ noted, a pencil sketch in the wavery hand BJ associated with old men. "This is kind of a quiz on what you learned in other rotations."

For a moment they relaxed, but only for a moment. None of them spoke during the ride; they were all trying to guess what they needed, and reviewing what they knew.

Fields met them at the turnoff. "Good morning, good morning! You don't get up with farmers, I see."

He smiled genially down on them. Annie had the grace to smile back even as she buttoned her blouse higher.

The shepherd's name was B'cu, with a click. He was human, though he didn't speak English; his original language was Swahili. Fields translated. "I have taught him, Stefan has taught him, but he wants to know what you can teach him."

At Sugar's prompting, they lectured in rotation—lessons on diet, dehydration, optimum breeding cycles, infection, precautions at lambing time, entropion in newborn lambs. For much of it he nodded politely; for some of it he listened with astonishment, and smiled with a dazzling gratitude.

There were some nursing lambs in B'cu's flock. He watched, amused, while they tried to catch them, then ran the lambs down with a long-strided ease that left them gaping.

While Annie was demonstrating a dental exam, BJ asked Fields, "Will he remember what we tell him?"

"Better than you remember what you read. He has never used a book."

Sugar did little to conceal his surprise; Annie was by far the best at teaching through Fields. She spoke slowly and carefully, repeated where necessary, asked for questions, apologized for being unclear. At the end of the lesson, B'cu bent down and put a hand on her blond hair, laughing and speaking a series of rapid clicks. She smiled back uncertainly and turned to Fields.

"Now," Fields said, "he will teach you."

B'cu scratched in the dirt and spoke in a firm, clear voice. He rapped his staff on a stone whenever one of them turned away, waiting for Fields to translate.

He spoke of nursing ailments, and udders torn by brambles. He held a sheep's head and made them watch it chew cud, explaining what the rhythm told about diet and health. He pulled a ram's horns back and forth, speaking in gasps about measures of strength and how to protect the weaker breeding rams from the stronger. He lectured them on hybrid crosses, showing knowledge each of them had received in undergraduate Biology 1100 but never applied.

Through it all, Sugar grinned smugly at them, but BJ noticed him taking notes on the inevitable scraps of paper from his pockets.

Toward the end of the lecture, BJ heard hooves on rock above them and risked turning around. Melina, homespun bag under her arm and walking stick in her hand, was watching from the rise. BJ caught Sugar's eye; he nodded. She excused herself through Fields and walked uphill, smiling.

Melina did not smile back.

BJ paused and stood awkwardly, wondering what to say. The now-familiar song of the blue-backs sounded in the distance. "Hello."

"Io." For someone who had kissed BJ on the lips, Melina was surprisingly distant.

"Your bag looks nice." It was Melina's only clothing today. Dave probably would have leered, but he was busy among the sheep, below. "Why don't you get a knapsack from outside, like Stefan?"

She stiffened. "This one I made myself. Stefan is more fond than I am of things from your world."

"How is he?"

"Fine, I suppose." Melina stared intently out at the meadow. B'cu was showing Lee Anne, Dave, and Annie the finer points of diagnosing ovine diseases from their stools.

"Have you seen him?"

"This morning. He keeps to himself now." Melina turned and looked angrily at BJ.

BJ swallowed and asked a question about what should have been a matter of indifference to her: "If you don't mind my asking, are you and he involved, or related, or anything?"

Melina considered the question and answered bluntly. "I'm not his sister. I'm not his lover. But we were lambs together, and I do not like seeing him hurt."

BJ had no response. Eventually, Melina shrugged and walked off toward Stein's, with the rapid steady pace of someone who walks every day by necessity.

BJ turned and saw Fields regarding her sadly, almost without sexual overtones. Her ears blushing red, she said hotly, "Do you have something you'd like to say to me?"

Fields shook his head slowly from side to side, barely disturbing his shaggy curls. "I do not need to. I think you are learning a great lesson from your world, that it is always the good and not the bad who create their own damnation."

BJ went down to the others, and was grateful when they all got into the van to go home.

It was past noon, and they were beginning to think in terms of something more than bread in their stomachs. Unless the Road Crews had changed this route as well, the road they were on would lead them past Stein's; BJ was willing to confront an angry Melina again for the sake of a hot meal.

Sugar stopped at the hill before Stein's, opened the truck door, and stood on the brake and clutch as he shouted over the cab and up the hill questioningly.

Carron was hard to miss, standing on the hilltop. He was

waving his arms, and his shout carried even against the breeze: "Polyta!"

Sugar, defying common sense, drove the truck straight up the hill. The truck rocked from side to side, clanking as boulders struck beneath it.

Lee Anne stared ahead and said, uncharacteristically, "Oh, shit."

Polyta was lying down, sprawled on her side. The entire mass of the foal bulged across her belly and upper side. BJ didn't understand why Lee Anne was so worried until she remembered that Polyta's reproductive system was equine.

Polyta was exhausted; if she didn't deliver the foal, she would die.

Without a word, Sugar went straight to the back of the truck and grabbed a sleeve. Lee Anne went straight to Polyta's flanks and lifted her tail.

Polyta's vulva was edematous—swollen from long labor. Lee Anne stroked Polyta's sides. "Relax now," she said soothingly. "We'll take care of it. You relax."

Polyta turned her head. "I can't." Her eyes were sunken and foreboding.

Sugar lubricated the sleeve, put his arm into her, and said almost immediately, "Yep." He withdrew his arm and said, "I guess you know that the . . . child is backward in the womb, what we call a bad presentation. Breech birth. You both know that means trouble."

"Can you shift it?" Polyta said, and cried aloud as another contraction shook her.

"Not really. Even a horse foal is way too long to twist around, and a centaur—no. I'm sorry, but I just don't see how."

"It's because we're different sizes," Carron said bleakly. "I did this, by choosing her."

"I chose you," Polyta corrected, and tried to smile at him. Carron wouldn't smile back.

"Size isn't the problem, sir." Lee Anne was at the truck now, scrubbing her arms down. "Horses don't always have trouble when the parents are different sizes—" She broke off, realizing that Carron didn't really care why it was happening. "Sometimes these presentations happen; we don't know why."

"Sometimes they happen," Carron agreed. He looked away from them all.

When he turned back, his face was set, his arms folded. "Do you still have the wire you used to saw the horse foal apart?"

"No," Polyta gasped. Droplets of sweat gathered on her face and trickled down. "Kill the mother, not the child. Cut me open."

"Caesarean?" Lee Anne said sharply to Sugar.

Sugar, watching Carron's deliberately impassive face, shook his head slowly. "I'll bet she has to be ready to travel soon."

"Two days." He said it faintly, but firmly. "Over rocks and streams, to river bottomland."

"And if she can't leave?"

"Then she stays and starves. We would kill her, to keep her from being hurt." He looked at them without apology, but would not look at Polyta. "I can't hold my people here, keep them hungry, simply because I love someone."

"Then kill me now, and save the child." Tears ran down Polyta's face, but she sounded no less determined for that.

"No." Carron ambled to just in front of her. "We save the mother."

"The child, or neither of us, Nesyos."

"Who is Carron here?" he said sharply.

"You," she said through clenched teeth, "but only till I kill you."

He looked down at her and suddenly smiled, grabbing for her hand. She made an effort and reached up to touch his fingers, and they locked hands, her arm muscles straining to hang on.

But she couldn't sustain it; soon her hand dropped and she sank back. Carron turned back to Sugar and the students. "Cut the foal apart," he said flatly. "Now."

Using her left hand, Lee Anne opened a cabinet on the truck. She stood staring at the Gigli wire for the fetotomy. BJ felt sick.

Instead, Lee Anne pulled out a cloth and laid the OB chains out on it. They were smooth, shiny link chains, with a rectangular open loop at either end.

Sugar said to her, "Ever pulled a foal?"

"A few." She jiggled the chains, checking for twists and kinks. "Mostly they just popped out."

"Any bad presentations? Backward?"

"Twice," Lee Anne said, as though it were a forced confession.

"Did they live?"

Lee Anne ignored him and turned to Carron. "With all due respect, sir, we intend to deliver the child."

"If you lose both mother and child," he said coldly, "it will be murder, by you. You will be killed, trampled, in the manner of the Hippoi."

"I will be killed," Sugar contradicted him. "These young people are . . . well, are my foals, in my charge, and nothing you can do about it."

Carron nodded once quickly. "I understand." He seemed less and less able to speak, more withdrawn and tense.

Sugar turned to the students. "Be a smooth team, folks. I'd like to drive home with you when you go." He nodded respectfully to Lee Anne. "She's been your case. You start."

She opened her mouth to say something, then changed her mind. "Okay. Ma'am, we'd like you to get up now. Come on. You can do it."

Polyta struggled tiredly erect. It was the only time BJ had seen either of the Hippoi wave arms for balance, a fairly useless gesture on someone with four legs. Her legs tottered like a newborn foal's.

Lee Anne put on a sleeve, lubricated it, and stood sideways, sliding her arm into Polyta's vagina, letting one end of the chain drape along her arm.

Carron's expression remained unchanged. Polyta's face was too taut and agonized to change.

Lee Anne, however, looked like a cartoon, grimacing and waggling eyebrows with each arm movement. BJ, watching, remembered her first year in vet school, the first time she had put on a palpation sleeve and slid her hand inside a cow's rectum. Dr. Laurien had ignored BJ's discomfort and said flatly, "Feel around in there till you can tell where the ovaries are. Should be under your hand."

BJ, face averted, had groped dutifully beyond the cervix, but had never found the ovaries. It had taken her three more tries until she was even faintly sure of herself.

Lee Anne was groping to check the other rear hoof of the colt, and she had no guarantee that it was within reach and not tucked up. If she didn't find it, nothing would enable them to pull the fetus out whole without tearing Polyta apart.

She stretched deep in, the cords in her neck standing out, and she said suddenly, "Got it."

And Sugar was there, his left shirtsleeve torn off, his arm glistening with disinfectant. "You know a half hitch when you see one?"

Lee Anne grinned at him, but her face was dewed with sweat, and her lower lip was bloody where she'd bitten it. "Can't see it, but I tied one around the leg."

"Okay. Keep tension on it, tight, and pull it up real slow."

She started. She closed her eyes, took a deep breath, and tried again. Finally she said, "It's not moving."

"Happens." Sugar stretched his left arm out, slid forward, and suddenly they were chest to chest, like dancers. Tall as she was, she looked as though she could put her head on his shoulder.

"Now," he said, "somebody hand me the second chain."

A second later his arm muscles twitched. "Okay. I've got the other leg, and I've got the chain. I'm pulling."

The other students watched helplessly: BJ unable to stand still, Annie with worried calm, Dave with clenched fists. Lee Anne, keeping tension on her chain, gasped a moment later, "All set?"

"Should be, but I ain't. Mine's stuck, too."

"Retropulse?" Lee Anne said. She didn't sound happy. She said to Polyta, "Ma'am, we're gonna push the foal back in for a second. Please fight us as little as you can."

BJ grabbed a basin, poured from the distilled water in the truck, and tapped Dave and Annie, pointing to Polyta's shuddering human torso. "I'd help, but Annie's lighter."

Annie looked blank, then got it. She hopped on Dave's shoulders and sponged Polyta's forehead and chest. "Hold on," she said soothingly. "Just hold on. We're going to make it."

Sugar said, grimacing, "Now."

Sugar and Lee Anne, keeping the free ends of the chains in sight, pushed in on the foal, then ducked simultaneously to unbend the rear legs.

The whole thing, BJ thought, was begging for disaster; she had only seen OB chains used on cattle, and none of the students but Lee Anne had worked on even a normal foaling.

Sugar did a last test of the chains, then said, "Front and center." Dave and Annie ran back. He passed the ends back to BJ, Dave, and Annie. "Okay, start soft and build up. Pull and keep pulling."

The tension at first was next to nothing, a slow, steady tug. Nothing happened.

"A little more," Sugar ordered. "More . . . more . . . hang on. Anything?" he said to Lee Anne.

She blew ineffectually at a strand of sweat-drenched hair, trying to keep it out of her eyes. "Maybe a little slippage. Nothing much."

"Still hung up. Try to reach it."

Lee Anne leaned against Polyta's buttock, moving her arm in as far as it would go. "Not on my side."

"Not here, either. Pull again," Sugar said, bracing his feet.

They pulled, gradually building up to the kind of strain that left the chain quivering in a straight line between the students and Polyta. BJ's arms were sore, and even Dave was making grunting noises and furrowing his forehead.

The tips of the hooves appeared.

"It's coming," Lee Anne said loudly.

Sugar barked, "Slow!"

They pulled still harder, trying not to get excited and overdo it. The legs gradually slid out between Sugar's and Lee Anne's hands, then stopped.

"Hindquarters coming," Lee Anne called. "Pull steady, pull hard, be ready to stop if we sing out." She caught herself and looked for reassurance to Sugar.

He nodded grimly. "From here it's work. Fingertips out, Lee Anne. How you holding up?"

"Real fine," she said loudly enough for Polyta to hear. "I bet we'll be done in a few minutes." Her eyebrows were pulled down and together with the strain on her inserted arm. More softly she said, "This is awful slow for a horse."

"Pull," Sugar said loudly.

Dave said, "Rolling," and leaned back from the chain, digging his feet in. BJ and Annie redoubled their efforts, BJ praying fervently that her muscles would all do exactly as she wanted them to.

Nothing happened. They increased pressure, and still nothing happened, and finally Sugar said, "Here we go. Heads up, Lee Anne."

Sugar and Lee Anne moved apart marginally, Polyta screamed, and the foal's legs moved all the way out. The hindquarters followed.

"We know it's a colt now," Dave said.

Sugar ran a hand up the leg, found the femoral artery, and said, "Hell of a pulse. He's still alive."

Suddenly none of them were tired. Lee Anne buried her arm almost to the shoulder inside and announced, "I got me the right front leg here. I'm straightening it. . . . Okay."

"Left front leg—damn." Sugar said nothing for what seemed a long time and finally said, "That's what's keeping us; it's hung up under the pelvic brim."

They considered in silence. The only sound was Polyta's breathing, coming in short, loud gasps.

Finally Lee Anne said, "Retropulse again."

But they didn't get a chance; Polyta groaned and her legs gave under her. Sugar pulled free and pulled Lee Anne away as Polyta's body collapsed sideways.

Carron dropped to his knees in front of her, his big hands holding her head out of the dirt.

"Can you get up, ma'am?" Lee Anne asked. There was no reply. Lee Anne dropped to her side and put her sleeved arm back inside Polyta. "I'm gonna try again."

There was no room for two. Sugar said dubiously, "You think you're strong enough to do it while she's lying down?"

Lee Anne licked her bloodstained lip, and finally said, "Don't know, sir. I want to try." She pushed.

The colt didn't move. Lee Anne's hand slipped, but she got her footing quickly. "I'm sorry about that, ma'am. You all right?"

There was no reply.

Carron said urgently, "Polyta!"

She made a confused sleepy noise, but that was all.

"We're gonna have to get back up," Sugar said almost pleadingly.

Carron bent down and put his arms on her human torso; his muscles flexed until the veins stood out in relief. "I'll help," he said between his teeth.

Her legs twitched, and she looked tiredly up at him.

"Up, love," Carron said. She didn't answer. He pulled on her body, straining. "Polyta, stand up. For the child."

Polyta angrily heaved her body up in one powerful motion, throwing Lee Anne flat in the dirt behind her.

Lee Anne lay on the ground, her sleeved arm straight up like a fallen center fielder holding a fly ball.

Carron held on to Polyta, helping her stay upright. Sugar helped Lee Anne up. "Sleeve still clean?"

"Yep." She moved back to Polyta's flanks.

Sugar joined her. "We'll have to retropulse one more time. Polyta, we're gonna push the colt back in a little; try not to fight us."

He turned around. "You on the chains, tug once and then relax." Sugar sounded, for him, frantic. They tugged, and he said almost into Lee Anne's face, "Now, dammit, now."

Lee Anne shoved on the colt, practically doing a handstand off it. Sugar looked like Atlas, pressing in on it. The muscles on his arms bulged.

The colt's body moved in three or four inches, and Sugar straightened up and all but dived against Polyta's hindquarters, twisting his arm this way and that inside her.

Finally he said shakily, "The left front leg's okay now, I think. Still okay on your side, Lee Anne?"

"Fine, I think." She was flat against Polyta, feeling as deep in as she could. "Ready to roll."

"Okay." He took a deep breath and said quietly, "Light pull on the chains."

They pulled.

After all the preparation, the birth took less than thirty seconds, the colt sliding out smoothly and quickly. Lee Anne and BJ grabbed him, lowering him to the ground and quickly untying his hind legs.

The human torso was stretched straight forward from the horse back, as though it were diving. BJ imagined that in a normal birth, the centaur colt would dive headfirst from the womb.

Sugar slapped the human part between the shoulder blades while it was still prone. The child coughed, shuddering, spat, cried for only a few seconds, and stopped.

"Is that good or bad?" Dave whispered.

"Bad for babies, normal for foals," Annie whispered back.

The colt struggled to its wobbly legs, spreading them wide and balancing precariously.

Slowly the human part of the colt straightened up, like a child pulling up from toe-touches.

He looked like a slightly babyish eight-year-old boy. His soaking hair was plastered flat to his head. His mouth opened, and he gave a baby's wail, oddly mixed with a whinny.

Polyta's breasts lactated suddenly, and she gave an inarticulate cry and grabbed for the head of the boy, hugging him tightly.

Carron, sidling up to her, seemed to be dreaming. He shook himself and turned toward Sugar.

"What is your true name?"

"Charles Franklin Dobbs."

"And yours?"

"Lee Anne Radford Harrison."

"Then those are his names," Carron said. "We'll put them in one name somehow."

He was bent almost double, wonderingly stroking the head of his son.

"That's too much for one child," Lee Anne said. "Why not just call him Sugar Lee?"

"Sugarly," Polyta said, making it one word. "It means sweet. Yes." She laughed weakly, happy but exhausted.

"Sounds good." Lee Anne slumped against the side of the

truck. The others walked back and forth mechanically, cleaning and storing the equipment, one eye on the nursing centaur colt.

Sugar walked over to her. "You're getting our truck all messy."

"That seems a shame."

"We can clean it later." He grinned at her. "Fine job back there. A little country know-how?"

Lee Anne, tired as she was, grinned widely. "You bet your ass," she said, and added, "sir."

He stretched. "Time to celebrate."

Lee Anne stood to go, then turned to Carron. "Do you want to come for a drink with us, Mr. Carron?"

He shook his head violently; BJ was reminded of a horse ridding itself of flies. "Of course not. I can't go inside a building."

But he reached in his purse and handed Sugar a fistful of coins. "Drink for me."

Sugar's hand dropped several inches with the weight. Dave peered over and whistled. "Man, you must drink a lot."

Sugar said, "Carron, we can't take half this."

"Please." He looked genuinely troubled. "I can't save your lives, and I can't feed you for life. Take this."

Sugar closed his hand unwillingly around the coins. "Thanks a whole lot." He dropped them into his left hand and offered his hand to Carron, wincing as the centaur's fist closed completely around Sugar's hand and clenched with emotion.

Carron withdrew wordlessly, turned to Lee Anne, ignored her outstretched hand, and picked her completely off the ground, hugging her tightly to his bare chest.

He set her down. "I'm sorry. That didn't show proper respect."

Lee Anne felt her ribs dazedly. "That's all right."

Carron quietly walked over to Polyta. He put an arm around her, cradled her head in his hand, and kissed her again and again, as passionately as if no one had been there.

Then he bent down swiftly and, laughing, raised the kicking colt in his muscular arms and held it straight up to the afternoon sun. "Bend down, God, and bless this child. This one is yours, but he is also Polyta's." He laughed louder, tears streaming down his face.

"And yours," she said mock angrily, trying to touch the colt held out of her reach.

Sugar signaled the students and they got in the truck quietly. With great restraint, not one of them whooped until they were back on the main road to Stein's. Sugar excused himself when Stein mentioned a message from Owen.

The party that night, catchlet fights, target games, and all, lasted far longer than it should have for people who needed to get up and practice medicine the following day. When they hit the roads at two in the morning to "drive and see the stars," only Dave was completely awake, and only Annie completely sober.

Dave had the driver's window rolled down, and was unnerving Annie by shouting at intervals out it: "Road trip! Road trip!"

"We'd better watch where we go," BJ said from where she was slouched comfortably against their dirty coveralls. "These aren't like roads in Virginia."

Annie said immediately, "Slow down."

Dave did, which probably saved the life of the person who stepped in front of the truck a moment later.

T·W·E·N·T·Y

FIELDS STOOD IN the headlights, waving his arms; he stepped to the side as they approached. Dave, driving (he never would have let the others drive), swung toward him quickly, nearly swiping Fields with the right side mirror.

Fields staggered back, holding out a sheet of notebook paper. BJ recognized Sugar's handwriting; one side had typical Dobbs notes to self about deadlines and meetings.

She turned it over and read: "I need you right away. Follow this map *exactly;* I'm going on ahead. If Fields wants, take him along. Come as fast as you can."

"What is it? Does he tell you what's wrong?"

BJ realized that Fields couldn't read. He was the first adult she had ever met, whom she had known about, who couldn't read.

She passed the note on. "How did you get this?"

"Stein's parrot," he said. "It does errands for food." He brushed self-consciously at his shirt, where he had already tried to rub off a white dripping spot.

Lee Anne scanned the note. "Dr. Dobbs doesn't say what's wrong, but says he needs us. I'm guessing it's an emergency case." She looked up. "Mr. Fields, he says we should take you along, if you wish."

"Can you—" He gestured at the truck. "Can I, to be fast—?"

BJ hopped over the seat into the back. "Hop in," Dave said.

Fields did. He found it hard to get in; he needed to grab tight with his hands, and his hooves clanked on the door. He pulled it shut; when it clicked he was apprehensive. He pushed on it; nothing happened. Suddenly his eyes were all whites.

"Pull on that little silver handle." Dave pointed at it. "Then pull it shut again."

Fields tugged at it. The door swung open; he looked considerably relieved. He pulled it shut again and said in a small voice, "The window?"

"Spin the little crank, sir," Lee Anne said.

He did. The window rolled down as Dave turned the ignition and started up. Fields stuck his shaggy head out the window and stared at the ground rolling out from under him, and for the only time that BJ had seen him, he didn't have an undertone of sex.

He stared at the windshield, and for a moment he was truly frightened. "Do you know where we are going?"

"Just about." Dave, holding the sketched map, grinned at him.

"No." He thumped the dashboard. "Never 'just about.' You know or you don't. The road is dangerous for people who say 'just about.' "

BJ said, "He knows where we're going." Dave looked surprised, then grateful. She added, "For a moment there, you sounded like Dr. Dobbs."

Fields laughed uncertainly. As the truck picked up speed and the cold air came in, he rolled up the window.

Suddenly it was quite close in the truck cabin. In seconds, the smell of sweat was everywhere.

More than sweat, BJ realized. Musk. It had to be coming from Fields. She shrugged. It was bearable. She'd smelled worse. . . .

In a few minutes, she was daydreaming about someone she'd dated as an undergraduate. Western Vee had had a ring dance for seniors, silly even in Virginia, but it had been fun, all dressed up. The air had been rich with the scents of Virginia spring: dogwood, lilac, wisteria.

She'd remembered how she'd felt after two hours of dancing, her silk dress rustling over her breasts as she pressed tightly against Jeff, feeling his shirt beneath his open tuxedo jacket and smelling a light undercurrent of fresh sweat, animal but not unpleasant, from both of them. . . .

With a start she realized that she'd been shifting back and forth on the seat. She glanced embarrassedly sideways at Lee Anne. Lee Anne, who was rubbing her hand quietly against the denim on the outside of her leg, hadn't noticed her. BJ looked quickly at Annie, who was staring straight ahead, holding perfectly still and looking at no one. Annie had a fine bead of sweat on her upper lip.

BJ looked back at Fields, who was gripping the armrest and the dash. He glanced back at her face, then smiled slightly and shrugged. "I really can't help it."

Dave said, "Huh?"

BJ smiled politely at Fields and looked away. In a few moments she was daydreaming about Jeff again.

They all concentrated more as they moved into the rocky valley; they were thrown back and forth. Lee Anne grabbed the seat in front of her and said, "Don't let the rocks pull you off-road."

Dave wrenched the wheel back and forth in response to the jolts. "I can handle it."

"Well, slow down if you can't." Lee Anne pointed meaningfully to the side lanes, which appeared suddenly out of the darkness at random and popped off the main branch. "Some of those roads will be hard to turn around on."

She didn't add that some of the side roads might not lead back at all. She didn't have to; Dave slowed down.

BJ stared at the ruts and gullies in the road ahead. "Why is this road so bad? Crossroads doesn't do this."

Dave was hunched over the wheel, concentrating. "Maybe they ran short of construction funds."

Annie shook her head. "It doesn't work that way."

Fields said shortly, "Those who live here like their privacy. They asked for a bad road."

"That makes no sense." Dave swerved to avoid a boulder. "What kind of people would want a road they can't use?"

"People who fly," BJ said suddenly. "They just need something to follow; they wouldn't walk. It's where the griffins live, isn't it?"

Fields smiled at her, but the smile was sickly. "Yes, miss. The griffins." He added, as though it were forced out of him, "And . . . others."

The road, such as it was, twisted through a canyon into a bowl-shaped valley. The rock fell away to either side; in the darkness they couldn't see any hills. Low stands of thick-trunked trees, twisted and bent by high winds, grew to either side of the road. The branches whipped against the windshield, flashing out of the dark and disappearing back into it.

Down and down they dropped, kicking up great clouds of dust. This part of Crossroads was dry and empty; BJ wondered what kind of life a creature could have here.

Dave rounded a sharp curve and slammed on the breaks, skidding in the rock and sand. The students looked in shock at the blood-flecked, fluffy ruin blocking the road in front of them.

The chick was half the size of the truck, its fuzzy down looking ridiculous on that scale, its pink skin in the featherless patches grotesque. Its eyes were still shut, and from time to time its beak moved soundlessly, opening wide enough to reveal the huge gullet below.

It was ugly in that half-naked, veinous way that some animals and most baby birds are. It lay helpless on its back, looking weak except for a pair of wicked-looking talons that appeared, if possible, stronger than the front feet of the Griffin himself.

Its left leg was twisted almost at a right angle. The muscle tissue was already purple, and the purple was spreading.

"Pretend it's a half-ton chicken with a bad attitude," a voice said sharply from in front of them.

Sugar stepped in front of the truck; Owen followed. Owen's cart, BJ saw, was to one side of the chick.

Sugar all but ran to the back of the truck and began throwing open panels, half tossing gauze and butterfly pins out. "Showtime. Everybody, get out and help. *Now*."

They leaped out. He added only slightly more calmly, "Leave the headlights on until we're oriented, then shut down."

"Can't we have them to work by?" BJ said.

"Think," Sugar said exasperatedly. "If our battery dies, how do we call Triple-A?"

It was like him to be sarcastic, unlike him to be rude. He also patted his shirt pocket several times; BJ hadn't been aware he used to smoke.

"Plus," he said more quietly, "I'd like to do this without much attention. And fast. Let's roll, folks." He looked strained. Sugar looked strained. "Dave, you were due for a case again. Start reading from Lao, the section on rocs." And, as Dave punched open the glove compartment, "Out loud."

BJ realized, belatedly, that Sugar wasn't prepared, either. This was not a case like the Griffin's.

Dave thumbed through *Lao's Guide* rapidly by the dome light, cleared his throat, and began: " 'The roc is symbolic of mythic force. God made Leviathan in the deep and Behemoth on the land; the roc is Islamic afterthought to Judeo-Christian oversight.' "

He looked cautiously, and unnecessarily, at Annie. "That's what it says. Sorry."

"Don't worry about it." Annie was kneeling by the chick, wiping moisture off its legs and wings. "Thanks, though. What else?"

" 'The power of the roc expands upon the brutal power of the Christian material world, in appropriate Middle Eastern fashion. If Allah is to be merciful, it is only fitting that even the air above the Faithful is cruel. The symmetry is terrifyingly sensible: *Allahu akbar, Rukh akbar.* God is great, and His rocs are the Great, cruelest of all birds of prey.' "

BJ heard in the dark, impossibly far off, the soft flapping of large wings.

" 'Their nests are on mountains, precipices, and promontories. Even so, there is no defense for a nest when the Great are away. The chicks have little balance; on foot, they are vulnerable. Their weight keeps them from escaping on foot or in the air.

" 'The chicks must have food constantly. Their hunger is terrible, in all senses. The chicks often starve in the absence of the parents or if they fall from the nest unobserved.' "

Dave paused, glancing at the open, working mouth of the chick. He went on: " 'As with the American condor, one or, rarely, two chicks are born in any season to the Great. They are not prolific. Any persistent predator could eliminate the species in a short time.

" 'It is for this reason that the Great defend their young ruthlessly, wiping out whole species in defense of a single nest. They are' "—he struggled with words he had read more than he had pronounced—" 'raptorial birds, not vermiforous. The Great, when they are not in balance with their predators, are an endangered and an endangering species.' "

He looked up, confused, as a sudden steady breeze ruffled the book pages. Fields stood by the roc chick, looking helpless for the only time BJ ever noticed.

Dave hopped out of the truck and went to Sugar. "Not much help in there."

"So give a hand here." Sugar was moving constantly, nervous energy translating into a tail-to-head exam of the roc chick. "Check for injuries. So far I'm finding no deep cuts, mostly contusions and hematomas."

Dave stepped in and began checking between feathers. "How big does it get?"

Sugar said, "We'll need rads. And steel pin plates. And a full theater; this is no job for field surgery."

"Jesus, this thing is as big as a Toyota Corolla; how big does it get?"

Annie looked nervously into the darkness. "What could do all this to it, and what could possibly have scared it off?"

Dave shivered as though something icy stabbed through him front to back. "How big are its *parents*?"

"This is bad," Fields said somberly. "This is very, very bad."

The flapping wings sounded louder, and the treetops began waving back and forth.

Suddenly the chick squeaked loudly and repeatedly, and struggled back and forth. Something was exciting it. Lee Anne and Annie laid hands on it from either side, trying to calm it and to keep it from rolling on its damaged leg.

Then, as suddenly, it sagged back in the dust, its stubby wings spread as if in supplication.

BJ noted, relieved, that the sound of wings had ceased. The only sound now was the unremittent crying of the chick and the soft sigh of the night wind in the trees.

Sugar said tightly, "Everybody, step back, real slowly, from the chick. Do it now."

They all retreated toward the truck. Sugar stayed perfectly still by the chick. "Pull on the lights again."

BJ leaned in the cab window and did. She heard a frightened gasp and realized that it was Lee Anne, frozen in the headlights like a rabbit on the road. She was staring straight up.

BJ's first crazy thought, looking where Lee Anne was looking, was, The moon has a hole in it.

But the dark spot was a pupil, in the center of a milky white iris larger than a tractor tire.

Slowly BJ saw the dark outline surrounding the eye: an enormous, nearly bald head, preceded by a beak the length of the truck. The head was cocked sideways so that the eye pointed straight at them.

Of course it is, she thought. Bird eyes don't move like ours; it has to move its whole head to follow us. She was half in shock.

She turned away from the eye and saw, above them on the other side of the clearing, another pale eye.

She came forward to stand with the others, stepping carefully to avoid startling the rocs.

Annie whispered, "How close are they?"

A feather spun down toward them; Dave reached out reflexively and caught it. He raised his left hand and shakily smoothed the feather upward. The barbules on the feather were as large as tuna fishhooks, and caught each other to make the feather a single glistening surface. It caught the night breeze, twitching in Dave's trembling grasp.

He looked up at the waving tip of the feather, and his eyes traveled beyond to the curved predator's beak, larger than the truck, outlined against the few stars still visible. The beak was so far from the eye that they seemed unrelated. He lowered his hand slowly, dropping the feather.

BJ swallowed and stepped toward the roc chick. The huge beak swung toward her, and a second beak, from the other side of the valley, swung with it.

"We want to look the chick over," BJ said. "To make it better."

The milky eyes stared at her silently.

"It's been hurt." She pointed to the leg. "Someone broke its leg."

The beaks bent lower. Maybe it was a motion to keep her in sight, but the hooks of both beaks tipped toward her, shining in the headlights. The beaks were long enough that they seemed completely dissociated from the staring eyes.

She finished shakily, "And we're—we want to be doctors. More than anything. Let us help your chick. Please."

"What we need," the Griffin said dryly from the dark, "is a system of chicks and balances."

BJ ran over, surprised at how glad she was to hear him. He was standing with one front foot raised and head up, staring unblinkingly into one of the giant eyes. His feathers were ruffled and the fur on his back was raised to make him look larger. His entire defiant form was smaller than the beak above him. BJ was reminded, absurdly, of a defiant chihuahua she had once seen attack a rottweiler.

She put a hand on his fur. It was dry, with that soft dusty quality some tawny cats have. Unconsciously, she tried to smooth him back down.

"Please move," he said gently. "At any moment, I may have to leap straight up, and it's fairly difficult."

BJ stared up into the huge, pitiless eye. "You wouldn't."

"I would."

"But you'd die."

The Griffin turned his head toward her very briefly. "And?"

Feet shifted in the rock near her, and Owen stood beside them. "One of us hurt your child," he said bluntly upward.

The beaks shifted away from the Griffin and toward him.

"Not someone here. But someone from Crossroads, someone whom . . . we can find."

The beaks hung in front of Owen. BJ thought they opened

slightly. Owen walked over to the chick, calmly and apparently without fear.

He knelt where Annie had been a moment before and laid a hand on the chick's head. It stirred, cheeping and waving its immense head from side to side with its mouth open. "This little one needs our help."

He stretched his hand back, as low as he possibly could, and waved Sugar and the students forward.

Sugar came forward, straight and tall. Annie tiptoed behind him and carefully slid a splint to either side of the chick's bent leg. Dave scuttled up, ducking, and began unrolling gauze. They worked cautiously at immobilizing the leg.

"Is the break at the joint?" Dave asked Sugar.

"No such luck," Sugar said, as if that were luck. "Tibia and fibula both. A clean snap, at least, and tough bones. Probably it fell at least thirty or forty feet." He held up the scored fold of skin on the upper thigh. "It was grabbed here, above the broken bones. See the teeth marks?" His fingers traveled lightly up the chick. "And all these scrapes? It was dragged here."

"The bone didn't break the skin." Dave put his fingers against the leg and probed delicately, probably more delicately than was necessary. "Can you imagine the blood loss if it had popped a vein?"

The blood loss didn't matter just then: the chick turned its head toward him pleadingly.

"Where'd it come from?" Lee Anne said. "Nobody'd build a nest down here."

"There is a mountain in the dark behind us," Fields said heavily. "Almost at the top is a cliff. The nest is there, built of tree limbs and trunks. On the face below, a trail—it is narrow, but it goes all the way to the river below. They must have come that way, and dragged it down."

Sugar looked around. "Who are 'they'?"

Fields pointed to the tracks. "The wolves." The tracks covered the dusty path, dancing, twisting, leaping across one another. The dragged claws of the baby chick ran across them.

Lee Anne said slowly, "They didn't stay to feed."

Dave glanced straight up. "Would you, if Mom and Dad came back?"

BJ said, "No, she's right. Look at the skin on the chick; they didn't even try to feed."

Fields grunted in surprise. "She's right." He bent down and measured the wolf tracks carefully against his palm. When he straightened, he looked angry, but said nothing.

"Pretty strange behavior for predators," Lee Anne said. "Push a chick off a cliff, drag it around, scare it, play with it . . ."

As Annie and Dave adjusted the broken leg, the chick flopped once, trying to pull away from them. Annie ran back to the upper body. "Nobody's going to hurt you."

She stuck her hand down and checked the stubby, nearly featherless wings. "There," she said. Her eyes were glistening. "It's all right."

BJ, looking at it, remembered an Easter at her grandfather's. Her grandpa, a country man, had given her a baby chick—well, he had tried. He had stretched his hand out, and had put the chick out in it, and at the last minute before handing it to her, his fingers slipped sideways. The chick fell to the ground, flapping crazily by instinct, and thumped onto the sidewalk.

Grandpa, staring slack-jawed and gaping downward at his own hand, had suddenly and mirthlessly started laughing, loudly and bitterly. BJ had knelt by the still-flapping baby chicken and wept.

Sugar, finishing off near the head, patted Annie's shoulder lightly. It was one of the few times BJ could remember his having touched a female student.

He straightened up and stepped back from the chick. "That's that. Everything but the leg is superficial." He frowned. "Surgery time."

"Here?" Dave looked around at the rocks and dust.

"Nope. Back home." Sugar looked wistfully down the road, as if wishing he were there again.

"Can't we just splint it and leave it here?"

"To do what?"

Dave shrugged. "Hey, if it can fly—"

"If it can fly, it has to land." Sugar pointed to the massive thighs on the baby. "Remember undergrad biology? Bird legs take a lot of impact; they're a lot of the bone weight in the body. How long do you think this thing would live if it fell over every time it landed? Or if it rebroke its leg on a bad landing? Plus it's a raptor; it hunts with those legs."

BJ, remembering the missing buck on the road earlier, glanced upward and shivered.

"Think we should euthanize it?" Dave said, and clapped a hand over his mouth.

"No," Sugar said, with the briefest of glances up into the watching eyes. "I don't think that would be a real good idea."

"Okay. So we take it with us." Dave looked around. "How?" He started for the truck, then turned and moved back, gesturing as he said loudly, "How about if we make a ramp out of branches, slide the chick up it to the top of the truck—"

He mimed pushing against the chick, then froze as the two huge beaks swung together overhead, blocking the sky. The tops of the beaks were far above his head. The points were almost touching the top of his head.

There was a skitter in the rock as the Griffin pulled Dave backward, a single sharp tug as his talon poked through the cloth shirt easily without touching Dave's skin.

Owen stepped up to the dark, shiny beaks. He tilted his head back and said quietly upward, "These people will take your child away now, to cure it. You don't need to come after them."

Owen spread his hands. "Don't you think that, if one of us did this, the Inspector General will find us? Don't you know what he'll do to the ones who did it?"

After a long, frozen moment, the beaks withdrew slightly, and more stars appeared between them. Sugar sighed. Owen sagged.

Sugar said, "That Inspector General must really be something."

Owen said, "They're the only species that isn't afraid of him."

BJ came up to Owen. "Thank you."

He smiled shyly. "I've had to learn how to talk to strangers, up and down the Strangeways. Some days it's all that keeps me alive." He glanced upward involuntarily. "Some nights, too."

He unfolded one of his blankets and tipped the cart onto it unceremoniously, shaking the content off the pegs. He folded the lids all the way out to form a wide table, then pulled a blanket from his knapsack-cabinet and spread it over the top to pad the pegs.

Lee Anne and Dave brought more pads from the truck, making a passable stretcher for the chick. Fields came forward for the first time, and even the Griffin, claws wrapped in two of Owen's shirts, crouched by the body. It took all of them to lift it on, with two of them immobilizing the leg.

Once it was on, Sugar wiped his brow. "Anybody have any ideas about how we handle it from here?"

But he was already pulling rope out of the truck, recoiling it without thinking about it, looking speculatively at the shafts of the cart.

Lee Anne said dubiously, "Will that thing hold together over the hills?"

"If I go slow," Sugar said. "Shoot, it held together over these roads; it must be tough."

"It should make it," Owen agreed, but added as lightly as he could, "I'd like it back in one piece."

BJ had found another blanket and was spreading it carefully over the chick. "Will you be coming with us?"

Owen shook his head. "I have work to do here." He gestured at his goods. "I'll watch these, and wait."

The Griffin cocked his head meaningfully at the dark above them. "I believe I'll wait here with him. Safe travel."

Sugar took the wheel; the truck lurched slowly back out of the valley. Behind them they heard the trees suddenly flatten and the wind pick up, then diminish suddenly. The Great had gone back to the mountains.

Lee Anne turned to BJ and said abruptly, "Were you scared?"

"Of course," BJ said.

Lee Anne looked at her closely. "You sure didn't look it. You looked ready to face death."

BJ closed her eyes. "Bedside manner." Annie looked at her sharply but said nothing.

The trip took the rest of the night; even on good roads, Sugar couldn't afford to drive fast with the cart thumping along behind. He slowed down as they came close to Virginia, double-checking to be sure that the roads hadn't been changed. As they came to the stone bridge, Sugar stopped. "Anybody got any bright ideas on how we can keep this cart inconspicuous, even at four in the morning?"

The others, half-asleep and exhausted, scratched their heads. Lee Anne said suddenly, "Got any large paper, or a sheet?"

A half hour later, they wheeled slowly into the left lane of 480 with the truck lights flashing: slow-moving vehicle. On the back of the cart, which looked like an antique piled high with goods, was a hand-lettered sign painted in brown Betadyne antiseptic solution: VISIT THE DUBLIN FLEA MARKET, SUNDAYS.

The two cars and one semi that passed paid them no attention.

T·W·E·N·T·Y·O·N·E

LAURIE STOOD IN the hall, her eyes shut. She was sleeping on her feet, an unlit cigarette in her right hand. Other people might have thought her strange; the vet students looked at her enviously for being able to sleep anywhere.

She opened her eyes as the cart creaked. "What's up?" She looked down at the cart. "Oh, my."

The roc chick turned its sightless head toward her and cheeped listlessly.

She scanned down the body and said flatly, "Just the leg?"

Sugar said, "Isn't that enough? Can you come in on this one?"

She lit a cigarette. "The night is young."

They watched Laurie check the anesthetic supplies from the raptor clinic, and heard her say, "Jesus, we could probably use it all."

Lee Anne, exhausted and brain-dead like the rest of them, said, "What concentration of gas to start with?"

"Gosh, I don't know," Laurie said innocently. "And the library's closed at this hour." Lee Anne shut up.

Sugar said, "Didn't we do an ostrich once, from the Mill Mountain Zoo?"

Laurie nodded. "Swallowed a doorknob some idiot fed it. First year we were both here."

"How about for eagles?"

"So far this year? Two bald, one golden." She considered. "One of those was a yearling, too. We used isoflurane."

"Okay. Give me somewhere around a yearling eagle the size of an ostrich."

Laurie sighed. "Well, thank God medicine's an exact science."

Dave chuckled. Sugar turned back to him. "I'll be doing this one myself. Dave, you'll assist."

They hustled the roc chick into OR. Lee Anne, scrubbing up, said quietly to Dave, "Watch your butt."

"I know it's a great butt to watch, but it'll do fine," he said. But he looked uneasy.

"Remember, it's like carpentry." As if to make the point, Sugar double-checked the Gigli wire, the drill, and the pin chuck.

He turned back to the table. "Dave, set up the IM pins."

That meant intermedullary pins, surgical steel rods with screw threads at one or both ends. Often, a pin would be drilled from the break point of a bone to the hard cortex bone end, after which the doctor would align the two broken bone ends and, from the upper end of the pin this time, drill the pin into the other bone fragment so as to reduce the gap between them.

Except that in this case, the broken thighbone was longer than any intermedullary pin they had.

Annie and Lee Anne, who had both scrubbed up also, had finished draping the patient and the table. Laurie double-checked the roc's breathing and nodded to Sugar, who said without looking up, "Dave, got those pins?"

Dave looked at the drawer of pins helplessly. "Which ones?"

"Look at the size of the cavity," Sugar said, surprised. "Which ones do you think?"

"They're none of them big enough," he said helplessly.

"Well, which one's biggest? It has to be better than the smaller ones."

Lee Anne, BJ, and Annie looked at each other.

Dave stammered, "But you—I—we don't have a pin long enough—"

Sugar turned around with annoyance. "You've always wanted to wing it?" He pointed to the limp chick. "Fine. Here's a wing. Hustle up. I'm opening." Laurie rolled her eyes.

The break on the roc's leg was transverse and not too badly displaced. Still, Sugar would need to improvise. He quickly outlined a procedure: two IM pins cross-pinning the bone fracture.

"While we're in here," Sugar said as he exposed the bone, "would you like to tell your colleagues about raptor bones?"

"Not really," Dave said with a short laugh.

"Don't know much about them?" Sugar pulled back the muscle tissue to either side of the break. "How about telling me about the rad?"

"What?" He looked around.

Annie, in scrubs, gestured quickly to the radiographs clipped to the display lights. BJ and Lee Anne had taken them while Dave was scrubbing.

"Right." Dave reached to scratch his head, remembering in time that he should stay sterile. "Um. The fracture is simple and transverse, according to the rad—"

"According to the open leg in front of us, too," Sugar said, dripping sarcasm. "Anything else?"

"Um." Dave checked frantically up and down the X rays. "Looks all right to me—"

The incision on the roc chick was filling up. "How about a little hemostasis on some of these bleeders?" Sugar said sharply.

Dave swung the hemostat in, too eagerly or too nervously. He bumped Sugar's scalpel. There was the quick grind of blade on bone, and Sugar swore under his breath.

"Sorry." Dave bit his lip. "Any harm?"

"I could have sliced a tendon." Sugar took the hemostat away and clipped the bleeder, then sponged so he could see. "Nope. It's fine. Just a little scratch on the bone."

Dave relaxed, then stiffened as Sugar added, "Go wash up."

" 'Scuse me?"

"Wash up, get into street clothes. Go on and get out. You're in the way." Sugar turned his back on Dave. "I'll manage."

BJ watched for a while, then excused herself and washed up. Sugar, possibly because he was already annoyed, let her go.

Dave was sitting in the conference room alone, wiping his eyes. BJ walked quietly behind him and put an arm around him.

"I did everything I could think of," he said hoarsely. "Every last damn thing. I just didn't know what to do." He sagged on BJ's arm. "Sugar's gonna fail me."

There was nothing BJ could say at first. Finally she said, "I've been where you've been. I've felt what you've felt. You know that Truelove failed me."

"Yeah." He looked up. "We were all kinda surprised."

"Why?"

"Because you're so good."

BJ, astonished, let that pass. "You're good yourself. Very good. He caught you when you weren't prepared; that's all." She added, because it was true, "You'll never feel good about this. Never. But I'll bet if he didn't think it would make you better, he wouldn't have done it. He's a good teacher."

She didn't like to stick her neck out, but she was sure of herself: "I'll also bet he passes you in the long run."

Dave looked at her miserably. "Is that why Truelove failed you, to make you better?"

"No." She hadn't realized it until just now. "Truelove failed me because he could. Failing people makes him look discriminating without his having to be.

"Do you need to talk?"

"Thanks." He reached up and patted her arm. "I think I'd like to be by myself."

"Call if you need anything." BJ left, remembering when she had been completely indifferent to Dave. This rotation was changing her.

Once home, her bed looked better than all the scenery in Crossroads, but she held off. She made herself a cup of coffee in her mini-pot, drank it, and thought of all the ways to say what she had to. Then she double-checked her address book and carefully dialed Peter's number.

It rang several times; she thought with relief, He's out. She wanted very badly to hang up. She knew that she had to tell him. She had been hurt deeply by finding out about their mother's illness only after their mother committed suicide; she couldn't let that happen to Peter.

On the eighth ring he picked up. "If this is a wrong number," he said sleepily and bitterly, "I'll track you down no matter where you live."

"It's a right number," she said. "Hi, Peter."

"BeeGee." He sounded confused and, she realized, frightened. "What's up? What do you want? Do you know what time it is?"

"I do." She hadn't; it was still predawn in the Midwest. "But I had to talk to you."

"What about?"

She took a deep breath and said carefully, "I wanted to tell you—I've taken the genetic test for Huntington's chorea."

She was completely unprepared for his response.

He let out a whoop that cut right through her brain. "Oh, thank God," he said, his voice cracking. "Thank God."

She listened as he went on: "I didn't want to say anything after my test. I didn't know how to tell you. I was so afraid to say anything until you'd been proved negative. How long have you known?"

"A few days, that's all," she said slowly.

"A few days? Why the hell didn't you call me? I've been worried sick about you, kid."

"I was afraid to call you until I knew."

He laughed. She could have told him she'd smashed up his car, and he'd still forgive her just now. "I can't argue with that, I guess. BeeGee, I've been so scared for you, ever since I first knew. . . ."

He babbled on, completely oblivious to her.

BJ finally said carefully, "How did you know I tested negative?"

"Oh, you had to," he burbled. "You just had to. Once I had my results, I knew."

"I could have been positive—"

"Don't talk like that," he barked, hurting her ears. "Jesus, what the hell do you need to talk like that for? I don't need that shit."

And before she was ready he shifted gears again, suddenly chatty. "Listen, we've got to get together and celebrate. I know I've been shitty to you for weeks, and I'd love to make up for it, show you around out here. What about after graduation?"

"We'll talk. Can it wait, though?" She tried not to sound pleading. "Right now I'm exhausted."

She hung up and laid her head in her hands. Now she understood why her mother had been unable to call and explain to her about committing suicide.

A half hour later, BJ woke up, asleep at the table. She crawled over to her bed and fell back to sleep with her clothes on.

T·W·E·N·T·Y-T·W·O

"NOT A BAD day, huh?" Dave was grinning. He was feeling better.

"It was all right," BJ said stiffly.

BJ's case, referred by Owen, involved nothing more complex than mastitis in dairy cows. The herd's owners turned out to be the little brown men. Communication had been a problem, but Dave had proved adept at reading their gestures, and through him, she had been able to recommend ongoing treatment.

The entire time that BJ was checking the herd, the brown men danced around her, chattering and screaming. During the examination, Sugar and Lee Anne had broken up three fights and a full-scale skirmish. Annie had been pinched five times, twice obscenely, and BJ herself had been squirted in the face at a moment when she was sure that she was the only one kneeling near the udder. The laughter was constant and uproarious.

There didn't seem to be any little brown women. Asked about it, the brown men looked sad and penitent, and said that the little brown women had left long ago. BJ didn't blame them.

Dave was in his glory. "What fun guys," he said for the fifteenth time. "Don't give a damn about anything. They just have a good time—"

"We're here," Lee Anne said woodenly as Sugar stopped the truck. They had arrived at Stein's for lunch.

They were barely out of the truck when Annie stopped dead and stared uphill.

224

Near the pond, a circle of gaunt men and women stood with their backs outward, poking at something small in the center. From time to time they laughed.

Lee Anne looked at them narrowly. "I've seen groups like that before, when I was a kid. I don't trust them much."

Sugar grunted, "Did you learn to stay away from them?"

The knot of people gave a sudden cry, laughed shortly, and half leaped to the right and re-formed.

The students left the side of the truck reluctantly and walked toward Stein's.

As they grew closer they could see that the circle had linked arms and was kicking inward with a great deal of grace but not in any particular rhythm. A man glanced their way casually and looked away; BJ recognized Vlatmir.

"Leave it alone," Lee Anne said softly.

From the middle of the jabbing circle of people came a squeak of pain.

Annie spun around and marched straight for the group. Lee Anne, grimacing, followed, the others behind her.

"Let it go," Annie said firmly.

One of the women laughed loudly. Vlatmir smiled. "Gredya wants it."

Sugar said calmly, "Annie, bring it back with you and get away from them."

Gredya scowled, and her upper lip twitched on one side like a dog's, exposing her perfect white teeth. "Don't touch it."

"You'll hurt it," Annie said.

"Yes. And you."

The other Wyr edged closer to Annie, gradually moving toward her until they formed a U-shaped barrier around her and the bleeding flowerbinder. A tall, very young man to the right of Vlatmir sniffed the air and laughed. "You smell weak."

"Try us," Lee Anne said. She had her belt off, swinging from her left hand.

One of the Wyr kicked the flowerbinder; it squeaked. Annie stepped inside the circle and bent double to scoop it up.

Vlatmir swung at her neck, chopping with the flat of his hand as though he were unused to making a fist. Dave and Lee Anne moved forward, but Sugar was there first, blocking the blow as he stepped forward. Dave and Lee Anne pulled her back.

Vlatmir launched himself forward, punching at Sugar's throat. Sugar ducked to one side, and Vlatmir growled with frustration.

Vlatmir was vicious but untrained in hand-to-hand fighting.

Sugar's years in rodeo and his time spent shifting and holding large animals had left him formidably muscled. His contact with cowboy bars hadn't left him shy about fights; he spoke of them casually from time to time.

Sugar feinted with his left, dropped Vlatmir's guard, and weighed in with a punch that started somewhere in Alabama and finished in Quebec, laying the Wyr out flat almost before he hit the ground.

Gredya dropped to the ground. The other Wyr formed a half-circle around her, but pressed forward at Sugar and Lee Anne. Lee Anne snapped her belt at them, buckle forward.

BJ turned and ran, awkwardly, into Stein's. She knew what the others were thinking and didn't care. She dashed through the corridor, startling the swearing parrot, and shouted in the main hall, "Melina!"

The faun, balancing a tray of steins on her hip, nearly dropped them. She wiped up the spillage with the towel she kept on her shoulder. "What?" She didn't look particularly happy to see BJ.

"Are any of the spits in the fire bare?"

"Two of them." She hurried over, set the tray down, and paused the turning wheels, letting the belt that turned them slip on the axle. The bare spits were in front. "Don't touch them!"

But BJ had grabbed the bar towel from Melina's shoulder and wrapped it around a spit end.

She opened her hand partway and scooped the end of the second spit into the towel. She lifted them both hastily and ran to the door, careful not to strike against anyone. The towel was already smoking.

Annie had pulled back, holding the flowerbinder; she was kicking at any of the Wyr who came within reach.

Vlatmir, lithe as a dancer, dodged her kicks. He was terrible with his hands, but extremely graceful on his feet. He moved toward her and pulled his arm back like a club, ready to swing it into Annie.

BJ slammed the spits down on Vlatmir's shoulder, resting them there.

He yelped aloud, not a human cry at all, and grabbed the spits, then yelped again, ducking away and letting them fall. BJ nearly dropped them, but held firm to the towel.

Sugar ripped his shirt off and grabbed one of the spits from her, grabbed the shirt-wrapped spit like a Louisville Slugger, and swung it, hard, across the row of the other Wyr. They fell back, snarling.

A deeper snarl sounded below and behind them.

BJ clutched the remaining spit like a bat, as Sugar had, but stepped forward unhesitatingly through the Wyr as though charging the pitcher. The first Wyr tried to strike her and she bounced the spit off him, swinging it sideways to clear a path through the rest of them. The Wyr parted in astonishment, unprepared for a charge.

Gredya lay pulsing and nearly covered in new fur. She raised her half-muzzle and snarled in pain and anger at BJ.

BJ held the still-smoking spit over the still-helpless Gredya. "Pull back from us," she said to the other Wyr.

Vlatmir braced to leap at her. Sugar was suddenly right behind her, holding his weapon like a policeman's truncheon. "Don't."

Vlatmir, rubbing his swollen jaw, looked over BJ at Sugar. "You hit hard."

"Not yet I haven't."

"Pull back," BJ repeated.

Vlatmir lowered his dark eyebrows and glared resentfully at her, but addressed Annie. "Give it back."

She held the struggling flowerbinder with difficulty; her shirt was streaked with blood. "No."

Vlatmir glared at her, then gave a sudden, full-toothed smile. "You like money?" he said. "You will pay. Soon." He gestured to the others, who moved to the fully transformed Gredya prior to leaving. "But not money," he added, and turned unhurriedly to jog downhill with the others.

BJ and Sugar dropped their weapons simultaneously, shaking their burned hands. BJ licked her red-streaked palm, feeling a little like a Wyr herself.

Lee Anne said shakily, "You cut that a tad close."

"That," Sugar said grimly to BJ, "was flat-out crazy."

"You did it too." She poked at the rapidly cooling spits with her foot.

Sugar shook his head. "No, getting the spits was bright. I meant running in like that; that was crazy."

BJ thought fervently, "Couldn't you have said reckless, stupid, or even unprofessional? Not crazy. Never crazy." Aloud she admitted, "It was a risk."

"Annie took a risk." Dave was kneeling, restraining the flowerbinder so that Annie could examine it. "You took your life in your hands." He grinned at BJ, but he was clearly shaken. "And you drop things too easy."

BJ grinned back at him. "Don't I, though?" This time, at least, she had dropped nothing. She stopped smiling. "If Gredya had finished changing, we'd all be dead."

"We've made enemies for sure now," Lee Anne said. To Annie she said, "Was it worth it?"

"Of course." Annie was cuddling the now-calmer flowerbinder. "This little guy needs treatment." She pulled her face back from the cat and looked imploringly at Sugar.

He scratched his head. "If you can keep him quiet in the truck and smuggle him into the vet school, I'll treat him. I can hide him till he's better. How's that?"

Annie nodded up and down vigorously like a small child. The others smiled involuntarily. Dave said, "I'll grab some take-out for us." BJ went with him, carrying the still-warm spits.

Stein himself was standing in the outside doorway. "Everything all right?"

"Sure." Dave made to move beyond him. The parrot chortled, "*Stooo*-pid."

Stein gave it a withering look and knocked on the inside door. As Melina unbarred it, he ushered them in, taking the spits from BJ. "We don't see much of those kind here. They like their food better if it's still screaming."

"That explains the locked door," Dave said. He gave his order to Melina, who smiled politely at him, looked indifferently at BJ, and returned with their food.

On the ride home, BJ had more worrisome things than Melina's behavior to wonder about: why was Sugar so willing to take an animal back with them?

For that matter, why would the Wyr, who had nothing but scorn for humans, have come so near Stein's? There was plenty of prey elsewhere. What were they looking for, and did it have something to do with the vet students?

BJ was too tired to think much about the questions. The sun was warm on the cab, and Sugar, concentrating on his map, was leaving the students to themselves. Soon they were all asleep, and until the clangor of the inevitable Road Crew and its turnoff changes woke them, the only sound was the thunderous purring of the injured but affectionate flowerbinder, snuggled across Annie and BJ.

T·W·E·N·T·Y-T·H·R·E·E

RETURNING TO ANAVALON was easy; returning to the camp proved impossible. Brandal stood facing the gaunt man who was not a man, whose people claimed to be the only true men.

"I need to go to Morgan's camp."

"No." His speech was sharp and short, even in Anavalerse.

"You can't stop me. Do you have a name?"

"Not for you."

Brandal said solemnly, "Don't be afraid of me."

The man scowled and spat out, "Vlatmir."

"Vlatmir." Brandal didn't recognize the name, but knew it to be a common one for the Wyr. "Let me by, Vlatmir."

Vlatmir folded his arms. Brandal heard a rustle in the grass by the roadside and realized, as he should have earlier, that no Wyr would stand guard alone in human form.

They were interrupted by an immense thrashing, coming from the underbrush at the other side of the road. A bulky figure crashed through the thornbushes, swearing in Anavalerse. "It's all right," Reize boomed. "Curly's with me."

"So he is—now."

Vlatmir smiled at him, but did not show his teeth—yet. "Morgan asked us."

Reize folded his hands over his belly, scowling at the slender guard. "You talk like a man with an eagle up his ass. She has human guards."

Now the teeth showed. "Humans take bribes."

Reize looked disgusted. "No."

"True."

He looked away, his face a study in contempt. "To think," he said bitterly, "that I was ever responsible for your safety, working side by side with men I trusted. With women I trusted—trusted with my body, in fact." He thumped his belly. A stray piece of scrip, tucked hurriedly into his belt, fluttered down; he stooped laboriously to pick it up. "And now you tell me that some of them were taking bribes." He folded the scrip, putting it away more securely this time. "Now, that sickens me."

Vlatmir said, "You were one."

Reize gaped at him. "You insult me?" He made to draw a weapon from his empty belt.

"Forgive him," Brandal said.

Reize glared down at him. "I cannot; I can never. My honor!" He roared. "Insulted! I'm so mad I could piss in a knot."

The rustling in the underbrush sounded again, softly, beside Reize.

Brandal said hastily, "Morgan wouldn't want him killed."

Reize looked outraged. Vlatmir looked scornful, but said only, "Perhaps not." The rustling in the grass stopped.

Brandal, surprised that it was so easy, said, "Are her wishes that important to you?"

Vlatmir said nothing.

Brandal thought of the line outside the stone shed. "She gives you something that you'd die for."

Vlatmir's face under stress was as nakedly expressive as a dog's. His face rippled through resentment, defiance, and an odd shame. Brandal saw something more: a nauseatingly, cringingly overwhelming desire.

The Wyr rubbed his own arm, and Brandal was confused by what he saw there: a series of tiny marks, as though someone had been poking Vlatmir with a needle.

"You're a slave now," he said flatly. "She's found a way to make slaves of the Wyr."

Vlatmir said, in a low, venomous growl, "Go away."

They did, straight into the grove of *thearnficht*. The thorns tore at them dangerously, and at that, Brandal felt safer there than he had on the road.

"It was kind of you, Curly, to save that silly bastard's life back there, even with such a poor excuse."

"I had to do something," he replied. "I'm surprised that you let him live."

Reize snorted. "I've had worse insults than that lately. Me, who should have been a king of thieves, a thief of kings! The turd of fortune, Curly; the turd of fortune."

He stopped and lifted his shirt. The weals were still visible on his otherwise smooth, featureless fat back.

Brandal winced and said sympathetically, "Felaris?"

"She flogged me, Curly," Reize said bitterly. "Thirteen lashes, with me crawling away on my bare belly in the dirt, while I yelled and everyone laughed. If I didn't believe in my own honor over other people's harsh judgment, I couldn't look anyone in the face again."

"What did she flog you for?" Brandal asked.

Reize looked pained. "Drunkenness."

"Were you drunk?"

"That makes it even worse. Integrity," Reize said pontifically, "is a delicate thing. It only takes one factual accusation to damage it irreparably." He finished with injured pride, "Which is why people ought to be more careful before making accusations public—particularly well-founded ones."

Brandal walked with him through the grove of *thearnficht*. "You mean, it would have been better if she had made a false accusation?"

"Absolutely." Reize thumped him on the shoulders for his perception, nearly dropping him to his knees. "If, for instance, she had accused me of raping fish or ignoring women or callously undervaluing other people's misplaced property, why, I could have cleared myself. But to pick a charge with evidence behind it . . ." Reize's unkempt mustache bristled. "It's a tactic as loathsome as snail snot."

"But you were guilty," Brandal protested feebly.

Reize waved a dismissive hand. "Now you're talking like a man with a paper nose *and* an eagle up his ass."

"How did they know to replace the sentries?"

"Jaeken. He tried to kill someone in a night fight; he had his sword. To save his unlovable, skinny, one-buttocked ass, he told how he saw me sneaking you back into the camp."

"But Felaris didn't kill you," he said thoughtfully.

"Of course not. My training is too costly." Reize swelled self-importantly, threatening to annihilate his own shirt. "I've been chosen for special duty."

He stood on the overlook and pointed downhill. "When that first group of puppies and their new strange friends lead the charge, I'll be right behind them. In a special group. Handpicked."

" 'Handpicked' . . . Who did the picking?"

"Felaris. But she was under Morgan's special orders." Reize poked Brandal with a stubby finger for emphasis, then thumped his own triangular shoulder patch. "Oh, I wasn't promoted—probably political, the usual infighting—but you watch me. This is only the start. I'll move up from here, and when I'm done . . ." His eyes were shining. "Curly, it takes my breath away." He sighed loudly.

Brandal blinked. Whatever took Reize's breath away could probably have gotten drunk off the fumes alone. He looked away and noticed for the first time that the path he had taken before was gone, chopped out of the steep hillside, now made steeper.

"She sent a work crew. Fifty diggers, and it took two days." Reize shrugged. "Waste of time, really. Now there's only one way into the camp."

"The road. And it's guarded." It didn't seem like a waste of time to Brandal. He squinted down at the camp. "Who are these 'strange friends'?"

"Not my friends. Just troops for the front line." Reize puffed his chest out until it almost equaled his stomach. "Just ahead of my own outfit."

Brandal was new to war, but Stein had explained the subdivisions of troop movement: "The ones who charge in and destroy everything, they're the shock troops. The extra bodies you send after them, especially if it's risky, they're the ones you don't care about. The cannon fodder."

Brandal didn't know firsthand what cannons were but he understood the principle, and he knew which troops Reize was assigned to. He stared downhill in silence.

The camp looked bigger: a large unfriendly grid of huts the same size. Brandal hadn't thought neatness and order could look so disturbing by themselves. Only one end of the camp was disorganized, where a large mound of trash shimmered in the late-afternoon sun. . . .

It wasn't trash. It was an exit mound, piled around a hole the size of one of the sheds. And the ground wasn't shimmering.

"From here," Brandal said with a chill, "they look like worms."

"From up close, they look like worms and women."

The forms along the ground writhed and coiled, never staying still. The human bodies at their heads turned this way and that, watching the rest of the camp. From time to time, two of them fought, twenty or thirty feet of scaled body constricting around another.

Presently one of them unwound, leaving the other one still. The winner one and another dislocated their human jaws and started at either end of the dead one, swallowing until they met at the middle and began fighting. The rest of the exit mound writhed around them, indifferent.

"Lamiae?" he said with disbelief and distaste.

"You know these women?"

He shook his head. "They're not really women—or men, either. They're—never mind. I've heard stories."

"I'm relieved," he grunted. "No man should want anything like that." He stared into space and said morosely, "When I was young I dreamed of the perfect woman. Now all I want in life is a woman who, if she shows up in your bed, you won't scream and smack her with a rock." He looked off into the distance wistfully. "A nice, friendly, selfless, dirty girl with no morals."

"You'll find one. Or she'll find you. Bring money." He shook his head, staring down. "I thought they were all gone."

"The bitch's brood Morgan recruited, a member of which I just faced down on the road"—Reize's ego had its own survival skills—"brought them back here. On orders, I'd guess."

"It wouldn't be hard." Brandal stared down, fascinated and repelled at the same time. "Promise them enough food and they'll do anything. They're the only beings I know crazy enough to follow the Wyr."

"The who?"

"The wolf-people." Brandal stood up. "You'd best go back."

"Curly, come back with me." He held a pleading, pudgy hand out. "There's no future for anyone outside the camp."

"It's too much work."

"We'll only be here a little longer," Reize said eagerly. "Everybody knows that."

"What if you lose?"

"She'll win; she's bound to. I can find an excuse for you; I can get you in. Flogging only hurts for a little; you can't be proud about these things if you want to get ahead. Please, Curly."

Brandal took the offered hand, shook it, let it go. "Trying would only get us both killed. Be well, Reize."

"Where will you go?"

"Off to seek my fortune, like you've always wanted," Brandal said lightly. "If I do all right, I'll be in touch."

Reize shook his head somberly. "Not you or me, boy. It's not in us to do all right. All wrong, is what we do."

Reize looked down at the smaller man and said suddenly,

"Here." He unslung his flask and passed it over. "The road is dry."

Brandal, moved, accepted it. Reize hugged him tightly. "Watch yourself, Curly. You're too nice to be a good thief."

Brandal stepped back on the road and looked dubiously at Vlatmir, who looked away. The Wyr was getting restless. Brandal looked back once to make sure no one was following him on the road, then turned onto a side road and faded out of view, in plain sight.

At the edge of Crossroads, Brandal reached for Reize's flask and discovered suddenly that his purse was missing. He grinned and drank from the flask. "To you, Oghannon Reize. Don't spend it all on wine."

The air was sweeter, and moisture hung in it. Blue backs sang in the evening sunlight. Brandal had walked back into Crossroads.

He glanced at the road behind him to be sure he hadn't been followed, then relaxed. Soon he would be back in other clothes, moving in a world at peace.

A form, still shivering with the pain of transformation, rose up from the grass by the roadside. She pointed a bony, still-growing finger at him. "I knew," she gasped, mumbling as her human teeth grew in. "I knew."

Brandal stepped toward her, then quickly back. "Why did you change? You know that I should kill you."

She grinned, her gums still trickling her own blood. Understanding in time, Brandal leaped away from her, putting his back to a rock outcropping.

If he had remained distracted by her, he would already have been dead. Two forms lunged out of the grass from either side, snarling. He ducked the first, but the body of the second smashed against his shoulder and spun him around. He held his sword out, hoping for contact rather than aiming a blow, and concentrated on keeping his feet.

He tossed the edge of his cloak around his throat and wrapped it, spreading his feet wide and shuffling in the dirt for his best balance. If I fall, he told himself calmly, they'll take my throat. He looked at them carefully, noting that one was gray in the muzzle, the other quite young.

Jaws half-open, the Wyr circled him. When they were opposite each other, or when Brandal's guard finally dropped, one of them would lunge at him.

A surprise attack is easier to repel if you can choose the moment when your enemy surprises you. Brandal shifted his feet, bracing, and lowered his sword fractionally, turning to look to his left.

The old wolf on his right sprang soundlessly at his sword arm—

Which was gone, spinning behind him to drop on the other wolf. Instead, the gray wolf took a dagger blow from Brandal's left hand. It scraped down the wolf's rib cage, leaving a lengthy gash but no real damage. The wolf snarled in pain and fury, dropping to the ground.

The young wolf rolled to avoid the sword; Brandal kicked the animal hard and backed against the rock again. He looked up.

The naked Wyrwoman, still shiny with the sweat of transformation, was stumbling back down the road to Anavalon, her head cocked as she sniffed for trail markings.

Brandal ran toward her. The Wyr, scrambling to their feet, bounded after him, thinking he was fleeing.

Before he raised his sword, one of the wolves thought to bark. It sounded to Brandal like all the other noises they had made in combat, but the woman jerked her head around suddenly and saw Brandal. She opened her mouth wide, curling her lips back in a completely useless combat reflex.

Brandal stabbed her in the chest with a single quick lunge, withdrawing his sword before she fell. She never put her arms up to shield herself, as a human would; she was still confused between woman and wolf. She bit futilely at him as she died.

One of the wolves howled and flung itself recklessly at Brandal. He leaped sideways and slashed with his sword, catching the beast's foreleg.

It was the young one. It fell, rebalanced on three legs, and limped back toward Brandal, rocking awkwardly. Brandal knew that as soon as it found its new balance it would be as deadly as before.

The old wolf barely glanced at his comrade, and streaked past Brandal to crouch in his path. He yipped several times to the other wolf, who had been running toward Brandal.

They circled again. This time Brandal had nothing at his back. The fight would be over quite soon.

Brandal loosened the cloak from his throat, exposing his bare neck. He slit his shirt with his own dagger, cutting his sword-arm sleeve free, and wrapped the rag around his left forearm. He tucked his dagger in his belt.

This time the older wolf was cautious, edging toward Brandal's

left, reacting to every movement by the man. Brandal heard a soft
scratch in the road gravel to his right, much closer than before.
He willed himself not to look and, instead of lowering his guard,
made as if to lunge at the gray.

The growl and the leap were simultaneous. Brandal stepped
quickly backward and dropped the edge of his cloak like a mata-
dor's cape, letting the cloak slide off him.

The young wolf, tangled in the cloak and falling on his back,
snarled and bit. Brandal smashed his sword blade down with all
his strength, dropped to his knees, and raised his padded forearm,
shoving it into the jaws of the charging gray.

The gray closed on it, ripping it left and right. Brandal dropped
his sword, grabbed his dagger with his right hand, and drove it
through the old wolf's throat.

He leaped aside, watching the grim twin metamorphoses. The
legend was true; what died a wolf would be buried a human.

Where the maimed wolf had fallen, there lay a teenage boy,
his chest wounded, clutching in his left hand the severed ruin of
his right.

Brandal bent down and closed the boy's eyes, but the face still
looked pained and furious. Brandal moved over and laid out the
other Wyr, a wiry man with short gray hair and a cut throat. The
resemblance between the two was more than tribal. Probably they
were father and son. He looked at the corpses sadly; neither could
be said to be at peace.

A cold, angry voice said, "I would have left them."

He turned. Morgan stood at the top of the hill, on the
Strangeway. It was hard to focus on her; she was standing
exactly on the border between worlds, ready to withdraw if
Brandal attacked.

"You look the same," she said. "Do I?"

A stray breeze behind her sent her long red and gray hair rippling forward, framing her face. A shaft of sunlight moved across
her face, and Brandal caught his breath at how she looked, again,
to him; how she always would.

Then she squinted in the sun, slit-eyed and brutal. Physically
she was still beautiful, but where he once saw passion, he now
recognized anger; where he once saw force of will, he now saw
only cruelty. "Yes," he said. "Exactly the same."

She began walking back and forth, her image rippling at Crossroads' edge. She could not hold still. "You still have no taste for
killing."

"That's the only reason you're still alive. Do you remember

how the Inspector General begged me to let him kill you when we found the graves you had filled?"

"Yes." Morgan smiled. "That I remember." But her smile showed too much teeth, and soon she was pacing and tight lipped again. "If memory were enough, I would never do anything new."

And she was suddenly lost, whirling in her own guilt and desire. Brandal watched, unable to help or stop her.

"Why? Why do I do it?" She paced, wringing her hands. "And I need to repeat. Old blood turns brown and crackles, and turns to no more than dust. New-spilled blood is liquid jewelry, ruby incarnidine. And I wear it and wear it and wear it, but it can never stay new."

She was arguing with herself. It was an argument she had lost, repeatedly, in the time Brandal had known her.

As suddenly she was controlled again. She smiled almost softly at Brandal. "Have you thought of me?"

"Often, and in many ways. Have you thought of me?"

"Too often, in too many ways." Her hands tangled in her purple cloak; her right hand drifted up without her seeming to notice and pulled and knotted her hair. "Maybe that's why I want to return. Because of you. I can't tell."

"When we met, did you want me, or did you only want Crossroads?"

She said nothing.

He asked, "How old are you?"

She wouldn't answer.

Brandal burst out, "I was young!"

She smiled coldly. "As you say, you were young. That made it easy."

"It did," he agreed. He sat beside the bodies of the Wyr, watching her and watching the grass for any movement. "You picked your allies well," he said.

"They were my only choice. Of all those in Crossroads, only the Wyr can find their way from world to world easily."

"That's not true. There are others . . . The Great go everywhere, we think. Perhaps you should have asked them, before asking their enemy."

Her lip curled. "I don't need their help." But she looked up cautiously.

"Possibly not. But you still picked well; of all those in Crossroads, only the Wyr kill and torture for fun."

He corrected himself, "Of all those still in Crossroads."

For a moment she looked empty. "You still haven't forgiven me."

"You're quite wrong," he said seriously. "You I forgave long ago. I can't forgive myself."

"For driving me away?"

"For not letting you be killed."

"Oh yes," she said bitterly. "You saved me. Dressed me in rags and had me driven, blindfolded, down one of your damned Strangeways. And sent me here," she said bitterly. "Where all the water is brackish, and every day is dusty. Where even queens grovel, and the living are ashamed of life."

"Is it better," he said softly, "now that you're there?"

And at that, something in her snapped. "Don't judge me. You're still no king. Look at you. Old boots, battered armor, torn field pack, a chipped field sword—"

"I've been in the field," he reminded her.

"But you're not going back to riches or power," she said, her lips pursed. "You have clothes just as plain, weapons just as shabby, hidden elsewhere. You wear poverty like honor. You haven't the least idea how to rule well."

Her hands drifted down and twisted the seam of her cloak, pulling it apart. Only the pin held it together.

He looked at the pin. "You're wearing it."

She glanced down at the brooch of a griffin being slain by a soldier. She turned it back and forth in the sunlight, smiling.

"This I remember."

But now Brandal was unsmiling. "I remember too well. Why did I let you do so much to so many?"

The answer seemed forced over her clenched jaw. "You loved me!"

He nodded tiredly. "And that made you angry. As so much does."

She turned away and vanished on the Strangeway.

The arms of both bodies were marked with small blue holes, as if pins or needles had been stuck in them.

Brandal turned the stiffening limbs, examining them carefully. There was nothing else to tell him what the marks were.

He would ask all his people to look for strangers with needles, and he would try to find out what the needles were for—before the Inspector General had the strangers killed.

He was a good ways down the road when he suddenly remembered: the veterinarians whom Fields had called in used needles in their work.

Morgan was right about the second set of clothes and equipment. He arrived shortly at a rock cairn by a crossroads; he pulled off one of the side stones and put on a new disguise, taking his soldier's clothes off. The rest of his traveling supplies were hidden nearby.

No one met him on the road; sensible travelers were making camp. Brandal walked all night, restless and unhappy, and only stopped to rest briefly at daybreak.

T·W·E·N·T·Y-F·O·U·R

BUMPING INTO DAVE near the main campus felt strange. Though they both had gone to Western Vee at the same time, they had never met before being accepted at vet school. Over three thousand students had made up BJ's and Dave's graduating class. Courses had generally included between forty and eighty students. Even in the vet school class, of only eighty-eight, they hadn't done much more than socialize enough to know each other on sight.

Truth to tell, BJ hadn't thought much of Dave's loud mouth and self-conscious maverick behavior. She also knew that, if asked, he would say she wasn't his type.

Now, BJ reflected, she felt more comfortable with Dave inside Crossroads than she did at the edge of the Western Vee campus. Dave shuffled from foot to foot, suddenly awkward. "What you been doing this afternoon?"

BJ had confirmed her bank balance, written three more farewell letters, and checked how much she owed on her beat-up Chevette. She had also consulted with a local lawyer on the best arrangements for her portion of her mother's estate, and what arrangements she should make in the event of her dying before the estate closed. She had taken her brother's address and a copy of her mother's will; the lawyer had reassured her, then commended her on being so sensible. "Running errands."

"Oh," Dave said. "Me, too. This block hasn't left us in town much." He fell silent. It was now four in the afternoon, and since neither of them showed any sign of leaving, the embarrassed shuffling could last all afternoon.

BJ glanced from side to side, trying to think of something to say. "Funny."

"What's funny?"

BJ pointed at the passing undergraduates, at the bench loungers in front of Mitch's Ice Cream, at the commercial vans on College Street.

"If any of these people were going in and out of Crossroads, how would we know?"

"If we saw them in Crossroads," Dave said disgustedly, "we'd know, wouldn't we?"

BJ could be patient, even with Dave. "If we saw them out here, how could we tell that they'd been over there?"

"Strange dirt in the tire treads," he said promptly, "if I were Batman."

BJ said as tactfully as possible, "Unless you're awfully good at disguise, we're out of luck."

"Okay: how about slips in conversation?"

"Bizarre, unexplained references to unicorns, centaurs, and satyrs? How many slips like that have you made?"

"None." He said a little defensively, "How would you catch them?"

BJ thought of Hetty's mural, but realized regretfully that it wasn't likely to be a universal form of evidence.

Or maybe it was. "If we can guess what they went in for, we'd know what to look for."

"Pretty vague." Dave pointed at Mitch's Ice Cream, with its toys and multiple dangly philodendrons and spider plants in need of repotting. "How about if he were taking ice cream in?"

"The mileage on the store truck," she said immediately, "And the extra orders of ice cream, and maybe special flavors."

"Like Roc Ripple. Makes sense." Dave was enjoying this. "And the Greek place?"

"Stan would have new recipes." BJ thought. "And he orders his lamb pre-spiced from Chicago."

"How do you know that?"

"We talk. Anyway, his orders would go up."

Dave screwed up his forehead, thinking. "Yeah. That's how the IRS tracks businesses that are cheating on taxes. . . ."

He snapped his fingers, BJ's eyes flew wide, and they said in unison, "The gold."

They turned slowly and stared at Ryerson's jewelry store. The window was stocked with class rings, watches with Roman numeral faces, smooth silver Jefferson cups with no engraved initials yet, and the inevitable display of engagement rings. BJ had learned as an undergraduate that she could make any date nervous simply by stopping and staring at the rings.

She shook her head. "Not this place. Too respectable." Wyatt Ryerson, the elderly man who had founded and still ran Ryerson Jewelry, sent a letter each term to the *WeeVee Times*, welcoming new students to Kendrick and urging them to avoid "Loud, vulgar, unsuitable deportment" during their stay. BJ had gone in to get the gold hoops she had planned to use on the unicorn horn, and had discovered that Mr. Ryerson was in fact quite nice, if a bit formal.

Dave scratched his head. "He doesn't make rings anyway, just orders them and sets the stones. What about the other shop, the new one?"

BJ looked blank. "Where?"

For answer, Dave led her to the staircase leading to the tier of shops above Mitch's Ice Cream and Ryerson's.

These were the marginal businesses, places with little chance of making street-level rent with display windows. Generally they came and went rapidly: health-food restaurants becoming Philly cheese-steak cafés becoming Lebanese take-out. BJ hadn't been up here since she had been a sophomore.

In the meantime, between the kite store and the movie memorabilia shop was a new place with its name etched on the glass door in flowing script: CRYSTALCRAFFT AND GOLDWERKE.

The etching below it, of a single iris, looked stylized and otherworldly in a way that BJ now realized was merely pretentious. Dave held the door open for her.

The windows to the west were hung with crystals and glasswork. The light fixtures all had pendants, earrings, and crystal balls in monofilament netting dangling below them. The shop sparkled and scintillated, and every swaying monofilament line brought a new rainbow on the floor and ceiling.

The glass display cases alternated between crystals and gold: wire work, filigree work, blocky rings with letters, runes, and figures incised into them.

Another display, of amethysts, rose quartz, and miscellaneous minerals, featured handworked wire gold stands, each designed for the particular stone.

BJ stared from display to display, as disoriented as she had been by anything in Crossroads. This was definitely not like the engagement-ring and graduation-watch shop on College Street.

The man behind the counter, smiling, watched her face. He was gangling and nearly bald, and the ends of his large mustache were waxed and curled.

When he spoke, it was with a consciously upper-crust version of the local accent. "I'm so very glad y'all took the time to come up the stairs. I surely hope I can make you feel that it was worth the trip." He smiled broadly, almost flirtatiously, and held out his hand. "I am W. Meredith Corliss."

From the way he said it, BJ felt as though she should say, "Not *the* W. Meredith Corliss?" She merely introduced herself and Dave.

"Are you here for a crystal?" he said sharply. "If so, you'd best plan to take a decent amount of time to select a stand: driftwood, gold, or wire suspension. I do say a good crystal is no earthly good without the proper stand, no matter what its miraculous natural powers."

To BJ he sounded disturbingly like an elderly female southern eccentric.

BJ said, "We have kind of a funny question."

He smiled at her, and for a moment he looked normal and friendly. "Honey, there are fewer funny questions left than you'd imagine."

BJ held out two triangular sixpieces. "I'd like to know, if I gave you these, how I could change them for money."

W. Meredith Corliss stared at the two of them for a moment. "I did think," he said in a hurt voice, "that your question might show a decent and sensible interest in crystals."

But he went on, "You have several choices, all of them lower tech than you might imagine. For gold-bearing ore, there's amalgam of mercury, a little like what happens with gold fillings, and a reclamation process. If the gold ore has tellurium in it, you roast the ore. A good heat-treating furnace, just a tabletop model with a door like an oven, could give you controlled heating and turn the trick.

"For previously extracted gold, the traditional refiner's fire, so popular in Scripture, melts the gold at fairly low temperatures. The gold, being heavy, sinks to the bottom of the crucible, you skim the top off, pour the rest into an ingot mold, and you have a nice shiny bar of nearly pure gold."

His smile was a trace cold. "You might be a little careful not to breathe in vapors, lead being a good old-fashioned additive to stretch out gold coinage; a kind of 'Gold Helper,' you might say."

He tapped on the glass counter to bring them back from, presumably, riotous mirth at his little joke.

"But why bother?" He held a hand out. "Easier still, y'all hand it to me, I perform a little sleight of hand with it for a small courtesy fee, and the United States Assay Office in Philadelphia will give your little bitty gold the attention and assessment it deserves. I'd submit it in fairly big batches, if it were a personal transaction of mine." He laid his hands palms up on the wood strip behind the glass counter, finished.

"Sounds pretty simple," Dave said, impressed. "I didn't know it was that easy to sell gold."

W. Meredith Corliss actually bowed. "If you have the expertise, most anything is easy."

BJ said, "How much is the courtesy fee?"

"Seven percent. If you think that's excessive, why, I urge you to try to do better." This time his smile was almost smug.

"I see." BJ looked through the cases, as though intrigued by the rock crystals, and said finally, "Thank you for your time."

"Come back anytime," he said pleasantly. "If I look in the right crystal, maybe I'll see y'all coming."

Once outside, BJ said, "There's our proof. Someone else has been in."

"You mean because he knew how to do it? Hey, he's a jeweler—"

"I mean because he knew his fee, without having to work it out first."

"Maybe it was Sugar, converting our fees into cash."

BJ shook her head. "He wasn't surprised enough, and he had his explanation down pat. We weren't the second people in there." But something else was bothering her. "Could you excuse me a minute? I want to run back and ask him something." She didn't want Dave to come. "Can I meet you somewhere for a beer?"

"You bet. Dart Club?" Dave looked hopefully across at the wooden stairs up to the second-story club.

"That sounds fine." He trotted off. She opened the street door again and went back upstairs.

He looked up when she entered and said with exaggerated surprise, "Honey, when I said 'anytime,' I had no idea it would be so soon."

BJ took a scrap of paper from her pocket. "I didn't think of this until I was outside. I would like to place an order." She handed the slip to him.

He read it and stared, all pretense gone. "Are you serious? I can do part of it, but once the casting's done, I'm not licensed to—"

"Can't you find someone to work with you?" She pulled out her checkbook, which for the first time in years was correct to the penny. "I can leave two-thirds of cost for a down payment."

He sized her up and wrote a figure on the scrap. BJ studied it and wrote a check for two-thirds the amount, tearing it off before he could rethink. "Would three days be too soon?"

"Four days," he said absently, staring at the check. "Gracious, I seem to be in the wrong line of work."

He snapped out of it, popped the check and the paper into his cash register, and said briskly, "Four days. I'll see you then." He looked up at her, glancing down the thong around her neck which had been exposed when she bent over the counter. "That amulet's a nice piece, honey. Would you let me see it?"

BJ reluctantly slid the thong off her neck and handed the stone over to him. He pulled his glasses down on his nose and squinted at the stone, turning it over. "Carved . . . old enough to be worn, or overpolished? Flecks of mica, maybe schist—metamorphic—it might have been representational once, but my Lord, that's long gone."

He passed it back to her. "It is indeed curious, my dear, but I'm sorry to say it doesn't have much value."

She slipped it back on. "I don't think so, either."

She couldn't find Dave till he waved at her from a table near the dart lanes. The post-classes, pre-supper crowd was here for drinks.

The crowd was gesturing, talking, some singing along with the sound system. Ten or twelve of them were in the darts lanes, chalking, throwing, and bragging. BJ felt as though she were at Stein's, and looked around wistfully for Rudy and Bambi. She saw only Western Vee undergrads and graduates, mostly blonde or brown haired, all depressingly similar.

The same could not be said of the beers on the menu. The Dart Club boasted over eighty imported beers, of several different shades. After looking at the menu for long enough to have downed a beer already, as Dave irritably pointed out, BJ ordered a nut brown ale from England.

When it came, she sipped it and discovered to her surprise that it tasted neither as strong nor as bitter as she expected; the ale at Stein's was changing her taste. The plastic beer stein, quite sensible for a college town, felt strange after the heavy steins she had used before.

She finished it and had another. Dave, still working on his first, looked at her interestedly.

She caught Dave looking around as though he were a stranger here in one of his favorite places. "Funny how things look different now."

He nodded. "This used to be my favorite place. It had more variety than the other bars in town." He looked wistful. "Now everybody looks the same here."

"They always did." As Dave waved an arm around the place, a waitress hurried over; BJ ordered another ale. "We've changed."

Dave, gulping beer in an effort to keep up, nodded. "Remember what we were like three weeks ago?"

"Or a month ago." BJ thought about those days, when she knew that her mother sounded strange on the phone but otherwise BJ's life was normal. She realized how much she was enjoying this afternoon, how badly she needed just to sit without thinking. All she wanted was to feel normal and healthy for a few hours.

She downed half of her stein, basking in the glow brought on by too much ale too fast. Life wasn't so bad. Maybe she wasn't really sick yet. Maybe the tests were wrong. . . .

She and Dave talked for nearly an hour more, aimless conversation: speculation about the book thefts and other petty losses at the vet school, gossip about classmates and the constantly shifting webs of romance, picks and pans of teacher performances. They ordered snacks to stand in for supper, and eventually even played a fairly wobbly round of darts. Dave won easily.

When they got back to their seats, BJ said, "Let me buy you another beer." She signaled, a sloppy overhead wave.

"Thanks." Dave beamed at her, clearly feeling the beer himself. "You're nice. How come we never got to be friends before?"

"I didn't think you made friends with women." But she was smiling at him over the ale; at the moment she liked him. "You were too busy playing predator after full-figured honey-hair blondes to bother with me."

He grinned crookedly, the old Dave back again. "I dunno. If you wore a halter top and lost ten pounds—"

"Ten pounds?" BJ stood up, half laughing and half angry. "Ten *pounds*?" She stood on her chair, still holding her glass, other hand on her hip. "I'll have you know, David Roy Wilson, that I am well proportioned, muscled, smart, fast, hardworking, and every last damn thing a woman ought to *be*!"

She knew, back in her mind, that this was not the behavior of a sober person. She knew also that she was speaking as loudly as Dave had spoken his first night at Stein's; she didn't care. Dave was looking up at her with his mouth hanging open, embarrassed but impressed. Women at the neighboring tables clapped and cheered. She turned, taking them in with her eyes.

"So here's to me, dammit." By now the whole bar was looking, and enjoying it. Several of the men and women raised their glasses to her. Some of the looks were admiring. She raised her own glass . . .

And it slipped sickeningly from her hand, spilling beer all over the table. BJ made a late, frantic grab for the glass and toppled sideways to the floor, knocking a chair over.

Laughter went up around the bar. A red-haired man at the bar snorted, "Here's to *you*!"

Dave, laughing and mopping up the beer with a pile of napkins, said, "Nice going. Are you okay?"

BJ stood up, holding the table. Her legs felt unsteady. She pulled out her money slowly and carefully, feeling acutely how clumsy her fingers were. "Let's leave."

He wasn't surprised. He was good natured enough to say, "Look, it was no big deal," but insensitive enough to kid her about it twice on the way to his car.

BJ said good night, locked herself in her apartment, and sat on the floor in a corner of the kitchen, bouncing a half-dead tennis ball for nearly an hour. She cried the entire time. She dropped it seventeen times.

T·W·E·N·T·Y-F·I·V·E

B'CU WAS TALKING rapidly, glottal clicks popping from him like distant gunfire. He waved his staff, gesturing at the sky, the stream, the grass, and his flock. The Griffin said calmly, "He believes that I'm translating all this. Much of it has to do with magic, a capricious rain god who long ago slept with the mother of his people, and a curse that he believes has followed him here. What shall I tell him?"

"Tell him we can't do much about curses," Sugar said. His face was grim.

The tall grass here was flattened, trampled from the stampede of panic-stricken animals. Much of it was dotted with blood. Annie, moving from sheep to sheep, was dictating the list of injuries. "Seven: superficial bite, ripping wool . . . front right leg, radius, and ulna crushed. . . . Eight: Nose bitten, sinus cavity exposed . . ."

She didn't hurry and she didn't waste time. She fastened improvised cloth tags to each sheep. BJ took notes as quickly as possible, barely worrying about her shaky handwriting.

Forty feet away, Dave and Lee Anne were doing the same thing, working their way toward the center of the flock.

Some of the sheep were still. Some still moved feebly. A few let out plaintive bleats and shifted uneasily; B'cu and Sugar went back and forth, holding them in place.

All four students brushed constantly at flies. BJ looked up nervously at a flying shadow, but it was only a carrion vulture, circling patiently.

Finally Annie said, "Thirty-two," and looked up at Lee Anne. "Have you done this one?"

"Who cares? It's already dead." But she finished tagging it. "That's all of them."

It was; not a single sheep was uninjured.

Under the Griffin's direction, they had made an X on the body of every animal who would not survive. That was all of them.

"Actually," the Griffin said calmly, "it's a bit like a nasty parody of Passover. Here, the Angel of Death has marked all the bloody lambs, and he hasn't passed over any."

The Griffin had come quickly when Stein's parrot, squawking annoyedly, had brought news of the sheep kill. The students had been politely respectful to him; BJ, at least, had been glad to see him.

Now B'cu was going from animal to animal, slitting throats. Sugar had argued for injecting T-61 (a euthanasia solution), but when B'cu had found out that the sheep wouldn't be fit for meat afterward he had insisted on butchering instead.

After watching the slaughter for a few minutes, Sugar silently helped B'cu tie the rear legs of each dead sheep together with twists of grass. Lee Anne fell in behind him. The other vet students joined in unhappily.

Together they moved the bodies to the one tree in sight. It was bent to the east, its lower branches rubbed off by grazing animals, and its twisted body had the stubs of many broken branches.

B'cu stubbornly insisted on hanging the butchered sheep by their legs on the higher branches, and letting them drain. With the same knife and with great dexterity, he gutted them all without breaking the grass twists that held them hanging.

The students found it hard to watch; slaughter and surgery are nothing alike. They stood looking at the bloodied field, now emptied of any bodies.

B'cu tore leaves from a nearby broadleaf shrub and washed them methodically.

"He's going to wrap the meat," BJ said suddenly.

"True. And he'll salvage most of it that way, but he knows the reality of the market. Most people raise their own mutton, Stein can't possibly use this much at once, and there's no refrigeration here."

"I've read of animal mutilations," Lee Anne said, and shivered. "In supermarket tabloids. I never believed in them before."

"My pastor says they're the work of Satanists," Annie said noncommittally.

"The tabloids say it's vampires or space aliens."

The Griffin waved a dismissive claw. "Honestly. A single fact should never be construed as proof of the absurd. There are no space aliens, to my knowledge at least, and there are—" he hesitated, "no vampires that I know of who would do this." The students looked at each other uneasily.

The Griffin went on, "All of this has a much more mundane explanation: werewolves."

"Just your everyday, garden-variety werewolf," Lee Anne said sourly. "Shoot, I feel much better. How 'bout the rest of you?"

The Griffin, thinking, ignored her. "All the same, that explains *who* and not *why*."

"I'm still a little lost on *how*," Lee Anne said, looking around her. "Between doing things like this, where do they hide?"

"Wherever a wolf or a human can hide," the Griffin said crisply. "More to the point, they can hide in places where most of Crossroads' inhabitants can never look."

He took up an affected stance, as though he were lecturing the students.

"Actually," he said thoughtfully, "the Wyr are among the few species who can navigate to and from Crossroads successfully without maps. Chimeras migrate here to breed." He said it with some disgust, as if the breeding of chimeras were a reprehensible practice. "Possibly, also, the Great can fly from world to world by eyeing the roads ahead. No one knows. But the Wyr . . ."

He paused, cocking an eye at the vet students. "Do you mind a disgusting detail of animal behavior?"

"Not at all," Annie said.

"It's practically all I read these days," Lee Anne said.

"Very well. The Wyr, at the borders of Crossroads, urinate almost constantly and smell the roads for other urine. In this manner, so long as they know where the others have gone, they can follow the pack from world to world."

"But what about the Road Crews?" Dave objected.

"Ah. I said it was disgusting. The Road Crews, in the course of a day's work, eat and drink. It follows, therefore, that they—"

"Crap and whiz," Dave said.

"I was going to say, defecate and urinate," the Griffin said coldly. "Moreover, they have, mmm, partaken of whatever can be had at the border. There is a small amount of barter there, and there is also a certain amount of overgrowth from adjoining worlds— seeds dropped by birds, encroaching tendrils—"

"Someday," Lee Anne said, "you're gonna have a kudzu problem like everyone else."

BJ said suddenly, "My God, are you telling us that the Wyr can tell where people have been by smelling their urine and stools?"

"Dr. Dobbs, you have my sympathies. It absolutely amazes me," the Griffin said bitterly, "that anyone attempts to teach an assembly of people who interrupt this often. That is exactly what I am saying, although I would have done it with considerably more style."

Sugar, returning from his work with B'cu, nodded tiredly.

BJ frowned. "Then why do people need to use—" She caught herself before mentioning *The Book of Strangeways*. "Then why can't people just follow the Wyr up and down the roads, instead of using up-to-date maps?"

The Griffin said dryly, "In order to follow the Wyr between worlds, one would need to trust them. Now that you have seen their recreation, would you care to?"

BJ said, "They're not evil, just . . . brutal. And cruel, when they play—and, no, I wouldn't. But what if you had some kind of hold on them?"

The Griffin leaned forward. "What sort of hold do you feel would be sufficient?"

She considered. "Something that would make a Wyr completely dependent on me. Is there anything like that?"

"I was hoping you knew of something."

B'cu returned to them. He made a quick nod, then spoke rapidly.

"He says he must go to Stein's," the Griffin translated. "He says he doesn't think your vehicle is fit for transporting meat."

"Or anything else," Lee Anne muttered.

"He says," the Griffin said heavily, with a disapproving eye on Lee Anne, "that you don't need to wait here."

"Knew that," Dave said. "Anything else?"

B'cu turned to Sugar, nodded several times, and said his one word in English. "T'ank." It had a loud click at the end.

"You're welcome," Sugar said, and they watched him move into the unmatted grass. He was short enough and the grass thick enough that he seemed little more than a head and shoulders. Soon there was nothing around them but grasslands, rippling intermittently in the breeze.

The Griffin turned his eagle eyes to Sugar. "Unless you can think of a specific need for me, I'll be going."

"Thanks for helping," Sugar said.

"People in Crossroads have a duty to help," the Griffin corrected. "Thank you, Doctor."

Sugar, watching him run to the crest of the hill to take flight, said uneasily, "Seems to me that somebody in Crossroads isn't taking his duty half serious enough."

"Or too serious," Lee Anne agreed.

The Griffin poked his head over the hilltop. "You're sure you don't need me?"

"Quite sure."

"Because I could stay if you needed me."

"We appreciate it."

The Griffin said uncertainly, "It's fairly isolated out here."

They looked around. Except for the grotesque tree with its burden of leaf-wrapped carcasses, nothing but hillocks of tall prairie grass broke the skyline except, in the far north, the dim blue masses of the northern mountains.

"We'll be fine," Sugar said.

"Just so," the Griffin responded, and was gone. BJ was disappointed; she had hoped to see him fly.

Suddenly they were very much alone. There were few sounds besides the hum of locusts and the occasional bird song. They looked at each other, trying not to stare back at the tree.

Lee Anne finally turned, unwillingly, and looked at it. The wrapped carcasses were hanging perfectly still. "Sir, if the Wyr attacked those sheep—"

"That's only an assumption," Sugar said.

"Yeah," Dave cut in. "Remember, when you assume, you make an ass of u and me."

Lee Anne said witheringly, "We were halfway there on your first birthday. My point is, why didn't they take the meat? Why just maim them and leave them?"

Sugar scratched his head. In this setting, he looked more than ever like a range rider. "I'd love to have a better sense of why they did this," he announced.

"Because they're brutal," Annie said firmly.

"Sure, but why this brutality? Why not some other?"

The grass waved at the crest of the hill.

"And why here?"

Dave blurted, "Well, it's isolated, for one thing. Even for Crossroads, we are out in the damn boonies."

The waist-high grass rippled down the hill, as it had in breezes earlier.

"Still, why did they do it?" Sugar said.

"I know why," BJ said suddenly, and went white, pointing at the tree. They turned.

The lowest line of sheep carcasses was swaying as if in a heavy wind; one body was missing.

The ripples divided, moving around them. There was no breeze at all.

Sugar said tightly, "In the truck. Now."

BJ lifted her arms parallel to the grass, like a wader in chilly water. She ran toward the truck, feeling like this was one of those dreams in which you know you will never move fast enough.

She was nearly there when, seemingly from nowhere, a wolf with gray patches shot up at BJ and snapped at her arm. BJ screamed and backed away from the door.

A moment later she was bunched with the others, looking in confusion at her arm. Her shirt wasn't even torn. She looked quickly at the others, trying to understand.

The others were staring, wide-eyed, at their own arms and legs, marked with red scratches from fangs. So far, none of the biting had broken the skin.

Sugar and the students, back to back, bunched together as tightly as, undoubtedly, the panicked sheep had earlier.

A muzzle with flashing white teeth darted out of the grass and snapped at Lee Anne's ankle. She yelled, backing into the others, and they jumped back with her. A moment later, the same thing happened to Sugar. BJ was reminded of a border collie herding sheep. . . .

They were being driven away from the truck, out into the field. The grass rippled back and forth; BJ caught a glimpse of a dark tail waving.

"I said so, remember? You would pay."

Vlatmir, in human form, was seated on a rock, smiling and watching.

Sugar said, "You son of a bitch."

Vlatmir laughed in sharp barks. Sugar didn't appreciate the humor.

The snapping jaws moved them.

"Are you gonna kill us?" Lee Anne said.

"In time, yes." He scanned the sheep massacre, moving his head from side to side more than a normal human would. "This was bait. We knew you."

A she-wolf darted at the tiny space between BJ and Annie; they moved apart instinctively. The wolf growled, deep in her throat, at Annie, who was suddenly apart from the rest, alone in the grass.

Lee Anne tried to move toward her, but suddenly faced snarling jaws that snapped at her fingers. She looked across helplessly at Annie, who pulled her arms in tight and stood staring into the grass, fingering the cross at her neck.

Annie cried out as the she-wolf passed, snapping sideways at Annie's calf and tearing denim and flesh easily. The Wyr had drawn their first blood.

BJ ducked instinctively as a shadow nearly the size of their truck sailed overhead. She looked at it as it passed.

Her first thought was, I hadn't been sure he could really fly.

Her second, immediately, was relief. She had no doubt at all that they were safe now.

One of the Wyr locked onto the Griffin's right wing and snatched it sideways. The Griffin, still trying to land, fell heavily. Two more wolves latched onto his body, tearing at it.

Another, making a desperate bid for a quick kill, leaped at Annie. Sugar hit it with his shoulder, a full-body block. It turned its head to snap futilely at him; its body slammed into Annie, knocking her down.

Dave stood over her. His belt was in his hand, and he was snapping the buckle end at the wolves, shouting. In a moment, Lee Anne and BJ were beside him, doing the same. They snapped the belts like lion tamers, trying to strike eyes, ears, and noses with the buckles. BJ knew that the students couldn't keep this pace up for long; the wolves would outlast them.

The Griffin, wolves still hanging on him and trying to bring him down, bounded across the grass, clawing them one at a time. He moved out of sight on the other side of the truck. Shortly, yelps and howls came from there.

The remainder of the pack abandoned their attack and darted quickly to the other side of the truck.

Vlatmir, scowling furiously, jogged away to the south, leaving the rest behind. Even in the confusion, that struck BJ as odd.

All noise died. The attack was over, as suddenly as it had begun. The humans stared wildly at each other, unwilling to let go of their weapons.

"Annie." BJ dropped to the ground beside Annie, checking quickly for a pulse.

"Move over." Sugar all but knocked BJ aside as he dropped to his knees. "Okay, help me do a top-to-toe check."

They went down her from top to bottom as thoroughly as they could without rolling her over to undress her. Sugar ran his fingers lightly over Annie's scalp, then quickly examined her arms and legs where her clothing had been torn. He unbuttoned her blouse and checked the impact point where the wolf had hit her. "Just one hell of a bruise," he said with relief.

Her eyelids fluttered. Sugar quickly checked her pupils and, still examining her, asked, "What bothers you the most?"

Annie looked blearily up at him. "Barking dogs," she said vaguely. "I never could stand barking dogs."

"You're in the wrong line of work, then." He helped her sit up. "That's it. We're not coming back here. This was too big a risk to begin with."

Annie dazedly buttoned her blouse, not asking how she had gotten undressed.

"There's nothing wrong with a few risks," Dave said, panting. One of his arms was scraped, but otherwise he was fine.

"If it's your own self you're risking," Lee Anne pointed out. "Sir, we all knew these trips were dangerous. It's not as if we're not adults; we consented to these trips—"

He shook his head. "I don't see it that way."

"Then why did you bring us in the first place?" BJ said. She walked over to where Vlatmir had sat on the rock.

In the grass, lying on its side, was an empty vial from the Western Vee pharmacy. She nearly bent to pick it up, then pushed it with her foot instead, reading the label without bending over. It had held injectable morphine.

She looked back at Sugar, who was watching her narrowly. "Why did you bring us?" she repeated as naturally as possible.

Sugar opened his mouth, closed it, and shook his head. "Foolishness." He stood up. "We're leaving for good. Now." He walked around the van, saying to the Griffin, "Thanks much for the assist——"

He froze in place. BJ, seeing him, ran around the van; the others followed.

The Griffin was lying on his side next to two disemboweled and one nearly decapitated Wyr. Written in blood on the side of the truck was a single word in English: JUSTICE.

The Griffin looked steadily up at them from a growing pool of his own blood. "You are more than welcome. And now, I would greatly appreciate some assistance from all of you."

T·W·E·N·T·Y-S·I·X

THEY USED EVERY scrap of bandage on the truck, then tore up their coveralls. They tied pressure bandages on the Griffin's fore-limbs, and packed the great gash on his chest with furacin, and bound it as tightly as they could. He stood patiently, blinking as they passed near his eyes. His third eyelid stayed visible for longer each time he blinked.

BJ knelt and wiped his beak with a damp cloth. Fur and drying blood, Wyr blood, came off on the cloth. "Open wide." Without fear she put her hand inside the mouth and dabbed at the inside of a beak with a gauze, then stuck her face to the opening and shone a penlight down his throat. There was little blood.

Then he coughed, cutting her wrist slightly. "I'm sorry."

"Don't worry. Open." She peered back down his throat and felt sick; there were now flecks of blood in his throat, coughed up from his lungs.

She pulled back and shut off the light as the others stepped away as well. The Griffin said flatly to Sugar, "I believe you'll need to operate."

Sugar hesitated, then said, "We'll need a full OR, if we do." BJ didn't like that "if."

"I understand." And clearly, he did. "Assuming for the moment that you can operate, we'd best be on our way. Stand clear."

He leaped to the top of the truck. He made no sound, but Annie cried out; the Griffin's dangling, mangled right wing snapped loudly against the truck body.

256

The shocks creaked and the tires settled. The Griffin scrambled for balance, then turned painfully back to Sugar and the students. "Could you bind me to the truck somehow? If it's no trouble, I mean."

There was something horrible in seeing the confident, nearly invincible Griffin asking for reassurance.

"Of course we can," Annie said, stretching up, and reached under the bloodstained beak to tuck her coveralls under the Griffin's head. "Rest for now; we'll take care of everything."

"Just one more thing," he said in a thin voice. "Dr. Dobbs?"

"Right here." He was pulling out the rope he had used to transport the roc.

The Griffin glanced around, barely focusing, at the others, and said in a near-whisper, "I don't mean to insult your students, for I think well of them. Highly, in fact." He gurgled, and a trickle of blood came out of his beak. "Nonetheless, I would appreciate your handling this one yourself. If you don't mind."

"You've got it," Sugar said.

They backed the truck up to the loading dock at the stable end of the school. The horses whickered nervously, then whinnied and pawed, but there was nowhere else to go.

Dave leaped out; Lee Anne followed, her long legs catching up with him before he was in the hall. They came back in rolling a steel table; they got it even with the truck, where BJ and Annie had undone the straps holding the Griffin in place, and stopped.

Sugar looked around. "We'll need slings and a rolling frame."

The Griffin raised his bulk up suddenly. "If I may," he said tightly, and before they could move he had lurched over to the steel table and leaped up. The table creaked.

But his rear legs didn't clear the tabletop, and the dark stain on his bandage blossomed suddenly. Sugar barked, "Move!"

BJ and the others found themselves careening down the hallway, pushing the cart as rapidly as possible toward the OR.

They spun around the corner on the dead run, then froze.

Sugar looked ahead and said tiredly, "Damn it, don't you ever go home?"

Laurie stood frozen in the hallway. "Asturiel," she said in a sharp whisper.

She moved faster than any of them had seen her move, and she had her hand lightly on the Griffin's neck. "Asturiel?" She probed for a pulse.

She found one and relaxed, then took in the bandages. "Jesus," she said softly, and shook. "Oh, Jesus, this is terrible."

The Griffin rallied. "Nonsense, my dear. It's simply the only excuse I could find to come see you again." He held one of his talons up to her. "I rather wish I'd found a better one."

She caressed the claws that could rip through stone and steel. "Next time, just send for me. I can make up better excuses."

"Ah yes," he said. "You've always been cleverer." But his voice was weak, and his leg dropped down far too quickly.

In the OR, BJ plugged a set of clippers in; Annie was shaving one of the Griffin's hind legs before the cord sagged. Sugar popped a pressure cuff that the students hardly ever used onto the leg, pumped the bulb briskly, and listened with a stethoscope that Lee Anne dropped onto his neck just in time. He checked his watch, scribbled two figures on paper, scowled, and pointed to a storeroom off the OR.

"Move him in here. We'll lock it tomorrow, and say it's being repainted."

They wheeled the Griffin in. Dobbs bent down. "Astu——I'm sorry. Griffin?"

"Yes," he said hoarsely. His head didn't move.

Sugar spoke loudly and slowly, as though to an elderly person or a foreigner. "We're going to keep you in here until you stabilize. We're going to put an I.V. drip on you, and change your bandages as needed, and see if we can go in on you later. We'll check you hourly."

"That sounds fine." He was barely audible.

Annie had the I.V. bottle, BJ the mobile hangar. Dave scrubbed the bare skin and BJ, grateful that the Griffin's veins hadn't collapsed, inserted the catheter stylet.

The Griffin turned his head toward them; he could no longer raise it. "Thank you," he said. His breathing was quick and shallow. "You are good children." He closed his eyes. They all held their hands to his side, checking his breathing. Even though it was easy to see his ribs rise and fall, none of them took their hands off for a while.

The others walked out the door through which they had rolled the Griffin. BJ, wanting to be alone, walked out the side door of the surgery. She was around the corner from the others, and the surgery door was recessed; a second swing door, by the sinks, had a small window in it. The door was still swinging slightly. BJ looked through the window.

Laurie was standing outside the surgery, chain-smoking. Her face was almost bloodless.

Beside her, Sugar shifted from one leg to the other, looking young and awkward. "If you want to go home, you can. Nothing's gonna happen for a while."

Laurie lit another cigarette on the butt of the first, stubbed the first out against the wall, and said, "If you lose him on the table, you son of a bitch, you're not walking out of the OR alive."

Sugar regarded her bleakly. "I don't dare cut him. He's lost way too much blood. I can pack the wounds, stitch him, apply pressure, and—well, that's all." His tone said it wasn't enough. He finished defensively, "There's nothing for him, Laurie; not even plasma."

Laurie stubbed out the second cigarette and threw it away. "I'm going to sit with him. I'm sorry about what I said."

"Forget it." Sugar held out his hand. "You got any of those left?"

She passed him a cigarette. He broke the filter off and smiled apologetically. "Camels smoker." He lit up, inhaled, coughed. "It's been seven years."

BJ turned back around and walked out the front OR door. She heard a sound from the cabinets in the prep room and turned back around.

Dave had emptied his books and notes from his duffel and was assembling supplies: fourteen-gauge needles, plastic hose, twenty donor bags.

She said, "I'll stash your books for you."

He whirled as she spoke.

BJ stared pointedly at the donor bags. Dave said defiantly, "I know I've done plenty of stupid things. This isn't stupid."

"Dangerous, though."

"So?" But it wasn't bravado, and it wasn't reckless. "If there's something smarter that will work, believe me, I'll try it."

BJ considered that. "I'm going to the library. Pick me up there. Fifteen minutes."

He looked at her blankly.

"Don't forget," she added, "we'll need a cooler."

T·W·E·N·T·Y-S·E·V·E·N

IF BJ HAD not been terminally ill, she would never have ridden behind Dave.

Not that he was inconsiderate; he had insisted on giving her his helmet. There was no way to explain to him that she had less of a life at risk than he had.

Once he left the main roads, her instinct for self-preservation outweighed any rational knowledge whatsoever.

His bike had a banana seat with a strap on it; she began by holding the strap. That worked well enough on the interstate, but once he turned down a dirt road, they were bouncing dangerously hard, and slewing sideways in the gravel mounds that even the best road-grading leaves to either side of the road crown.

BJ wrapped her right arm around his waist—tentatively at first, then tightly (with no desire whatsoever) as the gravel thinned and the rutted road became steeper. Dave didn't slow down at all, even for the switchback turns; they leaned from one side to the other in a desperate rhythm. BJ was grateful that her body seemed to be responding well enough to orders to follow his lead.

BJ pulled her chest tight against his back, leaned her head to one side, and scanned the photocopies she had just taken from *The Book of Strangeways*. At the awful, bone-jarring speed he was taking, she had barely enough time to twist her head forward, shift her gaze back to the map, and shout directions: "Left!

Straight! Right, then left, then straight! Center fork . . ."

Dave's last-minute slewing turns were wide enough to create quick glimpses of other views, down the side roads. BJ saw quick flashes of palm trees, saguaro cactus, burning windmills—and once, disturbingly, something with a leathery human body and a turtle's head, hunched over and peering down at them. It made no effort to snatch at them as they passed.

The worst stretch, past the stone bridge, was a section of cobbled road with no grass growing between the stones, and the earth at the roadside was still unsettled and half-damp. The Road Crews had been here within a day. BJ double-checked the map, hoped fervently that her map-reading skills had improved, and shouted, almost too late, "Right!"

Dave, without slowing down, veered right at the last instant. At the crossroad, they heard thousands of anguished voices whispering; abruptly, the voices cut off.

Presently they came out on the road above the river. BJ sagged against Dave's back.

They passed the place where BJ had treated the unicorn, then quickly swung by Stein's. BJ heard a snatch of music from something like a bagpipe, and rhythmically stamping feet. She fervently wished they could stop. Dave hunched over the handlebars and opened the throttle as wide as it would go.

Less than a half hour later they passed the point where they had picked up the roc chick. BJ looked up involuntarily; there were no signs of the Great. Now she was hanging on to Dave with both hands; a boulder every few feet sent him swerving from one side of the road to the other.

The cliff of the bowl valley rose to either side, and slowly began closing in. Before they blocked out the sky, BJ got a brief glimpse of mountains to the west. Several of them were topped by irregular mounds of sticks. BJ remembered the distances involved, and realized she was looking at nests made of entire trees piled together.

Finally Dave had to slow down as the road became nothing but two wheel tracks; he moved up one of them cautiously. The remaining thick-trunked trees thinned out, leaving nothing but gnarled dead trunks and lime rock, powdered with constant wind erosion. The cliff walls, powdery and pocked with caves, nearly merged; they were riding up a box canyon. The track became intolerably bumpy, crossed with natural faults and with gullies from rainwater.

Dave slowed and finally stopped as even that track ended.

BJ slid off the bike, but stayed beside it as she looked around. The cliffs to either side cut off the midmorning sun.

She checked her watch; they had been gone two hours. Back at Western Vee, the first- through third-year students would be in the second hour of morning lectures. A very few lucky, exhausted fourth-year students would be sleeping in, and the rest would be well into cases that seemed complex, baffling, and ripe with possibilities for ineptitude, neglect, and failure. BJ remembered feeling that those cases were the toughest problems in the world.

BJ and Dave stared to either side. BJ, with numb studiousness, began classifying the skulls on the limestone shelves around them. She recognized bats, raccoons, something with horns but very much like a rabbit, and further up a horse, a unicorn. . . . Long before the piles of human skulls she realized that there was a process of classification, by layer and horizontally, with a meticulousness that spoke of a great deal of killing and far too much time.

A deer dashed past them, desperately leaping its way up the gorge. It turned at the sheer wall ahead, the whites of its eyes showing. There was a flash of bronze and brown, and the deer made a noise that sickened BJ as its throat opened at a single talon stroke. The deer collapsed immediately, its legs heaving once.

The bronze griffin slashed across it, neatly gutting it with a single swipe, tossed the entrails aside with a flick eerily like a cat with a wet paw, and buried its beak in the still-pulsing chest. It met their eyes, raised its beak, and said clearly, "Oh, don't mind me. Please, carry on."

Dave made a gurgling sound much like the deer.

Griffins in flight were surprisingly graceful, but not fast. BJ suspected that they had to take off from a high point and glide down. They settled all around, on the rocks, and climbed down with feline grace.

Their plumage varied in color, but each was a single metallic color: gold, bronze, platinum, copper. Their heads were lowered, their eyes staring. BJ thought uneasily of cats at play with small animals.

"And where," the Copper said sharply, "are you from, and what do you want?"

Dave got off the bike and stood before them, palms up. He was nearly green with fear, and BJ was suddenly proud of him.

He cleared his throat several times and said, "We've come from Kendrick, Virginia, looking for griffin blood donors." He pointed. "All the way down this road," he said loudly in the voice he used unconsciously for foreigners. BJ winced.

The large Golden laughed and intoned: "Facilis descensus Averno est Noctes atque dies patet atri janua Ditis; Sed revocare gradum, superasque evadere ad auras, Hoc opus, hic labor est."

The small Golden chuckled.

Dave looked puzzled. "What does that mean?"

"No knowledge of Latin? Ah, me." The large Golden peered down at them contemptuously. " 'Easy is the descent to Avernus'—I was pointing out that some roads are easier to go down than they are to return back up."

The Bronze sniffed. "Try this, then: 'The shepherd in Virgil grew acquainted with Love, and found him a native of the rocks.' Your Dr. Johnson."

"They're American, not English," the small Golden corrected. "Listen to their speech."

"Tidewater Virginia is not far removed from Elizabethan English," the Copper objected. "Granted, Roanoke Island would be closer."

"You're very familiar with us." BJ was desperate to keep conversation open. "Do you read mainly from human writers?"

"Not always. For instance: 'All species covet each other's blood, differing only in the rate of exchange they desire.' That's from a very honest world." She bent down. "And what gives you such a pressing need for blood?"

BJ looked back at Dave; by rights, this was his case. He said, "Back on Earth—back in our reality—"

"Back where you come from," the Bronze corrected, not kindly at all.

"Right. We've taken in an injured griffin. Seriously injured. He's sustained a serious chest wound, plus we need to do exploratory surgery for intestinal and lung damage—internal bleeding from a blow, too, we think—and we need a blood supply, or the surgery will kill him."

BJ added, "And without the surgery, he'll die anyway."

"You seem to feel," the Copper said thoughtfully, "that one species has some sort of duty to save the lives of another. Why is that?"

BJ and Dave looked at each other helplessly. Finally Dave said blankly, "We're going to be veterinarians. That's what we do for a living. Sometimes we do it for free."

"Ah. Vocation." The large Bronze tucked an unidentifiable organ from the deer into his beak and finished, "But that's an important difference between us, don't you know. Except for the individual you are treating, whom we all suspect we know, griffins don't much care about other species. Fight, sicken, suffer, die, we just don't care." He gestured around. "Except at mealtimes, and the occasional intellectual amusement, such as now."

"Dinner theater," the Copper said.

Ignoring the implied threat, Dave said desperately, "But this isn't for one of us. This is for one of you."

The Golden nodded solemnly. "Ah. One of our own. 'The ashes of his fathers, and the temples of his gods.' And what sort of bona fides—I'm sorry; that's Latin, isn't it? What manner of *credentials* do you two have, that we should believe you and not eviscerate you?"

"We're veterinary students," Dave said. "What credentials do you want? Our transcripts aren't going to do you much good."

"Granted," the Bronze conceded, between dips of his beak into the deer carcass. "But we have no real need to help you establish credentials. Quite the opposite, in fact."

The other griffins sidled closer unhurriedly, making no attempt either to rush or be subtle.

"We have one credential," BJ said. "Proof that we know this griffin well—intimately."

"And what proof might that be?"

"His name," she said.

Dave looked at her in astonishment. So did several of the griffins.

Finally one said, "That would be more than adequate, if you are correct. What is the name?"

BJ shook her head. "What if the rest of you didn't know his name? You haven't shown me any *bona fides,*" she stressed it, "of your own. He might not want it confided in you." She corrected herself, for effect: "In you all."

Several beaks clicked loudly at that. A platinum-feathered griffin, off to one side, said annoyedly, "You're the one begging favors, biped. I don't much care for having my integrity questioned."

"Nor I." "Nor I." The others looked coldly at BJ, their eagle eyes clearly sizing up the distance between her chest and their claws.

A soft voice said from behind them, "She is not so much questioning your integrity as establishing her own."

Heads turned, and the winged bodies parted as a silver-feathered griffin, larger and more muscled than the others, strode toward BJ.

She gave him a nod which was almost a bow. "Are you the—" she fumbled for a word, "the ruler here?"

He dipped his beak in cursory acknowledgment of her bow. "By combat, of course." He came up to her, his great beak nearly touching her face. She did not flinch.

He turned his head to one side. "You may whisper the name to me. If you are wrong, I will tear you in half for the others to feed upon." He added more quietly, "By rights, it shouldn't be painless, but because I respect you, I will at least be quick."

She hesitated momentarily, then moved forward and whispered, where she thought the ear hole of the griffin's head would be, "Asturiel." She had a moment of dismay: if Laurie had not actually known the Griffin's name, or if BJ had misunderstood, then she and David would be dead shortly.

The Silver turned slowly toward her. "And did he give his name to you freely?"

She swallowed. "Actually, no. Someone else spoke it in front of us, inadvertently, when she saw how badly he was hurt." Dave closed his eyes.

But the Silver said quietly, "I believe you. No one would make up so reckless a truth. I am therefore inclined to believe the rest of your story." He raised his head and said to the others, "The name she gave was in fact correct."

The griffins regarded each other thoughtfully. The Bronze, with deer blood dripping from his raised beak, addressed Dave coldly and a trace disappointedly. "What are you waiting for, then? Take what you need."

Dave unstrapped the cooler and opened it, BJ beside him. "You stick, I'll tag," he said. She put a bottle of Betadine scrub in her shirt pocket, grabbed the packet of ten needles and ten tourniquets, and began.

She tied off one of each griffin's leonine rear legs, swabbed below the tourniquet, and slid a stylet cleanly and quickly into the veins below the tight bands. She was grateful that her hands, for once, were sure and quick; the veins were large, and she had no trouble.

David went behind her, attaching collection sets to the catheters. He wrote a number in grease pencil on each bag, then opened the cooler and waited.

But when Dave removed the first blood bag, the Bronze said, "Put on a second bag."

"We don't generally take that much blood from a single donor."

The Bronze said coldly, "I don't generally leave requests open to discussion. Put on a second bag."

Dave did as he was told. BJ, checking the connection, said, "You know, you *will* be weak for a few days."

The Bronze licked its stained front talons clean, like a cat. "How shall I ever get by?"

And so it went with the rest of them, a second bag from each. They did not appear significantly weaker at the end.

When the last donor bag was taken and the cooler filled, Dave cleared his throat and said, "I generally tell owners this, and not animals." The old Dave came back for a moment, and he glanced around innocently. "Do y'all have owners anywhere?"

There was a universal low growl, like thunder. Dave said hurriedly, "Okay. Rest up for the next day or two. Eat well and drink plenty of fluids. I don't know if you drink wine, but hold off any big parties for a couple days. I'll bet that flying is tiring; keep it to a minimum. Watch each other for fevers, listlessness, sepsis . . ." He had the grace not to patronize them by defining "sepsis" as "infection."

At the end of Dave's recital, the Silver nodded sagely. "We appreciate your cautions; now, go and save our associate." He raised an admonitory claw as Dave moved toward the bike. "We have, however, one more bit of business. Tell me," he said pleasantly. "If we discover that you were lying, how can we find you?"

Dave paled.

BJ said, "You can check with Fields. I'm not sure that's his real name. He's a satyr, and he's probably Greek. He knows how to find us at our school."

The Silver said, "I know whom you mean, and no, his name is not Fields. A fairly apt, if not literal, nom de guerre. His original name is Greek."

"They probably don't know Greek, either," said the Gold.

The Silver yawned. "Well, then, I suppose we'll have to provide them with a better translation. His name in English would probably be Al."

There was a ripple of laughter from the surrounding griffins. "Or All," one suggested.

The Silver raised a warning claw, and they fell silent. "Suffice it to say, we could find you, and you would owe us . . ."

He looked at the cooler meaningfully.

"Twenty pints of blood." Dave closed the lid. "And thanks for your kindness."

The Silver shook his head. "Never thank a griffin for kindness. We are never kind."

BJ strapped the cooler down and got on behind Dave. She was tired of threats, urbanity, and sarcasm. "Let's say instead that Dave and I set the appropriate value—to ourselves—on all this personal interest in honor."

There were several sharp hisses. The Silver said, amused, "At least your disapproval is articulate. Tell me, do you find us so evil?"

"Evil is at least active," she said. "You're indifferent, in all senses." They hissed again, but she didn't appear to notice. "Not one of you asked what had happened to him, or why we risked our lives to save him. Not one of you wonders if we'd do as much for you, even though that's what we're training for."

The Silver looked down at her. "If I were human, I would stand rebuked. You don't understand. Your patient is the youngest of us. He is my only offspring, in fact. If he had stayed with us, I had hoped he would rise—" He glanced at the others and sighed. "But life is cruel, and we are only just."

"Good for you. Ast——the Griffin we know is just and loving at the same time."

She looked around the bowl of unrelenting beaks and talons. "I suspect the rest of you aren't."

The Silver, when he spoke, spoke for all of them—by inclination as well as by right. "Take our blood and go."

Dave kick-started the bike so hard he stood off the seat.

Down the road he yelled into the wind, "You were great back there."

"So were you."

"No. I mean, you did everything perfectly. You didn't miss a single vein, and you knew just what to say, you were great."

"So were you," BJ screamed into the wind, and hugged his back.

Without knocking, Dave and BJ strode straight into Sugar's office, staggering with the full cooler. Sugar looked up, his face strained and unhappy, a half-smoked cigarette in his mouth.

"Is he still alive?" BJ asked.

"For now. Still bleeding."

Dave popped the bungee cord off the cooler and flung it open. "Griffin blood. Twenty pints, fresh."

Sugar threw aside the cigarette. "You and BJ get it into him." As they picked up the cooler, he added to Dave, "And scrub. Fast."

BJ carried the cooler to the OR with Dave. He was relieved now, close to babbling. "Weren't you afraid at all? I was."

They set the cooler down. "I was scared to death," BJ admitted, "but I figured you knew what you were doing."

"I did." But he looked awfully pleased. Suddenly he hugged her, with no trace of his usual hitting on women for sex. "Thanks for coming with me. I'd have been dead without you."

"I wouldn't have done it at all," she said simply. "None of us would but you. You were wonderful."

He let go of her and looked at her, and he looked about twelve. "I did good, didn't I?"

As BJ left, Dave was scrubbing up and singing tunelessly to himself. He was getting back some of his former cockiness, but BJ felt that this time he'd earned it.

Five minutes later, the Griffin received his first pint of whole blood. BJ helped Dave set up the transfer needle and line, then checked in with Sugar, in the main OR. "When can you start?"

He grimaced. "As soon as he's full, stabilized, and I can figure out an excuse to cover the windows in OR."

"A celebrity client needs privacy. Horse surgery." That had happened before.

"That'll work. Okay." He handed her a scribbled list, his faculty I.D., and a copied combination lock. "Head to the pharmacy."

She froze in place. "Sir?"

"Go to the pharmacy, sign out what I need there—" honesty made him amend, "what I think I might need, and get it back here. Don't tell anybody the combination."

"I'll be right back." She clutched the I.D. and papers, running into the hall.

But her mind was running even faster than her legs: I have the means to make it painless and controlled. I can go home and take it quietly. All it will take is a small, quick theft.

I may never get this chance again.

T·W·E·N·T·Y-E·I·G·H·T

BJ HAD NO intention of removing controlled drugs from the vet school dispensary until she was ready to leave the premises and inject them. Immediately before that, she would need to give the anesthetic drugs, the ketamine and Valium, to Sugar and to Laurie—who would normally have been signing for them, but were too busy with the Griffin.

Sugar would be setting up for at least half an hour. Beyond that, there was the problem of stabilizing the Griffin. BJ couldn't be sure how long he would take, but it would take a while to get the donated griffin blood into him.

She had several errands to run, and very little time.

First, she opened her locker and knelt at it, appalled; the books and notes wouldn't matter except to other vet students, who already had their own.

The amulet on her neck banged against the door. She slipped the stone off, laid it in the locker, and closed the door.

Next, she stopped by the kennels of her donor dogs—not really "her" dogs, but the ones she had cared for, Sam and Maizie. The two greyhounds leaped up, tails thumping against the cages, when they saw her.

She let them out briefly, ran them in the field adjoining the school, patted them both, hugged Sam and beeped his nose, felt guilty and hugged Maizie, and put them back. She checked their food and water, glad to see that they were well cared for, and left a note mentioning that she needed to be replaced in the feeding and walking schedule.

Finally, she tiptoed to the storeroom off OR and knocked timidly. "Griffin?"

After the briefest of pauses, a testy voice said, "If you're not supposed to know about me, come in anyway. It's boring, being ill." There was the sound of a bolt being slid back.

She opened the door.

Already, the Griffin's hospital room looked like a new wing of the university library, somewhere between the classics and literature departments with smatterings of biology and botany thrown in. Books were stacked five deep. Most of them had marbled covers, embossed or taped spines, battered corners, and the general look of overuse.

A quick glance through the stacks made clear that there was an immensely detailed organization to all this chaos. BJ, remembering the exhibitlike cataloging of skulls in the griffins' valley, was unsurprised.

Laurie, a pen in her teeth in lieu of a cigarette, watched her carefully.

The Griffin, his eye open, followed her examination of the stacks. "These are Laurie's handiwork," he said faintly but dryly. "By way of her office. I was quite concerned that her entire wages were being garnisheed in library fines, until I realized what a talented thief she is."

His blood catheter was still in place, though most of the donated blood had already been transfused into him. His new bandages were stained, but the stains were smaller than they had been on the old bandages. BJ was relieved.

"I'm sure Laurie's very talented," she said tactfully. "I'm glad to hear you speak."

"I'm not," Laurie said. "Be quiet and rest."

"I'd rather speak," he riposted. "I go into surgery in half an hour; I'll be silent enough then. Dr. Dobbs wants to make sure that I'm stable. You and your rash friend have bought me some time."

"Well." She shuffled from foot to foot; she hadn't really thought out this conversation. "I just thought I'd check in on you."

"And thank you for doing so."

"You're welcome." She came forward and, almost shyly, patted his tawny fur. "Well, good-bye."

More quickly than she had thought he could move while still weak, he whipped his left talon forward and caught her shoulder. Fast though he was, the talons did not prick her skin.

Laurie said quickly, "Don't strain yourself."

But the Griffin, gazing steadily at BJ, said only, "I apologize for my rudeness, Ms. Kleinman, but I really must speak to BJ alone. Now would be a good time for you to smoke a cigarette; you haven't had one in ages."

"I'm trying to quit." But the Griffin took no notice. Finally she said to BJ, "Don't excite him, and don't let him do too much. I'll be right outside." She slid through the door, saying warningly to the Griffin, "Right outside."

The door closed. The Griffin pulled BJ closer to the bed and looked directly into her eyes, his large golden eyes peering at her as though she were an unknown landscape many miles below him. He moved his head from side to side, looking at her from slightly changed angles.

BJ looked back fearlessly, with apparent indifference.

Finally he let her go. "Don't do it."

BJ said nothing.

"You have experienced a great many strange things in the past month."

She nodded.

"Many of them were almost completely beyond your imagination. Some of them were wonderful beyond belief, others frightening."

She nodded vigorously.

"Tell me: which of them would you willingly give up?"

She found her voice. " 'Willingly' is the wrong word."

"This is hardly a time for nice distinctions," he said sharply. "Which of them would you choose to give up by dying this week, if you weren't to have had the experience until next week?"

So much for pretending that she wasn't committing suicide. "None of them," she said stubbornly, "unless I were afraid that I might never again have the means to die and the mind to do it at once."

"You graduate in a short while."

"If I graduate." She still had to retake Truelove's small animal course, though that seemed a fairly unimportant problem just now.

"Oh, you will. I feel quite sure." He pointed a single claw at her. "And when you do, and when you take employment as a veterinarian, won't you have access to drugs?"

"I haven't sought employment," she said, feeling a bit silly at her own words. The Griffin's diction was catching. "I didn't think it would be right. I have . . . a health problem, which wouldn't make me a good long-term employee."

"I have my own health problem," he reminded her. "Unexpected solutions sometimes appear for these things."

"Not for mine."

"Nonetheless," he said sharply, "I counsel patience. Life can and does provide miracles. Why die now? Why not a month from now, or a year, or five years, or ten?"

BJ, who had not confided her fears to anyone, finally broke.

"Because I'm afraid to wait," she said, wringing her hands. "Because I don't want to wait too long, and end up paralyzed and helpless and crazy and—"

The Griffin blinked and looked dizzily at her. She wrenched herself free of him, which she never could have done when he was well; rushed through the door, said, "Better check him," to Laurie, and ran.

She took a syringe from the lab. It didn't need to be sterile, but it felt better to use a fresh one. There was a memo cautioning students and staff to be careful in disposing of needles, and directing them to the disposal bins, which broke needles. BJ took two, in case she somehow damaged the first. She took a tourniquet, though a belt would have done as well.

Almost guiltless, equipped, and her life in order, she walked the hall to the drug dispensary.

The door, equipped with a push-button combination lock, was propped open. A floor-to-ceiling metal grille divided the room in two; beyond the grille were several file cabinets, a refrigerator, metal shelves with bins on them, and a monitor's desk.

Marla Schmidt was working the student desk. At the moment, her face was buried in a copy of *Small Animal Medicine.* Her eyes had ugly bags; her clothing was wrinkled and, BJ suspected, slept in.

Dr. Truelove, bent over one of the file cabinets, turned suddenly when she entered. "Hello, BJ." He didn't ask how she was feeling, and he didn't look to be feeling very well himself.

"Dr. Dobbs wanted me to get this."

She showed Sugar's I.D. and handed over the slip of paper: Sugar's request for ketamine and Valium, Sugar's signature, and, between them, a carefully forged request for pentobarbital.

He looked at it again, looked unaccountably anxious, and said, "What would he need that for? And such a large dosage, especially of a euthanasia solution."

There were advantages to someone's thinking one a fool. BJ looked distressed. "I don't really know. He said he had a special client; he wouldn't discuss the case. Is that a problem?"

"A special client?" For a moment, Truelove's curiosity overcame his self-importance. "Well, I'll check for you."

He wrote Sugar's name and requisition number in the log, a black three-ring binder. He found and released the ketamine. He released the Valium, and annoyed her a great deal by saying, "Now, you will take this straight to Sugar and only to him, won't you?"

He released the pentobarbital, and BJ held her breath and tried to look casual.

He took her signature, frowning. "He should have sent the tech or come himself." He seemed to make that BJ's fault.

BJ said, "I think all the doctors do it."

He waved a hand. "Nonsense. I do it, but only on limited occasions, with very trustworthy people."

Marla, studying behind him, said nervously, "That's true. His signature is on nearly all of his own requisitions."

He looked at her strangely. She hastily turned back to her book.

BJ was anxious to leave now, but Dr. Truelove said, "Just to make a point." He opened the top drawer of requisition slips beside him and filed the slip. "I very occasionally send a student of mine down here. . . ." He rummaged through the drawer, pulling recent slips. He rummaged some more.

He left the file drawer and went to the shelves. He looked around: in the refrigerator, on the floor, in the boxes to be thrown out.

He came back, greatly troubled, and checked the printout of stock.

Turning to BJ, he masked his anxiety and said testily, "In fact, I can't find a single occasion when I've done it. Now, if you don't mind, I have my own work to do." He edged past her. "Very important research. Very important. Don't you think I wanted to send a student down here, instead of wasting my own time?" All pretense of his being kindly was gone.

Marla glanced nervously over her shoulder at him, afraid even to make eye contact with BJ.

Two things struck BJ immediately: One was that Dr. Truelove should not have left either her or Marla alone in the dispensary. The other was that BJ had not seen him put back the slips he had removed.

Did it matter? She had what she needed.

She thought of the Griffin, nearly killed, and the morphine bottle on the ground near Vlatmir's seat; yes, it did matter.

She said, "Marla?" and, a little louder, "Marla?"

"Hmm?" Marla, already having dropped back into her notes, jerked her head up.

"Sorry to bother you. Sugar wanted me to double-check the state files; he wanted to make sure I did the paperwork right. He's a little hazy on how the system works."

"Aren't they all," Marla said, looking over her shoulder automatically to be sure that Dr. Truelove was really gone. She gestured at a cardboard dead-storage file next to her. "That's why the dispensary takes care of it. Look at any of the records you want. God knows we have enough of them."

BJ lifted the lid, met Marla's tired eyes, and said kindly, "I'll do it right here, so you can keep studying." She moved the box over to a bare table and turned her back to Marla.

The state files were copies of the requisitions and releases of all drugs with potential for human abuse; essentially, all controlled substances with a street value. There were requests for amphetamines, for Valium . . .

There were far more requisitions for morphine than BJ had thought a veterinary hospital could use, no matter how many canine anesthesias required it.

The drug releases were all cosigned by faculty, by necessity. It was common knowledge that Dr. Truelove and Sugar Dobbs were nearly tied for highest number of requests; Sugar worked with large-animal surgery, Truelove with small-animal surgery and a phenomenal amount of drug research.

All of the morphine withdrawals were signed, in a careful, round hand, by Dr. Truelove.

A faint snort from the desk made her jump. Marla had dozed off over her text.

BJ closed the state files and looked around, eager to leave. She hesitated and looked back at the file cabinets.

Vet school had taught her thoroughness; she went back and examined the rest of the requisition file for the spring, checking the sequential numbering of the slips. Dr. Truelove had far fewer requisition slips than he had in the state box. She couldn't be sure that the missing slips were all morphine requisitions, but it seemed likely.

She looked through Sugar's requisitions as carefully. She found very few for controlled substances, and a great deal of care in entering. She was suddenly sorry that he might have to answer questions about her access to drugs for her suicide, but knew that it was a small betrayal, compared to those suicides normally make.

She pulled Sugar's requisition and wrote on it, "Per BJ Vaughan" next to the pentobarbital request and, under it in large letters, "Approved, Dr. Walter Truelove. See log entry." It might at least spread the blame. She double-checked the log entry to make sure that Truelove had done it correctly.

An entry near the top of the same page caught her eye:

#7089. Flexedine, 20 gm. For feline research. Applicant, Dr. Charles Dobbs. Co-applicant, Dr. Lucille Boudreau.

There was no Lucille Boudreau at the vet school. BJ went back to the requisition drawer and read the original request slip. On the bottom, in pencil, was a notation by Sugar: "2 P.M. Grass testing sta."

It was a typical Sugar Dobbs note to himself. BJ put the receipt back, locked the file cabinet, replaced the key, and left quickly. She left the requested anesthetic, and Sugar's borrowed I.D., with Sugar. He thanked her absently; he was reading standing up, scanning back and forth between an article on raptor surgery and a book on feline anatomy.

Dave said, "Are you going to scrub?"

"Not this time." She smiled at him. "Laurie and you are all the help he'll need. I'm going for a walk. Take care." She barely stopped herself from kissing him good-bye.

Something in her voice made Sugar glance up. She wouldn't look him in the eye; fortunately, he and Dave were preoccupied with surgical prep. Only Laurie looked at her curiously and, BJ thought, anxiously.

She was sure that she could feel and hear the pentobarbital and the syringes moving in her backpack. Only when she was away from the school—for the last time, she told herself—did she breathe easily.

Sneaking onto the grass farm was easy; a great many students, to the anger of testers, used the well-mowed hillside behind the NO TRESPASSING signs as a driving range. Even in the driest months, it was well watered and well tended, each plot carefully monitored and labeled. BJ walked on the access road between patches, nearly as carefully as she would have kept to the road inside Crossroads.

Then she suddenly turned and struck out over a patch that had a skull and crossbones over it, and hand-lettered signs that read HERBICIDE STATION. DANGER. The paint and the materials did not match the others in the area.

At the far edge of the ragged patch, gooseberry bushes and locust trees half hid a chicken-wire pen and a small shed built of scrap wood.

As she came closer, BJ could see that all the brush and even the high grass and tangled wildflowers were cleared away from the perimeter of the chicken wire fence. The area inside the fence was a square of the low, super-springy grass that the grass station was testing for putting greens. A tarp slung over one corner of the chicken wire provided shade. By the tarp were two dog dishes, one full of water, the other full of Hill's Science Diet, Feline Maintenance.

Padding back and forth behind the chicken wire, trying to stick an oversize paw through and mewing continually, was a clean, well-groomed flowerbinder.

BJ looked quickly at the road behind her. It still led to the Western Vee campus; she could see the athletic buildings in the distance and the tall metal poles of the football stadium lights. She was still in Virginia.

A black woman in her mid-thirties strode briskly out of the hut. Even in a T-shirt and jeans, she looked professional—or perhaps that was the clipboard. "Don't go near the fence," she said quickly, and looked anxiously at BJ. "You shouldn't be here." She spoke carefully and with authority.

BJ pointed to the flowerbinder. "Neither should he." She leaned over the fence and tickled his ears. "Do you miss your friends? Hmm? Do you?"

The flowerbinder rolled on its back, patting at BJ's hands as she scratched his belly.

The woman with the clipboard watched helplessly.

Finally BJ said, "Are you Lucille Boudreau?" She held out a hand. "BJ Vaughan. I work with Dr. Dobbs." The woman's face relaxed instantly, and she shook BJ's hand. Dr. Boudreau was quite attractive, though she had slightly bloodshot eyes. She also, BJ noted, had a wad of Kleenex sticking out of her left hip pocket.

"I'm sorry to be rude; I didn't expect you." She had a Carolina accent as strong as Lee Anne's.

"No, it's my fault," BJ said sincerely. "I came before Dr. Dobbs expected me to." Which was true enough. "I couldn't wait, I'm afraid; I wanted to see how this fella was doing." She toyed with the flowerbinder. "I've worked with them in the wild—"

"Lucky," Dr. Boudreau breathed. "Oh, you lucky, lucky girl."

Lucky? BJ thought. I'm arranging to kill myself later today. Aloud she said, "How's he doing?"

"Healing still." She pointed to the shaved patches, barely growing in, and the sutures. "Is that what this is about?"

BJ said with just the right degree of embarrassment, "I hate to bother you so soon—"

"I did promise Dr. Dobbs I'd return this little fella promptly after full recovery." She laughed. "He made me promise him three times, and when I finally said, 'Do you want it in writing?' he only said, 'If your word's no good, your writing's no good.' " She knelt by the flowerbinder and helped scratch his belly. "I wouldn't lie to Sugar."

As BJ had often noticed, women liked Sugar.

BJ checked the sutures carefully with her fingers. "There's no heat, no inflammation, no seepage. He'll be fine. Have you seen any problems with him?"

Dr. Boudreau frowned. "He's restless all the time. I see it, but I can't tell why. I feel as though I'm missing something important."

A meadowlark sang, clear liquid notes, somewhere in the line of brush at the edge of the grass station. The flowerbinder ran frantically back and forth, mewing and trying to reach through the chicken wire.

Dr. Boudreau looked at the pen with concern. "Why is the poor thing so nervous?"

BJ stepped to the tangle of daisies surrounding the nearby shrubs. "Two reasons," she said, pulling up flowers, stem, roots, and all. "One is that he has no shelter from predators in that pen." She had a brief image of the Great casually diving to carry off the flowerbinder and possibly the doctor. "The other reason involves feeding habits."

BJ dropped the plants inside the enclosure. The flowerbinder pounced on them eagerly, nipping the stems off at the root and twining the plants quickly into its fur. In a few moments he was nearly covered in greenery and blooms. He curled into a corner of the pen nearest the hedgerow, only his pink nose and mouth showing from under the leaves. A red-winged blackbird settled on the chicken wire farthest away from Dr. Boudreau and BJ;

the flowerbinder chirped invitingly at it.

Dr. Boudreau was charmed. "Do they all do this?"

"Oh, yes," BJ said. "And they're social animals, which isn't common for cats."

"Is that important?"

"He won't behave naturally away from the others. You're not a biologist, then?"

"I'm an M.D.," she said in that slightly supercilious tone BJ already associated with researchers in human medicine. "Allergy research." She watched BJ's face and smiled wryly. "I know, I know—'God, how exciting.' But this time it is."

She walked over to the flowerbinder's pen and, with a litheness BJ envied, doubled over the fence and inhaled deeply in the flowerbinder's fur. The flowerbinder purred loudly as she petted it.

She straightened. "See? And I'm tremendously allergic to cats."

"To the dander, you mean."

"All right, but I've taken samples from him, and there is not one bit of difference between cat dander and flowerbinder dander, and that's a fact." Her face wrinkled up suddenly. "What were those flowers you put on him?"

"Daisies."

"Ohhh, shit." She sneezed. "Well, that was certainly foolish." She walked into the shed. BJ followed, at least to the door; there was hardly room for two inside. A makeshift table—a door on sawhorses—held a microscope; the floor was stacked with aluminum suitcases. One of them, open, exposed a foam rubber insert with a hollow clearly designed to hold the tray of glass and rubber jars on the counter. The boxes had labels from a medical supply house in Raleigh, North Carolina; scribbled over them in marking pen was a laboratory address at Duke.

Dr. Boudreau pulled another fistful of Kleenex from a box by the door and buried her face in it. When she pulled back, her eyes were watering and her nose running. "Now you know why I went into allergy research," she mumbled.

BJ said suddenly, "That's right. I didn't sneeze at all in Crossroads, and I didn't even sneeze when I inhaled dust from—" She had been about to say, "from *The Book of Strangeways*," but stopped herself.

The doctor didn't notice. "Ohhh, shit." She sniffled, and fumbled on her desk for a Seldane. "Anyway, I'm trying to discover any reason that flowerbinder dander would suppress histamine reactions."

BJ said wistfully, "That's nice, but compared to some of the research you could do about Crossroads, it doesn't seem very important."

BJ had broken a cardinal rule: never imply that there is anything trivial about another person's research. Dr. Boudreau turned up her nose, then sneezed. "Allergies are extremely important," she said with muffled dignity from around the Kleenex. "And I intend to research other diseases and immunities in Crossroads as soon as I have the opportunity." She waved her pen at BJ patronizingly. "Where would you start?"

BJ realized that it was a rhetorical question, but she couldn't help herself. "With Huntington's chorea."

Doctor Boudreau stared at her without saying a word. "I have Huntington's chorea," BJ said. "I took the genetic test; it's confirmed. I started showing symptoms earlier this year."

Dr. Boudreau looked stunned for a moment, then smiled beatifically and picked up the clipboard and moved outside. "Lucky you."

As BJ's jaw dropped, the doctor added, "Tell me, have you seen any reversal yet?"

BJ stared at her while she walked around the perimeter.

"Dr. Dobbs might have told us. I have a colleague who would have given you a CT scan, an MRI, and a reflex exam every time you returned from Crossroads."

"It wouldn't have fit in with my studies," BJ said.

Dr. Boudreau frowned. "That seems like a pretty weak argument to me."

"But not to me," BJ said firmly. "Anyway, he didn't tell you because he didn't know. He chose four of us for a rotation of study in Crossroads, and he didn't choose for health. The reasons varied from person to person. I was just lucky." She considered. "Very, very lucky."

"Right," the doctor said dubiously. "God, we've got to get real doctors into that place. No offense," she added hastily. "I mean, nobody's realer than Sugar Dobbs."

"I wouldn't think so," BJ said vaguely. She was having trouble concentrating. "Well, I'd better go."

"Say hello to Sugar for me." She hastily transferred her Kleenex to her pocket and held out her hand. BJ took it dazedly.

A second red-winged blackbird landed on the chicken wire. The flowerbinder stalked the blackbird; Dr. Boudreau, Kleenex in hand, stalked the flowerbinder. BJ said lamely, "Nice meeting you."

Dr. Boudreau made a quick backward wave and knelt by the fence. BJ walked back through the grass station, downhill toward Kendrick and the university. She was too numb with astonishment to think clearly.

She walked with her tongue stuck out—a foolish thing to do, walking over an irregular field. She didn't stumble, and at the far end of the field, by the road, she was still holding her tongue out.

As she walked back out to the street, a thought hit her so hard that she leaned on the fence, shivering uncontrollably in the warm spring sunshine. I might never have known, she thought to herself. If I hadn't gone to the grass station, I would have died, and never known that I was going to be all right.

T·W·E·N·T·Y·N·I·N·E

BJ HAD NO idea how long she had been running.

She was in downtown Kendrick, a mile from the school. She had hopped on one foot a ways. She had picked up a rock and tossed it from hand to hand for two blocks without dropping it. She had danced for a block, spinning, and had gotten dizzy but not off balance.

"How long?" she said out loud, almost ready to sing. "How long have I been better?"

Looking back, she could see the change. She thought she had simply been lucky, or more careful; the games at Stein's had gone well recently, and she hadn't been stumbling as much.

She skipped past the stairs to the Dart Club. People were staring, but she was too happy to care. She glanced up at the entrance and said out loud, "I was drunk that night. I wasn't dying; I was drunk."

"You're drunk now," a stranger said, but she paid no attention. She broke into a trot, winded now but too elated to stop, and ran to the corner between Mitch's and Gyro's, trying to think which treat she wanted most, and decided on the gyro, and dashed across the street, barely looking—

And swerved at the last moment to avoid hitting someone.
" 'Scuse me," she said happily, reaching out to steady him—

She stared in shock.

Stefan looked at her emptily, then looked away. There were dark circles around his eyes, and the line of his jaw was sharp,

281

as though he had no body fat left. His once-graceful body was thinner, and it hung slack, like a marionette with loose strings.

He was clutching his backpack, which was full of something rectangular. His hands looked like blue-veined marble.

"Stefan?" She touched his cheek. "Are you all right?"

He broke away from her, running down the street without looking back. His legs wobbled several times, possibly from the padded sneakers. They hadn't bothered him before.

DeeDee came up to her. "Isn't that your friend I saw you with before? I thought he was a client." She looked interestedly down the street. "He's changed, hasn't he?"

BJ stared wildly at DeeDee, then back at the disappearing Stefan. Before she could run after him, DeeDee grabbed her shoulder in a gesture oddly like that which the Griffin had used earlier.

"I know that you're up to something," she said quietly. "Dr. Truelove knows, too. Sooner or later, I'll find out what it is."

"Like hell you will," BJ said, and shook her off. But it was too late; Stefan was gone.

She turned around, wondering where he had gone in Kendrick. He was past the door up to Crystalwerke, so it wasn't that. Mitch's was in the direction he'd run, and after Gyro's the campus started. . . .

The library.

Mrs. Sobell was not at her desk. BJ ran down to the map department, straight to the stacks.

Mrs. Sobell was slumped beside it, sitting on the floor, her back against the shelves as if defending them, too late. Her legs stuck straight out in front of her, and her hair was disarranged; she looked, BJ thought crazily, like Raggedy Ann's brokenhearted mother. Beside her, on the bottom shelf, was a gap several inches wide.

She said emptily to BJ, "I wondered if you'd show up."

"You could have called me," BJ said, forgetting that Mrs. Sobell had no way to get hold of her. "Did you look for it?"

"Oh, I looked, dear, but I knew that I wouldn't find it. After our last little scare, I put a spine rod in the book, so that it would set off an alarm if it were taken out."

BJ said, "All library books have that." She had set it off any number of times herself, walking through the security arch at the front door. Except during fire drills, there was no other way out of the building; even the windows were locked.

Mrs. Sobell held up a small rod with barber-pole stripes and what looked like a magnet at the end. "Only a very few books have a spine rod like this. It cues a special alarm, and gives a code number."

"I've never heard of that."

"You aren't supposed to. Only security—and, in this case, myself—knows to check the code numbers when the alarm goes off."

"And that alarm went off—"

"And security was upset, because the code number it gave didn't match any of their books." She looked bleakly up at BJ. "But it matched one of mine. Tell me, dear: do you have any idea who might have taken it?"

"Absolutely none," BJ said, looking directly into Mrs. Sobell's eyes.

"I see," she said after a short silence. "Well, it was worth asking."

She looked away from BJ and said to herself, "When an entire world is in jeopardy, it's worth asking a few questions."

BJ left quickly. She knew that Mrs. Sobell was now staring at her curiously, but didn't care; she had an urgent errand.

T·H·I·R·T·Y

SUGAR'S OFFICE WAS ajar, but Sugar was nowhere around. His black satchel lay on the desk.

BJ checked the surgery theater, the conference room, the halls, and, in a rare occurrence at the school, paged him, all without success.

She returned to the office and wrote a short note explaining what she was planning to do and why, turned it over, and wrote URGENT in block capitals underlined three times on the back.

"I should hope to shout that it's urgent."

BJ whirled. Lee Anne, looking over her shoulder, stabbed a finger at the note. "This book that's stolen, is that where he got the maps we ride in by?"

BJ nodded.

"And that's how you and Dave got to Crossroads and back without help; you knew about the book. Pretty sly."

But her grin faded. "If it's gone, how are you going?"

For answer, BJ unzipped the black satchel. It contained four photocopied articles (laminitis, bovine dystocia, surgical correction of left-displaced abomasum, and entropion in lambs), a copy of *American Rifleman* for last March, and a green spiral notebook labeled CLASS JOURNAL. BJ fingered the cover hesitantly.

"We shouldn't look in that," Lee Anne said flatly.

BJ picked it up by the spiral wire and shook it. The folded, photocopied map fluttered out.

BJ snatched it and said, "That's it. I'll check for Sugar one last time—"

But Lee Anne was gone.

BJ walked briskly through the building a final time, not finding Sugar.

She considered telling the Griffin, but decided against it; he would immediately leave his bed, and he wasn't ready.

There was, BJ thought unwillingly, a secondary reason for not telling him: the Griffin, through Laurie, would have access to the hospital's pharmaceuticals and equipment.

She trotted out to her car and froze. Leaning on it were Dave, Annie, and Lee Anne.

"Think you were going alone?" Dave asked.

BJ shook her head at him. "It could be dangerous."

"It's already been," Annie pointed out.

BJ held up the map. "What if this is a couple days old, and the roads have changed?"

They were silent at that. Finally Annie said simply, "Then you might need us."

BJ wouldn't let Dave drive, and it turned out that he was only a fair map reader.

After two harrowing last-minute decisions before they had even crossed the stone bridge, Lee Anne snatched the map and immediately said firmly, "Left at the next fork, then follow the curve, then right after the curve . . ."

BJ turned the radio on low, bringing in WVUR-AM Campus Radio. Dave raised an eyebrow at her, but didn't ask that she turn it off.

The signal faded, then shrieked back with a pulse of static.

"Good evening," the announcer said crisply. "Tonight on BBC One—"

At the fork after the curve, the radio blared rapid-fire Spanish, probably Latin American from the speed. At the next, a quick upturn on the switchback, the language seemed Oriental.

At the next there was music, high and keening, like nothing they had heard. It might have been a language.

By now they were crossing the bridge. All stations from here sounded faint and far away.

Lee Ann looked at the road ahead, then at the map. "Funny."

"What?" BJ slowed automatically.

"That's a three-way split ahead. On my map it's only two, and we take the left."

"Dynamite," Dave said. "So do we take the middle road, or the left?"

Lee Ann peered at it. Annie said, with barely a waver in her voice, "I took the one less traveled by, and that has made all the difference."

"Left," Lee Anne said finally. BJ rolled down it, her right hand tuning the now-silent radio up and down the scale.

The woods around them seemed fairly normal, if darker than Virginia usually was. BJ picked up speed.

Suddenly, the radio filled the car with a steady humming drone like a swarm of bees. The hair on BJ's arms prickled, and she slammed on the brakes.

The drone continued, unwavering, and the others stared out the windows uneasily. The road continued, but in the distance the rock pattern seemed hexagonal. The trees to either side were mixed with large, rubbery green plants.

Annie shrank back into herself, rubbing her arms as if cold.

BJ slid the car into reverse and, looking over her shoulder, backed up with extreme care, exactly in the faint tire tracks they had made in the remaining gravel.

When they were back at the familiar fork, BJ felt suddenly dizzy and realized she'd been holding her breath.

Slowly and carefully they took the middle road. A few minutes later they rolled around the edge of the river cliff, and the Road Crew, eyeing them narrowly, waved to them after recognizing their faces. None of the Road Crew smiled this time, and immediately behind BJ's car they began tearing up the road again.

BJ pushed her speed nearly as hard as Dave had on his motorcycle. "We've got to tell Fields."

"Why?" But Dave looked willing to go along with it.

"Because he'll know what to do." She rocketed past the unicorn valley, over the rise beyond, and toward the central Crossroads and Stein's.

Lee Anne said suddenly, "You're sending a message through that damn parrot, aren't you?"

"Probably."

"Then what?"

BJ looked at the other three beside her and felt as Sugar must have felt, responsible for risking lives other than her own. "Then we drive out. There's nothing more we can do here."

"And if there is?" Annie said.

BJ stared at the road ahead. "Then we'll all have to decide."

Stein himself was standing at the gap in the rocks around his inn. He waved BJ almost up to it, then raised a hand to stop her. "Leave it there." His other hand was out of sight.

BJ leaped from the car, followed by the others. "We need to send a message to Fields. Can your parrot—"

Stein shook his head. "He's too tired. Flown to the border twice today." His face was drawn and strained. "You shouldn't be here."

"You never discouraged us before," Annie said.

"We were never on the brink of war before."

They looked at him stupidly.

He opened the outer door. "You've heard of Morgan."

Lee Anne said, "Several times."

"She'll be bringing in a small force. I know you've met the Wyr; they'll be leading." He seemed to be talking half to himself, making plans. "With them she'll take any of the strange ones, the crazies and polyforms, that she can recruit. They make scary shock troops; they'll hit us first.

"The second wave will be any trainees she's willing to sacrifice for one reason or another, people she doesn't care about. She'll only bring in the army if she has a way in other than the Wyr—"

"Our copy of *The Book of Strangeways* has been stolen," BJ said.

Stein dropped his hands. "That's it, then."

He led them through the entryway. Small strips of board had been pulled from the side walls, leaving thin slits open to the main body of the inn. For the first time they could see how thick the walls were on the entryway, and that either wall was accessible from inside.

The parrot was on its perch with its head tucked under its wing. It looked up at them briefly, said quietly, "Hello," and went back to sleep. They had never seen it so civil.

Stein barred the inner and outer doors behind them. The windows, shuttered outside, had timber inserts that blocked all but a peephole. Melina barely looked up as they entered; she was bolting down the last of the window inserts.

He slumped on a bench, staring at nothing. When Annie came up to see if he was all right, he smiled sadly at her. "Do you know, I was really hoping that you were Morgan's spies? That way, Melina and I could kill all four of you, and except for Sugar Dobbs it would be over."

Melina came quietly over and rubbed his shoulders. He put a hand on top of hers. "We can leave."

Stein shook his head. "I did that, when I was young. I won't again." He turned and looked at her. "You, young lady, you should leave now."

Melina looked frightened, but shook her head firmly. Stein patted her hand and turned back to the others. "You, I don't know where you can go. There's no time to go back the way you came." He shrugged. "Hide here with me. We'll do our best when Morgan comes."

Lee Anne said, "Sir, can't the Inspector General—"

"Not this time." Stein looked openly worried. "He's been missing for over a week. No sightings, no bodies. If he stays away much longer, people will say he's dead, and who knows what will happen?" He added regretfully, "I'd kill somebody myself and pretend it was him, but he has a distinctive style. Hard to imitate."

BJ couldn't decide whether he was serious or not.

Dave peered out through one of the front peepholes. "Does King Brandal have an army?"

"Just us. And the Road Crews." Stein smiled grimly. "This morning they began tearing up all the roads out. By night, Crossroads will be cut off to everyone but the Wyr and people with *The Book of Strangeways*. Keep looking out the front, and tell me if anyone's coming."

"What else can we do?" BJ said.

He raised his hands and dropped them. "Now? We wait for trouble to come to us. It may not get here for a while, but it will come, you see if it doesn't."

He stood, looking around the inn and reviewing, as much for himself as for the students. "Food we've got. Not much of an inn without food. We're in a good location. With the pond above us, we have water enough to fight a fire or outlast a siege." He glanced behind them and said involuntarily, "And other uses maybe. We have a foot of front door between us and anybody else. We have thick walls, and the windows are covered. The entryway's set up for defense—"

"You've been planning for this."

"I *built* for this." He gestured to the walls, the barricaded windows, the front entry. "For attack, I built, really. You don't build for the end of your world; you build to postpone it."

He moved around the inn, double-checking the bars and bolts on the window inserts. "But her having the book, this changes things. If she didn't have the book, she'd come here first, hit us with everything she could afford to lose." He smiled at her, and for a moment he looked as he had when they first met him. "You've done so well guessing at things, young BJ; why do you think she'd do that?"

"Because she thinks she can get the book by coming here."

He said grimly, "Exactly. In some ways, in the short term at least, it will be easier on us."

There was a muffled pounding at the outer door. Stein cocked an ear. "Did anyone see who that is?"

Nobody answered. He sighed. "So our sentry system needs work. He must have come from the back. Melina, check the back for more."

She trotted to the ladder and climbed up carefully. BJ and Dave went to the inner front door and looked questioningly at Stein.

He gestured, and they opened it. BJ found that the passage made her feel claustrophobic and vulnerable now; she stared uneasily at the side slits between the boards. She hurried through, listening.

"Let me in," the voice said faintly through the plank and stud door.

Without looking at Stein, BJ lifted both bars off the door and slid the bolt back. Dave and, more reluctantly, Lee Anne helped her swing it open.

Stefan, gasping for breath and clutching his knapsack tightly, stumbled in and fell to the floor.

They slammed the outer door shut. BJ knelt beside Stefan; he was as close to chalk white as his olive skin would permit. He looked up at her piteously and turned his head away.

"Bring him in," Stein said levelly.

They looked. In his right hand he was holding a cleaver, in his left a carving knife. In his belt was a wide-hilted short sword.

"But he's injured."

Stein said, "Leave him there and he'll be dead."

They carried him as gently as they could. He was gasping for breath and trembling a great deal. He never relaxed his grip on the knapsack.

Dave took most of the weight, but it didn't seem to be a great deal. They laid him carefully down on one of the tables. "What the hell happened to you? Where've you been?"

"He was in Kendrick." They turned to stare at BJ, who went on, "I saw him. He must have run all the way here."

Lee Anne looked puzzled. "Why didn't we pass him?"

"There's another way in and out, on foot," Annie said. "It's fairly dangerous."

Stefan, deeply ashamed, said, "You should not be here. I was hopeful not to see you." He blinked back tears. "Never like this."

Dave repeated blankly to Stefan, "What the hell happened to you?"

The faun licked his lips and tried to focus. "She told me I'd be smarter." Stefan looked at BJ, the only time he had done so. "She promised me it would make me smarter, and I could be a veterinarian, be what would make me to be liked—and then later, when I wanted it more, she said I could only have it if I did something—I knew, I knew it was wrong, but by then I could not, could never—" He looked away again, crying bitterly.

BJ knelt closer, but it was Lee Anne who pulled on one of his arms at the wrist, twisting it free. The needle holes on his veins were ugly and fresh.

His knapsack came free of his grasp and slid on the floor. The flap popped open, and *The Book of Strangeways* lay on the floor in front of them.

T·H·I·R·T·Y-O·N·E

THEY PUT BLANKETS over Stefan and set him in the corner. BJ
brought his knapsack over and tried to speak with him, but he
turned his face to the wall.

Fields entered the inn, spoke quietly to Stein, and came over
and held Stefan, rocking him like a small child. Stefan wouldn't
embrace Fields back, and refused to speak. Fields set him tenderly back among the blankets and walked away, face troubled. BJ
remained.

Finally Stein came over to her and said gently, "Young lady,
we need you."

"For what?" Her face was tearstained, but she didn't care.

"As soon as Morgan knows that your friend didn't bring the
book to her, she will send someone for it."

"Who?"

"Everyone she can. Anyone she's willing to risk losing by sending them with the Wyr." He stretched out a hand. "The book."
When she hesitated, he added, "Please."

BJ rose to her feet, but dashed past him and threw it on the
hearth. Grease spattered across it, turning into a trickle of flame
that melted more grease and turned into a blazing pool on it.

Stein was annoyed. "Why did you do that? Now it will be
hard to pick up." He took the fire tongs from the right side
of the hearth and flipped the book out of the flames. After
the grease had stopped burning, he picked the book up easily.

291

He held it out for BJ's inspection; she touched it gingerly. The cover was still cool. A swipe of Stein's hand removed the ash from the grease; the book appeared no different.

"Isn't there any way . . . ?"

"Not burning, not acid, not even cutting or tearing." Stein took a page in his hands and pulled in opposite directions. His hands seemed to slide across the unsmeared map. "If it could be destroyed, I'd do it." He added ruefully, "I'll hide it with my own copy. I'll have to make sure I die if we lose; I'd hate to have them both found just because I was foolish enough to live."

"And if we're killed here," BJ said wonderingly, "if they burn us alive or pull the place down around us, the book will still be whole, and anyone could take it—"

"Not quite." Stein tapped the cover for emphasis. "There are a few people it would burn. Morgan is one of them. That's why she needed someone else to steal it for her."

BJ looked back pityingly at Stefan, then blinked. "Why would she choose him? He hardly knows the library, the place where the book was; he's been in it once."

Stein frowned, rubbing his chin thoughtfully. "He didn't need to know it. I think she had help from someone in your world, but I think," he finished obscurely, "it was someone she shouldn't have trusted." He tucked the book under his arm. "If you'll excuse me." He nodded to Fields, who went with him from the main hall.

They returned together a few minutes later, without the book. Stein clapped his hands and gathered the rest of the people together. "Thank you for staying," he said as formally as if he were introducing a concert. "I think we will need you all, plus more than we have if you want to know the truth. And now," he said, "for those of you who don't already know, I apologize."

"For what, sir?" Lee Ann asked.

"For hiding some of the truth from you. This place is more than it seems." He tugged at a floorboard, then stuck a small belt knife under the edge of it.

It flipped up like a chest lid. He began pulling out short-bladed swords that had long hilts with turned-up ends.

"Those look like the sticks from the game," Dave said naively.

"They are, but it's no game. He was training us," BJ said. "Are you a kind of field commander?"

He beamed at her. "So smart, and pretty, too."

"And the sharp buckled belts are weapons, too."

He pulled out a small pot with a green liquid in it. "Mostly they only wound. Dip the ends in this and they kill." He pulled out three more pots.

"Are you the Inspector General?"

His jaw dropped. "How could you think that?"

BJ had no answer.

He attached a rope to the pillar at the rear of the inn, and BJ noticed that there was fresh sawdust clinging to it and the saw cut at the middle was considerably deeper now.

"If I pull this"—he tugged the rope lightly—"and shout, 'Hold on,' then you hold on. Tight." He hung the end of rope carefully over a nail on the pillar.

He then deployed them to separate posts, as calmly and sensibly as though he had expected them all. Melina, in the upper room, was chief lookout. BJ ended up watching the road to the south, where the grasslands were. Lee Anne took her post beside BJ. From time to time, Lee Anne's hand drifted into her knapsack.

Melina called down, "Something is coming from the east."

Stein said sharply, "How many?"

"I don't know. It's hard to see."

The others scrambled to the east wall to peer out. Annie said with relief, "They're reinforcements."

The Griffin, his beak hanging down beside the truck cab, was giving directions. Sugar and Laurie were together in the cab; between them, BJ could barely see the top of someone's head.

"Who's the kid with them?" Dave said.

Annie said dubiously, "I never saw a child with gray hair before."

BJ smiled as Laurie hopped out of the truck and offered a hand to Mrs. Sobell, who slid down cautiously from the seat. Sugar and Laurie went to the back of the truck and helped the Griffin.

The students charged forward to undo the door.

Mrs. Sobell nodded politely to everyone, completely unsurprised by her surroundings. It was impossible to tell whether or not she had been there before.

Sugar, coming first, said, "You all right?"

Laurie, next in, said, "Typical. You want to find students, check in a bar."

The Griffin, squeezing through the hall with difficulty, said with weak dignity, "Nothing for me, thank you; I'm on medication." He made it as far as the center of the room before he collapsed, beak open and panting.

Laurie and Sugar were checking him out in seconds. The students moved in to help; Dave said, "How did you get him out of the school?"

"Snuck him to the loading dock, then hung a tarp over the back of the truck and barreled down the freeway." Sugar was rechecking all the sutures; they seemed to be holding. "The moment he was up from anesthetic, he pushed to come back."

"I had to," he said simply.

"If you try to fight," Laurie said bluntly, "I'll kill you myself."

"I gave my word," he said. "Only if the rest of you are dead." He dragged himself in slowly and painfully, and came to rest next to Stefan.

There was a tentative knock at the outside door; Rudy and Bambi came in. "Wow," Rudy said. Bambi said, "What's wrong? Can we do anything?"

Stein sighed. "Shut the doors."

They moved to their stations as before. On the south wall, BJ noticed Lee Anne fiddling nervously with her knapsack and sidled up to her. "I bought you something at the jeweler's."

Lee Anne looked blank. "That's real nice of you, but I don't much wear jewelry, and this doesn't much seem like the time—"

BJ dropped a box of cartridges into her hand: .22 shorts. Lee Anne nearly dropped it, startled at the weight. Even small bullets are heavy, but this box was exceptional.

She opened it and grinned. "Now, that's thoughtful. Silver suits me better than gold anyway."

"None for me, Doc?" Sugar said. They turned. He was holding a larger-caliber revolver. "Three fifty-seven karat, maybe?"

BJ said, "It's not proper for women to give jewelry to men."

Lee Anne loaded her .22, pocketing the remaining silver cartridges. From his pocket Sugar pulled a speed-loader and six bullets, and set it up to reload the revolver. Stein watched them sadly. "I always knew that guns would come here—and now, when they come, I'm helping the people who brought them. Well, it had to happen."

Laurie picked up a small sword and hefted it dubiously. "This is it? Swords and belts and two guns, to hold off whatever comes? How much chance that someone will bring reinforcements?"

Stein said, "It's almost certain, if we last long enough." He still looked unhappy. "We must try."

Laurie said, "How long do you think we can hold out here?"

"If she brings trained soldiers . . ." He shrugged. "We might last a few hours. Not more." He repeated, "We must try."

"Into the valley of death," Laurie said glumly. "Hot damn." She lit a cigarette.

The parrot woke up and strolled down the bar with a rocking gait. It regarded Stein solemnly.

"Well," Stein said to it, "here we are. Who would have thought, after all these years, we would die together?"

The parrot cackled, "*Stoo*-pid!" and flew upstairs. A moment later they heard his laugh as he flew out the window.

After a frozen moment, Stein said, "At least I'm rid of him."

It wasn't that funny, but Annie and Lee Anne laughed. Even Sugar joined in.

And suddenly, it was a party.

Rudy put an arm around Dave; Bambi hugged him. This time when she licked his nose, Dave laughed and licked hers back.

The little brown men crowded around Dave, patting his legs and chattering excitedly.

"Damn right," he said back to them. He raised his sword. "Kick ass."

They were delighted. They bounded up and down, waving their sharp-buckled belts in the air dangerously and shouting repeatedly, "Kee-kass! Kee-kass!"

Lee Anne was less enthusiastic. "It was never part of my life plan to die in the goddamn Alamo."

Stein nodded solemnly. "Mine, neither."

T·H·I·R·T·Y·T·W·O

THE WAITING WAS remarkably peaceable. Even the little brown men sat quietly, staring straight ahead.

BJ slumped in the corner, one arm wrapped around Stefan, one hand holding his. His hands were clammy, and shook. He whimpered with the withdrawal, and still wouldn't look at her.

She was barely thinking of him. She was thinking, bitterly, of how close she had come to having her life back.

Someone touched the bill of BJ's Orioles cap; BJ looked up, not very far, and saw Mrs. Sobell. "How nice. That's my own favorite team, you know. Do you like the Orioles?"

"I do." BJ felt foolish, talking about something so ordinary just before a war. "I listen to them on the radio sometimes while I study."

Mrs. Sobell beamed at her. "I'm so glad that I met you. When this is over, perhaps we can go to an Orioles game together."

BJ laughed, with small tears in her eyes. "I'd love to."

Sugar knelt by her for a moment. "How's he doing?"

"Badly." She let go of Stefan's hand and moved away to talk. "How could he get addicted so fast?"

Sugar grimaced. "Who knows? Drug reactions are tied to physiology, and his must be pretty strange." He looked at her narrowly. "Got any idea how long he's been shooting up?"

"No," she said slowly, "but I don't think it's been all that long."

He shrugged. "It doesn't matter. Unless we live, of course."

296

Sugar looked as bleak as BJ had ever seen him.

She said, "What's wrong?"

"Elaine's pregnant."

It took her a moment to remember that Elaine was Sugar's wife. "Congratulations."

"Right." He sat on a bench near the wall. "And I'm in here, and God knows if I'll ever get out. I can't even tell her what happened to me, if—" He cut off.

There was nothing to say to that. BJ watched him for a while, then moved back to Stefan.

A few minutes later, Stein, from the upper room, said sharply, "They're nearly here."

BJ peered beneath the shuttered and plugged window. She looked down at the creeping, striding, and crawling forces on the road below and thought bleakly, I'd love to go to an Orioles game. Or anywhere. Life seemed unbearably sweet.

A moment later they heard a wolf howl, and another.

Stein came downstairs. "They're only howling to upset you."

Dave said, "Gee, why would they think that would work?" Rudy and Bambi, weapons in hand, were huddling close to each other.

Lee Anne asked, "Sir, are there any plans about how we handle casualties?"

"Pull them aside and keep fighting," he said brutally, and peered out through one of the peepholes. After a moment, staring at the approaching force, he said quietly, "The casualties in this war have already happened. Stepfather God forgive us, we are going to be fighting them."

The hairs on the back of BJ's neck rose and moved at the nearly continuous wolf howling.

To either side of the road, the grass rippled and waved. From time to time there was a glimpse of a gray back or a waving tail.

Lee Anne said, "What in hell are those half-human snake things along the road?"

"Half-human snake things," Stein replied. "Lamiae. Constrictors. They're not very bright, so if you keep away from them—"

"No sweat there," Dave said. "I wouldn't come within a mile of them unless they cornered me."

He immediately looked sorry he had said it. BJ looked around her; Stein's suddenly seemed very small and close.

On the road from the east, a cadre of fifty or sixty humans (or comparative humans) was marching. Ahead of them, moving forward irregularly, a knot of men and women tugged at ropes against a huge, thrashing body.

BJ turned away, sickened. Carron, seven ropes around his neck and body, was being dragged up the hill.

Lee Anne pulled her gun out, looked through the peephole, and dropped it. There was no way to be of any help from this distance.

They were moving up the hill now. Some of the snake women, placid faced and indifferent, were gliding forward over rocks and ditches; the other soldiers were leaving them a wide berth. Carron, still struggling, was being half dragged uphill.

BJ saw a fat soldier stop and drink from a flask; a bony man who clearly outranked him smacked the flask from his hands. Other than that, the approaching troops moved steadily and with discipline.

They stopped just outside the ring of rocks around Stein's. One by one they edged past the vet school truck and BJ's car, pausing in between to peer at Stein's.

"They don't know that we're here or how we'll fight," Stein explained. "Now they'll bring in Carron."

They dragged the centaur between the vehicles; he was close to choking as they pulled him. The last soldier onto the crown of the hill carried a torch. He tossed it behind him.

The truck, and BJ's car, exploded into flame.

Sugar and BJ watched indifferently.

Stein tensed. "Be ready."

"What for?" BJ had to look to see that the speaker was Sugar and not Dave.

Six men and women, heaving at the nooses, dragged Carron ahead of the other soldiers. There was a commotion in back of them, and the troops parted.

BJ caught a quick glimpse as a slender woman in high-top tennis shoes, pleated canvas pants, and a rugby shirt rose unsteadily on a soldier's shoulders. The soldier plunged toward Carron and the woman slapped her hand quickly against Carron's neck. BJ saw a flash of silver and plastic in the sun.

The woman and soldier fell back, and the others dragged Carron within thirty feet of Stein's.

There they stopped. Carron stood stock-still; they slacked the ropes, and for one foolish moment BJ hoped that they intended to let it go.

Then his face contorted as he dropped his jaw and shrieked, flailing his arms, bucking and rearing.

Two soldiers, swinging with all their might, smacked the flats of broadswords into Carron's hindquarters. Carron, eyes wide and unseeing, charged forward at terrible speed.

Stein pulled Lee Anne and BJ back from the wall, one with each hand.

The wall thundered end to end as Carron's one-ton-plus body slammed into it without slowing. It buckled in the center.

"He's seizuring," Lee Anne yelled. "They must have pumped something into him. An opiate, maybe."

"He's their battering ram," Stein shouted back, and added with a bitterness that they had never heard in him, "Monsters, they must be. Kill them if you can. Monsters!"

Outside, Carron was still shouting. BJ risked peeking through the wall, aware that if Carron hit it as she did so she would be knocked cold at the very least.

The soldiers, dragging at the dangling ropes, had pulled Carron around. He was still leaping wildly and screaming unintelligibly. His face was bleeding, and his chest was cross-cut with splinters. The ropes had left vicious red burns on his flesh.

With an effort, they spun him back toward the wall again and drove him toward it, striking him and shouting.

This time the wall cracked in the center, four-by-four logs splintering and pulling apart at the impact.

From the shouting outside, the soldiers were having a hard time controlling the plunging, shrieking Carron. His face was a bloody ruin.

Sugar dropped down from the upper room, gun in hand. Stein snapped at him, "Now. Shoot."

"How?" But Sugar put his eye to one peephole and his gun through one below, and fired as best he could.

Two of the soldiers dragging on Carron dropped the ropes in astonishment, one staring at his side, the other holding his thigh.

"Not them. Shoot him, shoot the poor son of a bitch before—"

"I can't," Sugar said, pulling back. "I couldn't be sure of a kill, shooting like this."

Stein muttered with a mild disappointment that seemed out of place, "Well, save your bullets, then."

For a moment it seemed as though the handlers had lost control of Carron, but a red-haired woman strode forward. She gestured, and two more soldiers leaped to the dangling ropes.

She looked annoyedly down at the two wounded men. A dagger flashed in her left hand, and suddenly she was red to the elbows, rubbing her arms as though washing.

"Her," Stein snapped, unnerved. "Her, kill her."

"Goddamn right," Sugar said, and fired.

He missed completely, and at the sound she whirled, completely unafraid, and shouted another order in a strange language.

The new soldiers spun Carron face forward to the inn, dragging him toward it, and others struck his hindquarters again, and this time pursued him, cutting at his flesh, shouting and beating on him, and following him.

The red-haired woman waved one bloody arm and shouted another order in a cold, clear voice that carried even to the inn. Two wolves leaped forward and bit Carron's flanks.

He shrieked and, unbelievably, ran still faster, straight at the side of the inn.

There was a sound like a truck hitting a tree. The wall ruptured and breached in, and Carron's broken body dropped through the gap and shook the floor as it hit. He never moved.

Rudy gave an inarticulate bellow and charged forward and out, his head down.

Stein shouted "No!" but it was Dave who leaped forward beside Rudy, short sword ready.

The first wolf to leap at Rudy fell back, howling, one eye bloody. Dave dispatched it from its blind side, one quick stab over its shoulder and into its chest.

But the second wolf crawled below Rudy's antlers to snap at his throat. The stag-man pulled back sharply and stumbled, confused, against Carron's corpse.

Immediately there were four wolves at him, snapping at his frantically moving arms and legs.

With a leap that any ballerina would have envied, Bambi bounded forward in a high arc, landing between Rudy and the wolves. She swung the short sword ineffectually, and the wolves, more from surprise than anything else, stopped attacking for a moment.

Annie's yell astonished those who knew her more than it did the wolves. She spun the sword in her right hand and ran forward on Rudy's left. Dave, on his right, yelled back to her and hacked deftly, quickly at a fifth wolf who was circling behind them to cut them off.

Annie whacked a she-wolf with the flat of her sword; she bounced her sword off the first wolf and straight down the gullet of a second, hanging on tight as it shook her arm this way and that to rid its throat of the blade.

By the time she pulled free, the first wolf was tottering. Annie walked forward, not back, toward Bambi.

"No!" Stein said desperately. "Pull back, inside the wall."

Bambi, frustrated by her clumsiness with the sword, threw it aside. She dropped almost to her side and lashed out suddenly with her top leg.

A wolf dropped in place, its larynx kicked in. Bambi swung her hoof in a credible imitation of a martial-arts spin kick, gashing another wolf's nose and breaking one of his front fangs.

Rudy, back upright, grabbed one of her arms, and Dave the other, and they dropped back inside the wall as Annie retreated, just in front of them, slashing her sword back and forth to keep the snapping jaws away.

She turned as she stepped back in. Her eyes went wide as she dropped, and Sugar and Lee Anne stood firing into the wolves. The .357 sounded like dynamite in the empty inn.

Most of the wolves had probably never heard a gun, but they didn't panic. They ducked, growling, and yipped as the small bullets hit; they were knocked backward by the impact of the .357, but they kept moving in, snarling and implacable.

A wolf leaped in over the corpse, a blazing torch in his mouth. They all dropped back automatically, and it ran to one of the benches and carefully dropped the torch at the legs. Then it barked loudly, twice, at the door.

A gray wolf, a black wolf, any number of wolves of different sizes, charged in. Lee Anne shot one more before pocketing the gun and breaking out her sword.

The people inside tried to defend against the wolves, but inevitably a few of them broke through. Unlike real wolves, they didn't attack from behind; instead, they formed a semicircle around the now-burning bench and wall, guarding them from any attempts to douse the flames.

Any attempt at order among the defenders had collapsed immediately. BJ, alternately stabbing forward and parrying as she fell back, could barely grasp what was happening to the others.

The barking wolf watched them attentively, then turned from left to right, ears cocked, looking for someone.

A wolf, almost completely obscured by flailing brown men screaming, "Kee-kass! Kee-kass!" retreated hastily out through the breach. One of the little men gave a quick thumbs-up to Dave before attacking again. They were gone before BJ registered what she had seen: the limp body of a brown man held tightly in the wolf's jaws, the wolf shaking him like a rat.

Rudy, head lowered again for defense, was pressed against one of the side walls. Bambi, beside him, was kicking frantically.

The barking wolf pricked its ears up and dived for the center of the fight, where it nipped one of its comrades to drive it aside. Annie, her bloody sword barely pulled back from the last attacker, looked confusedly at the lead wolf.

It nodded at her once and barked, looking for all the world like it was laughing.

Annie said, "Vlatmir?"

He grinned with bloody jaws, moving toward her. She backed off.

BJ could do nothing but fight her own battle. She worked her way beside the fireplace, but the wolf, a female, was clever and cut her off from the hot cooking spits.

Vlatmir snapped at Annie again, herding her toward the burning wall, which was now half on fire.

Annie lunged at Vlatmir. With a deft snap, he grabbed at her wrist. She wrenched it free, but her sword fell from her hand.

Vlatmir grinned wider, snapping and dancing at her, pushing her half into the flames. She was nearly against the wall.

Stein shouted, "Annie!" His arm flashed up and back.

A knife quivered in the wall, above the flames and less than a foot from her left ear.

She stared at it for all of a second before reaching across with her right hand and grabbing it. Her hand was in front of her again when Vlatmir leaped, grinning jaws open wide, headed straight for her throat.

Her hand seemed to come up by itself, plunging against the wolf's chest. Without any apparent thought, she twisted her wrist and let the blade slide between the wolf's ribs.

Unable to stop, he smashed into the wall where she had been standing; he bit furiously at the floor and the benches as he died.

His body shivered convulsively as it began to change back to human. Annie looked blankly at him, and gazed with horror at the silver dagger in her hand.

Gradually the Wyr became disorganized, their attacks random. They lunged to and fro in the thickening smoke of the inn, getting in each other's way.

Just in front of the Griffin, Laurie swung the poker from the hearth into the ribs of a she-wolf; it whimpered and leaped back, colliding with another wolf. They snapped at each other, and crazy with the confusion, the smoke, and the loss of a leader, the Wyr degenerated into a leadership battle. One by one, snapping and growling, they leaped through the gap to move their battle outside.

The first of the swordsmen came in. He slashed his way to the rear wall with short, half-defensive strokes.

"Keep them back!" Stein shouted. But the advantage had been lost again.

Sugar faced off with the second man through the breach, the tall, bony man they had seen earlier. The tall man beat him back methodically, with repeated sword strokes from behind a shield, until there was room behind them for others to come in. They stepped in two at a time, steadily and unhesitatingly.

The defenders were on their home ground; they had all played the stick game many times in Stein's. Melina, her arm bandaged now, engaged a swordswoman around a pillar and used a tray from the tables as a shield. Stein himself fought constantly and carefully, disarming and killing fighter after fighter. Rudy came forward, coughing from the smoke, and took on a fighter. The advance through the inn slowed.

Casualties were high, but the invaders were winning, slowly and steadily. When one soldier was wounded or disarmed and fled or died, another came in. And the inn was burning more and more; the smoke was thicker now, the flames higher.

The smoke began drifting back in. A breeze from somewhere was fanning the flames.

"I can't stand it," Dave coughed, and whacked his way toward the breach, meeting surprisingly little resistance.

He stopped abruptly, overbalancing and tottering over Carron's body.

A stupid, passive, nearly blank female human face gazed at him fixedly as it glided past the breach on a snake's body. On its next pass it leaned in, opened its mouth, and simply kept opening it, dislocating its human jaw and expanding its gullet to expose a three-foot maw. Underneath it, the first of the snake coils rippled.

Lee Anne jerked forward and grabbed Dave, pulling him back. His face was white.

"Don't go out there," Stein ordered. "They're trying to force us out."

But the invaders were keeping the defenders back from the fire, much as the Wyr had done. The flames were being whipped higher by a wind through the breach. Sooner or later, the defenders would all be forced out or die in the fire.

And Morgan would win either way.

The wind picked up, and suddenly the breach exploded with bodies as everyone outside began scrambling into it, desperate to get inside.

The fighting lost all sense of order and discipline. Morgan's troops were slashing at each other as they climbed over Carron's body. There was no way to hold them back.

Stein shouted, "Go to the back wall." The remaining defenders moved there. Dave and Sugar grabbed the exhausted Rudy and Bambi and dragged them there.

BJ staggered into place beside Stefan. He had one of the swords and was trying shakily to wave it at the incoming troops.

BJ saw their attackers' faces: they were nakedly, unashamedly afraid.

An enormously fat man, puffing, fought his way to one side of the inn and disappeared in the smoke somewhere near the main door. BJ watched for his re-emergence, but lost track of him in the fighting.

A young man, stabbed in the back, fell in front of BJ, screaming; a woman stepped on rather than over him. For a single terrible moment, BJ was front to front with her: a coldly angry, red-haired woman who seemed to be six feet of implacable rage.

But under the rage was something even worse. The battle was going badly for her; half the blood on her arms was from her own men, and she was, mixed with the anger, as terribly and completely happy as she could ever be.

Morgan smashed downward with her bloody sword, uninterested in any but a killing blow.

BJ ducked to one side, caught the sword on the hilt of her own smaller weapon, and twisted the hilt as she would a catchlet.

Unbelievably, the sword spun out of Morgan's grasp. She froze, staring at BJ, who stood paralyzed, poised for a killing lunge but unready.

Then Morgan smiled, stabbing to the right at one of her own men. As he collapsed, she grabbed his sword, knocked BJ's weapon aside, and leaned toward BJ, reaching with her empty left hand. She marked BJ's forehead with a bloody imprint like a blessing, murmured, "Never hesitate," and strode back through Stein's, moving to the barred front door.

The wind from outside became a gale, and BJ turned away from her as Stein shouted in English, "Hold on. Now and for good." He tugged at the rope attached to the pillar. Nothing happened.

Dave and Sugar grabbed the rope and pulled with him. The pillar snapped in the middle. Stein grabbed each of them by a shoulder and pulled them backward as a section of roof dropped open.

BJ felt her ears pop as the water from the upstream pond shot through Stein's. She clutched at a roof support.

Lee Anne, stumbling in the current, stretched out a hand. BJ grabbed it and braced her feet, praying for good balance. Lee Anne pulled herself up BJ's body hand over hand, clutched her chest, then grabbed the pillar for herself.

Over the roaring water, BJ could hear the screams of those who were swept outside. She held on tightly, trying to see the others through the mingled spray and smoke.

The flood lasted for more than five minutes. When it finished, Stein's was a mess of knee-deep silt and water. Not surprisingly, the fire was out.

A Wyr, transforming back to human, lay choking in a corner. Dave and Sugar ran over to dispatch it.

"No." They turned as Fields stepped forward. "She has nothing left to fight for. Let her live, and let her heal."

She looked up as he spoke; it was Gredya. "Where is Morgan?"

They looked around. Fields said gently, "Gone or dead."

She looked even more gaunt and pinched than the transformation usually left a Wyr. She rubbed her arm nervously. "Did she give you—do you have any—"

He shook his head.

She threw her head back and howled, tears coursing down her cheeks. Fields held her, patting her head like a dog's. Stefan, in his corner with the Griffin, moaned in his half sleep.

Rudy and Bambi came forward, looking anxiously from side to side. "They're all gone?" Bambi said. She had a nasty scratch across her abdomen.

"They bugged out," Rudy said reassuringly. He was licking her abdomen to clean the wound, and he, too, had a ruminant's thick tongue. Dave shoved him aside and cleaned the wound with a bar towel.

"Where will they go?" Annie asked.

Sugar grunted. "The survivors? Down the nearest road, I bet. They don't have much choice."

"Reckless," Stein said disapprovingly. "This attack was terribly reckless. Morgan has lost most of the ones who got out alive, too."

The Griffin agreed. "Many worlds are about to learn new languages. Mostly profanity, I expect." Laurie was checking his sutures; for all the trouble he had been through in his first day out of surgery, he seemed to be holding up well.

Stein stepped outside and looked down at the nearby hillside, his face frozen with grief. BJ looked over his shoulder, braced for a prospect of the dead, the dying, and the wounded.

The hillside was bare of life. After a battle of this size that was impossible to imagine, until BJ realized what it meant and stared out at the distant flying silhouettes of the Great.

Fields put a hand on Stein's shoulder. The old man said huskily, "It's been a long time since I cried for the dead."

She turned away in pity and cringed automatically. One of the Great had landed on the other side of the inn, near the now-empty upper pond; it stuck out to either side of the building. The gigantic head and beak nearly touched the ground on the entrance side of the inn.

There was a man riding behind the head.

Owen slid down from the neck of the bird and dropped, sprawling in the dust. He rose shakily—flying had been alien—and bowed deeply to the roc.

With slow, ponderous wing flaps, the roc moved across the hilltop with long strides, gaining momentum. The wind of his passing flattened the grass around the wreckage of Stein's, and forced the assembled survivors to close their eyes and shield their bodies from flying debris. When they opened their eyes, it and the other Great were specks in the sky, far to the Southeast.

Owen turned to Stein. "Is *The Book of Strangeways* safe?"

Stein scrambled into the debris and returned shortly, carrying both copies. He held them out in front of Owen. "Yes, Lord Brandal."

"Then we've won, for now," he said simply. "Thank you, Commander." Stein bowed. Owen/Brandal said with more warmth, "Thanks also to the work of the Inspector General. Are you all right?"

Sugar and the veterinary students looked uneasily from human to human, waiting to see who might be the legendary dispenser of justice.

But it was the Griffin who knelt. "My liege."

T·H·I·R·T·Y·T·H·R·E·E

THEY HEARD A rumble of hooves. The Hippoi, led by Stein's parrot, were charging up the hill to Stein's.

The rest halted by the burned truck and car. Polyta galloped up, her face drawn and anxious. Sugarly, behind her, was laughing; galloping was fun.

She turned her body sideways, blocking Sugarly behind her.

Carron's body was wedged in the opening. His face, though battered, was clean of blood; his body and its wounds were scoured clean by the water and silt.

She knelt on her forelegs, bent tenderly, and kissed Carron's cheeks. She said once, softly, "Nesyos."

She gestured, and Sugarly came forward. He looked down uncomprehendingly at the mighty body, and became frightened because it wouldn't move.

Then his face looked stern and hard, very much like his father's would.

She rose and said to all nearby, "Now I am Carron."

She added briskly, "You will burn this place, with him in it. I'll stay to see it done."

Stein nodded mutely.

She put a hand on his shoulder, bending to do it. "You know you must do this, Stein. You know we will help you." Her mouth twitched, but she managed to say smoothly, "I am sorry for your loss."

They watched as Dave bent down by the breach and tenderly

carried a small body out into the sunlight. "Kee-kass," it said feebly. "Kee-kass."

"You bet," Dave said affectionately. "You did good, buddy." He wrapped the brown body in his shirt.

The vet students looked around the ruined inn and its grounds dazedly. Lee Anne said suddenly, "Where's that little old librarian who came in the truck? Did she get hurt? Poor little thing . . ."

A voice said politely, "If you don't mind . . ."

They turned. Mrs. Sobell, a sword carried awkwardly in her hand, was marching two wet, filthy prisoners around from the upper pond.

"They're quite fortunate to be alive," she said calmly. "They hid in the outside pantry; I saw the door and thought we should check for other survivors."

Dave said unbelievingly, "Dr. Truelove?"

BJ said with no expression, "DeeDee." She was wearing a mud-stained rugby shirt and torn, pleated canvas pants.

Truelove was babblingly grateful to see them. "Sugar, thank Jesus. I was arguing with DeeDee in the field behind the clinic— two wolves came"—he held his scratched wrist up pathetically— "they made me come here, they dragged me—I didn't want any part—"

Sugar frowned. "Arguing?"

BJ said calmly, "About the morphine. DeeDee forged his name on quite a few controlled-substance slips."

Truelove stared at her with astonishment. DeeDee was completely indifferent.

"Is that true, Walt?" Sugar said slowly. "And you didn't check on her until now?"

He burst out, "You let her get drugs for you. Scheduled drugs." He pointed to BJ.

"Once. And I checked up on the transaction after the surgery." He shook his head. "Walt, you were in charge of the dispensary this term. It was your turn to watch."

"I had my work to do," he said sullenly.

Fields looked at DeeDee in astonishment. "So you gave my Stefan and Carron—"

"And the Wyr," Brandal said. "That was Morgan's hold on them."

"She was also the one who gave Carron an injection just before he died."

"Sure," Sugar said flatly. "Morphine. Causes uncontrolled seizuring in horses." He glanced at Carron's body involuntarily.

The Griffin regarded DeeDee coldly. "I think we will deal with this later, when I have more time. Watch her, and let that ineffectual little man go."

Truelove scuttled gratefully away from DeeDee. Rudy and Bambi moved to either side of her, standing guard. The Griffin turned to the others. "In the meantime, are there any other survivors?"

BJ put a hand to her mouth. "Morgan."

Brandal whirled. "Where?"

"The entryway—she went to it just before the Great came."

Brandal strode grimly to the outside door, sword in hand. The Griffin, weak though he was, followed, with the others at a distance behind them.

The door was ajar; Brandal knew without looking that Morgan was gone. He walked to the door and stopped, staring.

Reize was lying against the wall, his leather jacket and his shirt a mass of blood across the belly. He was holding his stomach. He was staring across the valley behind Brandal in wonder. "So green. It's so beautiful here."

Brandal knelt beside him. "Reize."

The big man stared at him dazedly, not seeing him. "She cut me herself. She found me in here—didn't know I'd already come in to open the door—she cut me again and watched. Left when the fighting was all over." He coughed.

Brandal held his head up and gave him water. "Sorry it's not wine."

Reize finally focused on the face under the crown. He raised a bloody hand from his side and squeezed the king's shoulder. "You did it, Curly," he said happily. "I knew you had talent."

"Lie still." Brandal plucked at the mangled jacket. Strips of it were clawed into Reize's massive, badly torn belly. "You'll be fine."

Reize shook his head, never stopping smiling and not closing his eyes. "Don't talk like a man with an eagle up his ass. Can you imagine how you'd feel, putting a rope around my neck if I lived? Finding something big enough to swing this body from, and high enough so it wouldn't bounce?" He laughed lightly, and his great belly quivered lower in all directions. "Oh, you were a fine one. I thought you were a thief. I knew you'd be the best, if you wanted."

He looked down at himself and sighed. "Well, here it ends, Curly. No throne for me, eh?"

Brandal, his eyes filling, shook his head angrily.

"The Turd of Fortune, Curly, the Turd of Fortune. Ah, but with luck . . . think of it, Curly! With a little luck, what a man like me could have been!"

"It staggers the imagination," the Griffin said quietly.

"Exactly, sir. Worlds, passing gas with terror, and small dragons setting them off! Kings would have wept at my funeral. Ah, well," he said, and settled back. "Not this time."

He smiled peacefully, and Oghannon Reize, the Turd of Fortune, died almost without their noticing.

At least one king wept at his passing.

Stein was watching, but seemed to see nothing. Fields put a hand on his shoulder. "Stein?"

Stein's face was empty and tired. "Everything's lost. All gone. Look at it." He swallowed. "And when it dries, we have to burn it to the ground—"

"The Hippoi would understand—"

"No," he said firmly. "I won't add to their grief. Nesyos must have his due. He died in my building; up it goes. 'Up the chimney.' " His face twisted and worked as he looked at the ruins. "I'm too old for this, Lord. I swore, when I was young, that I'd never lose my home again."

"You can't rebuild." They turned to stare at Fields, who finished, "Not alone. And we wouldn't want you to." He stretched an arm out, not bothering to look at the others. "We can all help. You tell us; you know what you want."

"USF is out for the summer soon," Rudy said. "I was going back home, but hey, I could stay in Crossroads."

Bambi nodded timidly. "We both can."

Dave said, "We'd all come back—"

"No," Brandal said firmly to him. "Your term of study is over. Go home for good. I'm closing the road to your world, and keeping *The Book of Strangeways*."

The students looked at each other in shock. They had been allowed to see a world that held the cure to hundreds of illnesses.

Sugar said awkwardly, "Your Majesty? You can't possibly know what your world means to ours."

"Then you should approve. I'm saving it from you."

"My liege," the Griffin said diffidently, "I am hoping you will reconsider." He moved closer to Laurie, who put a hand on his back. "If they endangered us, they also saved us from danger. If they harmed us, we have harmed them." He glanced coldly at DeeDee. "And we may yet harm them more."

Truelove fidgeted nervously. DeeDee shrugged.

BJ spoke. "Actually, I know someone who could help Stein rebuild."

Stein, Brandal, and Fields turned to look.

"He's been in the restaurant business for forty years. He wouldn't tell anyone about Crossroads, because he hardly talks to anyone anymore. His health may not be good at first, but I think it will improve once he gets here. He can cook over an open grill while you rebuild, and run the inn for you while you supervise. And he could teach you new recipes."

Stein looked faintly interested. "What kind?"

"Mostly Greek food."

"Greek food," Fields said reverently.

Mrs. Sobell said suddenly, "Chris. Stan's father. What a perfect choice."

"Who?" Truelove said, looking around. "Stan who?" They ignored him.

BJ said quickly, "He'd have to do light work, and he speaks mainly Greek. Maybe Melina or someone could interpret." She said with studied reluctance, "Granted, he's pretty old—"

"Old is not a problem," Stein said with asperity. "All right, if the king says he can come in."

Brandal hesitated and finally said, "Melina, do you think you could bring him in?"

"Of course." She looked at the sodden ruin of Stein's, tears in her eyes. "I would do anything for this place." On impulse she ran up and hugged Stein.

Brandal looked around at the broken and disordered landscape. "All right," he said finally. "Bring him in. If you can, be fairly vague about the way in."

"That," BJ said, "will not be a problem at first."

After a brief silence, Brandal rubbed his hands. "Well, that's settled." He turned to Stein. "Now, if you will give me their copy of *The Book of Strangeways*—"

"Oh, no." Mrs. Sobell shook her head back and forth, a teacher correcting an errant pupil. "You can't keep it, you know."

He said to her exasperatedly, "It's the key to an entire world."

She said as exasperatedly, "And it's a library book."

The Griffin said, "My liege, I do not think you will win this argument."

He sighed. "You are reminding me that I shouldn't." He turned to Fields almost pleadingly. "Every sorrow we have ever known has come up the roads."

Fields said softly, "The sorrowful travel desperate roads. The book has always been there to help them find their way." He bowed his head. "It is your choos——your choice."

Brandal turned to Mrs. Sobell. "Will you take personal charge of the book, monitoring its use?"

She stiffened. "That violates the principle of libraries as allowing free use."

He said brittlely, "If people with principles were using the book, I would not be asking."

Sugar said to Mrs. Sobell, "Have you known anyone with MS, or Alzheimer's, or—"

She cut him off with an annoyed gesture. "I know how badly we need Crossroads, young man. All right, Lord Brandal; I'll monitor the use of the book. And I'll lock it up when I'm not there. For now." She emphasized the last two words.

He nodded. "Thank you. And I will tear up and close the Strangeways to your world, leaving only a path. For now."

Sugar, the students, and Mrs. Sobell looked bereft, but accepted it.

"That leaves," Brandal said, "one small problem." He turned to DeeDee and Truelove, still held prisoner by Rudy and Bambi.

DeeDee stared back, neither defiant nor guilty, as though life and death meant as little to her as did right and wrong.

The Griffin looked her up and down. "Apart from the obvious aesthetic difficulty in her demise, I don't perceive any problem."

"Let us take her back," Sugar said.

The Griffin cocked its head. "Nonsense."

"She's my responsibility—and Dr. Truelove's."

Truelove looked nervously around at the company. "That is— in a loose sense, I suppose she is my responsibility, since she's a veterinary student and I'm faculty—however, her actions—that is, what I've been led to understand of her actions—I can't be held accountable for such behavior from someone who was not directly operating with my imprimatur. . . ."

BJ was disgusted.

The Griffin cut him off in mid-ramble. "Are you releasing her to my custody, Doctor?"

Truelove paled. "Oh, I wouldn't say that—but I don't feel that I should interfere in your judicial process—"

"If we let him take her, he'll torture her to death, Walt." Sugar said to the Griffin, "She has to come with us."

Brandal stepped between them. "And will she face punishment there?"

"Not death, but punishment."

"Certain punishment, for the crime she committed?"

Sugar scratched his head and said uncomfortably, "Of course, if she's proven guilty."

The Griffin sat back on his hind legs, exposing both his present surgical scars and a jagged white line nearly a foot long across his chest. "Mercy," he said firmly, "is no kindness to the rest of us. My liege, you know that I've nearly died of your mercy before."

"I have never forgotten it," Brandal said steadily. "But this is not mercy; this is justice. We have no law for this crime; they do."

The Griffin looked around at the teachers and students. "And how will they enforce it?"

No one said anything.

"As I understand it," the Griffin went on, "your legal proceedings involve testimony under oath by witnesses. The witnesses, frequently inaccurate, are examined and cross-examined by articulate hirelings with no moral imperative, save the arbitrary conviction or acquittal of the prisoner, regardless of the truth or falsehood of the accusation."

He finished, "The answers to the hirelings' questions are then evaluated by twelve people of varied but equally narrow experience, on the assumption that diverse ignorance and partiality will somehow produce universal justice. Is that roughly accurate?"

Dave said, "Sometimes it's only six jurors."

"Much better. And you wish us to release this creature to that system?"

Polyta said, "Or to the Hippoi, for murder. Our justice is easier. And faster." She smiled calmly at Sugar, avoiding looking at the corpse of her husband. "In courtesy to you, I would see that her head was crushed early in the trampling."

"That does have merit," the Griffin murmured. "As compromises go. Not fitting, but final."

BJ said, "May I make a suggestion?"

Brandal smiled, despite the tension. "I wish you would." For a moment, he looked like the gentle, happy Owen he had been when BJ met him.

"It's a simple problem: you want DeeDee's punishment to fit her crime, and we—" she faltered, looking at Stefan, but managed to go on, "want her returned to our own world. But we need evidence to convict her of drug possession without referring to Crossroads in court."

Brandal said, "And your solution?"

"Inject her with her own morphine." Ignoring her companions' shocked looks, she went on: "Not enough to kill her, of course, but enough to be detected in her blood several hours later. When the police find her, she'll have syringes and drugs stolen from the vet school. Probably she has more at home, but I'm sure she has some in her knapsack still."

She saw DeeDee's sweetly defiant glare, and took a chance: "Plus the other things they'll find in her apartment. I don't think drugs and needles are the only things she's stolen from the vet school."

DeeDee's jaw dropped. Sugar stared, first at her, then at BJ, and scratched his chin thoughtfully. "The missing books and buckets and whatever."

"That's right. I don't know why she did it, any more than I know why she did this, but it won't help her case."

"Are you quite sure that she did these other things?"

"Absolutely," BJ said, not even needing to look at DeeDee.

The Griffin considered. "It is elegant. Her crime is still her undoing, despite your interference, and she has a small taste of what her victims underwent. Because of the drug, no one will credit any accusations of entrapment or any other stories she may tell of us, and it's entirely possible that she'll be wretched for life." He looked at BJ with respect. "You would make an adequate Inspector General."

"In certain cases, yes."

"That's right," DeeDee burst out, "show some guts here, surrounded by support, when at home you walk around whining and slacking in your work because your mother was just as gutless as you are and did the world a favor by killing herself. People like you," she finished bitterly, "you're just sheep, that's all. You shouldn't own anything, you shouldn't do anything, you should just keep out of the way of the people who really count."

She shut her mouth and gave BJ a tight little, mad little, triumphant smile.

"Morgan will always find people like her," Brandal said quietly. "And if Morgan hadn't found her, the chances are she'd have done just as much damage back in your world. Are you sure you want her back?"

Sugar blinked tiredly. "I'm sure we don't. But it's something we ought to do. I'm sure you have things that are your duty."

Brandal nodded. "Too many. This is one of them. All right, she can go—but I want to see the morphine administered here and now, by one of you, and I want the Inspector General's friend, if she has the expertise, to confirm that it is done correctly."

The Griffin murmured, "Bravo."

Laurie said, "No problem." She reached automatically for a cigarette, and looked uncomfortable when she couldn't find one. "Who gives the shot?"

The contingent from the university looked at each other uncomfortably.

Stefan cried out once. BJ rubbed his chest with one hand, using her other to wipe his forehead. "If no one else will, I'll do it myself."

"That's not your job," Sugar said flatly. He took a syringe and a small vial from DeeDee's backpack. "If I've learned anything this trip, it's that you have to take responsibility for what you don't do, as well as what you do."

He passed the syringe to Truelove. "Hit it."

Truelove took the syringe clumsily, staring at it as though he were a first-year student who had never given a shot in his life.

Sugar added, "Or you can leave her here, and bet that none of us will ever say anything about it."

Rudy and Bambi, each with an arm locked through DeeDee's, brought her forward. DeeDee, hair visibly mussed for the first time since BJ had known her, glared at Truelove.

Truelove dropped his eyes. He expertly tied off her arm with a thick string, swabbed the hollow of the arm where the vein throbbed, and shot a syringe of dilute morphine into her. His technique was flawless.

When he had finished, Sugar nodded. "I knew you would."

DeeDee stared unbelievingly at Truelove, who wouldn't look at her. Gradually she went unfocused and finally became unconscious.

There was little time left. At Polyta's direction, two centaurs tied poles to the sides of the burned-out truck and to BJ's destroyed car. Sugar shook hands with Fields and Stein, and nodded awkwardly to Brandal.

The students, feeling lost, made their own good-byes. Dave, Rudy, and Bambi hugged. Melina kissed Annie and BJ and, as an afterthought, Lee Anne and Dave. Stein shook each of their hands, patted the women's heads (he had to stretch for Lee Anne), and said a quick farewell.

BJ found herself alone with Fields. "Thank you for letting us see all this."

"Will you miss it?" he said, as though surprised.

"WILL I . . ." she found herself on the edge of tears. "Of course. You will let other people come back someday, won't you?"

"Ah, now. That is for the king to say." But he smiled slightly. "I will talk to him. You need us, and we may need you still."

She took his hand. He turned it and kissed hers, and for once not even his inevitable sexuality bothered her. "Care for Stefan," she said.

Fields said, "No one will have better care." He looked around with a mixture of relief and sadness. "We will all need care, for some time."

He walked away to speak with Stein again.

Mrs. Sobell was standing by the flooded lower pond, looking around with the same pleasant calm she usually had in the library. BJ came up to her. "Do you know Greek?"

"Only enough for medical suffixes, these days. Every reference librarian should know enough Latin and enough Greek to spell correctly in the sciences."

"That's probably enough. What's the Greek for 'all'?"

Mrs. Sobell dimpled. "You should have asked something harder. Panoply, Pan-American, Pantheon—"

BJ's stomach twisted and jumped. "So the word for 'all'—"

"Is *pan*." Mrs. Sobell added helpfully, "Like the God Pan."

"Yes," BJ said faintly. "Exactly like."

The Hippoi dragged the vehicles back to Virginia and gave rides to the returning humans. Polyta insisted on a travois for the sleeping DeeDee; she would not let the Hippoi touch her.

At the border, an exhausted Road Crew dug out a temporary roadbed. The centaurs disengaged the poles from the burned truck and car bodies and galloped back.

In Virginia, the large bearded man who had helped with the Road Crew before was waiting with a truck. He tipped his baseball cap to Brandal respectfully and said to Sugar and Truelove, "Y'all need rides?"

"Thanks," Sugar said. He turned to Brandal. "Don't forget; we're waiting to hear from you."

"I won't."

Sugar bowed awkwardly. Brandal ignored that and shook his hand.

Sugar carried DeeDee carefully to the back of the truck.

Brandal shook hands in turn with each of the students as they got in the truck. Lastly he said to BJ, "You didn't have to come back when the book was stolen."

"Of course I did."

Brandal considered, then went on. "I spoke to Stefan. Had it not been for you, he would have given the book to Morgan." He looked at her with amused wonder. "Heroes and villains. I thought you'd all be different."

"I think we will be," BJ said, "now. Give my love to the Stepfather God." She shook hands.

He turned and walked down the road. At the borderlands of Crossroads, he waved an arm. The Road Crews began tearing at the temporary bed; each moment they were fainter, and finally they were gone. BJ stared emptily at it.

She climbed into the truck and sat with the others; they were already yawning. The ride was bumpy and the truck noisy, but BJ's head sagged sideways almost immediately and she slept the sleep of the just.

E·P·I·L·O·G·U·E

BJ CLEANED HER locker a final time. There was remarkably little in it.

Clean-out was easy; it had only been a month. There were two bags from Burger King and three plastic forks. She put the trash in a small bag, and her remaining books in a large one.

The books looked completely different to her now; some of them were vital for reference and others would probably end up in a box at the back of her closet. Once, she would have judged them only on how easy they were to read.

Her own notebooks were worth their weight in plutonium or completely worthless, depending on what direction her career went from here.

She had retaken, and aced, small-animal medicine. She had gone through it with nearly perfect calm, forcing her to admit to herself that perhaps she had previously caused some of her own problems in Truelove's class.

Whether it had been the shock of her mother's death or a by-product of her own deterioration, she hadn't been an ideal student.

Now she was. Neither she nor Dr. Truelove had enjoyed that much; Dr. Truelove preferred nervous attention to excellence.

On the Saturday after small-animal rotation was over, Mrs. Sobell, BJ, and Annie had gone to the Orioles–Red Sox game. Inexplicably, the Red Sox won. Annie took it calmly; BJ and Mrs. Sobell shouted, screamed, complained, and had a thoroughly wonderful time.

Now she finished sorting her notebooks, checking each as carefully as she had the textbooks. She put them together in the bag, making sure that she had all of them.

But she knew that not one of the books contained a thing about unicorns, centaurs, rocs, or griffins. She knew that the class notes from her final rotation didn't, either. To her, the bag of books was interesting, but colorless.

At the bottom of the locker was the charm she had bought from Owen. She smiled and slipped it in her pocket.

BJ walked down the nearly empty hall. For the first time she realized how little impact any one class had on this building; it was exactly the same now that most of her classmates were gone and most of the faculty on vacation.

DeeDee had pleaded guilty to a misdemeanor drug possession, had filed suit against the school for her diploma after Western Vee had threatened not to graduate her, and had not only graduated but had taken a lucrative job with a poultry agri-business outside of Rockford, Illinois. The school had backed down when her lawyer, who was in possession of few but powerful facts in the case, suggested that Dr. Truelove had been negligent in controlling and documenting the narcotics. He attempted an entrapment argument, but backed down hurriedly when DeeDee offered more (true, but fantastic) depositions. As part of the settlement, DeeDee had agreed to a program of counseling for thefts.

Dr. Truelove was already tenured, plus which he had an incoming research grant and was up for a teaching award. Nothing at all adverse happened to him, and at graduation he was recognized for teaching excellence and made a touching statement about concern for students. BJ thought she heard Sugar chuckle.

Dave was headed for Cornell, to do research. In three years, BJ knew, he'd be riding herd on a graduate assistant and probably showing the first signs of male pattern baldness, and that raw wildness that had saved the Griffin's life would only come out on rare occasions and at parties.

Lee Anne, for all her complaining about how she would never get ahead, was drawing down one of the top salaries in the class, with an option to buy in. Her new boss, for some reason, felt that she could work with absolutely anything that came in the door. It was a small-animal practice—Lee Anne was sick of large animals.

She had called BJ and said that the turning point of the interview had been when, as she inspected the practice, a rottweiler had snapped at her and she had shouted back, cowing the dog.

"Beej, after a werewolf, a rottie's just a really big chihuahua."

Annie was headed for Chad, to work with famine relief and an incredibly primitive and disease-ridden agricultural program. She frankly and simply asked her classmates for support and donations, and hand-wrote delighted thank-you notes to everyone who contributed.

BJ's classmates all had jobs.

BJ hadn't applied anywhere. She really hadn't planned on living until graduation.

She was still brooding on this last when she came out of the hallway between buildings, turned a corner, and smacked into Laurie.

Laurie picked up the bag. "This time it's your fault."

BJ didn't think so, but only said, "Welcome back." Laurie had been on leave, reportedly caring for a sick relative.

Laurie said, "I just saw Astu——the Griffin. He's healing well." Her look went beyond gratitude.

BJ, embarrassed, said, "That's all right."

Laurie frowned. "It's one hell of a lot better than all right. Do you know what he means to . . . to that world?"

This was the Laurie BJ was used to. "I'm glad to help it."

"Well, you helped it a lot." Laurie looked at the bags. "Cleaning up again? Remember the last time I saw you?"

"And you said Dr. Dobbs wanted to see me." Six weeks ago? Was that all?

"*Plus ça change*," Laurie said, "*plus ça reste la même chose*. Sugar Dobbs wants to see you." She added slyly, "Lucky."

"Thanks." BJ now knew Laurie and took her humor for what it was: the kind of meaningless innuendo that makes dull moments more interesting.

The sign on the door was the same. The office was the same, and probably Sugar was the same, or nearly. BJ knocked at the half-open door.

"Same old BJ," Sugar said. "Come on in."

This time BJ came in without feeling nervous at all. Still in her early twenties, she felt worldly and unflappable; what was there left that could startle her?

"I figured you'd be long gone with everybody else," he said. "Did you say your good-byes?"

"All of them. Annie was the last, this morning. She left this noon."

Sugar nodded. "She came by just before leaving. Gave me her new address and asked for all the ag vet contacts I could give her.

She's off to get her shots and have a perfectly healthy appendix removed so she can go into the bush." He shook his head dazedly. "Calm as tomorrow's sunrise. Nothing I showed her fazed her in the slightest."

BJ said, "You were wrong about her."

He said deadpan, "Is that so."

"You thought her faith"—she stumbled over the word; why was faith embarrassing to talk about?—"made her narrow. It made her brave and good. Some things about her religion made her naive; you were right about that. But that wasn't much of a handicap, and the rest of us might not have made it through without her."

Sugar winced. "You've got me there."

"You were right about some other things, though," BJ said. "You wanted Dave to shape up and stop being reckless. You wanted Lee Anne to feel like a hotshot and be less self-conscious about being country and Southern. I think that's why you asked them to join the Crossroads rotation."

"And it worked fine for them."

"But you were wrong about those things, too," BJ said mildly. "If Dave hadn't been such a maverick, the Griffin would have died. If Lee Anne hadn't been and felt country, she wouldn't have been as good with the centaurs."

"I'm real pleased," he said dryly, "that you're here to point out my faults. I guess that's a difference between being a teacher and having a colleague."

"You've always wanted to hear what's on my mind," BJ said.

"I can't teach you much," Sugar said, "if you're not going to tell me what you got right and wrong."

"That's harder than just learning."

"It is harder," he agreed, "but it's the only real learning. The rest is just studying."

BJ thought about that. "That's pretty good. Are you ready to hear what's on my mind?"

He smiled uneasily. "I ain't sure. It's harder that way, now that you're teaching, too."

"Would you like to hear about my second genetic test?"

After a frozen moment, he nodded a fraction of an inch. "A whole lot."

"Negative," she said calmly. The news hadn't been calm at all; she'd had two retests, and practically an entire lab at Duke had groveled to her in apology. The first results must have been a mistake, it was extraordinary that it could happen, thank God she hadn't acted rashly ... and the subtext: *Don't sue us. Please,*

Jesus, Hermes, and Hippocrates, don't let her sue us.

Sugar sighed. "That's that, then."

"How did you know about my mother?"

"A real invasion of privacy." He sat back now, looking much more relaxed. "We had people at Duke working with us; you know that."

"I knew it after a while. I also knew that they were researching Crossroads and genetic diseases."

"Right. And after your mother killed herself—"

"Peter." She shook her head in amazement. "He got his tests from Duke?"

"Bingo. Right after the funeral. And his name turned up on a list we shouldn't ought to have had anyway, but we were thinking of taking a volunteer in on a kind of nature-or-nurture test, to see whether genetic defects healed in Crossroads—"

"No, Doctor. You already knew they did."

"I knew some of them did. Not all." He showed the most embarrassment BJ could remember. "Once I knew about your mother, I could guess what you might be planning. I wouldn't stop you, but I had my fingers crossed for you." He tapped a pencil on the desk. "So . . . what are your plans from here?"

BJ had a dizzying feeling of déjà vu, back to the time she had sat in this office not wanting to tell Sugar that she was going to commit suicide. She shook her head. "I don't—I haven't made any. Too much has changed." Her mouth quirked. "I can't even go home and think about it."

Sugar, studiously not looking at her, changed the subject. "Fields dropped by."

"How is he?"

"Fine." Sugar grinned. "He made a couple women nervous, just by being here."

BJ could sympathize with that. "Did he talk about Crossroads?" It felt odd to be talking about it, as though that part of her life was as irrevocably lost as an old romance or a part of childhood. She thought of her first view of a unicorn, and part of her ached.

Sugar looked scornful. " 'Course he talked about Crossroads. It's not like he was in the neighborhood and just dropped by." He paused. "You can't say things are back to normal, since 'normal' doesn't mean much there. Morgan's gone, for now, and people are putting life together again."

"And the Wyr?"

Sugar toyed with his pencil. "The ones who survived are all through withdrawal but still recovering. They'll mostly make it.

There's been some scrapping, but nothing major. Fields tells me the pack is going through dominance struggles every day." He added delicately, "You didn't ask about Stefan."

She'd been afraid to. She'd written letter after letter, sending them via Laurie, and he'd answered none of them. "How is he?"

"Weak, but recovered. He wants to come back out, but Fields doesn't think he should until he learns more about the risks out here. Laurie took him some pamphlets, and she's working with him. She's done some counseling before. Tough, tough woman. He'll make it okay."

He looked embarrassed again; personal issues weren't his forte. "Listen, BJ, don't be hard on him if he doesn't write; they call it 'withdrawal' for two reasons. Plus he feels ashamed; lots of addicts do."

BJ was relieved, but only said, "So things are settling down in Crossroads."

"Settling," Sugar said, "but not settled. A place like Crossroads doesn't rebalance itself overnight." He looked her in the eye. "In fact, Fields says they want a resident vet there, for a while."

There was a long silence. Finally BJ said shakily, "And you told him that the others all had jobs."

He shook his head slowly, enjoying the moment. "Nope. Didn't say a thing. They requested you, off the bat."

"Who did?"

"Brandal. Stein. Fields." He added casually, "And Stefan, but they figured he was prejudiced."

"Not the Griffin?"

Sugar said, "I wouldn't call his opinion a request. More a command performance. Some stuff about honor, right and wrong, sense of duty, obligation . . ."

"That's exactly how he'd put it," BJ said slowly. "When did they ask for me?"

Sugar said, "Right after I recommended you and agreed to bring you in and gave you the very first rotation case in front of Fields."

For once, BJ had nothing to say.

He looked away from her again, trying not to pressure her. "You know, you wouldn't get back here much. And you wouldn't have phones, or TV, or major-league baseball. You wouldn't be able to tell people, even friends, where you were working, and you'd go half-crazy trying to change your pay from gold to cash."

When she said nothing, he went on, "And it wouldn't be like out here, where eighty percent of your work is the same damn thing over and over. You'd see nothing but odd cases, and until things calm down in Crossroads, you'd be seeing mostly emergencies. God only knows what you'd be working on half the time, and guessing at what 'normal' meant for it."

He hesitated, then went on. "Probably your life feels precious to you now. Remember, Morgan's still out there, and she won't quit. If you got hurt, you'd be on your own. If you had a tough case, you'd be on your own. We'd help you get supplies and take the occasional major case, but that's it."

BJ clutched the paper bag of books to her chest.

Finally Sugar said, "Fields and I bought a used truck from the school. We left the title blank. He doesn't know how to drive it yet, but he'll buy what you need from the school and help you pack. I told him you'd want a week to rest and to make up your mind."

He finished, "He'll be by next Thursday to drive in with you. He said to give you these . . . gifts, not loans."

He passed her two books in battered cloth bindings. She looked at them dazedly.

One was a travel-stained copy of *Lao's Guide to Nonbiological Species.* She opened it and read on the flyleaf, "With thanks from P. Fields to BJ Vaughan, D.V.M."

She opened the other book and scanned the maps, half believing she was watching them change. She read again the last sentence of the warning: "For those lost at Crossroads, only a map will help them find themselves."

She dropped the books into her paper bag. "I'll be there."

ACKNOWLEDGMENTS

When you write a world, you owe a world of thanks. I gratefully acknowledge:

Jill O'Brien, roc anesthetist, griffin medic, and extremely patient, greatly appreciated D.V.M.;

Jenny Clark and Lynn Anne Evans, centaur birth coaches and D.V.M.'s;

Cathy Lund and James Tiede, patient and bemused D.V.M. and V.M.D.;

Sue Sokoloski, Mary Madeiros, and Stacy Nile, veterinary technicians;

Cindy Capra, nurse practitioner;

Syl Gookin, engineer and shootist.

Knowledge and practice detailed herein are mostly theirs. Mistakes are entirely mine.

I should also acknowledge quotes from that invaluable work, *Lao's Guide to the Nonbiological Species.* Several of the passages quoted herein are also cited in *The Circus of Dr. Lao,* by Charles G. Finney, which I purchased on a trip to England twenty-five years ago and have reread with enjoyment ever since.

Thanks and love to L.A. for her reading, constant expertise, and patience.

Thanks and love to my parents, my brother, and his wife and family for their love, support, and interest.

Two important notes:

1. Western Vee University and its personnel are entirely fic-

tional. I intentionally made no effort at detailing an existing controlled-substance program and how to steal from it. No vet school would ever allow students access to the drug racks as I described it.

2. For fictional purposes, I made Dr. Hitori the worst possible doctor to consult for a patient with Huntington's chorea. There is far better, more sensitive, expert, and qualified advice available for patients seeking testing for Huntington's chorea. For further information, consult the Huntington's Disease Society of America, Inc., 140 West 22nd Street, 6th floor, New York, NY 10011-2420.

The Huntington's Disease Society of America was not consulted in the research for this book and is in no way answerable for its contents. I am.

Finally, thanks and love to my in-laws, Bob and Anna Evans, Bob and Ann Evans, Bob and Marie DelGallo, and Brian (where'd *he* come from?) and Pat Lussier for their patience, love, support, encouragement, and, of course, food. This book is dedicated to them.